A STARLESS CLAN

WARRIORS

SKY

A STARLESS CLAN

A STARLESS CLAN

WARRIORS

SKY

ERIN HUNTER

HARPER

An Imprint of HarperCollinsPublishers

Library of Congress Cataloging-in-Publication Data

Names: Hunter, Erin, author.

Title: Sky / Erin Hunter.

Description: First edition. | New York : Harper, [2022] | Series: Warriors: a starless clan ; book
2 | Audience: Ages 8-12. | Audience: Grades 4-6. | Summary: "As a leaderless RiverClan faces
disaster, its warriors and its young medicine cat apprentice are determined to protect their
Clan and find its new leader-even if it means lying to the other Clans"--Provided by publisher.

Identifiers: LCCN 2022020973 | ISBN 978-0-06-305015-0 (hardcover)

Subjects: CYAC: Fantasy. | Cats--Fiction. | Clans--Fiction. | LCGFT: Fantasy fiction. | Animal
fiction. | Novels.

Classification: LCC PZ7.H916625 Sk 2022 | DDC [Fic]--dc23

LC record available at https://lccn.loc.gov/2022020973

Typography by Jessie Gang

22 23 24 25 26   PC/LSCH   10 9 8 7 6 5 4 3 2 1

❖

First Edition

Special thanks to Kate Cary

ALLEGIANCES

THUNDERCLAN

LEADER

BRAMBLESTAR—dark brown tabby tom with amber eyes

DEPUTY

SQUIRRELFLIGHT—dark ginger she-cat with green eyes and one white paw

MEDICINE CATS

JAYFEATHER—gray tabby tom with blind blue eyes

ALDERHEART—dark ginger tom with amber eyes

WARRIORS

(toms and she-cats without kits)

WHITEWING—white she-cat with green eyes

BIRCHFALL—light brown tabby tom

MOUSEWHISKER—gray-and-white tom

BAYSHINE—golden tabby tom

POPPYFROST—pale tortoiseshell-and-white she-cat

LILYHEART—small, dark tabby she-cat with white patches and blue eyes

NIGHTHEART—black tom

BUMBLESTRIPE—very pale gray tom with black stripes

CHERRYFALL—ginger she-cat

MOLEWHISKER—brown-and-cream tom

CINDERHEART—gray tabby she-cat

FINCHLIGHT—tortoiseshell she-cat

BLOSSOMFALL—tortoiseshell-and-white she-cat with petal-shaped white patches

IVYPOOL—silver-and-white tabby she-cat with dark blue eyes

EAGLEWING—ginger she-cat

MYRTLEBLOOM—pale brown she-cat

DEWNOSE—gray-and-white tom

THRIFTEAR—dark gray she-cat

STORMCLOUD—gray tabby tom

HOLLYTUFT—black she-cat

FERNSONG—yellow tabby tom

HONEYFUR—white she-cat with yellow splotches

SPARKPELT—orange tabby she-cat

SORRELSTRIPE—dark brown she-cat

TWIGBRANCH—gray she-cat with green eyes

FINLEAP—brown tom

SHELLFUR—tortoiseshell tom

FERNSTRIPE—gray tabby she-cat

PLUMSTONE—black-and-ginger she-cat

FLIPCLAW—brown tabby tom

LEAFSHADE—tortoiseshell she-cat

LIONBLAZE—golden tabby tom with amber eyes

QUEENS (she-cats expecting or nursing kits)

DAISY—cream long-furred cat from the horseplace

SPOTFUR—spotted tabby she-cat (mother to Bristlekit, an orange-and-white tabby she-kit; Stemkit, an orange tabby tom; and Graykit, a white tom with gray spots)

ELDERS (former warriors and queens, now retired)

THORNCLAW—golden-brown tabby tom

CLOUDTAIL—long-haired white tom with blue eyes

BRIGHTHEART—white she-cat with ginger patches

BRACKENFUR—golden-brown tabby tom

SHADOWCLAN

LEADER **TIGERSTAR**—dark brown tabby tom

DEPUTY **CLOVERFOOT**—gray tabby she-cat

MEDICINE CATS **PUDDLESHINE**—brown tom with white splotches

SHADOWSIGHT—gray tabby tom

WARRIORS **TAWNYPELT**—tortoiseshell she-cat with green eyes

STONEWING—white tom

SCORCHFUR—dark gray tom with slashed ears

FLAXFOOT—brown tabby tom

SPARROWTAIL—large brown tabby tom

SNOWBIRD—pure white she-cat with green eyes

YARROWLEAF—ginger she-cat with yellow eyes

BERRYHEART—black-and-white she-cat

GRASSHEART—pale brown tabby she-cat

WHORLPELT—gray-and-white tom

HOPWHISKER—calico she-cat

BLAZEFIRE—white-and-ginger tom

FLOWERSTEM—silver she-cat

SNAKETOOTH—honey-colored tabby she-cat

SLATEFUR—sleek gray tom

POUNCESTEP—gray tabby she-cat

LIGHTLEAP—brown tabby she-cat

GULLSWOOP—white she-cat

SPIRECLAW—black-and-white tom

FRINGEWHISKER—white she-cat with brown splotches

HOLLOWSPRING—black tom

SUNBEAM—brown-and-white tabby she-cat

QUEENS **DOVEWING**—pale gray she-cat with green eyes (mother to Rowankit, a ginger tom, and Birchkit, a light brown tom)

CINNAMONTAIL—brown tabby she-cat with white paws (mother to Firkit, a brown tabby tom, Streamkit, a gray tabby she-kit, Bloomkit, a black she-kit, and Whisperkit, a gray tom)

ELDERS **OAKFUR**—small brown tom

SKYCLAN

LEADER **LEAFSTAR**—brown-and-cream tabby she-cat with amber eyes

DEPUTY **HAWKWING**—dark gray tom with yellow eyes

MEDICINE CATS **FRECKLEWISH**—mottled light brown tabby she-cat with spotted legs

FIDGETFLAKE—black-and-white tom

MEDIATOR **TREE**—yellow tom with amber eyes

WARRIORS

SPARROWPELT—dark brown tabby tom

MACGYVER—black-and-white tom

DEWSPRING—sturdy gray tom

ROOTSPRING—yellow tom

NEEDLECLAW—black-and-white she-cat

PLUMWILLOW—dark gray she-cat

SAGENOSE—pale gray tom

KITESCRATCH—reddish-brown tom

HARRYBROOK—gray tom

CHERRYTAIL—fluffy tortoiseshell-and-white she-cat

CLOUDMIST—white she-cat with yellow eyes

TURTLECRAWL—tortoiseshell she-cat

RABBITLEAP—brown tom

WRENFLIGHT—golden tabby she-cat

REEDCLAW—small pale tabby she-cat
APPRENTICE, BEETLEPAW (tabby tom)

MINTFUR—gray tabby she-cat with blue eyes

NETTLESPLASH—pale brown tom

TINYCLOUD—small white she-cat

PALESKY—black-and-white she-cat

VIOLETSHINE—black-and-white she-cat with yellow eyes

BELLALEAF—pale orange she-cat with green eyes

QUAILFEATHER—white tom with crow-black ears

PIGEONFOOT—gray-and-white she-cat

GRAVELNOSE—tan tom

SUNNYPELT—ginger she-cat
APPRENTICE, BEEPAW (white-and-tabby she-kit)

NECTARSONG—brown she-cat

QUEENS   **BLOSSOMHEART**—ginger-and-white she-cat (mother to Ridgekit, a reddish she-kit with a white nose, and Duskkit, a white tom with brown paws and ears)

ELDERS   **FALLOWFERN**—pale brown she-cat who has lost her hearing

WINDCLAN

LEADER   **HARESTAR**—brown-and-white tom

DEPUTY   **CROWFEATHER**—dark gray tom

MEDICINE CATS   **KESTRELFLIGHT**—mottled gray tom with white splotches like kestrel feathers
APPRENTICE, WHISTLEPAW (gray tabby she-cat)

WARRIORS   **NIGHTCLOUD**—black she-cat

BRINDLEWING—mottled brown she-cat

APPLESHINE—yellow tabby she-cat

LEAFTAIL—dark tabby tom with amber eyes

WOODSONG—brown she-cat

EMBERFOOT—gray tom with two dark paws

BREEZEPELT—black tom with amber eyes

HEATHERTAIL—light brown tabby she-cat with blue eyes

FEATHERPELT—gray tabby she-cat

CROUCHFOOT—ginger tom

SONGLEAP—tortoiseshell she-cat

SEDGEWHISKER—light brown tabby she-cat

FLUTTERFOOT—brown-and-white tom

SLIGHTFOOT—black tom with white flash on his chest

OATCLAW—pale brown tabby tom

HOOTWHISKER—dark gray tom

QUEENS
LARKWING—pale brown tabby she-cat (mother to Stripekit, a gray tabby tom, and Brookkit, a black-and-white tom)

ELDERS
WHISKERNOSE—light brown tom

GORSETAIL—very pale gray-and-white she-cat with blue eyes

RIVERCLAN

MEDICINE CATS
MOTHWING—dappled golden she-cat
APPRENTICE, FROSTPAW (light gray she-cat)

WARRIORS
DUSKFUR—brown tabby she-cat

MINNOWTAIL—dark gray-and-white she-cat

MALLOWNOSE—light brown tabby tom

HAVENPELT—black-and-white she-cat

PODLIGHT—gray-and-white tom

SHIMMERPELT—silver she-cat

LIZARDTAIL—light brown tom

SNEEZECLOUD—gray-and-white tom

BRACKENPELT—tortoiseshell she-cat

SPLASHTAIL—brown tabby tom

FOGNOSE—gray-and-white she-cat

HARELIGHT—white tom

ICEWING—white she-cat with blue eyes
APPRENTICE, MISTPAW (tortoiseshell-and-white tabby she-cat)

OWLNOSE—brown tabby tom

GORSECLAW—white tom with gray ears

NIGHTSKY—dark gray she-cat with blue eyes

BREEZEHEART—brown-and-white she-cat
APPRENTICE, GRAYPAW (silver tabby tom)

ELDERS

MOSSPELT—tortoiseshell-and-white she-cat

A STARLESS CLAN

WARRIORS

SKY

TWOLEG NEST

GREENLEAF
TWOLEGPLACE

TWOLEG PATH

TWOLEG PATH

CLEARING

SHADOWCLAN
CAMP

SMALL
THUNDERPATH

HALFBRIDGE

GREENLEAF
TWOLEGPLACE

HALFBRIDGE

CAT VIEW

ISLAND

STREAM

RIVERCLAN
CAMP

HORSEPLACE

HAREVIEW CAMPSITE

SANCTUARY COTTAGE

SADLER WOODS

LITTLEPINE ROAD

LITTLEPINE SAILING CENTER

TWOLEG VI

LITTLEPINE ISLAND

RIVER ALBA

WHITECHURCH ROAD

KNIGHT'S COPSE

PROLOGUE

Two cats sat hunched together as if they were suffering the deepest cold of leaf-bare, oblivious to the warm breeze rippling their fur and the sunlight radiating from the blue sky that stretched above them.

The larger cat's thick black fur twitched nervously. "We must warn them."

"Believe me, Reedwhisker. I've tried." His mother tucked her paws tighter against her belly. "It's not possible."

Reedwhisker stared back at Mistystar desperately. "There *has* to be a way." Behind him, the reed beds rustled temptingly, rich with the promise of prey sweeter than any he'd tasted in life, but he didn't even glance at them. "RiverClan is in danger."

Mistystar shook her head. "There's nothing we can do."

"Then we must ask the other Clans to help," Reedwhisker urged. "I don't care how desperate we'd seem. We have to do *something*."

Mistystar shot him a warning glance. "Do you really want them to know how vulnerable RiverClan is right now?" She swished her tail. "I won't risk it."

"But RiverClan has no leader or deputy."

"They have the warrior code."

"The warrior code is changing," Reedwhisker argued. "And they have no cat to guide them. How can we watch and do nothing?"

Mistystar wrapped her tail around her paws. "We have to trust our Clanmates to find their own way out of this mess."

"What if they can't?"

"They've managed in the past."

"In the past they've had a leader!" Reedwhisker didn't hide his exasperation. "If only I were still with them. If only I hadn't died. I could show them a way. I could help them!"

"They must do this by themselves." Mistystar's mew was firm, but her eyes betrayed fear. She'd been a leader long enough to know how quickly quarrels could split a Clan into factions and how easily those factions could turn on each other. Just as fish needed the river's current to guide them, warriors needed leadership.

Reedwhisker let out a sigh, but nodded his acceptance and walked away.

Mistystar shrank deeper into her pelt as though the warm winds of StarClan carried the chill of the Dark Forest. She felt more frightened now than at any time she'd been alive. Without a leader or deputy to hold the Clan together, would RiverClan drift apart like a reed bed torn to pieces by a storm?

CHAPTER 1

❧

Sunbeam stared fiercely ahead, narrowing her eyes against the early morning light glittering through the pine branches. She felt her brown-and-white pelt prickle with irritation as Gullswoop trotted beside her, her tail high. She wished she were alone.

"Let's head toward the mossy stream," Gullswoop mewed brightly.

"Why don't *you* head that way?" Sunbeam had been trying since they'd left camp to persuade her denmate that they should split up and cover more ground in their search for prey.

But Gullswoop was determined to stick to her like a burr. "Cloverfoot told us to hunt together," she reminded Sunbeam.

"I don't think she meant we had to share the same paw steps." Sunbeam kept her gaze firmly on the path ahead. She didn't want to meet Gullswoop's inquisitive gaze. The white she-cat had been watching her like an apprentice watching prey, trying to guess her thoughts, as hungry for gossip as the rest of ShadowClan.

Sunbeam tried harder to relax, but she could still feel her

pelt twitching angrily along her spine. She couldn't blame Gullswoop for being curious. Her romantic humiliations had been
a topic of conversation in the Clan for a half-moon. But why
couldn't they move on? If they did, perhaps she would too.

She picked up her pace as the forest floor sloped upward.
At the top, she broke into a run. The thick layer of pine needles was spongy beneath her paws. She sent needles spraying
out behind her as she began to swerve one way, then the other,
dodging between the trees. Gullswoop would have trouble
tracking her paw steps as she zigzagged through the forest.

"Wait for me!" Gullswoop's plaintive cry was already distant.

Sunbeam didn't look back. She didn't want to lose her
stride. Exhilaration fizzed in her paws. This was the closest
she'd had to solitude for days, and for one shining moment,
she felt free of the sadness and humiliation that had stuck like
thorns in her belly since—

"Slow down!" Gullswoop called again. "You're too fast
for me."

Like a cloud blocking out the sun, her denmate's wail
dampened Sunbeam's excitement. She wouldn't feel better
if it meant hurting a Clanmate's feelings. She scrambled to a
halt, catching her breath as she waited for Gullswoop.

But Gullswoop didn't look hurt when she caught up.
Instead she blinked eagerly at Sunbeam. "You're so fast," she
mewed. "And graceful. The way you darted between the trees.
Like a sparrow hawk."

Gullswoop's flattery annoyed Sunbeam even more than

her curiosity. These days, *all* Sunbeam's Clanmates seemed
to be falling over themselves to compliment her, like she was
some timid kit who needed extra encouragement. She growled
at Gullswoop. "*Enough*, okay?"

"Why?" Gullswoop looked surprised. "I mean it. You're
really grace—"

"*Stop* it!" Sunbeam snapped. "You're just trying to make me
feel better, but it doesn't make me feel better to have every cat
tiptoeing around me, being nice. It feels too much like pity.
If you want to help, just give me some space and act like you
don't know I ever liked Blazefire."

She knew as she spoke that she must sound ungrateful. It
wasn't just nosiness that inspired her Clanmates' attention;
they were genuinely concerned. She hadn't been the only cat
to assume that she and Blazefire would be mates one day. She
and the white-and-ginger tom had always been close, sharing prey, sharing tongues, hanging out every chance they
got. They'd spent so much time together that it had never
occurred to Sunbeam they wouldn't end up together. But it
seemed that Blazefire hadn't felt the same way. To him they
would only ever be friends, and the hurt and embarrassment
she felt was made worse by the fact that everyone in Shadow-
Clan knew he'd rejected her. She'd decided that the only
thing to do now was to think about it as little as possible.
That's why she'd volunteered for every patrol that had been
offered. She was determined to stay busy and wear herself out
so that when she curled up in her nest at the end of the day,
all she thought about was sleep.

Gullswoop was gazing at her now sympathetically, and it was all Sunbeam could do to stop from bristling. "You'll get over him eventually," Gullswoop promised. "And I'm sure you'll find the right tom before long. A *real* ShadowClan cat—"

Sunbeam's eyes widened. "Blazefire *is* a real ShadowClan cat."

"You know what I mean," Gullswoop went on. "One who was *born* here. Blazefire's a great warrior, but he comes from a Twolegplace. He's not a *real* Clan cat. He's never going to think like a cat who was born here."

Sunbeam prickled defensively on Blazefire's behalf. She knew Gullswoop was trying to cheer her up. But it didn't make any difference where Blazefire had been born. He was warm and friendly and skillful and brave, and ShadowClan was lucky he'd chosen to join them. "Blazefire's a great warrior," she objected.

"I know," Gullswoop agreed. "I'm just saying there are perfectly good ShadowClan toms for you to like. And you and Blazefire will still be friends." She eyed Sunbeam curiously. "Won't you?"

"Of course we will." Sunbeam whisked her tail. She wasn't going to act like a kit and ignore him. Besides, he was still the good-natured tom she'd fallen for. She *wanted* to be friends with him, and she felt sure that, even though he hung out mostly with Lightleap now, there was no reason they shouldn't all get along.

It was just a coincidence that Blazefire had decided he didn't want to become Sunbeam's mate at the same time he'd grown close to her best friend. There wasn't anything between them. Still, the thought of Lightleap brought a sour taste to Sunbeam's mouth. It was Lightleap who'd let Blazefire get hurt in the first place. Her recklessness had gotten him caught in the rockfall that had confined him to the medicine den these past days. He could have *died*! And yet Blazefire was treating Lightleap like she was a better friend than Sunbeam.

Sunbeam turned away from Gullswoop, eyeing the forest. She'd come on this patrol to avoid thinking about Blazefire. And now she was thinking about Lightleap too.

The sun was scorching through the tops of the pines and warming the cold leaf-fall air. In the nursery, the kits would be stirring. Cinnamontail would be hungry after feeding her litter through the night, and Dovewing would be looking for something soft and juicy to give Rowankit and Birchkit. Both tom-kits had been sniffling and coughing for the past couple of days, so it was important to catch something fresh and tasty to tempt them.

Sunbeam shook out her fur. "Let's hunt," she mewed. Opening her mouth to taste for prey-scent, she headed down the slope.

Clouds rolled in, and by the time they had caught a piece of prey each and returned to camp, the clearing was nearly empty. Rain was beating down on the bramble dens. Only Fringewhisker and Cloverfoot had stayed outside. Fringewhisker sat outside the warriors' den, hardly blinking, though raindrops spattered her pretty, round face. Was she trying to prove that the weather didn't bother her, or were SkyClan cats simply mouse-brained?

The white-and-brown she-cat had come to ShadowClan from SkyClan to be with Sunbeam's brother, Spireclaw. Recently, the warrior code had been changed to allow cats to switch Clans to be with a mate. The former SkyClan she-cat seemed determined to show her new Clanmates that she was as brave and loyal as any ShadowClan warrior.

The rain didn't seem to bother Cloverfoot, either. She was swiping stale, blood-soaked dirt from around the fresh-kill pile, her fluffed-out fur the only sign that she felt the chill. All that was left from yesterday's catch was a frog and a shriveled rat that no cat had wanted when it was fresh and certainly wouldn't want now.

The frog and rat looked even more unappetizing when Sunbeam laid her plump starling beside them.

Gullswoop dropped her mouse next to it and glanced at the unwanted prey. "Should I dump them outside camp for the crows?" she asked Cloverfoot.

The ShadowClan deputy frowned. "Prey shouldn't be wasted," she growled. "Especially with leaf-bare so close. In another moon, we might be grateful for them."

"I'll eat the frog," Fringewhisker offered, heading toward them.

Cloverfoot blinked at her. "Save it for later," she mewed. "Right now, the nursery needs fresh bedding."

"I'll gather some." Fringewhisker brightened, and Sunbeam wondered whether she was truly pleased to help or just relieved to be given an easier way to prove her loyalty to ShadowClan than eating a stale frog.

"Take Yarrowleaf with you," Cloverfoot added. "She knows where the thickest bracken grows." As Fringewhisker headed away, Cloverfoot called after her. "The apprentices' den is empty. Put anything you gather in there so it can dry out before we make it into nests." She turned to Sunbeam and blinked encouragingly. "Nice catch," she mewed, patting the starling with her paw.

Sunbeam sniffed. Even the deputy was overcomplimenting her. "It's no better than any other prey."

Cloverfoot switched her gaze to Gullswoop. "Take the starling to the medicine den," she ordered. "Blazefire must be hungry." She looked back at Sunbeam. "You can take the mouse to the nursery."

Sunbeam narrowed her eyes. Was the ShadowClan deputy trying to protect her from having to see Blazefire, or was she trying to protect Blazefire from seeing *her*? "I caught the starling," she mewed defensively. "*I'll* take it." She was going to show her Clanmates that she didn't care that Blazefire had rejected her. Without waiting to see the deputy's reaction, she snatched up the starling and headed for the gap in the thick bramble wall of the camp that led to the medicine den.

She pushed her way in, hesitating as she realized that neither Puddleshine nor Shadowsight was there. Only Blazefire.

He sat up in his nest as she entered, the white patches on his ginger pelt glowing in the dull light, and she froze as he looked at her, her anger evaporating. Instead she became agonizingly self-conscious. What was she going to say? Would he think she'd come just to see him? That the prey was an excuse?

His nose twitched and he glanced at the starling dangling beneath her chin. "Is that for me?"

She carried it across the den and dropped it beside his nest. "Cloverfoot told me to bring you something to eat." She hoped he didn't find out that she'd *insisted* on bringing it. But as she stepped back, she felt a flash of defiance. Why *shouldn't* he find out? Was it a crime to care about him? They were still Clan-mates, weren't they? They were supposed to be friends. There was nothing wrong with wanting to bring him food. "How's your sprain?" she asked. "Does it still hurt?"

The paw that had been damaged in the rockfall was still swathed in leaves; the poultice beneath them smelled like the forest floor after rain.

"Only a bit." Blazefire leaned over the side of his nest and sniffed the starling. "Did you catch this?"

"Yes." Sunbeam shifted her weight from paw to paw. Aware that she must look fidgety, she forced herself to stand still. "I went hunting with Gullswoop."

"Just you and Gullswoop?"

"Cloverfoot didn't assign us to the dawn patrol," Sunbeam told him. "So I offered to go hunting by myself. Cloverfoot told me to take Gullswoop."

"Still keeping busy?" Blazefire looked at her.

"Yes." She stiffened. "I mean, *no*." Was it obvious that she'd been trying to distract herself from the hurt of losing her future with him as a mate? "A good warrior is always ready to hunt for her Clan."

Blazefire lifted his injured paw. "I wish I could still hunt for my Clan."

"You'll be able to soon."

"I guess."

Sunbeam glanced at the ground. For a while, Puddleshine had been uncertain whether Blazefire would be able to walk again. But thankfully, he was now recovering. The sudden silence between them seemed larger than the lake. She tried to fill it. "Has Puddleshine told you when you can hunt again?" As she spoke, her paws pricked with embarrassment. Her question sounded stilted. *He'll think I'm trying too hard to make conversation so I can hang around.* And yet, if she left, it would be obvious that she felt too awkward to stay.

"He said it will be okay in a few days," Blazefire told her.

The den entrance rustled, and Sunbeam felt a rush of relief. Some cat was coming. She could leave without seeming odd.

"Bring him in." Shadowsight, his pelt sparkling with raindrops, pushed his way into the den, then stood aside to let Dovewing through. Tigerstar was following, holding Rowankit by the scruff.

Sunbeam's belly tightened. Rowankit looked so small, his soft fur matted and unkempt and his eyes closed. He must be very sick. She forgot her awkwardness and moved quickly out of the way as Shadowsight motioned Tigerstar toward an empty nest on the other side of the den.

Tigerstar laid Rowankit inside it, and Shadowsight leaned in and sniffed the unconscious kit.

Dovewing's eyes were wide with fear. "He coughed half the night, and this morning, he was hot and wouldn't wake up."

"He'll wake once I've given him something for the fever," Shadowsight reassured her.

Tigerstar's pelt was ruffled. "It's only whitecough," he mewed. "He shouldn't have a fever."

Dovewing stared at Shadowsight anxiously as he sniffed Rowankit. "It *is* only whitecough, isn't it?" Her mew was barely more than a whisper, and Sunbeam felt a tingle of dread. She knew what Dovewing was asking—had the kit's whitecough worsened? Had it turned to greencough? The ginger tom-kit had always been smaller than his littermate, and now that he was ill, he seemed more vulnerable than ever. Would such a tiny kit be strong enough to survive greencough?

Shadowsight lifted his head and met Dovewing's gaze. "We can't be sure yet," he mewed softly.

Tigerstar hurried to Dovewing's side and pressed against her. "Don't worry," he mewed. "Shadowsight and Puddleshine will take good care of him."

"We'll do everything we can," Shadowsight promised.

"Will he have to stay here?" Dovewing's pelt was pricking with fear. "In the medicine den?"

"It's best to keep him away from the nursery now," Shadowsight told him. "We don't want his cough spreading there."

Sunbeam tensed. *What about here?* She glanced toward

Blazefire. "Perhaps Blazefire should move back to the warriors' den—" She paused, mad at herself for being so quick to worry about Blazefire. *He's not my mate and he never will be.*

But Shadowsight didn't seem to have heard her. He'd turned toward the herb store.

As he rummaged inside, Puddleshine slid into the den. The brown-and-white medicine cat glanced around, taking in Dovewing and Tigerstar and the sick kit in the nest before settling his gaze on Shadowsight. "What are you looking for?"

"Catmint," Shadowsight told him. "Rowankit might have greencough."

Puddleshine hurried toward the kit's nest and leaned in, running his muzzle along the kit's damp pelt. He lifted his head, his eyes dark with worry.

Shadowsight had pulled a thin bundle of leaves from the store and was looking at them in dismay. "Is this all we have?"

"Yes," Puddleshine answered grimly.

Dovewing looked from one medicine cat to the other. "I can fetch more if you need it."

Puddleshine's ears twitched uneasily. "The patch by the half-bridge has died back."

"Already?" Tigerstar looked alarmed. "But it's not even leaf-bare."

"The lake flooded there during greenleaf," Puddleshine reminded him. "The bush half drowned and never quite recovered."

"We can go to SkyClan," Shadowsight suggested. "They

have catmint on their territory."

"I'll go," Dovewing offered, her eyes bright with fear.

"It would be better for a medicine cat to go," Tigerstar told her gently.

"If Frecklewish has any catmint, she'll share it," Puddleshine reassured her. "I'll go at once. Shadowsight will give Rowankit something to ease his fever while I'm gone."

As he hurried out of the den, Shadowsight began shredding herbs.

"He'll be all right, won't he?" Dovewing fretted.

"He'll be fine once he's had some catmint," Shadowsight told her without looking up.

Tigerstar's fur was spiking along his spine. The Shadow-Clan leader was scared. "The catmint stock shouldn't be so low already," he mewed, half to himself.

Sunbeam felt a twinge of foreboding. Greencough was a greater danger than even hunger during leaf-bare. How would the Clan manage with their catmint store so low? She wondered whether to reassure them. Surely Puddleshine would return from SkyClan with a big bundle of the precious herb. And if he didn't, they'd find enough to last leaf-bare somehow, even if it meant asking the other Clans for help. But Dovewing looked so worried that Sunbeam felt her words might sound hollow if she said them out loud.

She glanced at Blazefire, hoping to feel reassured. He was always so positive and encouraging. But the ginger-and-white tom looked as worried as the others.

Tigerstar nudged Dovewing toward the den entrance. "I'll

stay here with Rowankit," he mewed. "You should get back to Birchkit."

"Cinnamontail is looking after him," Dovewing objected.

"He'll be anxious if you're not there," Tigerstar told her.

Reluctantly, Dovewing turned toward the entrance and Tigerstar sat down beside Rowankit's nest. As she left, Shadowsight looked up from his herbs and blinked at Sunbeam.

"You ought to go too," he mewed. "It's a little crowded in here. If it is greencough . . ." His mew trailed away as Tigerstar jerked his gaze toward the medicine cat.

Sunbeam felt a rush of heat to her pelt. She should have left already. She must look like she was hanging around Blazefire like a lost kit. Dipping her head politely, she hurried to the entrance and, narrowing her eyes against the rain, nosed her way out.

Lightleap was in the clearing, her ears twitching anxiously as she watched Dovewing hurry back to the nursery. She must have just learned about her younger brother's sickness. For a moment, Sunbeam wondered whether to reassure her best friend. But she hesitated. Their relationship was still fragile. Lightleap might not be ready to share her worries with Sunbeam yet. And Sunbeam still felt a prickle of resentment that might show in her mew. It would be better to avoid each other for a while longer. The friendship still needed time to heal.

CHAPTER 2

Though the sun was shining in a clear blue sky, a cold wind skimmed the ThunderClan forest, ruffling the oaks so that their leaves shimmered like the golden fur of an ancient LionClan warrior.

Nightheart puffed out his chest. At last he was patrolling on his own rather than training with his mentor. While Lilyheart was on the other side of ThunderClan territory helping mark the borders, Nightheart was hunting with Lionblaze, Birchfall, Hollytuft, Plumstone, and Finleap. He tasted the air. The first frost would come soon, and then leaf-bare, and ThunderClan would face hunger as the forest prey burrowed deeper into the shelter of the earth. But his Clan would begin leaf-bare with full bellies; he'd make sure of it.

Nightheart's paws had tingled with excitement when Bramblestar had told Lionblaze to let Nightheart join the patrol. He was determined to prove he was a good warrior and make every cat in the Clan forget that it had taken him three attempts to pass his warrior assessment.

It hadn't been his fault. It had been bad luck: Lilyheart and Squirrelflight had been so busy comparing him to Firestar that they'd judged him harshly over and over until he'd begun to lose confidence in himself. He hadn't *chosen* to be Firestar's kin. And now, with a new name less directly tied to his famous ancestor, Nightheart was determined to make his own paw marks in the forest instead of trying to fill Firestar's. That was why, at his warrior naming ceremony, he'd told his Clanmates that he didn't want the warrior name Bramblestar had chosen. *Flameheart!* It was too much like Fireheart, Firestar's warrior name before he became leader. Nightheart's black pelt didn't even *resemble* fire. His mother must only have named him Flamekit because she hoped he'd grow up to be like the fabled leader. It was an unfair burden to put on him, and he wasn't going to apologize for wanting to be himself instead of the pale shadow of another cat.

"Nightheart?" Lionblaze's mew jerked him from his thoughts, and Nightheart realized the rest of the patrol was looking at him. "Are you listening?"

He straightened. It was obvious he hadn't been, and his pelt grew hot. "Sorry."

Lionblaze looked at him sternly. "I thought you were excited to be on patrol."

"I am," Nightheart mewed.

Birchfall grunted. "We shouldn't have brought a warrior who still has the smell of the apprentices' den in his fur."

Nightheart glared at the light brown tabby tom, but Birchfall wasn't even looking at him. He was watching Lionblaze.

"We're going to take home two pieces of prey each," the golden warrior mewed. "There's plenty in the forest, but the closer we get to leaf-bare, the more alert the prey will be. We'll move more quietly if we split up into pairs."

"I'll pair up with Birchfall," Hollytuft mewed quickly.

"I'll go with Finleap." Plumstone moved closer to the brown tom.

Nightheart's claws itched. *No cat wants to pair up with me.*

Lionblaze glanced at him. "I'll take Nightheart, then." Was that disappointment in his mew?

Thanks for doing me a favor. Nightheart swallowed back resentment. He would show them.

"I want the fresh-kill pile fully stocked for the next moon," Lionblaze went on. "Leaf-fall is our last chance to eat well, and we should make the most of it."

Birchfall headed away, Hollytuft padding after him. Finleap and Plumstone looked around as though still deciding where to hunt.

Lionblaze whisked his tail. "Come on, Nightheart," he mewed. "Let's see if we can flush out some prey in the brambles near the SkyClan border."

"We'll come with you as far as the Ancient Oak," Finleap mewed.

The Ancient Oak. Nightheart pricked his ears. There would be squirrels there. Eagerly, he followed Lionblaze, Plumstone, and Finleap to the dip where the great tree stood. Leaves had gathered in drifts around its roots, and more rattled above each time a gust of wind shook its branches.

Nightheart looked up. The acorns ripening among the clusters of foliage had attracted prey. A squirrel was bobbing

along a high branch. Another skittered up the trunk. Nightheart licked his lips. "We could hunt squirrels too," he mewed
hopefully.

Lionblaze flicked his tail. "We should find something
closer to the ground."

Nightheart's paws pricked with indignation. "That's—" *Not
fair.* He stopped himself before he said it out loud. He didn't
want to sound like an argumentative kit. "Okay," he mewed
instead.

As Plumstone and Finleap headed toward the oak, Lionblaze motioned for Nightheart to follow him along the bottom
of the rise. As they left, Nightheart glanced back ruefully.
He'd been so excited to leave Lilyheart behind, but Lionblaze
was acting more like a mentor than a fellow warrior. He padded after the golden tom, crossing a hollow where dogwood
crowded the trail, until they reached a small clearing ringed
by beech trees. As they stopped at the edge, a squirrel darted
from behind a trunk and bounced across the leaf-strewn forest floor.

Nightheart's blood quickened. Quivering with excitement,
he dropped into a hunting crouch as the squirrel paused at the
bottom of a tree. It sniffed at the leaves piled there, clearly
unaware of the warriors' arrival, but its ears were twitching,
alert for any sound.

Nightheart forced himself to be still. Determination was
pulsing beneath his pelt. He hadn't spent all those moons in
training for nothing. He was going to prove he could catch a
squirrel as well as any warrior.

"Stay on the ground," Lionblaze ordered.

"But Lilyheart taught me how to hunt in trees."

"You're still inexperienced and I don't want to risk . . ."

Nightheart stopped listening. He wasn't going to miss this opportunity because he was arguing with a Clanmate. Pressing his belly to the earth, he drew himself forward, but he was aware of Lionblaze's gaze on his back. He hesitated. Suddenly it felt like an assessment. He narrowed his eyes. He had failed twice as an apprentice, both in assessments having to do with his judgment when it came to hunting. But he was a warrior now, and this time he wasn't going to make any mistakes.

The squirrel was rummaging in the leaves at the bottom of the tree, absorbed in its search for beechnuts. But its ears were still twitching. It was listening for any sign of danger. Nightheart lifted his tail so that it didn't drag along the ground. Keeping low, he put one paw silently in front of the other. *I can do this.* He was stalking perfectly. He could feel it. Every movement was slow, his breath was controlled, and every hair on his pelt lay smooth and still as he crept closer to his quarry.

Two tail-lengths away from the squirrel, he stopped. He was far enough away to remain unnoticed, close enough to pounce. Gathering his strength in his hindquarters, he pressed back a shiver of excitement and unsheathed his claws. *I can do this.* As he prepared to jump, a bird shook the branch above him. The squirrel jerked its gaze upward. Its eye flashed toward the bird; then, as though sensing there was another danger, it looked back over its shoulder and saw Nightheart.

Terror bushed its tail. It leaped for the trunk, but Nightheart was ready. He pounced, and as it skittered upward, he hooked his claws into the bark and hauled himself after it.

The squirrel fled toward the safety of a branch halfway up and raced along it. Nightheart scrambled from the trunk and pounded after it, leaves shivering around him. He could guess the squirrel's plan. The next tree was only a short jump away, and its weight would hardly bend the tip of the branch as it leaped for safety. Nightheart had to grab it before it got there.

As the branch narrowed, he pushed harder. Splinters showered down as the bark grazed his pads. Taking a deep breath and focusing his gaze on the squirrel, he leaped. He came down hard, gripping the squirrel firmly with his paws. As he did, the bark crumbled beneath his hind claws. One paw slipped, and his heart lurched as his leg shot downward, his fur ripping against the branch as he lost his balance and slithered sideways. The squirrel wriggled from his grip as his hindquarters dragged him down, and he gasped, hooking his claws into the branch with a yelp of panic.

For a moment he hung there, but soon he could not support his own weight. Pelt spiking, he lost his grip and plummeted downward. The branch below broke his fall with a thump that knocked the breath from him so hard that he didn't have a chance to grab it, and he fell again. Thinking fast, he spun in the air, tucking his legs under him so that he landed squarely as he hit the ground, and sank into his paws, letting them absorb the shock of his fall. He froze for a second, taking stock of his body, feeling for injuries. Relief swamped him. The only pain he felt was where the bark had grazed his pelt.

Lionblaze was watching him from the other side of the clearing.

"It's okay," Nightheart called. "I'm fine."

But Lionblaze didn't look relieved. His gaze was stern. "I told you not to leave the ground," he growled.

"I almost had it." Nightheart straightened and limped toward the golden warrior. His grazed leg stung, and he forced himself to ignore the pain, but he could smell his own blood.

Lionblaze could clearly smell it too. His gaze flitted over Nightheart as he drew closer, settling on the dripping wound on his leg. "You'll have to go back to camp and get that treated." He turned and called through the trees. "Finleap! Come here!"

"It can wait till our patrol is finished," Nightheart mewed quickly. He didn't want to be sent home yet. He hadn't caught anything.

Lionblaze's gaze darkened. "You'll go home *now*."

Brown fur flashed between the trees as Finleap raced toward them and skidded to a halt beside Lionblaze. "Is something wrong?" he panted.

"Nightheart's hurt," Lionblaze mewed. "Take him back to camp."

"Already?" Finleap blinked at him. "What happened?"

"It's just a scratch." Nightheart didn't want to tell him that he'd fallen while hunting a squirrel. It would be like admitting Lionblaze had been right. "I can keep going. Honest."

"You might be able to hunt today," Lionblaze growled.

"But I don't want that wound going sour." Nightheart tried to read his gaze. *Is he saying that because he's worried about me?* After all, they were kin as well as Clanmates. But Nightheart had learned that kin didn't always react as he expected, and Lionblaze was still staring angrily at him. "If it does, you'll be out of action for the rest of leaf-fall." The golden warrior lashed his tail. "Didn't Lilyheart teach you that this moon's hunting will decide whether we survive leaf-bare? It's our last chance to fill our bellies before newleaf, and we need every warrior to be fit and well."

Nightheart's heart sank. *He only cares that I'm hurt because it might affect the Clan.*

"Take him to the medicine den," Lionblaze told Finleap. "And ask Finchlight to join us in his place."

"But she was on the dawn patrol," Finleap reminded him. "She'll want to rest."

"She can rest after she's caught the prey Nightheart should have taken home today." His tail flicking irritably, Lionblaze headed between the trees.

Nightheart's pelt pricked uncomfortably. His sister, Finchlight, was quickly tiring of being caught in the middle between him and Sparkpelt after his name change. If she was dragged out of camp to finish his hunt, she'd be convinced that he only made mistakes. *Why couldn't I have proved Lionblaze wrong?* Shame wormed in his belly, and Finleap's sympathetic glance only made him feel worse. Had StarClan decided that no matter what he did, Nightheart was always going to look like the most incompetent warrior in ThunderClan?

* * *

Nightheart sat up as Jayfeather stopped beside his nest. "Can I go back to the warriors' den yet?"

"Wait until the poultice has dried," Jayfeather told him. "I want a good strong scab to form before you start walking on that leg."

Nightheart had been in the medicine den for two days. The graze on his leg wasn't deep, but it was wide, and infection had crept in at the edges. Jayfeather had kept it smeared with herb poultices that smelled so strong they had put him off his food. But the wound was clearly healing now.

"I'll be careful," Nightheart promised.

"I should hope so." Jayfeather's ears swiveled toward Brightheart. The white-and-ginger elder was wheezing louder than ever.

Alderheart was leaning into her nest, his ear to the she-cat's chest. "Take a deep breath," he told her.

Brightheart's lungs seemed to rattle with the effort, and she burst into a cough that sounded painful.

Alderheart sat back and frowned.

"Come outside," Jayfeather told him quietly. He flicked his tail toward the entrance, and as Alderheart nosed his way out, he followed the younger cat from the den.

Nightheart glanced at Brightheart as her coughing fit eased. Her eyes shone with fever, and she blinked at him wearily before settling down into her nest.

He could hear Jayfeather and Alderheart outside. They were talking in hushed mews about Brightheart.

"I'll keep an eye on her this afternoon," Jayfeather mewed. "You'd better fetch more tansy so that we can manage her fever."

"Do you think it's still whitecough?" Alderheart sounded anxious. "The fever suggests it might have developed into greencough."

"Let's not worry about that yet," Jayfeather mewed. "We'll keep treating her with tansy and coltsfoot and pray to StarClan that it's enough."

"We have a *little* catmint," Alderheart's mew lowered further, and Nightheart had to strain to hear as the younger medicine cat went on. "Should we give it to her now?"

"Not yet," Jayfeather told him. "We should use it only as a last resort."

"Perhaps we should ask Bramblestar to send another patrol to the abandoned Twolegplace," Alderheart mewed. "I know the last one said the catmint we planted there was nothing more than stalks. But I could go with them. They might have missed something."

"I doubt you'll find anything if the patrol didn't. Birchfall and Poppyfrost were on it, and they've been around long enough to know catmint when they see it. They wouldn't have missed the leaves if any had been there." Jayfeather sighed. "Whatever ate the leaves stripped the whole area clean."

"Do you think the bushes will recover before leaf-bare?" Alderheart fretted.

"We're too far into leaf-fall," Jayfeather mewed. "It'll be newleaf before they recover."

"But what if more cats get whitecough?" Alderheart's mew was taut with worry.

"Whitecough's not the problem," Jayfeather mewed. "We can treat it with tansy and coltsfoot—mallow if necessary. But if whitecough turns to greencough, catmint is the only herb that can treat it." He sounded grim. "If we have more than one or two cases this leaf-bare, our catmint supplies won't be enough."

Nightheart glanced at Brightheart, relieved her nest was too far from the entrance for her to hear the medicine cats' conversation. Jayfeather could be short-tempered and sharp-tongued, but Nightheart had never heard him sound *worried* before. It unsettled him. If *Jayfeather* was nervous, the situation must be bad.

"We should be on the lookout for coughs and sneezes, and we must isolate cats who are ill and treat them immediately," Alderheart mewed. "If we can stop whitecough from spreading, then we've won half the battle."

"Agreed," mewed Jayfeather. "The less whitecough, the less greencough. But if there *is* an outbreak of greencough, warriors will have to fight it with their strength alone. We must save our catmint for elders and kits."

Alderheart was quiet for a moment. He seemed to be absorbing Jayfeather's words. Then he spoke. "I'll gather as much tansy as I can this afternoon. And tomorrow I'll hunt for coltsfoot."

"I'll tell Bramblestar to ask all the patrols to keep a look out for catmint," Jayfeather added. "There might be a patch somewhere we haven't noticed. But I don't hold out much hope."

"If only we still had the territory we gave to SkyClan," Alderheart mewed. "There was catmint on it."

"We should have demanded foraging rights when we gave it to them," Jayfeather growled. "It's going to be a long leaf-bare if we can't replenish our store."

"We could ask them if we can gather some now," Alderheart suggested.

"We might have to," Jayfeather answered. "Let's just hope they're willing to share. If we're worried about greencough this early in the season, they might be worried too."

Nightheart's injured leg began to ache. He realized he'd been leaning on it to hear better. He shifted it into a more comfortable position. *Our catmint supplies won't be enough.* Jayfeather's words brought a chill to his pelt. In the quiet den, Brightheart's breathing sounded more labored than ever. Fear tightened his belly. What if she was only the first cat to fall ill? Without catmint, an outbreak of greencough could be enough to devastate all of ThunderClan.

A fiery evening sun glowed through the leaves at the top of the hollow and set the camp aflame. Nightheart scrunched up his eyes against the glare. After two days in the medicine den, he had grown accustomed to its gloom. But despite the golden wash of light, the air was cold, and his breath billowed a little as he padded slowly across the clearing, putting his full weight on his injured leg as carefully as he could, so as not to split open the scab. Dry now, it stung and itched at the same time, pulling on the skin around it. But he refused to limp.

Jayfeather had ordered him to stay in camp for a few more days, but he wasn't going to let his Clanmates think he was weak. No doubt Lionblaze had told every cat how he'd disobeyed orders and made a foolish attempt to catch a squirrel. But without bravery, ThunderClan wouldn't be the strongest Clan in the forest, and surely every warrior made a mistake now and then. It was just Nightheart's bad luck that every mistake he made was witnessed by a more experienced warrior, who was always eager to judge him by it.

Lifting his chin defiantly, he padded toward the fresh-kill pile. His Clanmates were already eating, settled in groups around the clearing, and there were only a few mice and a young rabbit left on the pile. Nightheart was hungry. His appetite had come racing back now that he was away from the pungent smell of the medicine den, but—although his belly was rumbling—he nudged the juicy-looking rabbit out of the way and took one of the mice. He couldn't eat the best prey when he hadn't helped catch it.

The mouse was small, but its sweet smell made his mouth water as he looked for a space to settle down to eat it. Sparkpelt and Finchlight were sharing a pigeon outside the warriors' den, and he padded toward them. His mother and sister looked up as he approached, but then exchanged a disapproving glance. Shock pulsed in his paws. *They don't want to eat with me.* He stared at them, stung by their unkindness. *Are they still angry that I changed my name to Nightheart?* He'd never been as

close to them as they were to each other—the impostor who'd
pretended to be Bramblestar had exiled them when he'd been
an apprentice, and they'd had to leave him in camp—but they
were his *kin*. Shouldn't they welcome him no matter what he'd
done, especially when he'd just recovered from an injury?

Perhaps Finchlight was just angry because she'd had to
finish his patrol the other day. Even so, it was unfair to hold
something so trivial against him *this* long. It had been days!
He dropped the mouse, feeling a fresh prickle of resentment.
"Aren't I allowed to *eat* with you anymore?"

Finchlight sniffed. "Oh, so you don't like it when kin turn
their back on you?"

Nightheart bristled. Did she mean *him*? "I never turned my
back on you."

Sparkpelt glared at him. His mother's green eyes were
flashing with anger. "You rejected your family when you
rejected your name."

"I only asked for a name that suits me better than Flameheart!" he objected. "What's wrong with that?"

Sparkpelt's ears flattened. "It's disrespectful, that's what's
wrong."

"To whom?" He stared at her. "To *you*?"

"To *Firestar*," Sparkpelt snapped.

"How can I be disrespectful to a cat I never met?" Nightheart tried to hold his anger in check, but it was impossible.
She was being so unfair. "You never met him either!"

"I don't need to have met him to know what a great warrior
he was," Sparkpelt snapped back.

"So what if he was a great warrior?" Nightheart's tail quivered. "Does that mean every warrior has to have a name like his?"

"His *kin* should," Sparkpelt growled.

"Why?" Nightheart mewed hotly. "Are you scared his kin will forget who he is? Or are you scared the rest of the Clan might forget we're related to him?"

Sparkpelt scrambled to her paws, her pelt spiking along her spine. "How dare you?" she hissed. "I gave you that name because kin is *important* to me, and it breaks my heart that it's not important to you!"

"If kin's so important to you, why are you giving *me* such a hard time?" he retorted.

"Because I don't understand why you're not honored to be related to Firestar!" Her tail was lashing with fury. "You chose to turn your back on his memory no matter how much you hurt your family. Firestar would never have done such a thing."

You don't know that. Nightheart swallowed back the words. She *wanted* to be angry. Nothing he said would change that.

Finchlight's ears twitched self-righteously. "You should find somewhere else to eat," she mewed. "If you stay here, you'll give Sparkpelt indigestion."

Nightheart stared at her in disbelief. Why did they care so much about his name? Shouldn't they care more about who he *was*? His heart was beating hard. He picked up his mouse and padded to the other side of the camp, relieved when

Myrtlebloom beckoned him with a nod and shifted to make room for him on the patch of grass where she'd been eating a sparrow. His pelt was ruffled with embarrassment. She must have overheard the conversation. Every cat in the *Clan* must have overheard it.

"It's fair for them to be upset," she mewed.

"Still?" Nightheart dropped the mouse beside her and sat down. He avoided looking around the clearing. His Clanmates were probably staring at him, and his pelt felt hot enough already.

"It was a shock," Myrtlebloom told him. "You changed your name in front of everyone. Without even warning Sparkpelt."

"It's not like I rejected my *father's* name," Nightheart grumbled. "I could understand Sparkpelt being angry if I'd done that."

"But you did reject Firestar's name," Myrtlebloom mewed gently. "In a way."

"Why shouldn't I? I'm nothing like him," Nightheart mewed. "My fur's not even ginger, it's black. Flamekit was a ridiculous name to give me. Anyway, I kept part of his name, remember? I'm Night*heart*." Myrtlebloom didn't look terribly impressed, and Nightheart's frustration hardened. "Can't any cat in the Clan just accept me for who I am?"

Myrtlebloom looked at her paws. "Do you know how many warriors would give their whiskers to be related to Firestar?" she mewed. "You might not think it's special, but it would mean the world to another cat. It's an honor even ShadowClan warriors would want. But you rejected it in front of the whole Clan, and that just seems . . ." She hesitated before she finished. "Spoiled."

"*Spoiled?*" Nightheart could hardly believe his ears. No cat had *ever* spoiled him. Sparkpelt hadn't even nursed him; she'd been too busy grieving over Larksong. The next thing he remembered, the impostor had exiled his mother and sister, so even if his kin had *wanted* to spoil him, they hadn't been around to do it. "I've never been spoiled in my life."

"But your kin are leader and deputy of ThunderClan." Myrtlebloom looked at him. "And no matter what you say, that affects you, and the way you're treated."

Nightheart stared at her. It might mean something to other cats, but he wanted to be respected for being *himself.* Not for being related to more powerful warriors. More than that, he'd much rather have a mother and sister who cared about him than be related to Firestar or Bramblestar or Squirrelflight. As it was, he was expected to be grateful for a family that didn't seem to support or respect him. He looked away. How could Myrtlebloom understand? Her kin cared about her. No cat would ever expect her to be anything more than an ordinary warrior. And if he kept trying to convince her, he might lose her support too. "It's not that I'm ungrateful for having such great kin," he conceded. "I'm proud of them. Firestar was a great leader—"

"See?" Myrtlebloom's eyes brightened. "You *can* see how important your kin are." She nudged him with a flick of her tail. "It's not too late. Everyone will realize that it was just a mistake and that you've changed your mind after thinking about it. You can go and ask for your real name back."

Nightheart glared at her. "Nightheart *is* my real name." Anger was throbbing afresh beneath his pelt. *I'm never asking for my old name back!* "No cat gets to decide what kind of warrior I am. Only *I* get to decide that."

Myrtlebloom looked disappointed. She gazed at him for a moment as though trying to understand. Then she gave herself a shake, smoothing out her fur. "What kind of warrior do you want to be, then?"

Nightheart hesitated. He didn't have an answer. Suddenly he felt angrier with himself than his Clan. Only a few days ago, at his naming ceremony, he'd been happy. For a few short moments, he'd felt as though he'd done the right thing. He'd finally stood up for himself and asked for a name that suited him, a name he could truly make his own. But that happiness was gone now. Once more he felt out of step with his Clan, as though what he was and what they wanted him to be were so far apart that he would never be able to bridge the gap.

Is there something wrong with me? Suddenly he wasn't hungry anymore. He didn't want to be Firestar's shadow, tied by his famous kin to an idea of greatness that had nothing to do with him. Was he wrong for not trying to become what his Clan expected him to be? Or was ThunderClan wrong for asking him to spend his life keeping alive a memory that it was time to let go?

CHAPTER 3

Every now and then, Frostpaw's grief lifted just enough to let panic rush in. What would she do now? How could she go on? Curlfeather was dead. Crouched deep in her nest, Frostpaw was barely aware of the medicine den rocking around her as wind swept the RiverClan camp. The reeds swished beyond the den walls, but her thoughts drowned out the noise.

The memory of her mother's death scorched through Frostpaw's mind: she saw the dog pack swarming like fish around Curlfeather, their backs jerking and twisting as they fought over the pale brown she-cat. Frostpaw had listened to her mother's screeches, powerless to help. The sound would never leave her, and yet it was the silence that followed that drove the sharpest thorns into her heart. The dogs had kept snarling, but Curlfeather had fallen silent, and Frostpaw had known with sickening certainty that her mother was dead.

Trust no cat. Curlfeather's final words lingered in Frostpaw's mind. Why had her mother left her with such a desperate plea? What had Curlfeather known before she died?

Frostpaw swallowed back a sob. *Trust no cat.* She was alone in a Clan with no leader or deputy, trying to learn how to become a medicine cat from a Clanmate who had no connection to StarClan. And every cat was watching and waiting for her to tell them who StarClan wanted to be their next leader.

She'd thought she had it right. But why had StarClan let Curlfeather die? Her mother would have been the perfect leader for RiverClan—she had always known what to do. When Frostpaw had felt lost or uncertain, her mother had encouraged her. And Curlfeather had been about to restore stability to RiverClan. Instead, she was gone.

Frostpaw's muzzle slid between her paws as she let grief flood in once more. At least the sorrow muffled her terror. *I miss you.* She wanted Curlfeather to come in and sit beside her. She wanted to feel her breath tickle her ears as she leaned down to comfort her. But that couldn't happen now. It could never happen again.

Paws scuffed the floor of the medicine den. *Is that*—Frostpaw lifted her head hopefully, her heart sinking like a stone when she saw Splashtail.

The tom's thick tabby fur was wind-ruffled, and his eyes glistened kindly as he laid a small, plump trout beside Frostpaw's nest. "You should eat," he mewed.

"I'm not hungry." Frostpaw laid her muzzle on her paws once more.

"But you haven't eaten since Curlfeather's vigil." Splashtail nudged the trout closer. "And that was days ago."

"I'm not hungry," Frostpaw mewed again, still not looking at him.

"You're a medicine cat," he pressed. "You need to stay strong."

She ignored him.

"For the Clan."

She closed her eyes. Why couldn't he go away and leave her alone?

But Splashtail didn't take the hint. "Mothwing is taking care of everything herself. She's even organizing the patrols. She could use some help. She must be worn out."

Frostpaw lifted her head, irritated now. "Are you trying to make me feel guilty? Isn't it enough that I'm grieving?"

Splashtail gazed at her apologetically. "I'm just trying to say anything that might persuade you to get up," he mewed. "You're never going to feel better lying here by yourself. You need fresh air and to be with your Clanmates. They care about you."

"If they cared, they'd leave me alone," she snapped.

"Maybe." Splashtail didn't move. "But I'm going to keep bringing you prey until you feel hungry again."

Deep in her chest, Frostpaw felt a glimmer of gratitude. It was the first warm emotion she'd felt in days. She pushed it away. And yet he'd managed to stir her curiosity. "Why is Mothwing organizing patrols?"

"No other cat wants to."

"Not even Duskfur?"

"Nope."

Why were RiverClan's warriors so reluctant to take responsibility? "What about Shimmerpelt or Icewing? I thought they'd *want* to take charge."

"Me too," he mewed. "Especially Shimmerpelt. She's been a warrior forever. And Icewing leads patrols better than any cat in camp." He looked bemused. "Mallownose sounded like he might volunteer after Mistystar and Reedwhisker died." He paused thoughtfully. "Perhaps he's in shock. Perhaps they're *all* in shock. Curlfeather's death might have been one death too many."

Frostpaw winced, fresh pain washing over her.

Splashtail's eyes flashed an apology, and he went on more gently. "It could have scared them."

"But surely *some* cat has the courage to take charge."

"We've lost our leader *and* our deputy," Splashtail pointed out. "Which means whoever takes over will have to make all the decisions. It's a lot to take on."

"Would it really be *so* hard for some cat who's been a warrior for moons?" Frostpaw just wanted some cat to make all RiverClan's troubles go away. "Warriors with experience, like Duskfur or Shimmerpelt, seem like the obvious choice. Why won't one of them step up?"

"I guess being a warrior isn't the same as being a leader," Splashtail mewed. "Experience might have taught them that the obvious choice isn't always the right choice."

Frostpaw felt too tired for this conversation. She was relieved when Mothwing padded in.

The dappled golden she-cat glanced at the trout Splashtail had brought. "I suppose she says she's not hungry."

She spoke to Splashtail as though Frostpaw were a difficult kit. But Frostpaw felt too exhausted to protest and rested her head once more. Mothwing and Splashtail could carry on talking about her so long as they didn't expect her to join in.

"Leave the trout here," Mothwing told Splashtail. "And go and join Owlnose's patrol. We need to keep the borders marked. It's important that the other Clans think nothing has changed."

Splashtail dipped his head and, with a final glance at Frostpaw, headed out of the den.

Mothwing sat down beside Frostpaw's nest. "Aren't you even going to take a bite?" She nodded at the trout.

"I'm not hungry."

"But you've been like this for *days*." Mothwing's mew was gentle, but there was an edge to it that had grown increasingly sharp since yesterday. "Curlfeather wouldn't want you lying here like this. You have responsibilities."

Frostpaw wanted to push her paws into her ears and block out her mentor's mew. It was true: she was training to be a medicine cat. But couldn't Mothwing give her a break for a little while longer? She was sure that she'd start to feel better soon. Just not now.

Mothwing tried again. "By helping keep RiverClan strong, you'd be *honoring* your mother," she mewed. "Isn't that better than grieving for her?" She paused as though waiting for an answer. Frostpaw didn't give her one. Mothwing softened a bit. "I know how you feel."

Do you? Frostpaw shut her eyes. *Did you watch your mother being torn apart by dogs?*

But Mothwing kept going. "When Willowshine died, I

thought my grief would never ease—"

Frostpaw flattened her ears against her mentor's mew. *You lost your* friend, *not your* mother! Was Mothwing so thick-furred that she thought those were the same thing?

"—but, at some point, it does. It *has* to. Life needs to get back to normal."

Frostpaw felt a rush of anger. *Leave me alone!* She sat up and glared at Mothwing. "Do you call this normal?" she snapped. "A Clan without a leader or a deputy? Whose next leader was killed before she could even get the blessing of StarClan? There's *no* normal. Not anymore. There's nothing to get back to. Why even try?"

Mothwing held her gaze. "Because our Clanmates are relying on us. Because no matter how bad you feel, they *need* you, and they'll keep needing you. And, if you let them down, then everything you've worked for until now—everything Curlfeather worked for—will be wasted."

Frostpaw heard her words. But they meant nothing to her. All her effort felt wasted already, and she wanted to lie down again. And yet she willed herself to stay upright if only to meet Mothwing's gaze, which seemed to reach for her with an urgency she couldn't ignore. The weight of her own body felt like more than she could bear—as though she were being pounded beneath a waterfall—but she forced herself to stay sitting up and lifted her chin. "What about the other Clans?" Hadn't Mothwing said, only a few days ago, that it was time to tell the other Clans about Mistystar and Reedwhisker? That RiverClan had kept their deaths a secret long enough?

"I thought you were going to ask them for help?"

To Frostpaw's surprise, Mothwing shook her head. "I've changed my mind."

"Why?"

"We've grown too vulnerable." Mothwing's pelt rippled uneasily. "You saw what happened to ThunderClan when Bramblestar's body was taken over by Ashfur. Without proper leadership, ThunderClan's warriors turned on each other. Some left, and some were exiled, so by the time they asked the other Clans for help, ThunderClan was so weak that it only made things worse. Every cat had an opinion, and every opinion seemed to tear ThunderClan further apart." She shook her head. "We've missed our chance to ask for help. We're too weak now to show our weakness. RiverClan needs to fix itself before we face the other Clans."

Mothwing's words filled Frostpaw with foreboding. She looked at her mentor. "How can we fix ourselves? Too much has happened. Curlfeather's death—" She paused to steady her breath, then forced herself to go on. "Curlfeather's death was the final reed that broke the dam." She felt more desolate than ever. "I'm not sure we *can* fix ourselves."

"We have to," Mothwing insisted. "We have no choice. We can't watch our Clan fall apart." Her eyes glittered with passion. "If we can just get StarClan to tell us who our leader should be, we'll be okay. We won't owe the other Clans anything. They'll never even know we were weak." She pressed on. "I need you to contact StarClan. You're the only one who can."

Frostpaw's belly clenched.

"You need to ask them to help us choose a new leader."

I already did, Frostpaw wanted to wail. *I chose Curlfeather and led her to her death.* Grief threatened to overwhelm her again. She breathed through the pain, trying to focus. RiverClan needed a leader, and if they couldn't choose one, they needed StarClan's guidance. Mothwing was right: she *was* the only cat who could reach their ancestors. She had no choice but to help.

Mothwing was staring at her hopefully. Outside, the wind rattled the dens. "I know this is hard for you and that you need longer to grieve," her mentor mewed. "But we don't have time. The Clan is barely functioning. No cat knows what to do, but every cat *thinks* they do. Gorseclaw and Havenpelt nearly came to blows yesterday over who was going to hunt in the water meadow, and half the Clan thinks we should be fishing downstream and the other half thinks we should fish upstream. It seems like the only thing any of our warriors are certain of is that they are right and their Clanmates are wrong. We need a leader to take control before the Clan falls apart."

Frostpaw narrowed her eyes. Her mentor's gaze burned now. Her muscles twitched beneath her pelt. Mothwing wasn't talking like a medicine cat. She was talking like a warrior. She clearly had wisdom beyond her knowledge of herbs. And hadn't she been the one organizing the patrols these past few days? Frostpaw leaned forward, her heart quickening. "Why don't *you* take charge?"

"Me?" Mothwing looked appalled.

"You've been the only cat giving orders."

Mothwing shook out her pelt. "I'd be happy to let some other cat make the decisions. I'd rather cure my Clanmates than lead them." She sounded so sure that Frostpaw felt foolish for even suggesting it. "You should speak with StarClan," she told Frostpaw.

Frostpaw stiffened.

"You need to go to the Moonpool." Mothwing's gaze seemed to bore into hers as she stared helplessly back at her mentor.

It was daunting enough to have her whole Clan relying on her alone, but the thought of traveling to the Moonpool again made Frostpaw sick with dread.

Mothwing leaned closer. "I know that's where Curlfeather died," she mewed. "But you need to go there. It's the best way to reach StarClan."

Frostpaw's mouth was too dry to answer. How could she face the journey after what happened last time?

Mothwing went on. "There was no sign of the dogs when Mallownose, Duskfur, and Splashtail fetched your mother's body and brought it home. And I've sent patrols to look for them over and over. They're gone. I'm sure of it."

Frostpaw looked at her bleakly, knowing she couldn't refuse.

"I'll come with you," Mothwing promised.

Trust no cat. Her mother's words echoed once more in Frostpaw's mind. She froze. *Why think of that now?* She searched Mothwing's gaze. The medicine cat's amber eyes were clear and eager. There was no cunning in them. Surely Curlfeather hadn't meant for her to distrust Mothwing?

Mothwing hadn't moved. "You have to go," she pressed. "We can take a patrol with us for protection if it will make you feel better. Splashtail can lead it. He's been worried about—"

Frostpaw cut her off. Fear was churning in her belly. "I don't know if I can," she whispered. "Perhaps in a few days. When I feel more—"

"You're going to have to save your grief till later. This can't wait." Mothwing was suddenly fierce. "RiverClan needs you to speak with StarClan." She turned and pushed her way out of the den, the wind whisking in where she'd been.

Frostpaw was trembling. She wanted to burrow into the bottom of her nest, but she couldn't burrow deep enough to escape the responsibility weighing on her like stone. *I just want to grieve in peace.* Her heart felt ready to split open. But Mothwing was right. Frostpaw knew that she was her Clan's best hope of finding one. She pressed her paws into her nest, forcing them to stop shaking. There was no time for her to be afraid. RiverClan needed a leader.

CHAPTER 4
❧

As she hauled a fresh bundle of bracken through the entrance tunnel, Sunbeam was grateful for the shelter of the brambles enclosing the ShadowClan camp. The wind was cold, and the pines above her rocked and creaked as it tore at the forest. This was the last of the bundles she'd gathered, and as she stacked it in the clearing beside the others, she wondered which of the dens needed fresh bedding first.

She was happy do such menial chores. Anything to keep herself busy. The past couple of days had been difficult—between avoiding Lightleap and worrying about Blazefire, she'd hardly relaxed for a moment. And now she was waiting anxiously for Puddleshine to return from his mission to ask SkyClan for catmint.

Blazefire had caught Rowankit's cough, and though it hadn't turned to greencough yet, it might at any moment. Rowankit was getting sicker by the day. This morning, he hadn't even woken up. Tigerstar and Dovewing's anxiety over their sick kit had infected the whole Clan until every warrior seemed to shoot a nervous glance toward the medicine den as they passed it. But Sunbeam couldn't help her thoughts flitting more often toward Blazefire. The few strands of cat-mint left in the medicine store had been used up, and now Shadowsight had only tansy and coltsfoot left.

Surely SkyClan would spare some catmint. Sunbeam's heart quickened at the thought. But she hardly dared hope. If Puddleshine's mission was a failure, Rowankit could die. And what would happen to Blazefire? She had to stop thinking. Grabbing one of the bracken bundles between her jaws, she began to haul it toward the nursery.

Cloverfoot was repairing a tear in the wall there. Around the clearing, ShadowClan's warriors were resting before the sunhigh border patrols. Snaketooth and Hopwhisker shared a mouse, while Grassheart and Scorchfur sat crouched in the long grass, their ears flattened against the wind.

As Sunbeam began to nose the bracken into the nursery, Puddleshine ducked into camp. She dropped the bundle and ran to his side. But before she reached him, she could see that the brown-and-white medicine cat's expression was grim, and he wasn't carrying any herbs. Sunbeam's heart sank.

Tigerstar hurried across the camp to meet Puddleshine, his eyes round with alarm. "Nothing?" he mewed. "Surely they had *some* to spare?"

Puddleshine shook his head. "Frecklewish said their cat-mint plants barely produced enough leaves for SkyClan."

Sunbeam's heart pounded with fear. *Blazefire needs help now,* she thought desperately, edging closer and swiveling her ears to hear more as Puddleshine went on.

"She's already refused ThunderClan foraging rights."

ThunderClan asked for foraging rights? Didn't they have catmint either? Sunbeam's fear hardened. If no Clan had catmint, they all faced a perilous leaf-bare.

Tigerstar's anxiety was bubbling into anger. "She's hoarding it!"

"Frecklewish wouldn't do that," Puddleshine objected.

But Tigerstar didn't seem to hear. "Did you tell her Rowankit has greencough?"

"Of course."

Dovewing pushed her way from the nursery, blinking hopefully. "Any news?" As she slid past Sunbeam, Birchkit scrambled out after her, but Dovewing shooed the light brown tom-kit back into the shelter of the den. "Stay with Cinnamontail and her kits," she told him as she hurried to join Tigerstar and the medicine cat. "What did Frecklewish say?"

"She refuses to share SkyClan's supply," growled Tigerstar.

"She doesn't have *enough*," Puddleshine corrected him.

"When she heard there was greencough in the Clans, she decided to keep all the catmint for SkyClan," Tigerstar growled.

Dovewing stared at him. "I guess she wants to protect her Clan," she mewed.

"She's turning her back on a sick kit!" Tigerstar's pelt rose angrily along his spine. "I should have gone to SkyClan myself."

"It would have made no difference," Puddleshine told him. "Frecklewish would have given it to me if she'd had it to spare."

"Even if Leafstar ordered her not to?" Tigerstar growled.

"Frecklewish is an honorable medicine cat. She wouldn't lie about her herb supply," Puddleshine insisted. "Fidgetflake took me into the woods and showed me where the catmint grows," he mewed. "There was nothing but a few bare stems." He shook his head sadly. "Some harvests are just poor, and there's nothing we can do about it."

Sunbeam pressed back the panic rising in her chest. Without catmint, Rowankit could die. And what about Blazefire? He was still recovering from his injured paw. That made him vulnerable, too.

Tigerstar was pacing back and forth, his tail lashing. "If SkyClan won't help us," he growled, "we'll go to the other Clans."

Cloverfoot had already paused from her work on the nursery wall. "Is that wise?" she asked now. "We don't want them to think we're weak."

"We're *not* weak," Tigerstar snapped. "I'm not letting Rowankit suffer for the sake of ShadowClan pride." He beckoned his deputy closer. "Organize three patrols," he ordered. "Send one to WindClan, one to ThunderClan, and one to RiverClan."

"We already know ThunderClan has no catmint," Puddleshine reminded him. "Why else would they ask Leafstar for foraging rights?"

But Cloverfoot simply dipped her head. "Okay," she mewed. "They'll leave as soon as the borders have been marked."

"The borders can wait," Tigerstar told her. "This is more important."

Sunbeam left the bracken bundle at the nursery entrance and hurried toward the ShadowClan deputy. "I'll go," she offered. Rowankit was in danger, she told herself. But in her heart she knew that the real reason she wanted to join the patrol was not for Tigerstar's kit; she wanted to make sure Blazefire was safe.

Sunbeam followed Scorchfur and Snaketooth along the winding path that led to RiverClan's camp. Hopwhisker was at her heels, glancing warily over the reeds, which hissed in the wind, their plumed heads bending low before each new gust.

"Should we have waited at the border?" Sunbeam asked nervously.

Snaketooth looked back at her. "This is medicine-cat business."

"But we're not medicine cats," Sunbeam pointed out.

"A kit is sick," Scorchfur mewed. "There's not enough time for Puddleshine and Shadowsight to visit every Clan, or for us to hang around on the border hoping RiverClan will spot us."

I just hope RiverClan agrees. Sunbeam remembered the last time they had encountered a RiverClan patrol this close to the river. The two RiverClan warriors, Lizardtail and Nightsky, hadn't been hostile, but they'd behaved strangely enough to put Sunbeam on edge. Hopwhisker had been injured, but Lizardtail and Nightsky had insisted he wait on the riverbank. Why hadn't they taken him into their camp so that Mothwing could examine him there? It would have been simpler than fetching the RiverClan medicine cat. She'd had to carry her herbs to the riverbank and treat the injured warrior in the open.

"Look out." Hopwhisker's warning came a moment before Mallownose and Splashtail crashed through the reeds ahead of them and blocked the path.

Mallownose's ears were flat. "Why are you here?"

Splashtail showed his teeth, his brown tabby pelt bristling.

Scorchfur held his ground. "Rowankit is sick," he mewed. "We need to speak to Mothwing."

Splashtail's pelt smoothed. Mallownose's ears relaxed. But they still seemed wary. Sunbeam noticed a stiffness in the warriors' shoulders that seemed more defensive than aggressive, almost as though they'd been caught on ShadowClan land rather than the other way around.

Scorchfur caught her eye. He looked puzzled. Was he wondering the same thing?

"Well?" Snaketooth's tail twitched with impatience as the RiverClan cats hesitated. "Can we see her or not?"

"Mothwing's gathering herbs," Mallownose told him. "But I can fetch Frostpaw."

"We're in a hurry," Snaketooth mewed. "It would save time if you took us straight to her."

"We won't be long," Splashtail promised.

"Neither will we." Snaketooth began to pad forward, but Mallownose blocked his path.

"Wait here," he growled.

Snaketooth narrowed his eyes. "Is there a problem in your camp?"

"Of course not," Mallownose mewed a little too quickly.

"RiverClan's doing great," Splashtail chimed.

Sunbeam frowned. These cats seemed to be tripping over each other to reassure the ShadowClan cats. "Lizardtail and Nightsky wouldn't let us near the camp last time we were here either," she told them. "Are you sure everything's okay?"

"Everything's fine." Mallownose and Splashtail exchanged an uneasy look.

Then Mallownose flicked his tail. Sunbeam sensed he'd come to a decision. "If you insist on sticking your whiskers where they're not welcome," he mewed irritably, "you'd better follow us."

He turned and headed along the path. Splashtail waited as the ShadowClan patrol followed, then fell in behind Sunbeam and her Clanmates.

They don't want to fight, Sunbeam thought, *but we're not welcome here.*

Her pelt was prickling uneasily as Mallownose led them into the RiverClan camp. She'd half expected to find it underwater or deserted. But RiverClan cats were dotted around the clearing. They seemed healthy and well-fed, their pelts as thick and glossy as ever, and they looked up as the ShadowClan warriors padded into the camp. Gorseclaw sat up. Sneezecloud got to his paws. Several cats glanced toward Mistystar's den. Was the RiverClan leader going to greet them? As Sunbeam looked expectantly toward her den, Mallownose whisked his tail. "Mistystar's not here," he mewed.

"She's out hunting," Splashtail told him.

Gorseclaw called across the clearing. "Why are they here?"

He sounded tense. *No Clan likes having visitors,* Sunbeam reasoned. And yet *something* felt strange. The dens seemed unkempt. Reeds stuck out here and there, with holes that should have been repaired this close to leaf-bare. She'd heard that RiverClan took pride in their camp, even decorating their dens with weird stuff they'd fished from the river, but it looked as though they no longer cared how their camp looked. Shells dangled limply from the walls. More lay like fallen leaves on the ground.

"Frostpaw!" Mallownose hurried toward the medicine den, looking relieved as the apprentice medicine cat nosed her way out. "These ShadowClan cats want to talk to you." He jerked his nose toward Sunbeam and her Clanmates.

Hopwhisker was scanning the RiverClan camp, while Scorchfur tasted the damp air, his nose wrinkling. Snaketooth was already crossing the clearing to meet Frostpaw. Sunbeam hurried after him.

Frostpaw looked a little dazed as she braced herself against the blustery wind that was tugging at her whiskers.

She looks exhausted. Sunbeam stopped beside Snaketooth. *Like she hasn't slept in days.* Frostpaw's eyes were clouded, her pelt unwashed. Was she sick?

Snaketooth didn't seem to realize or, if he did, made no allowances. "We need catmint," he mewed bluntly. "Rowankit has greencough and our supply has run low."

Frostpaw blinked at him. She looked puzzled. "Why don't you gather more? It isn't leaf-bare yet."

Snaketooth's tail twitched impatiently. "If we could, do you think we'd have come all the way here?"

"I don't know if . . ." Frostpaw hesitated, glancing toward the medicine den as though wondering what to do. *Doesn't she know if she has any catmint?* Sunbeam was surprised. Surely the young RiverClan she-cat had been training long enough to know what was in RiverClan's herb store.

The camp entrance shivered, and Mothwing padded in, a bunch of mallow leaves in her jaws. The golden dappled medicine cat's gaze swept around the camp, sharpening with alarm as she took in the ShadowClan warriors. She dropped the mallow. "What are you doing in our camp?" she demanded, staring squarely at Snaketooth.

"We need catmint," he mewed unapologetically, lifting his chin.

"Rowankit is sick." Sunbeam padded forward and blinked earnestly at the RiverClan medicine cat. Mothwing had spent time in ShadowClan when Mistystar had exiled her as a code-breaker. Surely she'd care about Tigerstar's kit.

Relief washed over her pelt when concern flooded Mothwing's large amber eyes.

"How sick?" The RiverClan medicine cat hurried forward.

"He hasn't woken up this morning," Sunbeam told her.

Mothwing stopped and glanced uneasily at the medicine den. "I—I wish we could help," she mewed. "But we don't have any catmint. I was just looking for some, but . . ." Her voice trailed away.

Snaketooth swished his tail. "We might be able to find some." He nodded toward Scorchfur and Hopwhisker. "There's none in the forest, but if we could search around the river—"

"No!" Mothwing stiffened, her pelt ruffling around her neck. "This is *our* territory. *We'll* search and let you know."

Snaketooth looked disappointed, but he didn't argue. After all, SkyClan had refused ThunderClan foraging rights. There was no reason to think RiverClan would allow ShadowClan to scour their territory. And yet Sunbeam couldn't help feeling that Mothwing had objected too sharply. The RiverClan medicine cat looked more scared than indignant. Was she hiding something?

No. Sunbeam pushed the thought away. Mothwing wouldn't do that to ShadowClan. She'd shared dens with them not long ago, and prey. "Perhaps Flaxfoot and Whorlpelt have managed to get catmint from WindClan," she told Snaketooth. Cloverfoot had sent the two toms on a mission to the moor.

"Let's hope so." Snaketooth's expression was grim.

"I'm sure WindClan will help you if they can." Mothwing looked relieved that ShadowClan hadn't fixed all their hopes on RiverClan.

But Mallownose's tail was flicking ominously. The River-Clan tom wasn't hiding his discomfort at having another Clan's warriors in his camp. He padded toward Snaketooth. "You need to leave now," he growled. "We have Clan business."

"Will you tell us if you find catmint?" Snaketooth asked him.

"Yes," Mallownose mewed curtly. "We'll show you to the border." He nodded toward the entrance.

Splashtail was waiting there. "Hurry up," he called to the ShadowClan cats.

"We don't need an escort," Snaketooth objected. "We know our way home."

"This is RiverClan territory." Splashtail turned toward the reed tunnel. "We don't let cats from other Clans roam where they please."

Sunbeam felt a chill in her pelt. *RiverClan clearly doesn't want us here—but are they hiding something?*

As they reached the ShadowClan camp, Sunbeam ducked through the entrance behind Hopwhisker and Scorchfur. Puddleshine hurried from the medicine den. His tail drooped as he saw the patrol's empty jaws, and Sunbeam felt a twinge of guilt. She blinked at him apologetically and headed for Tigerstar's den. What would the ShadowClan leader say when he heard that Mothwing, too, had refused to help?

Spireclaw and Fringewhisker were clearing away trailing brambles around the nursery.

Berryheart was sitting with Yarrowleaf and Stonewing outside the warriors' den. She got to her paws as Sunbeam passed her. "No luck?"

Sunbeam shook her head.

Hopwhisker and Scorchfur had already reached Tigerstar's

den, and the ShadowClan leader was listening to their report.

Tigerstar was frowning as she caught up to them. "Surely they must have *some*," he growled.

"Perhaps," Hopwhisker mewed. "But we couldn't exactly search their herb store."

"They couldn't get us off their land quick enough," Scorch-fur added.

"They were even weirder than last time, when they had Mothwing fix my leg on the riverbank," Hopwhisker chimed.

Sunbeam nodded. "At least they helped then," she mewed. "*This* time, they didn't seem to care whether we—"

Paw steps sounded at the camp entrance. Puddleshine snapped his gaze toward the sound, hope sparking in his eyes as Flaxfoot and Whorlpelt raced into camp. "You got some!" Puddleshine meowed, his voice thick with relief. But as Flaxfoot drew closer, Sunbeam could see that she was carrying only a few strands of the precious herb. Puddleshine's face fell. Sunbeam knew that the paltry stems were nothing like the thick bundles of leaves that ShadowClan would need to see them through leaf-bare.

Flaxfoot dropped the thick stalks at Puddleshine's paws. "Sorry," he grunted. "That's all they could spare."

Puddleshine blinked in dismay. "Doesn't *any* Clan have catmint?"

Whorlpelt was out of breath. "Kestrelflight told us that most of the leaves had rotted before they could be gathered."

Berryheart, Stonewing, and Yarrowleaf had drawn closer. Fringewhisker and Spireclaw had turned away from their work and were listening, too, their eyes bright with worry.

Tigerstar began to pace. "How in StarClan will we get through leaf-bare without any catmint?" The fear in his mew made Sunbeam's belly tighten.

Berryheart padded forward. "It wouldn't be so bad if there weren't whitecough in the Clan so early. It's usually another moon before we get our first case." She glanced toward Fringe-whisker.

Yarrowleaf followed her gaze. "Whitecough brings green-cough like rogues bring fleas." There was an edge to her mew that made her words sound like an accusation. "We should have done more to protect ShadowClan cats from catching it in the first place."

Fringewhisker moved closer to Spireclaw, who glared angrily at Yarrowleaf.

Tigerstar was still pacing. "Puddleshine." He stopped and looked at the medicine cat. "Call an emergency meeting of the other medicine cats," he mewed. "The Clans can't face leaf-bare with no catmint. We need a plan in place. If neces-sary, we'll have to send warriors beyond our borders to search for another source." He headed for the medicine den and, as Shadowsight peered out, called, "How's Rowankit?"

As he disappeared inside, Berryheart turned to face Fringe-whisker head on.

The former SkyClan warrior met her gaze steadily, but Sunbeam could see her pelt twitching uneasily along her flanks.

"Wasn't there an outbreak of whitecough in SkyClan before you left?" Berryheart mewed.

Sunbeam's eyes widened. Was that true? Had Fringewhisker brought whitecough to ShadowClan?

"If it turned to greencough," Berryheart murmured, still staring at Fringewhisker, "that *would* explain why SkyClan couldn't spare us catmint today."

Suddenly Sunbeam felt she understood why her mother had been so hostile to the changes in the warrior code that allowed warriors to move more freely between Clans. If cats could move freely, so could sickness.

Yarrowleaf and Stonewing leaned closer, their eyes narrowing.

Fringewhisker lifted her muzzle. "There was a mild case," she mewed. "But I didn't have it."

Berryheart turned away with a grunt. "That doesn't mean you couldn't have brought it to us," she muttered.

Yarrowleaf flexed her claws. "I always knew mixing up the Clans would cause trouble," she mewed.

Hopwhisker shot her a warning glance. "Clans have always had whitecough," he told her. "It's part of forest life."

"It's pointless blaming any cat," Flaxfoot agreed. "We just have to deal with it."

Stonewing glared at him. "We wouldn't have to deal with so much of it if warriors didn't keep crossing borders."

Spireclaw wrapped his tail protectively around Fringewhisker. "Come on," he told her. "Let's go hunt."

Berryheart watched them leave, her ears flattening angrily. "I remember when loyalty to the Clan you were born in was important," she mewed.

Sunbeam glanced at her mother. Was it really fair to blame Fringewhisker for bringing sickness to the camp? Warriors had mixed with other Clans even before the changes to the warrior code. Sunbeam herself had been to RiverClan this afternoon. Medicine cats met at the Moonpool each half-moon. And what about Gatherings? The Clans met on the island every moon. Sickness could spread there far more easily than if a single warrior switched Clans. But Berryheart had always been a loyal ShadowClan warrior. She wouldn't complain unless she was truly worried about the Clan.

Sunbeam spotted Tigerstar leaving the medicine den, no doubt having checked on Rowankit. That reminded her that Blazefire was still recovering there. Was he getting better? Had he developed greencough? She hurried across the clearing. If none of the other Clans had catmint to spare, greencough could kill him. And if anything happened to Blazefire . . . Grief sliced through her heart at the thought that she might lose him altogether. So what if he didn't love her? As long as he was around, they could be friends. But if he *died* . . . She could hardly breathe as she ducked into the medicine den. If Blazefire died, how could she ever be happy again?

CHAPTER 5

❧

Nightheart licked his leg. It stung where the squirrel had bit it, and though it had stopped bleeding, he knew he should have Alderheart or Jayfeather look at it. The flea-brained squirrel had managed to nip him with its sharp little teeth before it died.

Flipclaw and Thriftear, who'd been patrolling with him, hadn't missed the opportunity to tease him.

"You're meant to eat them; they're not meant to eat you," Flipclaw had purred.

Thriftear had winked. "Maybe Lionblaze was right to tell you to stick to ground prey."

Flipclaw had hooked up the squirrel's limp body with a claw and shaken it. "You shouldn't pick on *Nightheart*," he'd told it jokingly. "You might find yourself in StarClan having to answer to Firestar."

Nightheart had snatched the squirrel from him and carried it away, trying to act as though the bite hadn't hurt his leg or his pride.

"Where's your sense of humor?" Flipclaw had called after him.

"The elders say that even *Firestar* made a joke once in a while!" Thriftear added.

Nightheart had growled under his breath. "Yeah, but I bet no cat made *him* the joke." If being Firestar's kin was so important, why didn't his Clanmates treat him with more respect?

Back in camp, his claws itched with frustration. Squirrel hunting seemed to bring him nothing but bad luck. But he wasn't going to be deterred. He was going to prove to Flip-claw and Thriftear *and* Lionblaze that he could hunt as well as any experienced warrior and didn't need to stay on the ground like an apprentice with kit-fluff still behind his ears.

The sunhigh patrols had returned, and ThunderClan's warriors were sharing prey around the edge of the camp before they gathered for the last patrols of the day. Wind was rocking the trees at the top of the hollow, and leaves were fluttering like snowflakes into the camp.

Heading for the medicine den, Nightheart shook one from his whiskers. It drifted to the ground, where the breeze lifted it and tumbled it toward Sparkpelt and Finchlight, who were ripping apart a mouse outside the warriors' den. Nightheart's tail flicked irritably. His mother and sister still refused to share prey with him. But he was fine with that. He liked eating alone. He was used to it.

Bramblestar was lying on the Highledge, his eyes closed, his muzzle hanging over the edge. Was he asleep? Yesterday, Thriftear and Shellfur had been whispering about how the

ThunderClan leader barely slept at night but sat outside in the moonlight as though he was scared of the darkness inside his den. They said he was having nightmares. But Nightheart knew not to listen to Clan gossip. Why would the strongest, bravest warrior in ThunderClan be scared of the dark? He'd survived the Dark Forest. That must have been worse than any nightmare.

Squirrelflight was sitting next to him, gazing out across the hollow, her eyes blank.

As Nightheart reached the medicine den, paw steps sounded at the camp entrance. He stopped and jerked around. Who was coming? ThunderClan's warriors were all in camp. His nose wrinkled as he picked up the scent of ShadowClan. *Again?* They'd been here earlier, asking for catmint. What else did they want?

His pelt bristled crossly. How dare they come and go as they pleased, like this was ShadowClan land? He padded to meet them, fluffing out his pelt as Gullswoop and Flaxfoot raced into the camp. "You should have waited at the border," he growled.

The two warriors pulled up sharply, their flanks heaving, and looked at him.

"There wasn't time." Flaxfoot could barely speak. They must have run all the way.

Lionblaze got to his paws. "Has something happened?"

Bumblestripe and Cherryfall left the sparrow they'd been sharing and crossed the clearing to stand beside him.

Gullswoop struggled to catch his breath. "Medicine-cat business," he puffed.

"What is it?" Squirrelflight was bounding down the tumble of rocks.

Bramblestar opened his eyes and watched the ShadowClan warriors without lifting his head.

Flaxfoot whisked his tail. "Tigerstar says the medicine cats need to discuss the lack of catmint," he panted. "He wants Jayfeather and Alderheart to meet the other medicine cats at the Moonpool at moonhigh."

Squirrelflight's gaze flitted over the ShadowClan warriors. "Who does Tigerstar think he is, issuing orders to *our* medicine cats?"

"It's not an order." Flaxfoot shook out his pelt. "It's a request. But they have to meet tonight. It's urgent."

Jayfeather hurried from the medicine den. "That must mean he couldn't get catmint from the other Clans." He stopped beside Squirrelflight. "We already knew SkyClan didn't have enough to share, but if WindClan and RiverClan are also short, the Clans might be in trouble." His blind blue eyes darkened. "We'll come to the meeting at the Moonpool," he told Flaxfoot.

The ShadowClan warriors looked relieved.

Gullswoop dipped his head. "I'll tell Tigerstar."

Nightheart glanced up at the Highledge. Bramblestar still hadn't moved, though his gaze was focused on the Shadow-Clan warriors.

Squirrelflight nodded them away. "Lionblaze and Bum-blestripe will see you to the border," she told them.

As they headed for the thorn tunnel, Jayfeather turned back toward the medicine den.

"How's Brightheart?" Squirrelflight asked before he pad-ded away.

Jayfeather sighed. "She's still sick," he told her. "But it's not greencough yet."

"Good."

As she leaped back up to the Highledge, Jayfeather turned toward Nightheart. His nose twitched. "Are you bleeding?"

"Not anymore," Nightheart told him. "But I was bitten earlier. I was just on my way to see you."

"What bit you?" Jayfeather began to pad toward the medi-cine den. "Did you run into a fox?"

Nightheart fell in beside him. "A squirrel," he mumbled.

"A *squirrel*?" Jayfeather didn't bother to keep his voice down.

Gazes lifted around the clearing and flitted toward Nightheart. Hot with embarrassment, he ducked into the medicine den.

Alderheart was inside, tucking fresh moss into Bright-heart's nest while she ate a mouse beside it. "Hi, Nightheart," he mewed.

Nightheart sat down in the middle of the den and held out his sore paw. "Hi."

Jayfeather padded to the herb store. "He's been bitten," he told Alderheart, adding with a sniff, "by a squirrel."

Brightheart looked up from her mouse. "A *squirrel*?"

Nightheart scowled at her. "Prey have teeth too, you know."

Brightheart exchanged glances with Alderheart. "I guess." Her whiskers twitched with amusement as she returned to her mouse.

Jayfeather carried a bundle of dried leaves from the herb store and dropped them beside Nightheart. He began to crumble them together. "You and I are going to the Moonpool tonight," he told Alderheart.

Alderheart looked up from his work. "But it's not half-moon yet."

"ShadowClan, RiverClan, and WindClan have catmint shortages too," Jayfeather explained. "Tigerstar wants the medicine cats to discuss what to do."

"What *can* we do?" Alderheart mewed. "We can't conjure herbs from StarClan."

"No," Jayfeather agreed, "but we can work out how bad the shortage is." He lapped up the herb mixture and began to chew it.

Brightheart swallowed the last of her mouse. "Do you think the other Clans are really short of catmint?" Her mew was still hoarse, but she wasn't coughing anymore.

Jayfeather was too busy with the herb mixture to answer but Alderheart was frowning.

"Are you saying they lied?" he mewed.

"They might have *exaggerated*," Brightheart mewed.

Nightheart hadn't ever thought the other Clans would lie

about something so serious. But now that he thought about it, it seemed possible. "I can see why they might want to keep their catmint to themselves."

Alderheart grunted. "They're fools if they do."

Jayfeather leaned down and began lapping the herb mixture into Nightheart's wound. It stung for a moment; then the pain began to ease.

Alderheart went on. "If greencough takes hold in one of the Clans, it'll spread so far and so fast that, catmint or no catmint, every Clan will lose cats to it."

Jayfeather sat up. "I can't imagine any medicine cat hoarding catmint," he mewed. "But I wouldn't put it past some of the leaders to ask them to." His tail tip flicked crossly. "Warriors think with their claws, not their heads." He sniffed Nightheart's injury. "How does it feel?"

"Better." Nightheart realized the sting had completely disappeared.

"Good." Jayfeather brushed away the leftover herb crumbs. "Come back tomorrow and I'll put on fresh ointment."

Warriors think with their claws, not their heads. Nightheart should have felt insulted, but it was a relief to hear Jayfeather complain about his Clanmates. The medicine cat seemed to understand that being a warrior didn't automatically make you right. He wondered whether Jayfeather might understand how uncomfortable he felt in ThunderClan right now. His own mother and sister wouldn't share prey with him. Myrtlebloom had called him *spoiled*! And now Flipclaw and Thriftear had openly mocked him. His fur itched with indignation.

"Do you think *all* warriors think with their claws?" he asked Jayfeather.

Jayfeather blinked at him. "You must know. You share a den with them," he mewed. "All they care about is proving how brave and strong they are."

Nightheart was glad the medicine cat couldn't see him, because he startled a bit. *I'm a warrior. Is that what Jayfeather thinks of me?* The blind cat was not one to hold his tongue. "I guess," Nightheart murmured.

Brightheart hopped back into her nest. "There's nothing wrong with wanting to be brave and strong," she mewed. "After all, it's our strength and courage that protect the Clan."

"Sure." Nightheart agreed. "But there must be more to being a warrior than being strong and brave. Surely it's about what makes you unique. Like, your pelt doesn't define who you are. Or your name. So why should your strength alone decide how important you are to the Clan?"

Brightheart glanced at him. "True," she mewed. "But I guess ThunderClan cats can't help measuring themselves by their ancestors. After all, what other Clan has had a warrior like Firestar?"

Nightheart winced. If his Clanmates were always going to measure him against Firestar, he would always be found wanting. "That was the *past*," he mewed defensively.

Brightheart blinked at him. "Isn't it good to have a noble past to live up to?"

"I think it's better to focus on the present." Nightheart

looked at the ground. "We ought to care more about what warriors are like now." He felt heat rising self-consciously beneath his pelt. He was the only one in ThunderClan who thought anything should change. "Maybe that's why I don't fit in here," he mumbled. "Maybe I'd do better in another Clan."

Jayfeather turned toward at him. "Don't you think you should figure out who you are before you decide where you fit in?" His mew was suddenly gentle.

Nightheart lifted his gaze and looked at the blind medicine cat. "It might be easier to become a loner," he mewed. "Then I wouldn't *have* to fit in."

Brightheart and Alderheart had gone quiet, and he was aware of them watching him intently. He suddenly felt foolish. *I shouldn't have said that.*

"A loner." Jayfeather whisked his tail, his softness evaporating as quickly as it had come. "You wouldn't last a moon in the forest on your own."

Nightheart puffed out his chest. How would Jayfeather know what he was capable of? All Jayfeather could do was mix herbs.

Alderheart blinked sympathetically at Nightheart, and Nightheart hoped for a moment that the ginger medicine cat might understand how frustrated he felt. After all, hadn't he trained as a warrior before he decided to become a medicine cat? Perhaps he'd chosen to be a medicine cat so that no one could compare *him* to Firestar. After all, Alderheart was the great ThunderClan leader's kin too.

"You've only been a warrior for a few days," Alderheart

mewed gently. "You're still finding your way. Moving to another Clan or becoming a loner won't change who you are." He padded to Nightheart's side and nudged his shoulder with his nose. "Have faith. StarClan will guide you just as they guided me. You'll find your place in ThunderClan soon, and when you do, you'll understand that this is the only Clan for you. I'm sure you belong here."

Nightheart met his gaze. He could see that he'd been mistaken about the medicine cat; Alderheart hadn't chosen this path to avoid comparisons to Firestar. He'd been lucky enough to have a vision and let StarClan choose for him. Nightheart felt a twinge of envy. *It must feel good to be so sure of your place in the Clan.* But StarClan wasn't showing signs of choosing Nightheart for anything. He was going to have to figure this out for himself.

And yet the dark ginger tom was staring at him so kindly, his amber eyes glowing with encouragement. *He believes in me.* Nightheart felt a sudden rush of gratitude. *I just hope he's right.*

The wind eased as night closed around the hollow, and though the camp was cool, Nightheart decided to sleep outside. He preferred the fresh air to the stuffy den. And it wasn't as though his denmates would miss him. Besides, Jayfeather and Alderheart would be returning from the meeting at the Moonpool soon, and he wanted to know they were safe. Two medicine cats alone on the moor seemed risky after the dog attack on the RiverClan warriors, but even though Bramblestar had offered to send a warrior patrol to escort them,

Jayfeather had refused, reminding Bramblestar that his sense of smell was as good as any warrior's and that if any dogs were within a day's trek of the Moonpool, he'd know it.

Nightheart lay beside the warriors' den, his nose on his paws, relishing the night scents of the forest. The sound of the trees swishing around the hollow began to soothe him to sleep. But as he drifted off, paw steps brushed the earth outside camp. He jerked up his head and blinked into the darkness.

Alderheart and Jayfeather had returned.

Squirrelflight must have been waiting for them. She leaped nimbly down from the Highledge and hurried to meet them.

Nightheart frowned. Bramblestar was awake. Nightheart could see him pacing on the Highledge, moving in and out of the shadows. Why hadn't *he* come to greet them?

Wide awake now, he got quietly to his paws and crept deeper into the shadows. He didn't want Alderheart to know he'd been sleeping outside. He was supposed to be trying to fit in with his Clanmates, not avoiding them. But Alderheart didn't realize how hard it was to share a den with cats who didn't understand you or even seem to like you very much.

"It seems like every Clan is short of catmint," Jayfeather told Squirrelflight.

"ShadowClan has only a few stale stems left," Alderheart added.

Squirrelflight frowned. "Which is why Tigerstar organized the meeting."

"Rowankit is sick with greencough," Alderheart told her.

"He was the weaker of his litter to begin with," Jayfeather mewed. "Without catmint, I don't think much of his chances."

Alderheart's eyes reflected the moonlight. "Puddleshine says the Clans must send out a patrol to find catmint beyond the lake."

Squirrelflight's tail twitched impatiently. "Why didn't Tigerstar call a meeting of the leaders? They're the ones who'll decide whether to send a patrol."

"I guess he wanted an accurate idea of how much catmint is left," Jayfeather mewed. "Medicine cats are less likely than leaders to lie to each other."

Squirrelflight glanced at him but didn't comment on Jayfeather's theory. Instead she mewed, "In this case, I think Tigerstar is right. A patrol is a good idea."

"It'll need to travel a long way to find enough catmint for all the Clans," Jayfeather warned her.

Alderheart looked worried. "Will the other leaders agree?"

"They'll have to," Squirrelflight mewed. "Without catmint, one case of greencough might trigger an outbreak that could devastate the Clans."

"Frecklewish says she knows of a Twolegplace that SkyClan passed on their way to the lake," Alderheart told her. "The Twolegs there surrounded their nests with every kind of plant and took care of them like they were kits. She thinks we'll find catmint there even in a bad growing season like this one."

"How far is it?" Squirrelflight asked.

Jayfeather answered. "A day away, maybe two? She says the

journey could be dangerous, but she's bound to say that. Sky-Clan still acts like their journey to the lake was some kind of heroic adventure. The truth is the trek will simply be long and tedious."

"We decided that WindClan and RiverClan don't need to join the patrol," Alderheart mewed. "If Kestrelflight and Mothwing came with us, it would mean leaving an apprentice in charge at home. A patrol made up of cats from Shadow-Clan, SkyClan, and ThunderClan should be enough."

"That sounds wise," Squirrelflight agreed.

Alderheart whisked his tail. "I'll represent ThunderClan."

Jayfeather sniffed. "I guess I can handle all the work while you go adventuring."

Squirrelflight blinked at Jayfeather. "I'm glad you'll remain in camp," she told him diplomatically. "ThunderClan needs you." Her gaze flicked to Alderheart. "Who would you like to take with you? What about Twigbranch? She led SkyClan to the lake. She'll know the way."

Jayfeather answered for him. "He should take Nightheart."

Nightheart swallowed back a gasp of shock. *Me?* It didn't make sense. As Lionblaze enjoyed pointing out whenever he got the chance, Nightheart was the least experienced warrior in ThunderClan.

"He seems restless," Jayfeather told Squirrelflight. "After failing his assessment so many times, he needs a chance to prove himself."

Nightheart felt the sting of the medicine cat's words and

bristled. He shouldn't *have* to prove himself. *ThunderClan should have faith in me just as I am!*

"Very well." Squirrelflight's ready agreement took Night-heart by surprise. His tail twitched nervously as she went on. "It's a good choice. And Bramblestar will agree. He thinks Nightheart has the makings of a good warrior."

Happiness fizzed in Nightheart's chest. Bramblestar had faith in him! Suddenly he *wanted* to prove himself. This was a chance to show his Clanmates that he was more than a name; he was a warrior, good as any cat—and not because he was related to Firestar. He thought about what Jayfeather had said back in the medicine den. Some time away from the Clan might give him a chance to figure out who he was.

Nightheart's thoughts whirled, but Jayfeather was still talking.

"The oddest thing about the whole meeting," the blind medicine cat mewed, "was Mothwing and Frostpaw."

Alderheart was nodding. "They were at the Moonpool before we arrived."

Nightheart pricked his ears. The medicine cats sounded puzzled.

"Before *any* cat arrived," Jayfeather added.

"They seemed surprised that we'd come," Alderheart went on.

Squirrelflight tipped her head to one side. "Do you think they were there for another reason?"

"Yes," Jayfeather told her. "They stayed behind after every cat left, too."

"We think they were there to share with StarClan," Alder-heart mewed.

"*Frostpaw* was there to share with StarClan," Jayfeather corrected him. "Every cat knows Mothwing has no connection with them. I don't know why Mistystar didn't send a warrior with Frostpaw and keep Mothwing in camp to look after the Clan."

Squirrelflight's eyes narrowed. "If they weren't there for the meeting, what else could be so important that Mistystar would send both her medicine cats to the Moonpool? Did they give any clue?"

"No," Jayfeather mewed. "They barely spoke at all. Even when Puddleshine suggested the mission to bring back cat-mint, Mothwing seemed more irritated than worried. As though she had something else on her mind."

Squirrelflight sat up straight. "It's pointless guessing," she mewed. "We just have to hope that if it affects the other Clans, Mistystar will tell us at the next Gathering. Until then, it's not our problem." She glanced around the dark camp. "I need to report to Bramblestar what happened at the Moon-pool. Go and get some sleep."

Nightheart ducked closer to the warriors' den as Jayfeather and Alderheart headed for the medicine den. Squirrelflight shook out her pelt and turned toward the Highledge. As she did, she hesitated.

Nightheart froze as she caught his eye. She'd seen him listening in the shadows. He braced himself for a scolding. But Squirrelflight didn't speak. Instead she nodded to him and bounded lightly up the rock tumble.

He watched her go and realized that he was trembling. Not because he'd been caught, but because soon he'd be leaving Clan territory for the first time and embarking on a mission that might save all of ThunderClan.

CHAPTER 6

♣

Frostpaw watched the other medicine cats file up the slope to the rim of the Moonpool hollow. Starlight gleamed on their pelts, so they looked a little like StarClan warriors as they disappeared one at a time over the ledge.

Frostpaw had been surprised by their arrival. She and Mothwing had left camp before Tigerstar sent the messenger to fetch them, so they hadn't even known about the meeting that had brought the other cats here. Now, as the other medicine cats left, having decided to send a patrol beyond Clan borders to search for catmint, Mothwing murmured that she hoped their Clanmates had covered for them well, and not revealed that they were already on their way to the Moonpool. Frostpaw mewed her assent. She was glad that the mission didn't need RiverClan's help. RiverClan had its own crisis, and couldn't spare any of its warriors or medicine cats right now.

Alderheart was the last to leave, lingering to help Jayfeather down onto the steep boulders beyond. But Jayfeather shooed him away with a hiss, and Frostpaw thought how fond

Alderheart must be of his former mentor to still want to help the ill-tempered tom.

"Are you ready?" Mothwing shifted nervously beside her, and Frostpaw dragged her attention back to the Moonpool. The water lay unruffled in the shelter of the cliffs, reflecting the star-flecked sky.

"I'm ready." She braced herself. *Please, StarClan, help me this time.* When she'd tried to contact her ancestors before, they'd been vague, giving her no clear path forward. This time, she hoped it would be different. Perhaps Mistystar would be able to speak to her. If not, any cat would do, so long as they could tell her who to choose as RiverClan's new leader. Last time, a curled feather left on the path was all she'd had to tell her that it should be her mother who led the Clan.

Her heart ached with fresh grief as she thought of Curlfeather. She wanted more than anything to see her and to know that her mother was safely with StarClan now. But she wasn't here for that. She was here to help her Clan. Clearing her mind, Frostpaw crouched and touched her nose to the water, waiting for a message from StarClan to flood her thoughts.

Pelts swam before her, shrouded in mist, their scents overwhelming. *StarClan?* Frostpaw tried to call out, but her voice was muffled. *Mistystar?* As she peered through the fog, straining to see familiar fur, her own pelt began to feel heavy. A terrible tiredness began to drag at her bones, pulling her deeper into her vision, and she felt her head dip as the mist thickened and swallowed her.

A scent touched her nose, so warm and comforting that her throat tightened. *Curlfeather.* Like a fish swimming from the cloudy depths into crystal-clear water, her mother padded from the sea of pelts.

"Frostpaw." Curlfeather's eyes shone with welcome. Stars sparkled in her pelt.

"Are you okay?" Frostpaw hurried forward and touched her mother's nose, her heart swelling with joy and relief.

"I'm fine."

Frostpaw scanned her mother's pelt, looking for the injuries the dogs must have left, but there were no bitemarks or torn flesh, only stars and her thick brown fur. Relief swamped her. She could hardly speak. But she had to. "I'm sorry," she blurted. "I'm sorry I couldn't save you. I should have done better."

Curlfeather's eyes brimmed with sadness. "It's not your fault, Frostpaw. I would willingly die countless times if it meant keeping you safe."

"Don't say that!" Frostpaw pressed her cheek against Curlfeather's, wishing with all her heart that her mother weren't dead. "I miss you so much. I don't know if I can—"

"Hush," Curlfeather mewed gently. "There's no time now for your grief. You have to think of your Clan."

"But—"

"You can grieve later." Curlfeather echoed Mothwing's words.

Frostpaw knew she was right and pulled away, forcing herself to focus. "Okay." She steadied her breath. "I need to ask about RiverClan's next leader. Who should it be?"

"I can't tell you that."

Alarm sparked beneath Frostpaw's pelt. "Why not?"

"The living Clans must find their own path," Curlfeather told her.

"But how will we know we're following the right one?" Frostpaw's heart was pounding. Her mother couldn't leave such a huge decision in her paws.

"You'll know," Curlfeather told her.

"But *how*?" she mewed helplessly. "No cat in RiverClan seems to want to be leader."

"You have to look beyond the obvious choices."

Frostpaw stared into her mother's clear amber gaze. Hadn't Splashtail warned her, too, that the obvious choice might not be the right choice? StarClan must agree with him. "So it's not Shimmerpelt or Duskfur?"

Curlfeather returned her gaze fondly. "I'm so proud of you, Frostpaw. And I believe in you completely. RiverClan is going to be okay. I trust you to protect them."

Her mother's words sparked a memory. *Trust no cat.* "What did you mean?" She blinked at Curlfeather, whose eyes were glowing with love. "You told me to trust no—" She realized with a jolt that her mother's pelt was fading, the brown fur melting into the mist so that only the stars sparkling in it remained. "What did you mean?" she cried again, but Curl-feather closed her eyes and, as she did, disappeared.

Panic gripped Frostpaw. "Curlfeather!" For a moment it

felt as though her mother were dying all over again.

"Frostpaw?" Mothwing's anxious mew jerked her from her trance, and she blinked open her eyes and saw the Moonpool rippling where her nose had touched it. The vision must have been deep, because her thoughts felt fuzzy, as though she'd just woken from sleep. Her mentor was staring at her expectantly. "What happened? You called your mother's name."

Frostpaw scrambled to her paws. "I saw her."

"Did she tell you who our leader should be?"

"No." Frostpaw's pelt itched with frustration. She felt weary once more. "She says we must choose."

Mothwing growled under her breath. "What's the point of StarClan if they can't help us when we need it?"

"She said the living Clans must choose their own path," Frostpaw mewed.

"They probably have no more idea who to choose than we do," Mothwing grumbled.

"She did say we must look beyond the obvious choices," Frostpaw told her.

"That isn't exactly helpful." Mothwing began to head toward the spiral path that led out of the hollow.

"I guess StarClan trusts us to decide." Frostpaw hurried after her. *I believe in you completely.* She remembered Curlfeather's words and wished for a moment that her mother didn't believe in her quite so much. It felt like every cat expected too much of her.

Mothwing slid over the edge of the hollow and leaped

down the boulders to the path below. Frostpaw followed, concentrating on not losing her footing. She reached the bottom, breathless and relieved to feel soft grass beneath her paws once more, and they began to follow the stream that led across the moor to the edge of their own territory.

The moon hung between clouds, silvering the heather. It would be full again before they knew it.

Worry pricked in Frostpaw's pelt. "We're going to have to decide who should lead RiverClan before the next Gathering."

"I know." Mothwing eyed the moon. "Otherwise we'll have to tell the Clans what's going on. There's no way they'll believe Mistystar and Reedwhisker are both sick two moons in a row."

Look beyond the obvious. Curlfeather had clearly been hinting at something. But what? "Who's not obvious?" she wondered out loud.

Mothwing glanced at her. "That's up to you to decide," she mewed. "You're the one guided by StarClan. I trust you more than any cat to make the right decision."

Frostpaw's belly tightened. *Why does it have to be me?* Mothwing was far more experienced in Clan matters. Was her mentor just like Shimmerpelt and Duskfur? Scared of taking responsibility? And yet she knew that Mothwing's choice would never carry the same weight as her own. Every cat in every Clan knew that Mothwing had no connection with StarClan. If Mothwing made the choice, it might be questioned. Frostpaw was the only RiverClan cat who could share with StarClan. She was the only one whose words would carry the authority of RiverClan's ancestors.

The wide moorland sky seemed to press down on her back. *I have no choice.* Mothwing wasn't hiding from responsibility. Frostpaw was the only one who could make this decision.

CHAPTER 7

Sunbeam shifted nervously from paw to paw, fluffing out her fur against the predawn chill. Mist was hanging between the pines, and the birds were beginning to find their voices. She'd been proud and excited when Tigerstar had told her she would be joining the patrol to travel to the Twolegplace beyond the Clans' borders in search of catmint. She was still excited, but waiting to set out was making her nervous. She felt like she'd been waiting since moonhigh. Dawn was coming and there was still no sign of Puddleshine. Surely he wasn't still asleep! ShadowClan would be waking soon for the dawn patrols. And Nightheart, Alderheart, Rootspring, and Fidgetflake must already be waiting at the end of the old Thunderpath where SkyClan territory met the ThunderClan border. She should go and make sure Puddleshine was awake.

She began to head toward the medicine den.

"Sunbeam." Tigerstar's mew took her by surprise. She hadn't thought he was awake. Had he come to see them off? She turned to face him as he hurried through the gray dawn light toward her, stiffening as she saw Lightleap at his heels. Was her former friend coming to see them off too? Her pelt prickled self-consciously. She still wasn't entirely ready to act like friends again.

Tigerstar stopped a tail-length away.

"I was about to make sure Puddleshine was awake," Sunbeam told him.

"I've decided Puddleshine should stay in camp," Tigerstar mewed. "With Rowankit sick and Blazefire still coughing, it seems wise to keep both him and Shadowsight here. There'll be other medicine cats in the patrol who can identify catmint."

Sunbeam's paws pricked with surprise. "So I'm going by myself?" It would be strange traveling alone with Thunder-Clan and SkyClan cats.

"Lightleap will go with you," Tigerstar mewed.

Sunbeam's pelt bristled before she could stop it. Lightleap was looking at her hopefully, but there was wariness in her amber eyes. This was going to be awkward for them both. Sunbeam swallowed back irritation. She'd been looking forward to getting away from Lightleap and escaping the Clan's pity for a while. Now the mission seemed more like a chore than an adventure. Why had Tigerstar chosen *Lightleap*? Hadn't he heard about their quarrel? Or perhaps he was very aware of it and hoped that forcing them to travel together would fix their relationship.

Then she remembered something Berryheart had once said. *Tigerstar always finds a way to involve his kin in everything Shadow-Clan does.* Was the ShadowClan leader using Lightleap to keep one paw in the mission? She eyed Lightleap. If Tigerstar was employing her as a spy, was she happy to go along?

"Be careful." Tigerstar nodded to Sunbeam then turned and licked Lightleap's ear. "Don't either of you take any unnecessary risks."

"We won't," Lightleap promised.

Sunbeam twitched an ear uncomfortably. It wasn't so long ago that Lightleap's "unnecessary risks" had caused major problems for a cat she loved. But she pushed down the irritation. "We'll be back as soon as we can," Sunbeam told him. Suddenly she didn't want to make this mission last any longer than it had to.

Tigerstar dipped his head and headed toward the medicine den. He must be going to check on Rowankit.

Lightleap called after him. "We'll bring back catmint," she mewed. "I promise."

She sounded so earnest that Sunbeam felt a twinge of guilt. Perhaps she'd only come because she wanted to help her younger brother. *Or Blazefire.* Sunbeam tensed. Blazefire might need catmint as much as Rowankit soon. She knew Blazefire had told her he didn't care for Lightleap as a mate, but . . .

Her heart lurched. Had Lightleap begged her father to let her come so that *she* could be the one to save him?

Jealousy pricked in Sunbeam's belly. "Come on." Avoiding Lightleap's eyes, she headed for the camp entrance.

They hardly spoke as they padded to the lakeshore and followed it past ThunderClan's territory. Lightleap mewed something about being excited and how cool it was to be on a mission. Sunbeam just grunted and pulled ahead, hoping that

Lightleap wasn't going to try to make conversation all the way. At the SkyClan border, she headed into the trees and followed the scent line toward the old Thunderpath.

"Watch out!" Lightleap mewed suddenly.

Sunbeam jerked her muzzle toward Lightleap. The dark brown tabby was looking up at a branch, her eyes wide. Clean white wood showed where it had cracked, and the end dangled above their heads.

Sunbeam carried on walking with a sniff. Why did Lightleap have to make such a fuss? The branch was broken, but it wasn't *falling*.

Lightleap followed, her tail fluffing out self-consciously as Sunbeam pulled ahead. "You don't have to be—"

Sunbeam cut her off. "I'm not being anything," she mewed. "But we're late and we don't have time to make a drama out of every snapped twig."

"If it had fallen, it would have really hurt you," Lightleap mewed earnestly.

"But it didn't, did it?" Sunbeam quickened her pace. The sooner they met the rest of the patrol, the sooner Lightleap could talk to someone else.

She kept her pace brisk as they followed the abandoned Thunderpath, always staying a little ahead of Lightleap and making sure they were both so breathless that it was hard to talk. One of the ThunderClan cats—a handsome tom with crow-black fur—was waiting in the middle of the track, and he lifted his tail as he saw her, calling to the others.

"They're here!"

Rootspring and Fidgetflake padded from the trees, Alderheart with them, and stopped beside the black tom, their eyes widening in welcome.

Fidgetflake hurried to meet them. "How's Rowankit?"

Lightleap took a moment to catch her breath. "He's still very sick."

Fidgetflake's eyes darkened. "We'll find catmint," he promised. "He just has to hold on until we get back."

Sunbeam glanced at the black tom, surprised to see it was Flamepaw, the ThunderClan cat she'd talked to at the last Gathering. He'd grown. "Hi, Flamepaw," she mewed, pleased to see him.

His scowl took her by surprise. Alderheart gave her a warning glance.

"What's wrong?" She stared at Flamepaw, confused. Had she mistaken him for another cat?

"I'm *Nightheart*," he grunted.

"But . . ." Her voice trailed away. *Nightheart?* She'd been so certain it was Flamepaw.

"I *used* to be Flamepaw." He lifted his chin defiantly. "But I'm a *warrior* now. And Flamepaw never suited me, so I asked Bramblestar to name me Nightheart instead."

It was strange he hadn't carried his kit name into warriorhood. But perhaps ThunderClan did things differently. Besides, hadn't Sunbeam herself once said that he didn't look like a *Flame*paw? She glanced along his black pelt. "I guess *Night* does suit you better."

His fur smoothed and she felt relieved that she'd said

something right at last. It was bad enough traveling with Lightleap. It would be worse if she offended another warrior in the party.

"Come on." Rootspring turned toward the trees and began to head away. "We mustn't waste time."

"Sorry we're late." Lightleap hurried after him. "Tigerstar decided at the last minute that I should replace Puddleshine."

"Puddleshine's okay, isn't he?" Fidgetflake followed them.

"Sure," Lightleap told her. "Tigerstar just wanted two medicine cats in camp."

"That's wise with greencough in the Clan." Alderheart fell in with the others.

Sunbeam glanced at Nightheart. "Ready?"

Nightheart whisked his tail. "I'm looking forward to it," he mewed. His eyes were bright now, and he held his tail high as he followed the patrol between the trees. He seemed happy to be heading away from his home. Sunbeam padded after him, suddenly feeling happy too. This adventure could still be fun, even if it meant sharing a patrol with Lightleap.

On the moor, the mist lingered in dips and hollows where the early morning sunshine hadn't burned it away yet. They'd crossed into WindClan territory, and the breeze smelled of peat and moorland prey.

The musky scent of rabbit touched Sunbeam's nose. Her belly rumbled.

Nightheart looked at her. "Hungry?"

"The fresh-kill pile was still empty when we left," she told him. "We haven't eaten."

Nightheart called to Rootspring, who was leading the patrol between high walls of heather. "We should hunt."

"Not until we've left WindClan land," Rootspring called.

"But we're making this journey for them as well as ourselves," Nightheart argued. "They could spare us a rabbit or two, surely?"

Rootspring kept walking. "We don't have time to stop and explain if we meet a WindClan patrol."

"It's not far to the Moonpool from here," Alderheart promised. "After that, we'll be out of Clan territory. We can hunt then."

Sunbeam's paws prickled with excitement. What would the land look like beyond Clan borders? Would there be forests? Or rivers? *Bigger* rivers than the one that ran through RiverClan territory? Perhaps they'd see mountains—the mountains the Clans had crossed on their journey to the lake. "I'm happy to wait," she mewed.

Lightleap looked back over her shoulder at her. "I bet prey beyond the Moonpool tastes even better than at home," she mewed eagerly.

Sunbeam looked away. Trust Lightleap to barge into the conversation.

"Some of it's great," Alderheart agreed. "But nothing tastes as good as prey from your own land."

Sunbeam fell back a little as the rest of the patrol chatted like Clanmates. Lightleap's voice always seemed to be in the center of the conversation, but then Lightleap had always enjoyed the sound of her own mew.

The sun was reaching high into the sky as they trekked around the Moonpool, avoiding the hollow and following a track through the heather instead. The path sloped upward, and Sunbeam found herself breathless when they finally reached the top. As the patrol broke through the thick bushes, the land fell away, and they stopped and stared out over a wide plain.

Sunbeam pricked her ears. Mountain peaks sat jagged on the distant horizon. Fields and woods, dotted with Twoleg nests and crisscrossed by Thunderpaths, stretched toward hills on either side. She blinked at Fidgetflake. "Can you see the Twolegplace from here?" she asked. "The one with the catmint?"

Fidgetflake was already peering into the distance. "I think that might be it." He nodded to a jumble of Twoleg nests and paths that covered a stretch of land in the distance. To Sunbeam, it seemed a very long way off. The SkyClan medicine cat went on. "I'll know for sure once we reach the bottom of this slope. SkyClan got a little lost on the way to the lake, but then Twigbranch found us and guided us the rest of the way. I'm sure I'll recognize the route she showed us when I find it."

Sunbeam's nose twitched as prey-scents touched it. Her rumbling belly suddenly seemed more important than the long journey ahead. "We're out of WindClan territory, right?" she mewed.

Rootspring nodded. "We passed the border a while back."

Sunbeam purred. "Good," she mewed. "I can smell rabbit." The scent washed her tongue as she spoke, and her mouth watered. Narrowing her eyes, she scanned the slope, her heart quickening as she saw two small brown shapes crouching in the grass. "We can hunt now, right?" She looked hopefully at Rootspring.

He nodded, and she dropped into a hunting crouch. Fixing her gaze on the rabbits, she began to creep forward over the grass.

Lightleap padded past her, her tail quivering with excitement. "Should we catch those two first?" She was heading for Sunbeam's catch.

Anger flared beneath Sunbeam's pelt. *They're mine!* She swallowed the words back. She wasn't going to argue. That would mean talking to Lightleap. It would be easier to find another rabbit. She straightened and padded angrily away, her pelt itching as Rootspring headed after Lightleap and together they began to stalk *her* rabbits.

"There's rabbit dirt here." Nightheart fell in beside her, the wind rippling his thick black pelt. He nodded toward the small, dark pellets of dung on the grass. Beyond them, Sunbeam saw tracks in the grass where small paws had trampled it. Dropping low, she scanned the slope once more, delighted as she spotted movement farther downhill. Pale brown ear tips twitched in the long grass. She caught Nightheart's eye. "Head that way." She signaled with her tail. If he followed the curve of the hillside, and she rounded on their quarry from the other, it would be caught between them.

There was only one rabbit, but she could see, as she closed in on it, that it was a large buck and plump too. Enough to share with the medicine cats and still fill her own belly without having to take a single bite of Lightleap's catch. She could barely see Nightheart's pelt in the grass beyond, only a ripple of shadow that might have been caused by the wind. *He's a good hunter.*

She focused her attention on the rabbit. She could hear it chewing, munching the sweet, soft grass, unaware it was being hunted. The wind was blowing downhill, carrying her scent away, and she took a few more paw steps forward before waiting for Nightheart to reach pouncing distance. As he did, he lifted his amber gaze above the grass and blinked at her questioningly. He was asking if it was time to close in for the kill. She gave a tiny nod and, with her next breath, surged forward.

The rabbit saw her and kicked out against the ground, its movement wild with panic as it darted away from her. Nightheart cut off its escape. It saw him and swerved, but he was fast and dived onto it, grabbing its neck between his jaws and killing it with a single bite.

Sunbeam straightened and swished through the grass to meet him. The scent of rabbit blood was sweet on her tongue. "Nice catch," she told Nightheart, and glanced back along the hillside.

Lightleap and Rootspring were carrying two small rabbits toward Alderheart and Fidgetflake, who were waiting at the top of the hill.

Sunbeam helped Nightheart drag their catch to join them, pride swelling in her chest as they let it drop beside Lightleap's tiny offering. Then, after Rootspring had thanked StarClan for the catch, she settled beside Nightheart and ate hungrily, focusing on her food while the others talked between mouthfuls.

Lightleap was busy telling them about finding the rocky tunnel and how brave she and Blazefire had been. She didn't mention that she'd been the one who'd made him venture so deep that they'd been caught in a rockfall and that it was her fault he'd nearly lost the use of one of his paws.

"And then I raced to fetch help," Lightleap mewed breathlessly. "I've never run so fast in my life."

Sunbeam swallowed her last mouthful and got to her paws.

"I don't know how Blazefire stood the pain." Lightleap seemed so enthralled by her own story that she'd lost interest in eating. "But I'm relieved he didn't have to put up with it for long."

Sunbeam padded down the slope to wash by herself. The less time she spent listening to Lightleap's chatter, the better.

When they set out again, the sun had begun to slide toward the horizon. Fidgetflake led the way, stopping every now and then to sniff the air and explore one path, then another, until he felt sure he'd found the right track. They followed meadows and trekked through woods, crossing streams and overgrown Twoleg tracks.

Sunbeam's paws were sore by the time night began to drain the color from the trees and bushes.

When the shadows grew too black to see into, Alderheart pulled up. "We should make camp for the night," he mewed.

Lightleap blinked at him. Her amber eyes reflected the

darkening sky. "We have to keep going!" She sounded alarmed.

"We can't make it all the way to the Twolegplace without sleep," Alderheart mewed.

Lightleap stared at him. "But what about Rowankit?"

"If we get too tired, we'll make mistakes," Rootspring mewed. "We need to stay safe."

"We're *warriors*," Lightleap objected. "We don't need sleep! We should push on."

Sunbeam felt a flash of pity for her Clanmate. She clearly cared about Rowankit. If they'd still been friends, she'd have tried to comfort her. But they weren't. Lightleap would just have to deal with it by herself. It was *obvious* they couldn't make it all the way to the Twolegplace without resting, and it was mouse-brained to think they could. Why did Lightleap have to make such a fuss? Sunbeam glanced at Nightheart. Could *he* see how unreasonable Lightleap was being?

But he was watching Lightleap, concern in his eyes. "Rootspring and Alderheart are right," he told her softly.

Rootspring blinked sympathetically at Lightleap. "I know you're worried," he mewed. "But it's at least another full day's trek, and once we're there, we'll have to deal with Twolegs and monsters. And where there are Twolegs, there are dogs. We might need to outrun them. We have to rest."

Alderheart ran his tail along Lightleap's ruffled spine. "Rootspring's right," he mewed gently. "If we rest now, we can face whatever's ahead more safely. And getting back is more important than getting back quickly."

They were making such an effort to reason with her.

Sunbeam swallowed back irritation. Why did every cat try so hard to make Lightleap feel better? Just like Blazefire had. Were Lightleap's feelings more important than everyone else's? She was the only cat here who didn't want to rest. She'd just have to accept that the rest of the patrol needed sleep.

Fidgetflake was gazing ahead, his brow furrowed. "There's a Thunderpath ahead," he mewed. "It'll be quieter at night. We can cross it and rest afterward."

Rootspring nodded. "That sounds like a fair compromise." He looked at Lightleap encouragingly. "Would you be okay with that?"

Sunbeam stifled an indignant sniff. They didn't need Lightleap's approval. She padded away before Lightleap could answer, pleased when Nightheart fell in beside her. He opened his mouth as though tasting the air for the scent of monsters, and she copied, her nose wrinkling as an acrid tang bathed her tongue.

"Is that what Thunderpaths smell like?" she asked Nightheart.

"I guess." He narrowed his eyes, peering into the darkness ahead.

A hedge blocked their view. As they reached it, the rest of the patrol caught up. Rootspring slid past them and wriggled underneath. Sunbeam followed, branches scraping her spine. As she scrambled out the other side, a roar sounded a little way away. It grew louder, and eyes as bright as suns lifted above a rise and sped toward the patrol, lighting the smooth, black track ahead of it.

A *monster!* Sunbeam had heard about them in nursery tales. With a howl, its eyes bore down on them. Sunbeam backed away, terror shrilling through her, and cowered against the hedge as the monster streaked past. The bitter fumes of its breath rolled over her and made her cough.

Lightleap was trembling beside her. Nightheart had flattened his belly to the earth while Rootspring pressed Fidgetflake and Alderheart back toward the bushes, protecting them from the grit the monster had sprayed with its flank.

Sunbeam straightened, a little embarrassed that she hadn't been braver. Especially in front of Rootspring. This must seem like nothing to him after the Dark Forest.

The Thunderpath was quiet now, and she padded to the edge.

"Be careful," Rootspring warned, nudging her back.

As he did, another roar sounded beyond the rise, and a monster bounded over it and rattled past. This time Sunbeam held her ground. She wasn't going to cower again. Lightleap, too, kept her head high, and Nightheart stared after the monster as it disappeared into the darkness, his gaze hard, as though watching an enemy patrol flee.

Alderheart shook out his pelt. "They're not traveling in packs tonight," he mewed.

"Good," Rootspring mewed. He looked around the patrol. "Cross when I tell you to."

Sunbeam dipped her head. Rootspring wasn't the oldest cat here, but his experience in the Dark Forest had given him an authority none of the others could match.

The patrol lined up along the edge of the Thunderpath. Sunbeam glanced up and down the smooth track nervously.

Rootspring's pelt rippled along his spine, his eyes wide, his ears pricked. A roar was rumbling in the distance. "Let it pass and then run," he told them.

Sunbeam bunched her muscles, ready to dart across the path. She slitted her eyes against the glare as the monster bumped over the crest; then it howled past them and roared away.

"Go!"

On Rootspring's order, she pelted across the Thunderpath. The smooth black stone burned her paws. Her heart pounding, she kept her gaze fixed on the far side. It was only a tree-length away, and she pushed harder, racing toward it.

Light flashed against her flank, catching the edge of her vision. She jerked her muzzle toward it as a howl ripped through the air. A monster was charging toward her, coming from the other direction. Her heart seemed to explode as it raced toward the patrol. Lightleap was running faster than prey. Alderheart was close behind her. But Fidgetflake was trailing. Rootspring pulled up and shoved the medicine cat forward with his muzzle. Nightheart swung in behind and steadied him with his shoulder.

Sunbeam's thoughts whirled as the blazing eyes of the monster scorched the patrol. Blinded, she stumbled, losing direction. She hesitated, suddenly not knowing where to run.

"Keep going!" Rootspring yowled. She felt his broad head against her shoulder and scrambled forward, letting him guide her, her heart nearly bursting through her chest. Then she felt grass beneath her paws, and shadows swallowed her as she reached safety beyond the Thunderpath.

She dropped into a crouch and fought to catch her breath as, behind her, the monster raced past, its paws screeching over the stone. She looked around, still too dazzled to see clearly. "Lightleap? Nightheart?" She was surprised that, having felt annoyed with her all day, her first thought was for Lightleap. She struggled to make out the rest of the patrol. Her paws were trembling as though the earth was shaking. "Did every cat make it across?"

Sunbeam held her breath. Blinded by the dazzle of the monster's eye beams and deaf from its roar, she shook out her pelt, trying to clear the ringing in her ears. Relief flooded her as she saw Fidgetflake, Alderheart, Rootspring, Nightheart, and Lightleap crouching along the strip of grass beside the Thunderpath. She hurried toward them. "Is every cat okay?"

Alderheart nodded. Lightleap coughed.

Nightheart lifted his tail. "We're all safe."

"Come on." Rootspring nodded toward the bushes. "Let's get out of here." He waved the others through with his tail.

As they disappeared between the branches, Sunbeam paused, the last one to pass through. "Will we need to cross many Thunderpaths before we reach the Twolegplace?" she asked the yellow tom, hoping he'd say no.

"I don't know," he mewed. "But we'll get used to it. You can get used to anything."

There was a grimness to his mew that filled Sunbeam with

foreboding. Rootspring was younger than her, but he sounded a lifetime older. Had losing Bristlefrost made him like this? Or did the Dark Forest have that effect on every cat who set paw there? She ducked quickly through the bushes after the others.

Fidgetflake led the patrol along the edge of a field. As they neared a small wood on the far side, he nodded toward it. "We can rest there for the night."

Bracken sprouted between the trees, and Alderheart took the lead, pushing his way through the fronds until he reached a small clearing. The trees here sheltered them from the wind, but Sunbeam fluffed out her pelt anyway. The night had brought a chill with it.

At the foot of an ancient oak, twining roots created natural nests lined with leaves. As Fidgetflake, Alderheart, and Lightleap settled into them, Sunbeam tasted the air and wondered whether to hunt before she slept. Nightheart was scanning the forest as though already searching for prey.

Rootspring looked around, his pelt prickling uneasily. "We should take turns keeping watch while the others sleep," he mewed. "We don't know this territory or what might live here. Two cats for every watch."

"I'll take first watch," Nightheart offered.

Rootspring nodded his thanks. "I'll join you."

Sunbeam turned her head. "I can sit watch with Nightheart," she volunteered. It was the best way of ensuring she didn't have to share a watch with Lightleap.

"Are you sure?" Rootspring looked at her.

"Please," she mewed. "I'm not sleepy yet. I was thinking about hunting."

"Is it safe to hunt here?" Lightleap blinked from her makeshift nest. "We don't know the territory, like Rootspring said. I think we should stay together."

Sunbeam's claws itched with annoyance. Why was Lightleap interfering?

"Let's hunt in the morning," Fidgetflake suggested. He glanced at Alderheart, who had already tucked his nose between his paws and closed his eyes. "It's been a long day. We need sleep more than food."

Sunbeam sniffed and changed the subject. "How far is it to the Twolegplace from here?"

"A day's walk, maybe less." Fidgetflake circled in his nest. "I just hope the catmint's still there."

Nightheart's ears pricked. "Do you think it might have died like the catmint at the lake?"

"That's not what worries me," Fidgetflake mewed. "You know what Twolegs are like. They may have dug it up."

"Twolegs can't leave anything unchanged for more than a few moons," Alderheart grumbled in agreement.

Sunbeam felt a flicker of worry. "What if we can't find any?"

Lightleap's eyes rounded anxiously. "We have to take some back," she mewed. "Rowankit will die without it."

Sunbeam felt a pang of sympathy for her former friend but didn't show it. Instead she watched Rootspring as he hopped into a gap between the roots.

"It's pointless worrying before we're even there," he told Lightleap, and began to wash.

"We'll find some." Nightheart padded around the clearing, tasting the air.

"I guess Twolegs like change," Alderheart conceded. "But they're also lazy. Digging up catmint would be hard work."

Sunbeam was struck by the thought that these cats—talking so easily and settling down for the night as though they'd shared the same den for moons—were from different Clans. They seemed so like ShadowClan cats. She suddenly wondered what Berryheart would think if she could see them getting along so well.

"I just hope the Twolegplace kittypets won't mind us taking their herbs," Lightleap fretted.

"Why would they care?" Nightheart mewed. "Don't the Twolegs fix them when they're sick?"

"Twolegs do everything for them," Fidgetflake told him.

Sunbeam frowned. "But kittypets would still fight to protect their dens, wouldn't they?" she mewed. "They're cats, after all."

"They might protect their dens," Fidgetflake reasoned. "But I can't see them fighting over herbs."

"Are you sure?" Lightleap blinked at the SkyClan medicine cat. "Have you met many kittypets?"

"A few, when I lived at the gorge," he told her. "Most of them are okay."

Lightleap's gaze grew curious. "Do kittypets have a code?" she asked. "Like the warrior code?"

"No." Fidgetflake purred with amusement. "They don't need to make rules."

Rootspring sniffed. "Their Twolegs make rules for them."

"I couldn't follow Twoleg rules." Nightheart shuddered.

Sunbeam looked at him. "But you don't mind following the warrior code."

"Of course not," he mewed. "We decide the code for ourselves."

"StarClan decides it for us," Fidgetflake corrected him.

"Yes, but they let us change it if we want," Nightheart reminded her. "That's why we're allowed to switch Clans now."

Sunbeam's eyes widened. Her mother would be shocked to hear him talking so casually about changing the warrior code and switching Clans. "Do you think it's a good idea to change the code whenever we want?" she asked.

Nightheart looked surprised. "Don't you?"

"Of course she does!" Lightleap answered before Sunbeam could speak. "Why wouldn't she? It saves every cat a lot of grief if we let warriors choose who they want to be with."

Sunbeam dug her claws into the earth. Lightleap used to answer for her when they were friends too. She hadn't minded so much then, but how could Lightleap be so sure what Sunbeam thought now, when they hardly spoke?

Lightleap went on. "That's what we believe in Shadow-Clan anyway," she mewed. "Dovewing and Tigerstar had to go through so much to be together. Their Clans would never have accepted their relationship if they'd known about it, so

Dovewing and Tigerstar were forced to leave. Then Rowan-claw gave up his leadership, and without a deputy to take his place, ShadowClan became part of SkyClan until Tigerstar returned. All because of the warrior code." She blinked earnestly at Nightheart. "I'm just glad they had the courage to come home." She shuddered. "Otherwise, I'd have been raised as a *city* cat!"

Sunbeam growled to herself. Trust Lightleap to make the changes to the warrior code all about *her*.

Alderheart was snoring gently now, and Fidgetflake had curled into his makeshift nest.

Rootspring stopped washing and gazed into the darkness. "I'm glad StarClan let us change the code." There was sadness in his mew. "I just wish they could have done it sooner. I would have had a chance to be with Bristlefrost before she . . ." His mew trailed away for a moment. "Before she died." Nightheart was watching him solemnly. Lightleap's and Fidgetflake's ears were swiveled toward the SkyClan tom as he went on. Every cat knew what he'd been through in the Dark Forest, losing Bristlefrost, the cat he'd loved enough to consider switching Clans to be with her. "We were destined to be together," he went on. "But leaving our Clans would have been a huge sacrifice. Whichever one of us had done it would have always felt they'd betrayed their Clan."

"Not if you loved each other, surely!" Lightleap protested.

Sunbeam sniffed. Just because Dovewing and Tigerstar chose their own happiness over their Clans didn't mean *every* warrior would.

"We'd have broken the code," Rootspring explained. "Which meant we couldn't ever have been the best warriors we could be. We wanted to be true to each other, but we needed to be true to ourselves. The warrior code made us choose."

Fidgetflake looked at him gravely. "Because of your suffering, no other cat will ever have to make that choice again."

Nightheart seemed lost in his own thoughts. "Do you think there will ever be *other* reasons we're allowed to move to another Clan?" he wondered.

"*Other* reasons?" Sunbeam stared at him. No wonder Berryheart was so worried about the changes to the warrior code. It might just be the beginning. "What's the point of a warrior code, if we alter it whenever it suits us?" She stiffened, suddenly aware of how harsh she sounded. If only she didn't have her mother's voice running so loudly through her head!

Nightheart eyed her warily. "I was just wondering," he mewed. "That's all."

Rootspring curled down into his nest. "I guess every cat's entitled to their opinion, but right now we should get some sleep." He closed his eyes. "We've a long way to travel tomorrow."

Lightleap yawned, and Fidgetflake rested his nose between his paws.

Sunbeam padded to the edge of the clearing. She felt unsettled. She seemed to be the only cat here who was unsure about cats being allowed to switch Clans so easily. Every other cat sounded glad that the code had been changed. Was she wrong to worry? Had she been listening to Berryheart for too long?

Nightheart crossed the clearing and sat beside her. "Don't you approve of the changes to the warrior code?" he mewed softly.

She shifted her paws, acutely conscious of being the odd cat out. "I'm not sure," she mewed. "Berryheart—my mother—keeps saying it's wrong to change the rules that warriors have lived by for moons. She says that ShadowClan is for Shadow-Clan cats." Then she paused, thinking. "Fringewhisker isn't really like a ShadowClan cat. She finds it hard to hunt in such thick forest, and I don't think she'll ever eat frog. But she tries really hard. She takes extra patrols and brings back two pieces of prey when everyone else brings one. I guess, in her case, the changes to the code have made her try to be a better warrior. A *true* warrior. And that's good, right?" She looked at Night-heart, but he was staring into the trees.

"I think being a true warrior isn't decided by what Clan you belong to," he mewed. "It depends on what's in your heart."

Heart? Was he talking about love? Sunbeam glanced at him. "Would *you* leave your Clan for a mate?"

"I don't see why not." He sounded so casual. Her tail twitched uneasily as he went on. "Fernstripe seems happy to be with Shellfur. I suppose she misses WindClan, but she never mentions it. And ThunderClan doesn't seem to mind having a WindClan cat around. And Twigbranch and Fin-leap have been together for moons without any trouble. No cat even remembers he was a SkyClan warrior once."

"So you think it doesn't matter which Clan you live in?" She stared at him.

"It's not that it doesn't matter." He looked at her thoughtfully. "But warriors can adapt. They can change to fit their new Clan, and their new Clan can learn to accept them, even if it takes a while."

"What about loyalty?" she demanded.

"A true warrior is loyal to the cats who've put their trust in them." He glanced behind him at the sleeping cats and lowered his voice. "I believe in loyalty. I'm as loyal as any warrior. It's just that I'm not really comfortable in ThunderClan these days."

Sunbeam looked at him, surprised. She'd imagined she was the only one who was irritated with her Clanmates right now. Then she remembered—he'd had problems during his apprenticeship, right? He'd told her about them at the last Gathering. "You've passed your assessment now, though," she mewed. "Are you still annoyed it took so many attempts?"

"*Three.*" Nightheart's hackles lifted. "It only took *three* attempts."

"That's not so bad," she mewed encouragingly.

"You make it sound like I was taking assessments for *moons.*"

"I didn't mean to." She rounded her eyes apologetically.

He looked at her for a moment, then gazed into the forest once more. "Sorry," he mewed. "I guess I am still touchy about it."

"I'm not surprised." She shifted her paws. "It sounded like your mentor was really hard on you."

"She was. And so was Squirrelflight. *Every* cat in ThunderClan seems to be hard on me," he huffed. "They're angry about my changing my warrior name, and the whole Clan thinks I should be something I can never be."

Sunbeam glanced over her shoulder, glad to see Alderheart still asleep. He probably wouldn't approve of his Clanmate complaining to a ShadowClan warrior. But she felt a pang of sympathy for Nightheart. "That feels like a lot to deal with."

He glanced at her, as though surprised by her kindness. "I don't even get along with Sparkpelt and Finchlight," he added. "And they're my *kin*."

"But they're not your only kin," Sunbeam reminded him. "You have kin in ShadowClan, don't you?" Had she remembered right? "Tawnypelt."

"Yes!" His eyes brightened. "I hadn't thought of that. Perhaps I'd get along better with Tawnypelt than with my kin in ThunderClan."

"That's not what I meant," she mewed quickly. Nightheart sounded like he was ready to switch Clans right away. But she couldn't help liking his openness. "I guess every cat feels at odds with their Clan from time to time," she reassured him. "Right now, my Clanmates pity me."

"Pity you?" He sounded surprised. Then he seemed to remember something. "Oh yeah. There was a tom you thought you'd be mates with, and he started hanging out with your friend."

"My *former* friend." Sunbeam scowled at Lightleap. She was fast asleep.

Nightheart followed her gaze. "Is that her?"

"Yes."

Nightheart nudged her shoulder with his muzzle. "I'm sorry you haven't patched things up yet. But I can see why. You must feel pretty hurt."

She appreciated his sympathy. "I guess we can't tell our hearts what to feel," she sighed.

"I guess not."

"You'll probably feel better about your Clan soon," she told him. Nightheart was handsome—as handsome as any ShadowClan warrior—and good-hearted too. There had to be some cat in ThunderClan who thought so too. "Once you fall in love with some pretty Clanmate, you'll feel differently about everything."

He grunted. "I can't see that happening anytime soon."

She glanced at him. His glossy pelt was as black as the sky and gleamed with moonlight, but his brow was furrowed, and she wished it weren't. It seemed unfair that he should be unhappy. "It won't always be this way. Just give it time," she mewed softly. Perhaps time was all *she* needed to feel better too.

CHAPTER 8

❧

Nightheart stirred, his thoughts slowly untangling themselves from sleep. The oak rustled above him, and birds were beginning to chatter. He opened his eyes. The bracken was pale in the half-light of dawn and the air was chilly. He wanted to stretch his paws, stiff from the long walk yesterday, but something warm and soft was draped over his hind leg, and he lifted his muzzle to see what it was.

Sunbeam was nestled in the leaves beside him. Last night, after they'd woken Fidgetflake and Rootspring to take the next watch, they'd settled against the same curving root. Sunbeam was still fast asleep, her flank rising and falling, her face peaceful. It was her tail that was wrapped casually over his leg. He swallowed back a purr. This ShadowClan cat was so comfortable in her own pelt. He'd feel jealous if he didn't like her so much. She'd quietly listened to him complain about his Clanmates last night without judging him. *Did I say too much?* He felt a prickle of guilt. Sunbeam was from another Clan, after all. But he hadn't told her anything important. And even if Tigerstar *wanted* to know that one of ThunderClan's warriors had been arguing with his kin, Sunbeam wasn't the type to run and tell him.

Gently, he slid his leg from beneath her tail and pushed himself to his paws.

Fidgetflake and Rootspring were still asleep. Lightleap and Alderheart were sitting guard on either side of the clearing. Lightleap looked as though she was dozing, hunched against the cold with her eyes half-closed, but Alderheart turned and nodded a silent greeting to Nightheart.

In reply, Nightheart nodded toward the trees, hoping Alderheart would understand. He wanted to hunt before the others woke up. Hopping as quietly as he could from the nest of leaves, he tiptoed into the bracken. Mouse-scents hung in the air, and he followed them, pleased when he picked up a trail.

By the time sunlight was cutting between the trees, he'd caught two mice and a shrew and carried them back to the others. They were all awake now. Fidgetflake was washing his paws while Alderheart, no longer on guard, stretched in a pool of sunshine. Sunbeam didn't seem to notice Night-heart arrive; she was too busy plucking crumbs of leaf from her glossy pelt with her teeth. Rootspring had caught a spar-row and was tearing it apart for the others. He looked pleased when he saw Nightheart push his way from the bracken and drop his catch onto the ground.

Lightleap crossed the clearing. "Hey, Nightheart," she mewed. She winked at him playfully. "Are those for me?"

Sunbeam didn't look at him, but Nightheart noticed her soft brown-and-white fur bristle irritably.

"They're for every cat," Nightheart told Lightleap. He turned toward Sunbeam. "Do you want the shrew?"

She looked at him now, then down at the shrew. "Yes, please."

He half expected Lightleap to joke that *she* wanted the shrew. But the ShadowClan she-cat eyed Sunbeam warily and padded toward Rootspring instead.

"Should I give the wings to Fidgetflake and Alderheart?" she asked.

"Give them the breast to share," he told her. "We can share the wings among the three of us."

"You can have a mouse too." Nightheart tossed one toward them, and Lightleap dipped her head in polite thanks.

He crouched to eat beside Sunbeam, who ate hungrily, then sat up and licked her lips. "Shrew is my favorite," she mewed. "Thanks, Nightheart—and sorry I slept so late. I should have helped you hunt."

"That's okay," he mewed. "I'm glad I didn't wake you. You were sleeping so peacefully." His whiskers twitched with amusement as he remembered her tail.

She purred. "I thought I could only sleep well in the ShadowClan warriors' den," she mewed. "I must be better at sleeping than I thought."

He purred back. "You seem to have a talent for it."

Once their bellies were full, the patrol set off, Fidgetflake leading the way. All morning, they trekked through empty meadows, but as sunhigh came and went, they found themselves skirting more and more Twoleg dens. Thunderpaths crossed their route, narrow here and mostly empty, but there were more and more of them as the afternoon wore on. After a while, the air seemed to change scent, from the sweet, reassuring odors of forest and field to a sharper scent with an unfamiliar tang that made Nightheart's pelt twitch uneasily. They must be getting closer to the Twolegplace.

As they followed a wide track where grass grew on either side of deep ruts in the dirt, a low growl sounded beyond the hedgerow. Nightheart ducked away from the patrol, his hackles lifting, and peered through the hedge. In the field beyond, bare earth had been churned into long rows as though massive claws had raked it, and in the middle, a large monster was trudging along, its growl drowning out the sound of the birds. Its huge paws bumped over the field, casually throwing up dirt and leaving a fresh trail of earth behind them.

Nightheart watched it nervously, his heart skipping a beat as he noticed a Twoleg sitting high up on the monster, riding it like a kit badger-riding on its mother's shoulders. He jerked his gaze away and hurried to catch up to the patrol. "Did you know Twolegs ride on monsters?"

"What do you mean?" Sunbeam hurried to look. Fidgetflake and Lightleap followed and ducked to peer underneath. Alderheart watched them, but Rootspring sat down and gazed along the track.

"If we're going to stop and look at every strange monster," the SkyClan tom mewed, "we'll never make it to the Twoleg-place."

Nightheart blinked at him. How could he be so calm? "It looks like the monster is patrolling," he warned. "What if it sees us on its territory?"

"It won't be interested in us," Rootspring told him. "So long as we stay away from the monster, it'll stay away from us."

"But what if—"

"What?" Rootspring looked at him. "Do you think it might be scared we'll steal its prey?"

Sunbeam looked at him. "What *do* monsters eat?"

"It can't be mice and birds." Lightleap sat up.

Sunbeam eyed her sourly. "Perhaps they eat *cats*."

Lightleap's eyes widened for a moment. Then she shook out her pelt. "Of course they don't," she mewed. "If they did, we'd know about it."

"Don't tease your Clanmate," Fidgetflake chided Sunbeam.

But Nightheart felt a pang of sympathy for Sunbeam. Lightleap's betrayal had clearly hurt her. He wondered if she felt betrayed more by Blazefire or by Lightleap. They were both supposed to be her friends, but now it sounded like they preferred to hang out with each other. He fell in beside Sunbeam as Rootspring began to lead the patrol along the track once more.

"We need to head that way." Fidgetflake stopped as they reached the end of the hedgerow, and he nodded toward the field where the monster was still patrolling. It was at the far end now but turning to trek back toward them. "If we move fast, we can get to the other side before it reaches us."

"Okay." Rootspring glanced around the patrol. "We'll need to be quick." He ducked beneath the hedge and the patrol followed.

Nightheart hung back until the others were safely through, then squeezed after them. The rich, damp smell of soil flooded his nose as Rootspring led the patrol along the ditch that ran between the hedge and the churned ridges of soil. Ahead, the field was rimmed by a high fence made of Twoleg web. It glittered like water rippling in the late afternoon sunshine.

"How do we get over that?" Nightheart asked, feeling a twinge of worry.

"It's too high to climb," Fidgetflake mewed. "We'll have to burrow underneath."

Sunbeam glanced along the field. "What about the monster?"

The beast was still a good distance away, but it was moving steadily toward them.

Nightheart fluffed out his fur, refusing to be intimidated. "We'll be through by the time it reaches us." He hurried to the fence first and sniffed along the bottom, relieved to find that the earth around it was loose. "This will be easy to shift," he told them. He clawed up a pawful of soil, and the others began to dig beside him, working fast.

The growl of the monster grew louder, and Nightheart dug faster, scooping out earth, one paw after another. Beside him, Sunbeam burrowed faster than a rabbit. Her flank pressed against his, and he could feel the smooth, hard muscles working beneath.

He glanced at her. "Are you sure you're not a WindClan cat?"

She paused, looking puzzled.

"They used to tunnel beneath the moor," he explained.

"There's no time for talk." Fidgetflake jerked his muzzle toward the monster. Its dull, blank eyes seemed to be staring at them as it prowled closer.

Lightleap was examining the hole they'd dug beneath the silver fence. "I think I can squeeze through now," she mewed excitedly. As the others sat back, she nosed her way underneath and popped out on the other side. "Ouch." She jerked her muzzle around and began to lick her spine.

Rootspring blinked at her anxiously. "Are you okay?"

"It snagged my pelt." She straightened. "But I'm okay."

Nightheart could see a tuft of her dark brown fur left behind at the bottom of the fence. "Be careful," he warned as Fidgetflake squeezed after Lightleap.

The SkyClan medicine cat scrambled out, unharmed, and Alderheart followed.

Rootspring nodded Sunbeam through, and she dropped onto her belly, slithering into the gap. Pushing with her hind legs, she scrabbled forward, then froze with a yelp. "My pelt!" Alarm edged her mew. "It's caught!"

Her fur spiked along her spine and Nightheart could see where the long hairs at the base of her neck were caught on the jagged webbing.

Behind them, the monster rumbled closer.

"Hold still," he told her, reaching forward with his muzzle. He tried to nip the fur free, but she was writhing like captured prey, a yowl building in her throat. He couldn't get a grip.

"Try to stay calm," Alderheart soothed from the other side of the fence.

"We'll get you free," Fidgetflake promised.

But Sunbeam's panic was spiraling. Fear-scent was pulsing from her pelt, her writhing turned to jerks, and with each jerk her fur grew more tangled. The yowl she'd been pressing back escaped as a low, desperate moan. The bitter tang of the monster's breath rolled over them, and the ground began to tremble.

"Stay still!" Rootspring's command was sharp, but the monster's growl drowned it out.

Even if she'd heard it, Sunbeam was too panicked now to obey orders. Nightheart pressed back his own panic. Sunbeam was scrabbling desperately with her forepaws, trying to tear herself free. If she didn't hold still and let him help her, she would injure herself badly. He could hear her pelt begin to rip. Pain hardened her mew.

"It's okay." He leaned down close to her ear and rested his paw on her spine. "I'm going to get you out of here."

He saw her gaze flash toward him. "The monster—"

"It's not here yet." He glanced behind her, struck with an idea, then leaned closer. "But Lightleap is watching you." His mew dropped to a whisper. "Don't let her see you panic."

She grew still at last.

Hope flickered in Nightheart's chest. "That's great," he encouraged. "Just hold still for a moment longer. I can see where you're caught. I can untangle you."

"Is it here yet?" Her whimper was only loud enough for him to hear.

"Not yet." Nightheart was glad she was too tangled up to turn and see the monster's paws, now only a tree-length away. "I'll get you out before it reaches us." He stretched forward and began to nibble at Sunbeam's fur.

The monster growled, rolling inexorably toward them on its huge black paws. Nightheart ignored it. He was going to make sure Sunbeam was safe. He bit through a strand of fur, then another. She whimpered. He was hurting her. But he had no choice. He forced himself to keep plucking, strand after strand, until he felt the tangled fur loosen from around the webbing. "Can you move now?" he mewed in her ear.

Sunbeam pulled herself forward, tentatively at first, testing for pain. Then, with a gasp of relief, she hauled herself through the tunnel and out the other side.

"Thank StarClan." Rootspring swished his tail with relief and nosed Nightheart toward the gap.

Nightheart resisted. "What about you?"

The monster was a few tail-lengths away, its paws swiveling as it turned.

But Rootspring nudged him harder. "Just go!"

Nightheart scrambled beneath the fence, his heart pounding. As he burst out the other side, he turned and stared at Rootspring through the webbing. "Hurry!"

The monster's massive flank swung toward Rootspring, but the SkyClan warrior was fast. Like a mouse escaping beneath a root, he shot under the fence and scrambled out beside the rest of the patrol.

Sunbeam blinked at him guiltily. "I'm sorry," she mewed. "I put you all in danger."

Rootspring shook his pelt out. "You did fine," he told her. "Are you hurt?"

"It just stings a little." Her gaze flitted toward Nightheart, glittering with gratitude. "Thanks."

"No problem." Nightheart tried to sound casual, but his heart was still pounding so hard in his ears he could hardly hear her. He dipped his head to her, pleased he'd been able to help.

Lightleap was weaving around them. "I thought you were monster food," she mewed anxiously.

Alderheart nosed past her and began to examine the scratches on Sunbeam's neck. "There's just a little ripped fur." He glanced at Nightheart. "What did you say to calm her down?"

"Nothing, really," Nightheart mewed. "I just encouraged her a bit." He caught Sunbeam's eye.

Her ears twitched self-consciously. What he'd really told her would be their secret.

The sun was beginning to slip behind the distant mountains, their shadow deepening toward night.

"The Twolegplace is close now," Fidgetflake told them. He looked at Sunbeam. "Do you need to rest?"

"No," she assured him. "It doesn't hurt that much."

Alderheart flicked his tail. "I'll make some ointment for you as soon as we find a few oak leaves," he promised.

Rootspring was staring at the unnatural yellow light that glowed now in the distance. "The Twolegplace will be quieter at night," he mewed. "We should be able find the catmint and get out quickly."

The patrol headed onward, and Nightheart was pleased when Sunbeam fell in beside him.

"Thanks again," she whispered.

"No problem." But he wasn't really listening. He smelled prey-scent. He lifted his muzzle, his mouth watering. He didn't recognize the smell—it was nothing like he'd ever smelled before—but it made him want to taste the prey desperately.

Ahead, a meadow rose to a small wood, and beyond it colored lights flashed against the darkening sky. Nightheart narrowed his eyes. Had they reached the Twolegplace already? The prey-scent was growing stronger, and he could hear the hum of Twolegs mewing and, with it, the low rumble of monsters. Occasional yelps split the air, as though the Twolegs were calling to each other.

His pelt prickled warily. The others seemed nervous too. They slowed their pace as they reached the wood, and Rootspring slid into the lead. He signaled the patrol to keep quiet with a swish of his tail and picked his way between the trees. They followed him across the wood, where the sounds were louder and the smells were even stronger.

As the trees opened ahead of them, Nightheart's belly tightened. Brightly colored Twoleg nests crowded a wide field. Lights flashed around their roofs, and Twolegs thronged around them.

"This isn't the Twolegplace." Fidgetflake stopped beside him, his eyes wide with alarm.

Alderheart and Lightleap hung back, their ears swiveling as they tried to make sense of the noise. The air seemed to vibrate as the dens pulsed with a cacophony of thumping and squawking. Nightheart flattened his ears and screwed up his eyes, dazzled by flashing lights the colors of every greenleaf flower. And the whole time, the scent of warm, sweet prey bathed his muzzle. Twolegs were swarming between the dens. He could see them eating as they walked, cramming prey into their mouths, their eyes glazed with excitement, reflecting the colored lights.

"Look!" Sunbeam's alarmed yelp made him jump. She was staring at one of the nests. "It's a *monster*!"

The brightly colored Twoleg nest had the big round paws of a monster. Nightheart shuddered. Did Twolegs *live* inside monsters as well as ride them?

"I've never seen a Twolegplace like this before." Fidgetflake peered at the crowded field as though trying to see beyond it. "We should go around it. The real Twolegplace must be on the other side."

As he spoke, one of the Twoleg dens began to turn. It twisted on its paws, and Nightheart realized with a gasp that Twolegs were crammed in rows around the edge of its wide, round head, which was spinning faster and faster. The Two-legs trapped on it began to yowl. Their panicked shouts turned to wails as the monster's head lifted slowly and rose from its body, turning around and around. Was it trying to kill them? He tried to make out their faces, but the monster was spin-ning so fast now that their features became a blur, their voices screaming as it twirled them. He shrank back, horror gripping him. This place was terrifying.

Even Rootspring's pelt was spiking. "This way," the Sky-Clan tom ordered sharply, leading the way between the trees and following the wood as it curved around the field.

Nightheart hurried to catch up, Sunbeam beside him, her eyes wide. "Why don't the Twolegs run away?" she hissed. "Don't they realize the monsters are dangerous?"

"Perhaps they can't resist the prey-scents," Nightheart guessed. The smells wafting from the Twoleg dens were more enticing than any prey he'd hunted beside the lake. He licked his lips. This place was scary, but he longed for a mouthful of whatever was making such scents. Would it taste as good as it smelled? Better? "Perhaps we can hunt here on the way back."

Rootspring glanced at him. "Warriors don't eat Twoleg food," he growled.

"Even when it smells this good?" Nightheart objected.

Sunbeam leaned closer. "I'd certainly like to taste some," she whispered in his ear.

He caught her eye happily and flashed her a conspiratorial look.

Where the trees ended, they found a stretch of scrubland

clear of Twolegs and monsters. Keeping low, Rootspring headed across it. Nightheart took the rear, one eye on the patrol, but he couldn't help glancing back toward the bright nests. He was glad they'd put some space between themselves and the Twoleg crowds, but the smell of warm prey had made him hungrier than he'd ever felt.

"Hurry up," Rootspring called to him, and Nightheart realized he'd slowed, distracted by the tantalizing scents. The rest of the patrol had already ducked into a gap between two high wooden fences that edged a row of large, square Twoleg dens. The dens were swathed in shadow.

"Is this the Twolegplace?" he asked as he caught up.

"Yes." Fidgetflake looked relieved. "I've definitely been here before." He leaped onto a fence and peered down the other side. "Follow me," he mewed.

One by one, they leaped up after him. Nightheart could see fences crisscrossing each other and, between them, neat patches of grass. He tasted the air but smelled nothing famil-iar. Only the faint tang of Thunderpaths and stone. "Where are the catmint bushes?" he asked.

"We need to go deeper in to find them." Gingerly, Fidget-flake picked his way along the fence tops. It was like crossing a forest aboveground, following one branch, then another. At last, Fidgetflake paused. The patches of grass were larger here and edged by flowers that were tattered and dying in the leaf-fall chill.

Fidgetflake leaped down and headed toward them.

"Can you smell catmint?" Alderheart called, following him.

Fidgetflake didn't answer but flicked his tail, his attention fixed on the thick bushes ahead.

Nightheart jumped down and opened his mouth, tasting the air as he crossed the grass. The medicine cats were looking for catmint, but Nightheart was alert for any scent that signaled danger. Through the lingering stench of monsters, he could detect cat-scent, but it was faint and edged with a sweetness that warrior scent lacked. *Kittypets?*

At least there's no dog-scent here, he thought as he nosed his way through the flowering bushes after the rest of the patrol. The leaves were soft and fragrant as they brushed against his pelt. "Can you smell catmint?" he asked Sunbeam as he caught up to her.

"I can't smell anything but flowers," she told him.

Lightleap was ahead of them. She glanced back, her eyes bright with worry. "What if we can't find any?"

"We will," Fidgetflake mewed from the head of the patrol. He broke from the bushes and the others followed him out onto another wide stretch of grass. A Twoleg nest stood to one side, square and silent, and plants spilled from borders around the edge.

As Alderheart and Fidgetflake began to sniff their way around them, Nightheart pricked his ears, listening for sounds of danger. Monsters were murmuring quietly in the distance. Wind whispered around the Twoleg nest.

Sunbeam stopped beside him, her pelt twitching along her spine.

"Do the scratches still sting?" he whispered.

"A little," she breathed back. "It would hurt worse if you hadn't—"

A tiny hiss interrupted her.

Nightheart stiffened. Were there *snakes* here? He jerked his muzzle around, unsheathing his claws.

A small furry head poked out from beneath a bush. "Go away!"

A *kit!*

It was glaring at them furiously. "This is our garden!" it squeaked. "You're not allowed here!"

The patrol turned to look.

"What kind of cat is that?" Lightleap mewed in surprise.

The kit was gray and had strangely rounded ears, like a mouse.

Its eyes widened in alarm as the patrol faced it, but it held its ground. Nightheart didn't know whether to admire its courage or scold it for being so reckless. They were *warriors*, for StarClan's sake. Did it really think it could chase them off?

Alderheart blinked at the kit calmly. "We're sorry to trespass," he mewed. "But we're here on an import—"

"Go away or I'll tell my mother!" The kit stuck out its chest.

Fidgetflake and Rootspring exchanged glances.

Sunbeam purred. "It's so cute."

"No I'm not!" the kit hissed at her.

Nightheart dipped his head politely. "We promise we're not here to—" As he spoke, the leaves around the kit rustled, and a large she-cat slid out. She had the same odd, round ears as her kit, and she was clearly a kittypet—she had the strangely sweet cat-scent Nightheart had smelled earlier.

She flattened her ears as she saw the patrol and stepped quickly in front of her kit, glaring at them. "What are you doing here?" she spat.

Nightheart took a step back, surprised by her vehemence. "We—we—" he stammered.

The kittypet narrowed her eyes to slits and unsheathed her claws. Was she really prepared to fight them? Surely not! There wasn't a scar anywhere on her thick, soft pelt. She looked as though she'd never fought in her life.

Alderheart dipped his head. "We're looking for catmint," he told her. "There's greencough in our Clan."

The kittypet looked puzzled.

"One of our kits is very sick," Fidgetflake explained.

The kittypet's fur flattened a little and her round ears twitched. "And you think catmint will help?"

"He will die without it." Lightleap's amber eyes glittered anxiously.

The kittypet sheathed her claws. "Where is this kit?" she asked, her mew gentler now.

"Beside the lake," Alderheart told her. "Where we live. Beyond the moor."

Her own kit slipped beneath her belly and peeped out between her forelegs. Nightheart could see now that it was a she-kit. "What's catmint?" she asked.

"It's a plant," her mother told her. "There's none in our

garden." The kittypet turned her wide blue gaze toward Alderheart. "But there's some a few houses down." She pointed her muzzle toward a hedge. "That way."

"Thank you." Alderheart blinked at her gratefully. "We promise that's all we came for."

"We'll leave as soon as we've gathered some," Rootspring assured her.

The kittypet looked relieved. "I hope your kit recovers soon." She ducked her head and grabbed her kit by the scruff.

"Hey!" The kit struggled as her mother lifted her and ducked back between the leaves. "I can walk!" Her paws churned crossly in the air as they both disappeared into the bushes.

Nightheart glanced at Sunbeam. "I didn't know kittypets were so brave."

She frowned. "I just hope those two never run into rogues."

The air was fragrant with the scent of flowers. After the muskiness of the forest and the tang of the lake and moor, the sweetness of it was dizzying.

Lightleap looked around. "I can't imagine rogues here," she mewed.

"Come on." Fidgetflake headed toward the hedge the kittypet had pointed to.

The patrol followed. As they pushed their way through border after border, Nightheart's breath quickened. For the first time since they'd left the field of colorful dens, a scent touched his nose that made him forget the delicious smell of Twoleg prey. He opened his mouth to let it bathe his tongue.

It smelled like Jayfeather's den. Catmint?

Fidgetflake had clearly smelled it too. The SkyClan medicine cat quickened his pace, breaking into a run as he crossed the grass and disappeared between more bushes.

Nightheart's paws pricked with alarm. "Be careful," he hissed. Who knew what might be lurking beyond the shrubs? "Slow down!" He shouldered his way among the bushes, trying to keep up with the medicine cat. The smell was unmistakable now, and as Nightheart burst out once more onto grass, he saw it—catmint. The plant was far bigger than the catmint bushes around the lake. It frothed with purple flowers and spilled from the border onto the grass.

Fidgetflake was already wading through the stems, his tail whisking with triumph. Lightleap plunged in after him with Alderheart and Rootspring.

"Collect the tips," Fidgetflake told them. "They're the most potent part."

Sunbeam stopped beside Nightheart, her mouth open and her eyes sparkling as though the very scent of the catmint had filled her with fresh energy. She pushed her way into the bush, glancing back at Nightheart. "Come on," she mewed. "Let's help."

Nightheart's mouth watered as he followed her in. The heady fragrance filled his nose and mouth. He fought the urge to drop onto his belly and roll in the delicious leaves.

Alderheart's pelt was fluffed with joy. "There's more here than we could ever need!"

Fidgetflake blinked in agreement. "And it smells much stronger than the plants in the forest."

Nightheart bit off a juicy stem, delighted by the taste. He tossed it onto the grass nearby and bit off another. The rest of the patrol worked around him, and soon they'd gathered a pile of stems.

Alderheart stepped back and looked admiringly at the heap. "That's plenty."

Fidgetflake sat back on his haunches. "Enough for all the Clans."

Rootspring shook leaves from his whiskers. "And now we know exactly where it grows," he mewed. "We can come back if we need more."

"Let's hope we won't have to," Alderheart mewed.

Nightheart was already gathering a bunch of the stems between his jaws. He was eager to get back to the field of colored dens. The catmint had sharpened his appetite even more, and he was determined now to hunt among the Twoleg dens for a taste of the delicious-smelling Twoleg prey. He wondered whether to share his plan with the rest of the patrol. But his mouth was full. He'd wait until they reached the field before he mentioned it.

Nightheart trailed the patrol as it skirted the scrubland beside the colored dens. Twolegs were still crowding between them. *Don't they ever sleep?* he wondered. Sunbeam was in front of him. He was so busy watching the Twolegs that he didn't notice when she slowed, and his claws grazed her hind paw.

She flinched and he pulled back.

"Sorry!"

She glanced at him in surprise, a bundle of catmint between her jaws.

In explanation, he nodded toward the Twoleg dens. Surely she could smell the prey. Did she want to taste it as much as he did?

She tipped her head, her eyes questioning, then hurried after the others as they neared the woods.

Nightheart followed. As he reached the shelter of the trees, he dropped his bunch of catmint. "I'm going to hunt," he announced. "We need to eat before we sleep."

Lightleap blinked at him. "There'll be no prey here."

Rootspring nodded in agreement. "The Twolegs will have scared it away."

"Don't worry." Nightheart looked at the colored dens. Mouthwatering scents wafted from them. "I'll bring something back."

Sunbeam dropped her catmint. "I'll come with you."

Before anyone could object, Nightheart headed for the Twoleg dens. Sunbeam trotted after him.

"Nightheart!" Rootspring was calling after him, but Nightheart pretended not to hear, and soon the SkyClan tom's yowl was lost amid the chatter of the Twolegs and the hum of the den-monsters. Rhythmic thumping seemed to throb from every nest, and Nightheart was glad Sunbeam had come with him. He motioned for her to stay close with a flick of his tail and ducked behind a den. She darted to his side, and together they peered out at the swarming Twolegs.

"Can you see prey?" Sunbeam's eyes were wide.

"Not yet." Nightheart strained to see past the Twolegs parading in front of them. A yellow and red den-monster stood a tree-length away. Its paws were sunk in the muddy grass, and Twolegs clustered at the front, taking something from the outstretched paws of the Twoleg inside. He narrowed his eyes. "Is that prey?" He nodded toward it.

Sunbeam followed his gaze, her nose twitching. "I think so," she mewed.

Nightheart's belly growled longingly. He wanted to taste whatever the Twoleg was passing to its Clanmates.

Beyond the forest of Twoleg paws, he could see a shadowy space beneath the den-monster's belly. He pointed his muzzle toward the space. "Do you think you can make it over there?" he asked Sunbeam.

She hesitated.

"It's okay if you want to stay here," he told her. She'd probably never seen so many Twolegs in her life. He certainty hadn't. And the noise and bright lights were almost overwhelming.

But she blinked at him eagerly. "You're not leaving me behind," she mewed.

Nightheart crept along the side of the den to the edge of the Twoleg path. Sunbeam followed, keeping low as Twolegs swarmed ahead of them. Nightheart dug his claws into the muddy grass, preparing to dart between them.

"Wait." Sunbeam touched her tail-tip to his spine. She was looking along the path; he followed her gaze. The crowd, flowing past like a river, was thinning. A few moments later, a gap opened in front of them, and Sunbeam nodded. "Now!"

She darted from their hiding place and hared through the gap. Nightheart tore after her, his paws slithering on the grass as he followed Sunbeam around the Twolegs bunching in front of the yellow-and-red den-monster and ducked after her into the shadows underneath.

He crouched beside her, his flanks heaving.

Her eyes were shining. "I don't think they even noticed us."

"You're fast!" Every hair on Nightheart's pelt was quivering with fear and excitement. Then the delicious scent of Twoleg food washed over them. He blinked happily at Sunbeam. "Do you smell it?"

She licked her lips. "Of course I do," she mewed. "But how do we get our paws on it?"

Nightheart looked up at the dark underbelly of the monster. There weren't any openings there. But there was a Twoleg inside, so there must be an entrance. He crept from the shadow of the monster and peered up at the side, looking for a way in. They might be able to sneak through it without the Twoleg noticing and grab a piece of prey.

"Nightheart!" Sunbeam's excited mew made him turn. She was jerking her muzzle toward something on the grass in front the monster.

His eyes widened. A huge lump of prey was lying on the

ground. Twoleg paws shifted around it. At any moment they might crush it into the mud.

"I'll grab it," he told Sunbeam, thinking fast. "Then we both run for the trees."

"Okay." She nodded.

"Stay close!" Nightheart darted from beneath the monster. He zigzagged between the Twoleg paws, his heart pounding in his ears, his gaze fixed on the fallen prey. He reached it and sank his teeth in. Surprise pulsed beneath his pelt. It was *hot*! He nearly dropped it, but the juice running into his mouth was so tasty he didn't want to let go no matter how hot it was.

Yelps sounded above him. The Twolegs had seen him and shied away like frightened horses. Shock showed on their round pink and brown faces. Nightheart raced for the trees. *Sunbeam!* He glanced back, relieved to see her at his heels. As he caught her eye, triumph sparkled in her gaze.

The rest of the patrol was watching from beneath the undergrowth. They stared at Nightheart as he crashed through the bushes and slowed to a halt in front of them. He dropped the prey and licked his lips, his belly growling as the sweet, sticky juice sang on his tongue. The prey he'd stolen looked like a massive blackbird, but fatter, and with legs as plump as pigeons.

Rootspring sniffed. "Twoleg prey," he sneered.

"What is it?" Lightleap stared at it, puzzled. "It's too big to be forest prey."

"Who cares?" Fidgetflake padded around it, his tail swishing happily. "It smells delicious!"

Sunbeam sat down and caught her breath. "There's enough to fill all our bellies," she mewed.

Alderheart was hanging back, his gaze wary.

Nightheart blinked at him. "The juice tastes great," he mewed.

Alderheart looked doubtful. "Warriors shouldn't eat Twoleg food."

But Fidgetflake had already taken a bite. His expression melted into pleasure.

Lightleap's tail twitched excitedly, and she ducked forward to take a bite too. Her breath, warmed by the meat, billowed around her muzzle. "It tastes amazing."

Nightheart wanted to taste it so badly it was almost impossible to hold himself back. But he wanted to convince Rootspring and Alderheart first. "You can hunt for forest prey if you want," he told them. "But we'll be home quicker if we don't waste time hunting. The catmint will hardly have the chance to wilt."

Rootspring's tail twitched. "I guess eating this would save time," he conceded.

Sunbeam pawed a lump toward him. "We've already stolen it," she coaxed. "It would be a waste not to eat it."

Alderheart wrinkled his nose. "It's no better than carrion."

Lightleap looked at him, her mouth full. "It's *way* better than carrion."

Rootspring and Alderheart exchanged looks.

"I guess we didn't beg for it like kittypets," Alderheart mewed.

Rootspring padded closer to the carcass. "Since it's here," he mewed begrudgingly, and dipped his head to tear off a piece.

Nightheart swallowed back a purr as Rootspring's eyes lit up. The SkyClan warrior took another bite, his pelt smoothing. Pleased, Nightheart ripped a wing from the carcass and settled down to eat it. The sweet taste filled him with warmth and satisfaction. He caught Sunbeam's eye. Her chin glistened with grease and she blinked at him happily. With full bellies, they'd sleep well and be ready for the journey home in the morning.

Nightheart woke first, the warm pelts of the others pressed around him. When they'd finished the Twoleg prey, the patrol had snuggled like kits in a hollow between the roots of a beech and drifted to sleep despite the drone and thump of the Twoleg gathering. Sunbeam was still snoring, and Rootspring's tail was twitching as though the SkyClan warrior was dreaming.

Nightheart got to his paws and hopped from the makeshift nest. He scanned the woodland, looking for somewhere to make dirt. It was barely dawn, and there was no noise coming from the field of brightly colored dens. He padded to the edge of the trees and looked out, wondering if the colored lights would still be shining while the Twolegs, exhausted at last, slept among the monsters. He blinked, surprise sparking through his fur.

The monsters were gone, and there wasn't a single Twoleg in sight. Mist hung thickly over the wide, empty field. In the woods, the birds were waking, beginning their morning song as though nothing had ever disturbed them.

Nightheart scanned the deserted field. The trampled grass was littered here and there with scraps the Twolegs had left behind, and paw marks showed where the monsters had crept away. What had driven them from here?

Paw steps brushed the earth behind him, and Nightheart jerked around, relieved to see it was Sunbeam. As she reached him, her gaze flitted around the field. She stopped next to Nightheart, her ears twitching uneasily. "Where did they go?"

"I don't know." Nightheart felt a shiver along his spine.

"Did we dream it?" Sunbeam looked at him.

"No." Nightheart knew from his belly, still full from last night's feast, that they hadn't. He even still had some sticky, sweet juice around his mouth. He swiped his tongue around it now.

"Nightheart! Sunbeam!" Alderheart was calling them.

Sunbeam blinked at Nightheart. "We'd better go."

As she turned to leave, Nightheart hesitated. A small part of him didn't want to return home.

"Our Clanmates will be pleased to see us," Sunbeam mewed. "Especially when they see how much catmint we've brought." She headed toward the others, who were waiting beneath the trees.

Nightheart watched her go. Traveling had made him feel close to his patrolmates, even Lightleap. But he felt a special sort of kinship with Sunbeam. They'd hunted, eaten, and sat watch together, and shared confidences he'd never shared with his own Clanmates. They were friends now, and he couldn't help hoping it was a friendship that would outlast their return to the lake.

CHAPTER 9

Frostpaw stared at a patch of reeds on the roof of the medicine den. Her Clanmates' names were spinning in her mind like leaves caught in a whirlwind, and they had been doing so all night. She must have dozed a bit, but mostly Frostpaw had spent the night torturing herself with questions: Which warrior should she choose to lead RiverClan? Breezeheart? Sneezecloud? Havenpelt or Nightsky? Any of them could be okay. They were experienced enough to be taken seriously, but were they "beyond the obvious choices"?

She sat up. *Obvious choices.* Her mother's words were stuck in her thoughts. They meant she couldn't choose Shimmerpelt or Duskfur. Or Icewing or Lizardtail. In fact, she couldn't choose any of the cats she truly trusted to lead RiverClan. Instead she must choose a cat who no warrior would think could be Clan leader.

Irritation buzzed in her chest once more. Why had Curlfeather told her to look beyond the obvious choices? Did StarClan have bees in their brains, or did they simply enjoy making life difficult for the living? She shook out her fur. *Don't doubt StarClan,* she told herself sternly. It was bad enough

RiverClan had *one* medicine cat who believed that their ances-tors had no business controlling the lives of the living. They didn't need two. Especially now. She had to keep the faith and believe that StarClan guided the Clans with wisdom and compassion.

Just make a choice! She curled her claws into the moss at the bottom of her nest. StarClan wouldn't have left this decision up to her if they'd thought she'd get it wrong.

Splashtail?

Too young.

Mallownose?

Too old.

With every name, a reason popped into her head as to why they wouldn't be the leader RiverClan needed right now. She discarded one idea after another until her head spun.

Dawn light was seeping into the den, and Mothwing stirred in her nest. Her mentor would be awake soon, asking if Frost-paw had decided.

Frostpaw's heart began to pound. *I have to decide. The Clan needs to know.*

Then, like a fish suddenly breaking the surface of the river, one name leaped ahead of the others. She narrowed her eyes, focusing her thoughts on it, waiting for a reason—any reason—to knock it back again so that it could languish among the other discarded names. But no reason came. She stiffened. Could it be? Had she finally thought of a warrior who might be RiverClan's next leader? Hope sparked in her paws. Yes! This was it. The warrior StarClan had meant. At last. She knew who to choose!

She hopped out of her nest, her tail twitching excitedly. "Mothwing." Outside, she could hear her Clanmates beginning to move around the camp. "Mothwing!"

Her mentor lifted her head, her eyes opening sleepily. "What is it?"

"I know who to choose."

But Mothwing didn't seem to hear. She was staring at the sunlight pooling at the entrance. "Is it dawn already?" She scrambled to her paws. "I need to send out the patrols."

"It's okay." Frostpaw blinked at her. "You won't have to. I know who our leader should be!"

Mothwing looked at her. Her gaze widened. "Who?"

Frostpaw couldn't wait to hear what her mentor thought of her choice. But before she could speak, the entrance rustled and Splashtail padded in.

"The warriors are awake," he told Mothwing. "They're waiting for you."

"Good." Mothwing hopped from her nest. "I have news for them!"

"Really?" Splashtail's ears pricked. "What is it?"

"Frostpaw has chosen our next leader," Mothwing told him.

Splashtail turned excitedly to Frostpaw. "Did StarClan finally send you a dream?"

"Not exactly." Frostpaw shifted her paws. "But they told me at the Moonpool that they trust me to decide," she mewed. "And I've given it a lot of thought and I think I know who they wanted me to choose."

"Who?" Splashtail was staring at her so hard that Frost-paw's pelt burned. She'd been happy to share her decision with her mentor, but it didn't seem fair to tell one warrior before the others. And yet she wanted to get this over with. If she told Mothwing, and Mothwing objected, she'd have to start again. It was better to tell the whole Clan and let them decide.

"If you gather the Clan, I'll announce it," she told Moth-wing.

"Now?" Mothwing looked surprised.

"Now." Frostpaw fluffed out her fur decisively, but her heart was pounding. What if her Clanmates asked her to explain her choice? Was it enough to say that she felt sure? Would they need more proof that she was speaking for StarClan?

Mothwing held her gaze for a moment, as though checking if Frostpaw was certain, and when Frostpaw dipped her head, the medicine cat ducked out of the den. "I'll call a meeting at once," she mewed as she disappeared.

Splashtail was still staring at her. "Making such a big deci-sion was a real responsibility," he sympathized. "The past few days must have been hard for you."

"StarClan guided my thoughts," she told him, hoping it was true.

"Of course," he mewed. "You're our medicine cat. Whoever you choose, RiverClan will support you." He dipped his head and left the den.

She watched him go, her paws suddenly trembling. *I'm not your medicine cat yet,* she thought. *I'm just an apprentice.* But she was still the Clan's best link with StarClan. She was the only cat who could speak for their ancestors. Keeping her fur fluffed out despite the anxiety churning in her belly, she padded from the den.

Her Clanmates ringed the clearing, their expectant gazes widening as they saw her.

Duskfur's tail-tip was twitching. Icewing paced between her Clanmates, while Shimmerpelt hung back beside the reed wall of the camp, her silver pelt gleaming in the early morning sunshine. Splashtail alone blinked encouragingly at Frostpaw as she padded to the center of the clearing.

She felt sick. Her words would shape the future of River-Clan. She took a breath, steadying her mew. "StarClan told me to look for a leader beyond the obvious choices," she began. "I've thought a lot about which warrior they could mean, and now I think I know."

"You *think* you know?" Duskfur frowned.

"I'm *sure* I know," Frostpaw corrected herself. If this was going to settle the issue once and for all, she needed to sound as certain as she'd felt earlier in the medicine den. This was the right decision. It had felt right when she'd thought of it. It had to be right now. She scanned the hopeful faces of her Clanmates. "Our new leader will be . . ." She glanced at the sky. StarClan would send a sign if she was about to make a mistake, surely? But the sky was clear and blue for the first time in days, while the reeds rustled in a fresh breeze that brought the promise of a fine leaf-fall morning. "Our new leader should be Owlnose."

The brown tabby tom stiffened. He was the right choice, wasn't he? His shoulders were broad, and muscle showed beneath his thick, glossy pelt. He'd been her father's littermate and was a strong fighter and good hunter, just like Jayclaw. And if he flared into anger from time to time, that was good, wasn't it? It meant he'd fight for his Clan.

Owlnose didn't move, but only stared back at her, his eyes glittering with shock. *"Me?"*

Murmurs rippled around the clearing.

"He's never had an apprentice," Gorseclaw mewed.

"There are never enough apprentices for every cat to be a mentor," Mallownose pointed out. "And anyway, *deputies* need to have had an apprentice. Not leaders. So . . ."

Nightsky narrowed her eyes. "It's an *interesting* choice, for sure," she mewed doubtfully.

"It's certainly not an *obvious* one," Shimmerpelt muttered.

Frostpaw felt her confidence ebb as her Clanmates exchanged glances.

Then Icewing nodded. "*I* think it's a good decision."

"Owlnose is a true warrior," Fognose added.

Relief flooded Frostpaw's pelt. At least some of her Clanmates liked her choice.

Brackenpelt nudged Owlnose forward.

The brown tabby tom padded hesitantly toward Frostpaw and dipped his head. "Thanks for this honor," he mewed earnestly. "I will do my best to serve my Clan."

"It's what StarClan wants," Frostpaw told him, hoping it was true. "Tomorrow night, I'll take you to the Moonpool to receive your nine lives. Then you can choose a deputy." Despite her Clanmates' doubts, she felt a wash of satisfaction. Soon RiverClan would have a leader and deputy again, and life could return to normal. It was natural for Owlnose to look nervous. Becoming leader was a big step for any warrior.

Frostpaw glanced at Duskfur. The tabby warrior was watching Owlnose closely. Did *she* approve of Frostpaw's choice? And what about Shimmerpelt? The silver she-cat was sitting quietly in the shadow of the reeds, her tail swishing back and forth over the ground.

Mothwing padded to Frostpaw's side. "Well done, Frostpaw." She ran her tail along Frostpaw's spine, then dipped her head to Owlnose. "I think Frostpaw has made the right decision."

"Th-thanks," Owlnose mewed haltingly. He glanced around his Clanmates. "I hope I will lead you well."

Duskfur stared at him for a moment, then addressed the Clan. "Frostpaw has consulted StarClan and made her decision," she mewed. "We have a leader, and we should respect his decisions and honor his wishes. Owlnose has always been devoted to RiverClan, and I'm sure he has RiverClan's best interest at heart." She dipped her head to the brown tabby tom and signaled to Shimmerpelt with her tail. "Let's hunt," she told her. "Leader or no leader, RiverClan's bellies are still empty."

Frostpaw felt a chill in her pelt as Duskfur and Shimmerpelt padded out of camp.

Mothwing looked brightly at Owlnose. "Perhaps you should

organize the other warriors into patrols," she prompted.

"Um." He blinked at her. "Yes." He sounded sorry he hadn't thought of it himself. "Splashtail." He called his denmate over. "Take Brackenpelt upstream to fish," he mewed. Then he seemed to change his mind. "Wait. The river is running fast, and Brackenpelt is a good white-water fisher. She should fish in the gorge. Take . . ." Owlnose hesitated and glanced around their Clanmates, who were watching him expectantly. "Take . . ." His gaze flitted from one warrior to the next, but he seemed unable to make a decision.

"I could take Mallownose," Splashtail suggested. "He fishes well in slow water."

"Yes." Owlnose sounded relieved at the suggestion. "Take Mallownose."

"And Podlight?" Splashtail prompted.

"Yes," Owlnose agreed.

"What about taking Sneezecloud too?" Splashtail added. "There's a wide stretch of river. A large hunting party would catch more fish."

Mothwing cleared her throat. "We'll need enough warriors for the border patrol," she reminded Owlnose.

The brown tabby warrior's gaze darted toward her, then back to Splashtail. "The border. Of course." He nodded to Havenpelt. "Can you and Harelight mark the border?"

"Which one?" Havenpelt asked.

"WindClan." Owlnose's pelt was ruffled. "Wait. Um. ShadowClan. No. *WindClan*."

Havenpelt exchanged looks with Harelight. "We'd better

leave before he changes his mind again."

Mothwing blinked at Owlnose sympathetically. "It's only your first day," she told him. "You'll get the hang of it."

Frostpaw felt a wave of pity for Owlnose. Perhaps she should have given him some warning before naming him in front of the whole Clan. But even if he didn't know what to do right away, he'd soon learn. Why else would StarClan have nudged her toward choosing him?

She headed to the medicine den as the warriors drew closer around Owlnose, waiting for his orders. Her paw steps felt suddenly light. She'd made the decision that had weighed her down for days. Now she could be an ordinary medicine-cat apprentice again and worry about her Clan's health, not their future. She might even have a chance to earn her medicine-cat name.

"Frostpaw." Splashtail caught up to her as she neared the den. "That must have been scary."

"It was." She purred at him. "I'm just glad it's over."

"It was a good choice," he mewed.

"Do you think so?" She searched his gaze, eager for reassurance.

"Of course," he told her. "Why else would StarClan have led you to it?"

Frostpaw reached to the back of the herb store and pulled out the last bundle of dried leaves. They were so old she had to sniff them twice to guess what they were. *Marigold.* A faint tang was still there, but Frostpaw wasn't sure they'd have enough strength left to drive away infection.

She laid them beside the row of other bundles that needed replacing before leaf-bare set in. She and Mothwing should have checked the herb stocks sooner, but the crisis in River-Clan had kept them busy. Now, at last, they had a leader, and after Owlnose received his nine lives tomorrow at the Moon-pool and chose a new deputy, life would finally return to normal. She and Mothwing could focus on gathering herbs to replenish their supplies.

RiverClan had been lucky to be free of greencough so far. They hadn't even had the season's first case of whitecough yet. Frostpaw wondered suddenly how Tigerstar's kit was doing. Had the patrol to collect catmint from beyond Clan borders returned? Had they found catmint? She hoped so.

She looked around the den. One of the reed walls was sagging. If they repaired it, there would be room for another nest. The other nests looked a little unkempt and needed fresh moss to line them. Luckily, there was still time to fix everything before colder weather arrived.

Frostpaw sat back on her haunches and breathed out, feeling suddenly weary after so many long, anxious days. Her heart began to ache, and she welcomed the sensation. It felt right. The grief she'd pushed away had found room once more to unfold. She needed to finish mourning her mother, and now, at last, she could.

The entrance to the medicine den darkened as Mothwing slid in.

Frostpaw blinked at her. "How's Owlnose doing?"

"Not bad." Mothwing looked cheerful. "He organized all the patrols."

"Do you think he can ask some warriors to fix our den?" Frostpaw nodded toward the sagging wall.

"I'll mention it to him when he gets back," Mothwing mewed.

"Gets back?" Frostpaw was surprised their new leader had left. The medicine den wasn't the only den that needed fixing. The nursery roof had holes in it, the apprentices' den entrance was unraveling, and the camp wall was looking a little tattered after the recent wind and rain. "Where's he gone?"

"He joined Splashtail's patrol."

"Shouldn't he focus on getting the camp into shape first?"

Mothwing looked suddenly distracted. "He needs to check the borders," she mewed. "ShadowClan has been sniffing around. I ran into some of their warriors yesterday on the other side of the river, and they started asking if we'd had any cases of greencough and if we'd found catmint yet. I had to call Gorseclaw and Mallownose to stop them barging their way into our camp. I don't know why they keep pestering us when I've already told them we don't have catmint."

Frostpaw's belly tightened. "Do you think they're using catmint as an excuse to nose around?" she asked. "Perhaps they've guessed we're in trouble."

"We're not in trouble anymore," Mothwing told her firmly. She shook out her pelt. "We've got a leader. Let Owlnose deal with ShadowClan. You can take a break from worrying." Her eyes rounded sympathetically. "You still need to mourn

Curlfeather properly. You'll have time now."

Frostpaw's throat tightened. "Yes," she mewed quietly. She wanted to be away from RiverClan and all the worries that had been pressing down on her. But Mothwing was right: more than anything, she missed her mother. She needed to spend time grieving the cat who'd made her everything she was. Earlier, Frostpaw had dreaded going to the Moonpool, because she wasn't ready. But now that the business of choosing a leader was done, she felt excited to try to reach her mother and focus on saying good-bye. She wanted to be alone with Curlfeather. "I want to go to the Moonpool."

"I understand." Mothwing dipped her head. "Would you like to take some cat with you? Graypaw, perhaps, or Mistpaw. They're mourning too."

Frostpaw hesitated. She should ask her littermates to join her. After all, they'd lost Curlfeather too. But they'd had a chance to grieve over the past few days, while Frostpaw's thoughts had been consumed by choosing RiverClan's next leader. "No," she mewed. "This is something I want to do alone."

Mothwing touched her nose to Frostpaw's ear. "Okay," she mewed. "But perhaps spend a little more time with Graypaw and Mistpaw while you're in camp."

"I know—" Frostpaw's mew was cut off by paw steps pounding into camp. She smelled wet fur and fear. "Something's wrong."

Mothwing was already hurrying from the den, her tail spiking with alarm.

Frostpaw ducked out after her, stiffening as she saw Mallownose scrambling to a halt in the clearing. His eyes were wide, his wet pelt prickling as he looked back toward the camp entrance. Splashtail was helping Brackenpelt walk. The tortoiseshell she-cat's eyes were clouded, and she was having trouble staying on her paws.

"What happened?" Mothwing padded around her.

"The riverbank collapsed," Splashtail mewed. "Brackenpelt got swept away. I think she hit her head."

"Take her to the medicine den," Mothwing ordered.

As Splashtail helped Brackenpelt away, Frostpaw realized he was limping too. She hurried to his side and sniffed his paw. It wasn't twisted, but she could see swelling around his claws. "Are you okay?"

"It caught on a branch as I fell," he told her.

"Frostpaw!" Mothwing called her name and she turned.

Sneezecloud and Owlnose were helping Podlight into camp. Their wet pelts were slicked against their frames, and Frostpaw was struck by how small Owlnose suddenly seemed. He was trembling as he let Podlight slide to the ground.

She hurried to check the injured warrior. His eyes were open, but he looked dazed. She ran her paws over his legs and along his spine. "Nothing's broken," she told Mothwing.

Mothwing leaned down to look him over.

"I think he just swallowed a lot of muddy water," Sneezecloud told her.

"He'll need yarrow and then watermint," Mothwing mewed.

"Should I fetch some?" Frostpaw asked.

"No." Mothwing flicked her tail toward the medicine den. "You see to Brackenpelt. She'll need thyme."

Frostpaw tried to remember if there was any among the herbs she'd sorted earlier. She felt sure there were a few leaves left.

Mothwing was looking at Owlnose. "We need to get Podlight to the medicine den," she mewed.

But RiverClan's new leader didn't move. His eyes seemed to be glazed with panic.

Mothwing turned to Sneezecloud. "Can you help me?"

Sneezecloud nodded and shoved his muzzle beneath Podlight, pushing him to his paws.

Frostpaw hurried to the medicine den. Brackenpelt was leaning against a nest, her eyes still misted. Splashtail was gingerly licking his injured paw. Frostpaw grabbed some comfrey leaves from the herb pile. She dropped them beside him. "Wrap those around it while I see to Brackenpelt."

He lifted one with his teeth and draped it over his paw as Frostpaw turned back to the pile and picked out the few remaining thyme leaves.

As she crumbled them beside Brackenpelt, Sneezecloud helped Podlight into the den.

Mothwing hurried after them. "Lay him here." She nodded to a clear patch of earth and hurried to the herb pile, where she picked out yarrow and watermint. She darted back to Podlight and dropped the herbs at his paws. "Eat these."

Podlight stared at them reluctantly.

Mothwing was looking at Sneezecloud. "Didn't you realize the riverbank was unstable?"

Splashtail answered. "Owlnose told us to cross where the current wasn't too strong. We just assumed it would be okay." He winced as he wrapped another comfrey leaf around his paw. "I can't feel my claws," he mewed. "Is that normal?"

"I'll take a look at it once Podlight swallows this yarrow." Mothwing nudged the bitter leaves closer to the gray-and-white tom. "Eat them," she ordered as though he were a reluctant kit. "Who knows what else you swallowed with all that mud. It's better to be sick once now than to spend half a moon in the medicine den throwing up."

Brackenpelt was still dazed, and Frostpaw used a claw to delicately hook open her mouth. As she pushed the crumbled thyme leaves between her lips, Owlnose padded into the den.

"Is every cat okay?" His mew was so quiet, Frostpaw hardly heard him.

"We don't know yet." Mothwing padded to Frostpaw's side. Brackenpelt was struggling to keep her eyes open. Mothwing examined the swelling behind her ear. "It doesn't look too bad, but we won't be sure for a while."

Owlnose's eyes glittered with guilt. "I'm sorry," he mewed. "If I'd known the bank was unsafe, I wouldn't have—"

Splashtail interrupted him. "How could you have known? We haven't sent patrols to check the shorelines in a quarter moon."

"Should we do that now?" Owlnose blinked at him.

Sneezecloud's eyes widened. "Of course we should do that now."

"O-okay." Owlnose's gaze was flitting distractedly around his injured Clanmates. "I'll send a small patrol out once the border patrols get back."

"A *small* patrol?" Splashtail looked at him questioningly. "What if they get swept away too?"

"A big patrol, then," Owlnose corrected himself.

"Every riverbank needs checking," Splashtail told him.

"Then I'll send out *two* small patrols," Owlnose mewed.

Sneezecloud frowned. "Only two?"

Owlnose looked from Sneezecloud to Splashtail, his ears twitching uncertainly. He hesitated, and Frostpaw felt a twinge of dread. He was out of his depth. She willed him to make a decision.

"I'll send two small patrols out today and a bigger one in the morning," Owlnose mewed. Sneezecloud and Splashtail exchanged glances, and Frostpaw's heart sank. It was clear to everyone that Owlnose was trying to please them both instead of deciding what the Clan needed.

She turned to examine Splashtail's paw. He'd done a good job of wrapping comfrey around it. She began to neaten up the leaves, grabbing a reed to tie them in place. "I can give you poppy seeds for the pain," she mewed, but her thoughts weren't really on his injured paw. She was wondering if she'd made the right decision after all. *Look beyond the obvious choices.* Was that the only reason she'd chosen Owlnose? Because he seemed the least likely choice? Was that really what was best for RiverClan? What had made her so sure that *he* was the cat StarClan had wanted her to pick?

She forced herself to focus on her work. The reed was fiddly, and by the time she'd secured the comfrey in place and fetched the poppy seeds for Splashtail, she'd managed to push away her doubts. But outside the den, once the injured cats were stable and comfortable, she found it harder to distract herself.

The sun was sinking behind the distant moor as she crossed the clearing to the fresh-kill pile. It was well-stocked. Wasn't that a sign that Owlnose was a good leader? After picking a small carp from the heap, she carried it toward Graypaw and Mistpaw, who were already sharing a trout. Graypaw pricked his ears happily as he saw her approach, and Frostpaw felt a surge of guilt that she hadn't spent more time with her littermates since their mother's death.

"I heard he was going to send a big patrol and then changed his mind." Duskfur's mew made her pause. Her ears swiveled toward the brown tabby she-cat, who was picking at the bones of a salmon beside Gorseclaw. They were clearly talking about Owlnose. "One word from Splashtail and he decided a small patrol would be better."

"*Two* small patrols," Gorseclaw reminded her. There was an edge to the white tom's mew. "And then a big one tomorrow."

Duskfur sniffed. "I guess he covered every possibility," she mewed. She sounded unimpressed. "Unless he changes his mind again in the morning."

Frostpaw forced her pelt to stay smooth. It was inevitable that the Clan would have doubts about Owlnose at first. He was new to leadership. They all needed time to adjust. She wondered again if she should have warned Owlnose that she was going to choose him before telling the whole Clan; he could have prepared better. *If I'd told him, the change might be going smoother.* And yet, if he was the leader she hoped he'd be, shouldn't he be able to cope with the unexpected? Her pelt prickling uneasily, she settled down between Graypaw and Mistpaw.

Her littermates chatted amiably, and she tried to join in, but the conversation between Duskfur and Gorseclaw had unsettled her. Her thoughts kept flitting back to her choice. Perhaps she'd misunderstood StarClan. Perhaps they'd been trying to direct her to a different cat.

She wasn't surprised when Duskfur followed her back to the medicine den as the moon rose over the camp.

"Can we talk?" Duskfur mewed softly.

"Sure." Mothwing had already gone to her nest, and the clearing was nearly deserted as their Clanmates retired to their dens for the night.

Frostpaw faced Duskfur, wondering what the tabby she-cat would have to say. Duskfur was Curlfeather's mother, and Frostpaw hoped that she would be supportive despite what she'd said to Gorseclaw earlier. But as Duskfur seemed to hesitate to speak, Frostpaw felt anxious. *Does she think I'm wrong? Am I wrong?* "Is everything . . . okay?"

"Not exactly," Duskfur mewed quietly. "I'm glad you came

to a decision. The Clan needed a leader, and it couldn't have been easy being the one to decide."

"StarClan guided me," Frostpaw reminded her.

"That's what I've been wondering about," Duskfur mewed. "*How* did they guide you? What did they say?"

Frostpaw lifted her chin. Was Duskfur questioning her decision? "It was *Curlfeather* who spoke to me," she mewed. She hoped that would settle the matter, and Duskfur's gaze seemed to soften as she heard her daughter's name.

"I'm glad she's still trying to help you," she mewed. "But what exactly did she say?"

Frostpaw hesitated. She needed to choose her words carefully. She had never said that Curlfeather named Owlnose, but she had certainly given the impression that she had led Frostpaw in that direction. "She told me that StarClan couldn't make the choice for me, but that they trusted me to choose, and that I needed to look—"

"We know that," Duskfur interrupted her. "You needed to look beyond the obvious choices. But did they say *why* you needed to look beyond the obvious choices?"

Frostpaw shifted her paws nervously. Should she tell Duskfur that her mother had warned her to trust no cat? Right now, that was the only thing she felt certain of. Except, if her mother was being truthful, she shouldn't trust Duskfur, either. Frostpaw suppressed a shudder. *How am I supposed to make sense of this myself?* "Curlfeather didn't explain why," she mewed. "But I went through every Clanmate in my mind, and Owlnose was the one who felt right."

"*Felt* right?"

Frostpaw tried to explain. "I didn't have any doubts when I thought of his name," she mewed. "And I thought . . . well, StarClan must be *willing* me to choose him. You know? Because it wasn't obvious, but it . . . felt right." Frostpaw stopped herself. *Am I talking too much? Am I even making sense?*

Duskfur looked thoughtful. "It sounds like you made the right choice . . ." She paused. "But who exactly wanted you to look beyond the obvious choices?"

Frostpaw blinked. "What do you mean?"

"Was it Curlfeather or StarClan?"

Frostpaw stiffened. "What does it matter? I mean . . . wouldn't Curlfeather's wish be the same as StarClan's?"

Duskfur was looking thoughtful. "I suppose so. I'm just surprised Curlfeather agreed with them."

Frostpaw stared at her. *What does that mean?* "Why wouldn't she?"

"Curlfeather was always very direct, that's all," Duskfur mewed. "And she was fiercely protective of you. I'm not sure why she'd go along with forcing you to make such a hard decision by yourself."

Frostpaw felt a fresh wave of doubt. Had she misunderstood Curlfeather? Perhaps her mother had been trying to tell her something else. *What if I'm just not the right cat to make this decision?* She pushed the thought away. What did *Duskfur* know about what StarClan wanted? She was just a warrior. "Curlfeather trusts StarClan," she mewed. "And so do I. Because they understand more than living cats."

Duskfur gazed at her. "Perhaps." She sounded unconvinced. Then she shook out her pelt. "I'm sorry. I shouldn't be worrying you. You've made your decision, and now it's our duty to support Owlnose." She looked around the clearing. They were the only ones here. "But I hope he starts acting like a leader soon. If he doesn't, you might have to accept that you've made a mistake."

"When StarClan gives him his nine lives, you'll see I chose right." Frostpaw looked defiantly at Duskfur, but her paws were trembling. She watched Duskfur pad to the warriors' den and slip inside. Once she was alone, she felt her heart sink. She'd *made* a decision. It had been harder than she'd ever imagined. But it was done now. Couldn't that be the end? She closed her eyes, feeling suddenly tired to her bones. Owlnose's leadership hadn't brought certainty to the Clan after all. It had unsettled them even more. And cats were already coming to her with questions. Clearly her role in deciding the leadership of RiverClan was far from over.

CHAPTER 10

🍀

Sunbeam's paws ached. The patrol had been traveling since dawn yesterday and had kept moving through the night. But the sun was already rising as they reached the high moor and crossed the border into WindClan territory. Would they be in time to save Rowankit?

She could barely smell the catmint bunched between her jaws anymore. She must reek of it—the leaves had barely wilted—but as they'd traveled, she'd only laid the precious leaves down to drink from puddles, and their pungent odor seemed right at home among the familiar scents of leaf-fall.

Sunbeam ignored the soreness in her muscles and pushed harder as the patrol reached the great swaths of heather that stretched down toward the lake. Rowankit must be growing sicker by the moment, and though they weren't ShadowClan warriors, Rootspring, Fidgetflake, Alderheart, and Nightheart kept up their relentless pace as though it were their own Clanmate who was ill. As they grew closer to ShadowClan territory, Sunbeam's pelt began to prickle with anxiety. What would they find in the medicine-cat den? Would they return in time to help Rowankit?

They reached the shore, tracking it past ThunderClan territory, where Nightheart and Alderheart peeled away from the patrol and headed into the forest. Alderheart dropped his catmint for a moment and mewed, "I'll take some to WindClan and RiverClan later. You two must hurry." With their mouths full of catmint, it was impossible to say a proper good-bye, but Lightleap purred her thanks to Alderheart, and Sunbeam caught Nightheart's eye and hoped he understood how grateful she was that he'd traveled so fast right until the end.

He gave her a friendly nod in return before he disappeared between the trees. Alderheart whisked his tail and hurried after him. At the SkyClan border, Fidgetflake and Rootspring headed inland, making for their camp, and Sunbeam and Lightleap hurried on toward the pine forest alone.

Sunbeam could see, by her sharp movements, how nervous Lightleap was, and it made her heart ache. Lightleap had been annoying her lately, but they had been close friends since Sunbeam was a kit. Suddenly she imagined what her friend must be thinking. Was she frightened that Rowankit had become so ill that even the plentiful catmint wouldn't be able to save him? Sunbeam couldn't imagine feeling that worried about Spireclaw, or any member of her kin. She wanted to reassure her friend; their quarrel over Blazefire seemed suddenly petty. But Lightleap kept a few steps ahead, pushing ahead as though she didn't dare waste another moment.

At last they were following the trail that led to the Shadow-Clan camp. Sunbeam's heart began to pound. *Please let Rowankit be okay.* And what about Blazefire? At the thought of his name,

Sunbeam startled—she hadn't thought about her friend in days. What was going on with her? Now she wondered . . . had his whitecough become greencough? What if he was even sicker than Rowankit by now? She wished suddenly that the patrol had never stopped to sleep or hunt. They should have kept going, no matter the hardship.

Lightleap ducked through the entrance tunnel first. Sunbeam followed. Would the Clan be awake yet? She was relieved to see they were. Yarrowleaf and Snowbird were sitting beside the fresh-kill pile. Gullswoop and Stonewing stood near the warriors' den, their heads bowed as they talked in hushed whispers. All ShadowClan's warriors were awake. Were they waiting for Cloverfoot to organize the morning patrols?

Sunbeam's heart leaped. Blazefire was crossing the clearing. He looked well. He must have recovered while she'd been away.

There was no sign of Rowankit.

She blinked happily at Blazefire, but his expression sent a chill along her spine. His amber eyes were solemn. Suddenly she realized that the other warriors *were* waiting, but not for Cloverfoot to send out patrols. Despite the tantalizing chatter of birds in the trees around the camp, there was no eagerness in her Clanmates' movements, no excitement in their mews, only a kind of stillness and a hush that filled Sunbeam with foreboding. Cloverfoot sat as still as stone at the edge of the clearing.

Automatically, Sunbeam turned to look at her friend, and she could see her own fear and sadness reflected in Lightleap's eyes. *No!* Sunbeam drew closer, wanting to offer support, but before she could speak, Lightleap hurried past her and pushed her way into the medicine den.

Sunbeam slowed and met the ShadowClan deputy's gaze. There was grief in it. *He's gone.* She felt sick as Lightleap's wail sounded from the medicine den. She hesitated, her paws growing heavy with dread, before she forced herself to follow Lightleap inside.

She could make out Puddleshine, his light blue eyes like moons in the darkness. Tigerstar and Dovewing were beside him, hunched over a nest.

Lightleap stared into it, her pelt flattened against her slim frame as though slicked by rain, her tail curled fearfully between her legs. Her bundle of catmint lay scattered around her paws. "When did he die?" Her mew was thick with grief.

"Just before dawn." Dovewing ran her tail limply along Lightleap's spine.

"We should have traveled faster." Lightleap looked bleakly at her mother, then her father, guilt glittering in her eyes.

"It wouldn't have done any good," Puddleshine mewed softly. "He was too sick for even catmint to save him."

Sunbeam laid her bundle of leaves beside the entrance, aware now of other shapes in the nests around the edge of the den. The scent of sickness touched her nose. Blazefire might have recovered, but other cats had fallen ill. She recognized Oakfur in one of the nests; the elder's brown pelt was matted and unwashed. Cinnamontail was blinking from another nest, her eyes bright with fever, and it was just possible to make out Streamkit and Bloomkit in the nest beside her.

Shadowsight padded from the gloom beside the herb store. He crossed the den, glancing at Sunbeam before leaning down to sniff the catmint she'd brought. "I'm glad to see this," he mewed quietly. "I knew the greencough would spread, but not this quickly."

"But Blazefire is okay, right?" Sunbeam wanted to be sure.

"He recovered as soon as you'd left," Shadowsight told her. His gaze flitted anxiously toward Oakfur, then to Cinnamontail and her kits. "But the others will need this." He picked up the catmint and carried it to Cinnamontail's nest. As he began to shred the leaves, a sob burst from Lightleap's throat.

"Why didn't we travel faster?"

Dovewing pressed her nose to Lightleap's cheek. "I'm sure you went as fast as you could," she mewed huskily. "And you've given the others a chance."

Sunbeam didn't want to intrude on her Clanmates' grief. She felt terrible. She'd spent most of the quest avoiding Lightleap and having fun with Nightheart, and now her best friend had lost her brother and Sunbeam could do nothing to comfort her. *I should have been kinder.* Their dispute over Blazefire was no excuse to push Lightleap away when she needed her. With a last regretful look at her friend, she nosed her way from the den.

Outside, Berryheart padded toward her and touched her nose to Sunbeam's head. "I'm glad you're back safely."

Sunbeam blinked at her. "I thought Rowankit would survive until we got here," she mewed bleakly. "And so many other cats are ill."

"They'll be okay now that you've brought the catmint," Berryheart soothed.

"Will they?" She stared hopefully at her mother. Did she know best? "Puddleshine said that catmint wouldn't have saved Rowankit." She waited for her mother to reassure her, but Berryheart was frowning, anger prickling through her black-and-white fur.

"It was too late for Rowankit," she mewed. "Even before you left. I just wish he hadn't gotten sick in the first place."

Does she resent StarClan for letting this happen? wondered Sunbeam. But her mother's gaze was reaching across the clearing, hardening as it found Fringewhisker. No, Sunbeam realized. Her mother still blamed the former SkyClan cat for the sickness that had come to ShadowClan.

The day seemed to last a quarter moon. Cloverfoot sent out patrols, who brought back prey, but no cat seemed hungry enough to eat more than a mouthful. At last, as the sun began to set, Tigerstar carried Rowankit's body from the medicine den and laid it in the middle of the clearing, ready for his vigil. Flowerstem and Snowbird had collected leaves along with the last flowers of the season, and, with Dovewing, they laid them around the kit's stiff body.

As Sunbeam watched, Shadowsight crossed the clearing and stopped beside her.

"Was the mission dangerous?" he asked.

"Not really," she told him. "We kept out of sight." She didn't mention stealing food from under Twoleg noses in the field of brightly colored dens.

"While you were gone, Tigerstar started wondering why WindClan and RiverClan hadn't sent cats on the patrol with you," Shadowsight mewed.

"They didn't want to leave apprentice medicine cats in charge at home." Sunbeam wondered how he'd forgotten.

"So they said," Shadowsight mewed. "But they could have sent *warriors*, like we did."

"I guess." Sunbeam glanced at him. What was he getting at?

"Did the other cats on the mission talk about them not coming?" Shadowsight probed.

"No." There was clearly something bothering the medicine cat. "Is there a problem?"

"It's just that Tigerstar started wondering if they didn't need catmint as much as we did," Shadowsight mewed. "So he went to see Kestrelflight, and Kestrelflight showed him how little catmint he had left and even took him to see the shriveled catmint patches on the moor." Shadowsight paused. "But when he went to see RiverClan, Mothwing wasn't so helpful." Shadowsight glanced toward the ShadowClan leader, who was sitting at the head of the clearing, watching Dovewing scatter rowan leaves around their dead kit's body. "She wouldn't let him near the camp. She even sent for warriors to stop him crossing the border, and when he asked her if greencough had reached RiverClan, she said it wasn't any of his business."

The ShadowClan medicine cat sounded worried. "Something strange is going on there. We need to find out what it is before it starts affecting the other Clans. Tigerstar thinks—" Before he could go on, Tigerstar's mew rang across the clearing.

"Let's begin." Most of the Clan was already ringed around the clearing. The others joined them, taking their places among their Clanmates as Tigerstar started to speak. "Greencough has come early to the Clan," he mewed. "And taken a life that was only just beginning."

Dovewing pulled Birchkit deeper into her belly fur and wrapped her tail around Firkit and Whisperkit. She was taking care of Cinnamontail's kits while their mother and their littermates were in the medicine den. Firkit and Whisperkit looked lost and frightened, but Birchkit wriggled free of his mother and padded closer to his littermate's body.

He stared desolately at Rowankit. "I'll miss you," he mewed.

Tigerstar padded to his son's side. "He's safe now with StarClan. We'll see him again one day."

Sunbeam's throat tightened. If only they had traveled a little faster.

Lightleap was sitting on the other side of the clearing. Blazefire was beside her. As the Clan began to share stories of Rowankit's short life, he touched his nose to her ear from time to time, while Lightleap's eyes glistened with grief.

Sunbeam felt a jab of resentment. *She* should be the one comforting her friend. The thought surprised her. Shouldn't she be jealous of *Lightleap*, not Blazefire? *He's supposed to care about me.* But Rowankit was dead. Life was too precious to waste arguing. This quarrel had gone on long enough. She should apologize once the vigil was over.

And yet, what exactly would she be apologizing for? She *was* the one sitting alone while Lightleap and Blazefire comforted each other. That wasn't *her* fault; it was theirs.

She dragged her attention guiltily back to Rowankit. She should be thinking about him and his kin, not herself.

"Rowankit was the sweetest of all my kits," Dovewing was saying, her voice hoarse. "While his littermate was eager to play, eager to explore the camp, Rowankit was always content to be snuggled up to my belly." Dovewing blinked. "I know I'll still reach for him in my sleep. I just can't believe he's gone."

As Tigerstar moved to nuzzle his mate, Puddleshine stood to speak about Rowankit's sweet disposition while he was ill. Sunbeam felt heavy with grief. She carefully listened to the rest of her Clanmates' touching tributes to the young tom, wondering if she should add her own, but the ceremony was over before she could find the words. The Clan began to melt away, heading for their dens or the shelter of the bramble wall. Hopwhisker guided Birchkit, Firkit, and Whisperkit back to the nursery. The wind had grown chilly as night set in, and it was too cold for kits to stay outside until dawn. But Tigerstar and Dovewing stayed beside Rowankit, preparing to sit vigil through the night. Lightleap and Pouncestep joined them, Blazefire too, and Sunbeam couldn't help noticing that he sat so near to Lightleap that their pelts touched.

She glanced around the moonlit camp, wondering whether

to take some prey from the fresh-kill pile and eat before she slept. Padding to the heap, she sniffed a mouse. As she wondered if she was even hungry, paw steps brushed the earth behind her and she turned.

Berryheart stopped a nose-length away, blinking at her through the darkness. "Did WindClan and RiverClan really send no cat on the mission?" she mewed.

"We didn't need them," Sunbeam told her. "If the patrol had been any bigger, it would have been harder to sneak through the Twolegplace."

Berryheart sniffed. "I'm not really surprised they left us to do the hard work," she mewed acidly. "WindClan is always the first to turn its back on the other Clans, and RiverClan cats only ever think of themselves."

"There might be more to it than that," Sunbeam ventured. *Something strange is going on there.* Shadowsight's words had stuck with her.

"More to it?" Berryheart's gaze sharpened. "What do you mean?"

"They said they couldn't spare their medicine cats," Sunbeam mewed. "Perhaps they couldn't spare any warriors either." But even as she said it, she began to wonder if she should be encouraging her mother's doubts. Berryheart seemed angry enough already.

"Couldn't spare any warriors?" Berryheart sounded amazed. "What nonsense! It's just selfishness. They're happy to change *our* warrior code when it suits them, but when it comes to saving our kits, they're not interested."

"The warrior code's not just ours," Sunbeam mewed. "It's every Clan's."

But Berryheart wasn't listening. Her fur was ruffling along her spine. "I'm sorry Rowankit died"—she lowered her voice—"but he might still be alive if Tigerstar hadn't agreed to change the warrior code. I *knew* he shouldn't have gone along with it." Her tail was flicking angrily. "Doesn't he know he's meant to keep ShadowClan safe from outsiders? Not invite them in. He should know as well as any cat what happens when strangers join a Clan."

Sunbeam saw fear flash through her mother's gaze. She blinked. Berryheart was *scared* of outsiders. "Don't forget Dovewing," she reminded her mother gently. "She joined ShadowClan, and it's been fine."

"It's probably Dovewing who made him soft." Berryheart fluffed out her fur. "Don't get me wrong. I've nothing against Dovewing. She's a true warrior. But taking her as a mate might have given Tigerstar the idea that every cat from every Clan is a true warrior. I remember a time when any cat who wasn't a Clanmate was considered an enemy. And with good reason. If Tigerstar doesn't remember, it's up to his senior warriors to remind him." Berryheart glanced across the clearing to where Fringewhisker and Spireclaw were sitting in the shadows beside the nursery, as though guarding it while Dovewing sat vigil. "Outsiders mean trouble."

Sunbeam shifted her paws uneasily. Spireclaw and Fringewhisker seemed suddenly very alone as they sat in the darkness, and Sunbeam realized that they'd eaten alone earlier and returned from hunting alone. Were *all* their Clanmates avoiding them? Did everyone think the former SkyClan cat was a threat? It could be true. There was a chance Fringewhisker had brought infection to ShadowClan. She'd admitted there had been whitecough in SkyClan when she'd left. . . . Sunbeam found herself trying to remember which ShadowClan cat had the first cough of the season.

Her mother was watching her now, eyes narrow with interest. "It makes you wonder, doesn't it?" Before Sunbeam could answer, Berryheart went on. "You should come to the meeting tonight."

"What meeting?" Sunbeam blinked at her.

"Some of ShadowClan are meeting to discuss all this Clan-swapping."

Clan-swapping? Sunbeam had never heard switching Clans called *Clan-swapping* before. It made it sound feckless and petty, something only a fox-heart would do. Should she attend the meeting and find out exactly what her Clanmates were saying? Perhaps she could tell them what Nightheart had said about how well Fernstripe was settling into ThunderClan. The WindClan warrior hadn't spread whitecough or green-cough. In fact, it sounded like she'd brought new skills and fresh energy with her. So-called Clan-swapping had only seemed to make ThunderClan stronger. ShadowClan must've been unlucky, that was all.

"Come with me." Berryheart headed toward the dirtplace tunnel.

Sunbeam followed her into the forest, to a small rise a little way from camp. She felt uneasy joining a gathering with her Clanmates while Tigerstar sat vigil for his dead kit. Did the ShadowClan leader know they were meeting?

Snowbird and Whorlpelt were waiting at the top of the slope. Stonewing, Yarrowleaf, and Snaketooth were with them, and Grassheart came running up behind Berryheart as she reached the others. Sunbeam hung back a little as Berryheart addressed the group.

"Rowankit should still be playing with his brother," Berryheart told them.

Approving murmurs rippled among the others.

"The medicine den should be empty, not full," Whorlpelt mewed.

"It's not even leaf-bare and we've had our first greencough death," Yarrowleaf chimed.

"And we all know why." Berryheart looked around the gathered cats.

Sunbeam was shocked that these cats were so angry. Did they blame Fringewhisker too? "All Clans have greencough sometimes," she argued.

"But they used to keep it to themselves," Whorlpelt growled.

"I bet SkyClan has had greencough since *greenleaf*," Yarrowleaf mewed.

"We don't *know* that," Sunbeam pointed out.

"They've had *whitecough*," Grassheart chipped in. "And everyone knows that greencough follows whitecough like a fox stalking a rabbit."

"Fringewhisker brought it with her." Snowbird spoke now,

her white ears twitching angrily.

"She wasn't sick when she arrived," Sunbeam pointed out.

"She might have recovered but still been carrying the infection," Whorlpelt mewed to growls of agreement from his Clanmates.

Grassheart snarled. "If she hadn't come, Rowankit would still be alive."

Sunbeam's pads were itching with alarm. "He died because he had no catmint," she mewed. "Not because Fringewhisker joined ShadowClan. If our patrol had returned earlier . . ." Guilt flared fresh in her belly. "If we'd traveled faster—"

"We shouldn't even have needed catmint this early in the season," Snowbird snapped.

Berryheart swished her tail. "I just hope this makes Tigerstar realize he made a mistake allowing Clan-swappers to switch Clans whenever they feel like it."

The others growled in agreement.

Clan-swappers. That expression again! Sunbeam blinked at them in dismay. "It's still not easy switching Clans. There's a test. And—"

"A *test*!" Whorlpelt cut her off. "All she had to do was roll a rock up a hill. An apprentice could have done it. For a warrior, it was too easy! Tigerstar made it easy because he didn't want to be the one leader who was willing to stand up to the changes in the code and turn an outsider away."

Sunbeam's pelt bristled with frustration. These cats weren't listening to reason. Perhaps if she conceded something, they would hear her out. "Even if Fringewhisker *did* pass whitecough to Rowankit, she didn't *mean* to."

Snaketooth's eyes narrowed to slits. "Do we really know that?" she mewed.

Stonewing blinked at her. "Do you think she did it on *purpose*?"

Snaketooth gazed at him coolly. "She met Spireclaw in secret, didn't she? Perhaps she *set out* to trick him into loving her just so she could join ShadowClan."

"But she loves him!" Sunbeam argued. "Any cat can see that."

Snaketooth eyed her sharply. "SkyClan has a *lot* to gain from weakening the other Clans," she growled. "Infecting us on purpose might have been Leafstar's plan all along."

"That's absurd!" Sunbeam stared at the brown tabby she-cat.

But Stonewing was nodding now. "It makes sense," he mewed. "SkyClan could become the strongest Clan around the lake without lifting a paw. They could finally divide up the lake territory how they wanted. Don't forget how much land they demanded when they first moved here."

Whorlpelt's tail twitched. "*They've* probably got enough catmint to ensure they don't die."

"Perhaps SkyClan sabotaged every other Clan's catmint supply," Grassheart mewed. "That's why we don't have enough to protect ourselves."

Sunbeam could hardly believe her ears. She'd heard about evil cats like Darktail and the first Tigerstar. And she'd seen for herself how Ashfur had tried to harm the Clans. But *SkyClan*? They'd never shown signs of aggression toward

ShadowClan. And they'd actually helped fight off Darktail and Ashfur. Why would they want to hurt the other Clans now? "SkyClan sent cats on the mission to find catmint," she reminded them. "Why would they do that if they wanted us to be sick?"

"To cover their tracks, of course," Snaketooth mewed.

Sunbeam looked desperately at her mother. Surely Berryheart could see that such outlandish talk could lead to fighting that could cost cats their lives.

But Berryheart's eyes were glittering with outrage. "I always knew SkyClan couldn't be trusted. They never should have sent a cat to ShadowClan when they had sickness in their camp." She looked at Sunbeam. "I'm surprised you're defending them."

"I traveled with SkyClan cats on the mission," Sunbeam mewed defensively. "They don't want to hurt anyone."

Berryheart narrowed her eyes warily. "Were any of them sick? Has Puddleshine checked you over since you got back?"

Sunbeam stared back at her. Was her mother accusing *her* of spreading infection too? "He doesn't need to check me over. Rootspring and Fidgetflake weren't ill, and I feel fine."

And yet she sensed her Clanmates shrinking away from her.

Berryheart turned back to the others. "I just feel very strongly that the Clans should not mix like this. It's dangerous."

Grassheart grunted in agreement. Snowbird nodded.

Whorlpelt growled. "We should have learned by now that

the Clans should stay *more* separate, not less."

"We saw what happened when we got involved in Thunder-Clan's problems with Bramblestar and Ashfur," Yarrowleaf mewed. "It nearly destroyed all the Clans."

Sunbeam felt helpless. She wished these cats could have seen how well she and Nightheart had worked together. They'd hunted and even stolen food from Twolegs. It hadn't been any different from being with a Clanmate. The Clans could be *stronger* if they stopped protecting their differences and focused on what they had in common. But Sunbeam could see from these angry faces that nothing she said would make them see that. And she was suddenly aware that she was out-numbered. As anxiety pricked her pelt, Sunbeam wondered how she'd gotten here. How could she feel that way? These were her *Clanmates*. They were supposed to be on the same side as her. And one of them was her own mother.

Berryheart lashed her tail. "We have to make Tigerstar see that he's made a mistake," she told the others. "We are war-riors because we *respect* rules, not because we change them."

A chill rippled through Sunbeam's fur. She wasn't part of this. She didn't want to be, and she wished, with all her heart, that her mother weren't part of this either.

CHAPTER 11

♣

Nightheart felt restless in the ThunderClan hollow. After the wide openness of the valley meadows, the enclosing cliffs and forest seemed oppressive. And yet he was glad to be home. The familiar scents and pelts comforted him, and he suspected that his Clanmates respected him a little more now. After all, he'd brought back catmint, and Brightheart was already feeling better. Hadn't Squirrelflight said that thanks to him and Alderheart, Tigerstar might stop bothering them for a while? Was it possible even *she* respected him more?

A fresh wind was whisking the clouds across the morning sky. It would bring rain later, but Nightheart didn't mind. He was looking forward to being out in the forest. Squirrelflight was organizing the dawn patrols, and most of his Clanmates had already left. He shifted from paw to paw as he waited for his name to be called. Myrtlebloom was fidgeting beside him while Flipclaw paced in front, his tail swishing. From the edge of the clearing, Birchfall caught Nightheart's eye and acknowledged him with a nod before turning back to Squirrelflight. Finleap blinked at him approvingly.

Nightheart's chest swelled with pride. *They think of me as a real warrior now.* What patrol would Squirrelflight assign him to? A border patrol, perhaps? Or maybe she'd send him squirrel hunting with Lionblaze and Finleap again, and he could show them just how much he'd learned while he'd been gone.

"Fernsong." Squirrelflight called the yellow tom's name. "Take Ivypool and Birchfall to mark the SkyClan border."

She'd be calling Nightheart's name next. He puffed out his fur.

He hadn't had to prove anything to Sunbeam. She'd treated him like a true warrior from the start, and it had given him confidence. They'd caught the rabbit without having to speak, working as though they'd trained together for moons. She'd trusted him to block the rabbit's escape, and he'd trusted her to run it down. Hunting was far more fun without his Clan-mates second-guessing his every move.

Perhaps they'd stop second-guessing him now. The medi-cine den's herb store was filled with catmint because of him. He blinked eagerly at Squirrelflight, waiting for her to look at him.

"Myrtlebloom."

He leaned forward excitedly. He was one of the last to be chosen. Was she saving him for a special mission?

"Flipclaw."

She'd call his name next for sure.

"Go with Lionblaze and Finleap and see what you can catch around the beeches," she told the pale tabby.

What about me? Nightheart lifted his tail. Perhaps she hadn't noticed him. And yet, how could she miss him? Only Bayshine,

Shellfur, and Fernstripe remained with him in the clearing.

"Nightheart!" His heart leaped as Squirrelflight called his name at last. Was he going to *lead* a patrol? He pictured himself heading out of camp, Bayshine, Shellfur, and Fernstripe at his heels.

Squirrelflight whisked her tail. "I want you to clean out Bramblestar's den."

He stared at her, wondering if he'd heard right. "But that's an apprentice duty."

"Yes," she mewed briskly. "But since we have no apprentices at the moment, our warriors must take turns to do their chores."

"But I just got back from a mission—" *To save the Clan!* He stopped himself in time. But surely she must be thinking the same. "And I've probably cleaned more dens than any cat in ThunderClan." Squirrelflight had made sure of that by failing him on his *second* assessment and keeping him an apprentice long after his denmates had moved to the warriors' den. "Don't I deserve a place on a patrol?"

Squirrelflight looked at him sternly. "*Every* warrior in ThunderClan deserves a place on a patrol. But after your long journey, you could use a rest."

Cleaning dens isn't restful! Nightheart bit back the words.

"You'll be hunting with your Clanmates soon enough," Squirrelflight told him. "For now, there's dusty bedding that needs replacing." She looked past him to Fernstripe and Shellfur. "I want you to clean out the warriors' den."

"Should I clean out the nursery?" Bayshine offered.

"Daisy and Spotfur can take care of that," Squirrelflight mewed. "I want you to start patching the walls of the apprentices' den."

As she spoke, Daisy nosed her way from the nursery. The long-furred cream she-cat was dragging a bunch of tattered bracken. Stemkit, Bristlekit, and Graykit scurried after her, each proudly carrying a leaf scrap.

Squirrelflight gazed at them warmly. "I can see they've already started."

Shellfur's eyes sparkled with amusement. He nudged Nightheart. "Cleaning out dens doesn't have to be boring," he purred. "Look how much the kits are enjoying it."

Nightheart sniffed. "Nothing's boring when you're a kit." He couldn't help thinking of the time he'd allowed these same kits to help him with his apprentice chores, and gotten in trouble for it. Anyway, he was a warrior now. He should be doing warrior work.

Tail flicking with irritation, he climbed up the tumble of rocks to Bramblestar's den. He wondered what the other cats who'd helped bring catmint back to the Clans were doing right now. Had they been congratulated by their Clan by being given apprentice chores? Was Rootspring cleaning out dens? Or Sunbeam? He bet *she'd* been treated with respect ever since she'd returned. She'd probably always been treated with respect. It was just *ThunderClan* that didn't appreciate its warriors—or at least any warrior who had a mind of his own and didn't think that being related to Firestar was the greatest thing that could happen to a cat.

He reached Bramblestar's den and pushed his way into the sandy cave in the cliffside. His whiskers twitched with surprise as he saw Bramblestar inside. The Clan leader was sitting in his nest, his gaze vacant as he stared at the wall.

Is he sick? Nightheart hesitated in the entrance and tasted the air. It was stuffy in here, but the air wasn't sour. Shouldn't the ThunderClan leader at least be in the clearing while his warriors were hunting, not lazing in his den?

Nightheart cleared his throat, but Bramblestar didn't seem to notice that he'd arrived. He tried again. "Hi," he mewed tentatively. "Squirrelflight sent me to clean . . ." He paused as Bramblestar turned his muzzle toward him. The Thunder-Clan leader didn't seem to recognize him.

"Squirrelflight sent me," Nightheart mewed again.

Bramblestar blinked, as though coming to his senses. His eyes were suddenly bright—almost too bright—and glittering with anxiety.

"I've come to clean your den." Nightheart slid inside and tried to hide his awkwardness by making a joke. "I know, right? Den cleaning is apprentice work, but I guess Squirrel-flight figures that I must be bored of being out of camp, after having traveled almost to the mountains to fetch catmint for the Clans."

Bramblestar watched him without replying, and Night-heart felt even more awkward. That was a mouse-brained thing to say. He sounded like a sulky kit. He grabbed at a strand of bracken dangling from Bramblestar's nest. "So, she probably wants me to replace this?" He tugged it cautiously.

"What?" Bramblestar blinked at him. "Oh, yeah, of course." He hopped out of his nest. "I'm sorry. I'm in the way." But he didn't leave.

Nightheart hooked his claws into the side of the nest and tore away a clump of bracken. He dragged it out of the cave and left it beside the entrance. He hoped Bramblestar would follow him out and head down the rock tumble, but Bramblestar was still sitting inside when Nightheart ducked back in.

Nightheart grabbed another clump of bracken and tore it from the nest. He was acutely aware of Bramblestar watching him. Did the ThunderClan leader find this interesting? Nightheart's pelt burned self-consciously. He dragged the bracken outside and headed back in for more. Bramblestar's gaze followed him, but it was misted, as though the Thunder-Clan leader was lost in thought. Nightheart focused on his work, trying to pretend Bramblestar wasn't there as he dismantled the nest.

Then Bramblestar seemed to jerk from his daydreaming. "Perhaps you can settle a dispute for me," he mewed.

"A dispute?" Nightheart paused, shuffling the bracken together with his paws. What did he mean?

"Something Harestar said about a vole at the last Gathering."

Nightheart let the bracken fall from his grip. He knew exactly what Bramblestar was talking about. The Thunder-Clan leader had noticed Harestar's dig at Squirrelflight.

Bramblestar went on. "Squirrelflight says it didn't mean anything, but I'm not so sure."

A hollow feeling opened up in Nightheart's belly. Bramblestar had ordered Squirrelflight not to approach WindClan about a vole stolen when a WindClan warrior had chased it into ThunderClan territory. But Squirrelflight had disagreed with his decision and taken Nightheart and Sparkpelt anyway, to remind the WindClan leader about the rules over borders. Had she still not told him? She'd said it was the right thing to do. But suddenly Nightheart felt very uncomfortable.

Nightheart stared nervously at Bramblestar, hoping that his expression was giving nothing away. If he said nothing, Bramblestar might assume he knew nothing.

But Bramblestar seemed determined to tease out an answer. "At the Gathering, I distinctly remember Harestar saying that everything must be fine in ThunderClan 'because of that tasty vole from WindClan.'" He frowned. "Like WindClan had given ThunderClan a vole. But why would they do that?"

"Maybe it was a gift?" Nightheart mewed weakly.

"Maybe." The ThunderClan leader's eyes fixed on him like a hawk's.

Nightheart wanted to back out of the den and run. But he was stuck there. His thoughts whirled. *Does Bramblestar really want me to tattle on the deputy, his* mate? He looked away, more annoyed than ever that he'd been given this stupid task. If Squirrelflight wanted him to keep secrets from Bramblestar, she shouldn't make him work right under the ThunderClan leader's muzzle.

Bramblestar dropped his gaze. "Sorry," he mewed. "I'm

keeping you from your work." Relief washed over Night-heart's pelt. The ThunderClan leader must have realized how uncomfortable this was. He began clearing away the last strands of bracken. But after a moment, Bramblestar's mew took him by surprise once more.

"Of course!" The ThunderClan leader sounded relieved. "I remember now. Squirrelflight *did* mention talking to Hare-star."

Nightheart glanced at him. Was Bramblestar losing his memory? "We spoke to *Crowfeather*, not Harestar." He was pleased Squirrelflight hadn't kept the visit to WindClan secret after all. It could have been really awkward. He began to drag the final clump of bracken out of the den. "And Crowfeather was pretty nice about it, so I don't think Harestar meant any-thing serious at the Gathering. He was just poking fun at us." He looked at Bramblestar, his belly tightening as he saw the ThunderClan leader's expression.

Bramblestar's eyes glistened. He looked *hurt*. Nightheart's stomach sank. He'd never meant to cause his leader pain. But then his jaw clenched. Had Bramblestar been *pretend-ing* to know something he'd only suspected? Nightheart felt hot. Anger pulsed in his paws. He wouldn't have made such a mouse-brained mistake if Squirrelflight hadn't given him apprentice work. As it was, he'd confirmed Bramblestar's sus-picions and betrayed her. He quickly swept the bracken from the den. He should get out of here before he made things worse. But before he could slip outside, Bramblestar spoke.

"You went with her?"

Nightheart faced him, his paws suddenly heavy. "Yes," he confessed.

"Who else?"

"Sparkpelt." He swallowed, guilt welling in his chest. He'd betrayed Squirrelflight and tried to lie to Bramblestar. The ThunderClan leader's gaze was hardening. "She thought it was the right thing to do," he mumbled.

"I'm sure she did." Bramblestar was glaring past Nightheart as though he could see Squirrelflight beyond the wall of the den. Fury burned in his eyes, and Nightheart felt a glimmer of relief. Bramblestar was right to be angry; Squirrelflight had lied to him. At last the ThunderClan leader could confront his deputy, they could argue and talk it out, and things could return to normal.

Then Bramblestar seemed to deflate. His shoulders slumped. His head drooped. He looked like an elder, moons older than he was. Nightheart's heart sank. This wasn't how a great leader should react. Where was the Bramblestar he'd heard his Clanmates talk about so often? *This* Bramblestar looked defeated, as though the conversation had drained what little energy he'd had.

Nightheart glanced at the empty patch where Bramblestar's nest had been. "I'd better get some fresh bracken," he mewed clumsily.

"Bracken?" Bramblestar seemed to only half hear him. Then he blinked at Nightheart. "Forget it. Just leave. I'll fix the nest later."

"Really?" Nightheart tried to search his gaze, but Bramblestar looked away.

"Just go," he mewed. "I need to rest."

"But you don't have a nest." Nightheart was suddenly worried about the ThunderClan leader.

"That's okay."

"You must be hungry." Perhaps food would make Bramblestar feel better. "I could fetch you some prey. Or I could fetch Squirrelflight. You could talk to her and we could explain—"

"Get out!" Bramblestar's snarl took Nightheart by surprise. He backed away, his fur spiking as the ThunderClan leader's eyes blazed for a moment. Then Bramblestar looked exhausted once more and slumped onto his belly, staring blindly ahead.

Nightheart hesitated for a moment. Should he fetch Jayfeather? Was something wrong with the ThunderClan leader? He backed out of the den. Perhaps Bramblestar just needed to rest, like he said.

As he descended from the Highledge, Nightheart realized that his paws were trembling. He remembered when ThunderClan was ruled by the impostor. Ashfur had been a powerful and unpredictable warrior, and being an apprentice under his leadership had been scary. At least Ashfur hadn't been a true Clan leader. Everything the impostor had said and done—the orders that had nearly destroyed ThunderClan—were the orders of a fox-heart and a liar. But the impostor was gone. There was no Ashfur to blame this time. This was the *true* Bramblestar. And yet he wasn't acting like a leader. What was wrong with Bramblestar? Would he ever return to being the leader Nightheart had heard so much about—the cat he had been before Ashfur?

Nightheart's thoughts spiraled as he dragged the old bracken down to the clearing. If Bramblestar wasn't fit to lead the Clan, what was the alternative? The new warrior code allowed warriors to depose a leader, but if ThunderClan chose that path, Squirrelflight would become the new leader. If she did, Nightheart's life could be even worse. Squirrelflight was the one who'd failed Nightheart on his second assessment, and now, even though he'd passed, she still treated him like an apprentice. Why else did he spend so much time clearing out dens?

He dragged the bracken out of camp and dumped it, then sat down. Was he wasting his time in ThunderClan? His Clanmates already didn't take him seriously, and if Squirrelflight became leader, they never would. He'd probably be cleaning out dens until he was an elder. His heart began to pound as the future seemed to race away along a path he didn't want to follow.

If he were still on the mission, he could tell Sunbeam how he felt. She would listen and understand far more than any of his Clanmates. He gazed between the trees, wondering how far the ShadowClan camp was from here. Was she even there, or was she out hunting with her Clanmates?

"What are you doing?"

Bayshine's mew made Nightheart look up. The golden tabby tom was staring at him from the camp entrance.

"I was just dumping the old bracken from Bramblestar's den," Nightheart mewed.

Bayshine padded toward him. "You look like you chased a rabbit and caught a bee."

Nightheart looked at him thoughtfully. He needed to talk to some cat. But how much could he say? "Do you feel like you *belong* in ThunderClan?" he asked, watching Bayshine closely.

"Of course I do." Bayshine looked back, puzzled. "Can you imagine being a WindClan warrior and living up on that cold moor?" He shuddered. "Or eating fish in RiverClan? No, thank you."

Nightheart swished his tail. "For sure, no cat would want to be a *RiverClan* warrior," he mewed. "But what about"—he paused—"a Clan like, say, ShadowClan?" He tried to make his question sound casual. "After all, Tawnypelt left Thunder-Clan to go there, and so did Dovewing."

Bayshine stared at him. "What in StarClan is wrong with you?" Nightheart shifted self-consciously, but Bayshine hadn't finished. "We're *ThunderClan* cats, and we're lucky that we are. For StarClan's sake! ThunderClan is the best Clan! And you're a descendant of *Firestar*. Are you seriously thinking about becoming a *ShadowClan* cat?"

Nightheart's ears twitched uncomfortably. "No," he mewed quickly. "Of course not. That would be mouse-brained." He got to his paws and padded past Bayshine, heading back to camp. "Who'd want to be anything but a ThunderClan cat?" His heart felt as heavy as his paws. Was there no cat in ThunderClan he could confide in without getting his ears shredded? *No cat in the whole Clan understands me. I'm totally alone here.* He felt a twinge in his chest. If only he were still on the mission with Sunbeam. Then at least he'd feel like he had one friend he could talk to.

CHAPTER 12

❧

"Will it hurt?" Owlnose stopped on the track that led to the Moon-pool.

Frostpaw didn't know whether receiving nine lives from StarClan would hurt. A pale moon shone through thin clouds above the moor. Banks of heather on either side bathed them in shadow. She and Owlnose were nearing the hollow now, and her heart was racing. This would be her first time over-seeing a nine-lives ceremony. She looked back at him. "It . . . *might?*" She was guessing. Hadn't Kestrelflight said once that Harestar seemed a little shaken after his naming ceremony? It sounded like it might hurt a lot, but she didn't want to scare Owlnose.

"Let's hurry." She pushed on.

Owlnose glanced at her doubtfully, then followed, his eyes sparking with worry.

The moon hung bright and clear in the night sky. The stream chattered beside them and the moor stretched away, quiet but for the wind rustling the heather. They were close to where Curlfeather had died. Frostpaw had never had the opportunity to return to the Moonpool and try to contact

Curlfeather, as she had hoped; she'd been too busy dealing with the injuries from those disastrous hunting patrols. Her heart ached at the memory of her mother's horrible death, but she forced the memories from her mind.

Ahead, the cliffs enclosing the Moonpool cut into the sky. They were close now, and Frostpaw's heart was beating fast. Owlnose had walked silently beside her for most of the trek, but as they neared the hollow, he'd begun asking questions about the ceremony that had clearly been on his mind since they'd left the RiverClan camp. How long would it last? Would he be asleep or awake? Did he have to say anything special?

"What actually happens?" Owlnose asked now, his mew taut.

"I'm not sure." Frostpaw gave the same answer she had to his other questions. She wished she could be more help, but Mothwing hadn't told her anything useful, only to keep her eye on Owlnose and make sure he was okay. And she was eager to get Owlnose to the Moonpool, so that he could be given his nine lives and she could feel satisfied that she'd chosen the right cat. *And quiet Duskfur and any other skeptical Clanmates,* she thought. "I'm pretty sure some of your ancestors will be there."

"My kin?" For the first time, Owlnose's eyes lit with something close to excitement.

"I think so." Frostpaw was pleased to see Owlnose look enthusiastic. She wanted to encourage that. "They'll probably be the ones to give you your lives." *So let's get going!* "Along with some of the important cats from RiverClan's past," she added encouragingly.

But Owlnose looked nervous again. Frostpaw's stomach sank, but she pretended not to notice and kept moving. When Owlnose saw StarClan, she told herself, all his doubts would disintegrate. *We just have to get there.*

He hung back as she climbed the boulders to the Moonpool hollow, and she stopped at the top and waited for him to leap after her. But he hesitated so long at the bottom that she feared he'd changed his mind.

"Come on," she encouraged. "Almost there!"

He paused a little longer, then jumped up the rocks and landed lightly beside her.

She looked at the Moonpool. The smooth water reflected the stars like the great, round, black eye of a LeopardClan warrior. Surely this was where RiverClan's problems would be put to rest. "Ready?" she mewed softly.

Owlnose swallowed. "This is a terrible idea," he mewed suddenly. "I'm not a deputy. How can I become a leader?"

"It's what StarClan wants," Frostpaw told him. *Please, please just believe me.*

"Are you sure?" Owlnose searched her gaze. "Do you really think StarClan will approve of me?"

"I've had visions," she told him, hoping he wouldn't ask exactly what the visions were. They'd come this far. They couldn't turn back now. RiverClan needed a leader. "If StarClan didn't approve, they'd have sent a sign by now."

Owlnose seemed unconvinced. "But when has it ever

happened this way before?" he demanded. "When has a cat who wasn't deputy—or even a senior warrior—been made leader?"

"We have to *try*." Frostpaw flicked her tail impatiently. If she was right, these questions were wasting time. If she was wrong . . . She pushed the thought away. She looked directly at Owlnose. "I'll speak to StarClan first, okay? If there's a problem, they can let me know." She felt a flicker of resentment at StarClan. *It's not like they gave me much to work with.* "Once I've explained my decision, I'm sure they'll understand. They must see that RiverClan needs a leader, and you're as good as any cat."

Owlnose blinked at her, looking a little hurt. "As good as any cat?"

Frostpaw fluffed her pelt, feeling flustered. "I mean *better*," she corrected herself. *What am I doing?* First she'd struggled to explain her choice to Duskfur, and now she was offending their future leader.

"So you think they'll accept me?"

"Of course." Frostpaw's pads itched guiltily. She didn't feel sure of anything right now.

"And they'll give me my nine lives?"

"Why shouldn't they?"

"And I won't be struck by lightning or anything." Owlnose's pelt ruffled as he glanced toward the Moonpool.

"You'll be fine." Frostpaw padded toward the spiraling path of ancient paw prints that led to the bottom of the hollow. She felt relieved to have a chance to consult with StarClan first.

She hoped Curlfeather would greet her. Her heart ached with longing at the thought. RiverClan still felt strange and lonely without her mother, like a bad dream she wished she could wake up from.

Owlnose followed Frostpaw down and waited silently beside the Moonpool as she crouched on her belly and touched her nose to the still, black water. She closed her eyes and opened her thoughts to let StarClan's vision in. But all she saw was blackness.

StarClan? She tried to relax. *Curlfeather?* Her call echoed through silence. Panic started to swirl at the edges of her thoughts. She ignored it, focusing harder on the darkness ahead, willing it to fill with star-specked pelts. *Please! Please help me!* Why didn't StarClan come? Did they think she could do it without them? Or had they turned their back on her because she'd made the wrong decision? *I tried my best to do what you wanted.* She felt as helpless as a kit lost in the reed beds. *You can't abandon me! I need you. I can't do this alone. It's too much for me!*

Fear gripped her. What would Curlfeather say? She imagined her mother's stern mew. *Don't lose your nerve, Frostpaw.* Owlnose would be watching her. She mustn't scare him. She curled her claws against the stone and steadied her breath. Then she opened her eyes and stood up.

Owlnose was staring at her expectantly. "What did they say?"

"Nothing." She kept her mew light. "But that's not surprising. This ceremony is for you, not me." She hoped she was right and that their silence wasn't because she'd made the wrong choice. RiverClan had been without a leader for too long.

Owlnose's gaze flitted from her to the water then back. "Are you sure?"

"I'm sure."

He didn't seem reassured, his tail trembling as he held it high, but he padded to the edge of the pool. "I guess I need to try," he mewed, crouching beside it. Taking a deep breath, he closed his eyes and touched his nose to the water.

Frostpaw watched, her heart thumping so hard that her body seemed to ring with the sound. She padded a little way away and sat down, watching Owlnose and praying that the warriors of StarClan were already gathering in his vision. His pelt was twitching. Was that a good sign? She took in a few nervous breaths, and still he didn't move. Were they giving him his first life?

The breeze lifted her fur and she glanced nervously over her shoulder. Her thoughts flashed back to that night with Curlfeather. The thunder of the dogs' paws on the earth. Their hot breath. Their wild eyes. Her mother's shriek. She felt sick. What if the dogs had tracked them here? She scanned the rim of the hollow, half expecting to see dark silhouettes rising against the sky as the dogs hauled themselves over the edge. But there was no sign of life and no scents on the wind apart from the earthy smell of heather. *Mothwing sent out patrols to search the area,* she reminded herself. *There was no trace of the dogs.*

And yet Curlfeather's last words rang in her mind. *Trust no cat.*

Fresh grief sliced through her heart. Her mother had been the cat she'd trusted most, and now she was gone and, with her, the sense that Frostpaw could ever trust another cat so completely. As she remembered her mother's kind gaze, her warm breath, paw steps brushed the stone. She stiffened and raised her muzzle. Owlnose was padding away from the Moonpool.

Frostpaw stood up and hurried to meet him. Had they given him his nine lives already? He seemed shrunken beneath his pelt. Had the ceremony affected him the same way it had affected Harestar? She blinked at him hopefully. "How was it?"

He shook his head. "They weren't there," he mewed. His eyes were round with concern, but she thought she could detect relief in his mew. "No cat was there. No cat spoke to me. I didn't see anything."

Disappointment dropped like stone in Frostpaw's belly. She stared at Owlnose, her mouth growing dry. *What now?*

Dawn was breaking as Frostpaw followed Owlnose along the reed-bed trail that led to the RiverClan camp. They'd hardly spoken on the trek home. Now, as they neared the entrance, Owlnose slowed. He looked anxiously at Frostpaw, and she realized he was waiting for her to take the lead.

The doubt that had clawed her heart since they'd left the Moonpool hardened. Had her choice of Owlnose been entirely wrong? *No.* She had to have more faith in herself. She'd picked him because she'd sincerely felt he was the cat StarClan wanted her to choose. She lifted her chin and padded past him. She understood why he was hanging back. He'd never led more than a patrol until now, and StarClan had let him down. But she'd show him how to take responsibility.

Her nerve nearly failed her as she padded into camp and saw her Clanmates clustered around Duskfur. What would they say when she told them Owlnose hadn't been given nine lives? Then she paused. *Duskfur* was organizing the morning's patrols. The brown tabby she-cat, one of RiverClan's most experienced warriors, was finally taking charge. *If only she'd stepped up earlier,* Frostpaw thought. *Would my decision have been different?* Curlfeather's words rang in her mind. *Look beyond the obvious choices.* She shook out her pelt. Her decision to name Owlnose as RiverClan's new leader would have probably been the same.

If only StarClan had backed her up. She wondered again why they were silent. Had the connection between StarClan and the living Clans been broken again, like it was when Ashfur's spirit returned and possessed Bramblestar's body?

Frostpaw lifted her chin. There was no point scaring herself. Pushing through the crowd, she stopped beside Duskfur. Her belly tightened as her Clanmates blinked eagerly at her, but she waited for Owlnose to follow her through the crowd. As the brown tabby tom stopped beside her, Shimmerpelt was the first to call out.

"Did it happen?" asked the silver-gray warrior. "Are you our leader now, officially?"

Other Clanmates chimed in excitedly before Owlnose could reply. "Hooray for Owlstar!"

"Welcome home, Owlstar!"

"We've cleaned out the leader's den for you. . . ."

"Was Mistystar there?"

Owlnose's gaze flitted nervously around his Clanmates. He didn't speak.

Graypaw, standing beside Breezeheart, swished his tail eagerly. "Can we get our warrior names now?"

Frostpaw suddenly realized that her brother's shoulders were broader than his mentor's now. Mistpaw looked stronger than her mentor, Icewing, too. Her littermates should be warriors already, but without a leader, who could give them their warrior names? She glanced at Owlnose. Without StarClan's blessing of nine lives, *could* he?

"Well?"

Frostpaw realized that Mothwing was staring at her.

"What happened?"

"Nothing," she said regretfully, glancing at Owlnose. "I'm afraid Owlnose wasn't given nine lives. StarClan wasn't there."

Shocked mews rippled through the Clan. Owlnose stared at his paws.

"Have they deserted us?" Shimmerpelt gasped.

Fognose's ears twitched uneasily. "Why would they leave us without a leader?"

Minnowtail was frowning. "They clearly didn't approve of such an inexperienced warrior leading the Clan." She caught Duskfur's eye.

Duskfur shifted her paws. "They must want us to choose again."

Frostpaw's heart sank.

"They would have said so if that's what they thought!"

She was relieved to hear Splashtail's mew from the back of the crowd. The brown tabby tom shouldered his way to the front.

"Perhaps they're waiting to see him lead the Clan for a while," Splashtail went on. "If you go back in a half-moon or even a quarter moon, they may be ready to give him his nine lives."

Frostpaw felt a wave of gratitude toward the tom, especially when Graypaw, Mistpaw, Breezeheart, and Brackenpelt mewed in agreement.

"We can't assume silence is disapproval," Breezeheart mewed.

"This might be a test," Brackenpelt called. "To see if we are certain of our choice."

Duskfur's tail flicked crossly. "It seems clear to me that they don't approve and we need to think again."

Shimmerpelt seemed to agree. "StarClan has never refused to give a *true* leader nine lives," she mewed pointedly.

Fognose nodded. "Remember Nightstar," she mewed. "He *never* got his nine lives, because he was never a true leader."

Splashtail glared at her. "That was because ShadowClan's former leader was still alive. This is different. Mistystar is dead."

"So why hasn't StarClan given Owlnose his lives?" Duskfur snapped. "Without them, he's nothing but an ordinary warrior."

Frostpaw looked at Owlnose, hoping he'd speak up for himself. But the brown tabby tom's eyes were glittering with uncertainty, as though he almost agreed with Duskfur.

Mothwing padded forward. "StarClan's absence was unexpected," she mewed.

"To you, maybe," Duskfur muttered under her breath.

Mothwing ignored her. "You all know that I think the Clans give far too much weight to the words of StarClan. I know tradition is important, but we're *living* cats, and we don't need the approval of the dead. *We* must live with the consequences of our decisions, so *we* must make them." Frostpaw's pelt prickled self-consciously as her mentor's gaze turned to her. "I believe Frostpaw is leading us in the right direction. And, until StarClan speaks to us again, I will support her." Shimmerpelt grunted and Duskfur's gaze darkened. But Mothwing went on. "Owlnose is the warrior she chose, and he will continue to be our leader. We will simply have to ask for StarClan's blessing another time."

"They'll give it next time," Splashtail mewed. "Once they've seen we're certain Owlnose is the right choice."

Breezeheart and Brackenpelt murmured approvingly.

Frostpaw's shoulders relaxed. Grateful for Mothwing's support, she gazed hopefully around her Clanmates. Many of them looked as relieved as she felt that a decision had been made.

Harelight, who had been lingering at the back of the crowd, lifted his muzzle. "Onewhisker had to wait to become Onestar," he mewed encouragingly.

"And StarClan still gave him his nine lives," Breezeheart chimed in.

Owlnose, at last, began to look brighter. He lifted his tail a little and faced the Clan. Was he going to speak? Frostpaw leaned forward hopefully. But Owlnose only blinked at them, then looked at Mothwing, clearly waiting for her to speak again.

The medicine cat dipped her head to him. "You will need a deputy," she mewed.

Frostpaw noticed Duskfur straighten a little. Was she hoping to be chosen? Was that why she'd been organizing the dawn patrols?

Mothwing went on. "You're our leader," she told Owlnose. "It must be your decision."

Duskfur's pelt ruffled along her spine, but she said nothing as her Clanmates' gazes fixed expectantly on Owlnose.

The brown tabby tom shifted his weight from one paw to the other. He scanned his Clanmates, looking more anxious than thoughtful. This was clearly difficult for him. Frostpaw wondered who he'd choose—an older warrior would be more experienced, but a younger cat would have more energy. She was relieved that this time it wasn't her responsibility.

As Owlnose hesitated, sparrows flitted among the reeds on the other side of the river. Curlews called to each other as they skimmed the distant water meadow, and the pale dawn light began to give way to sunshine. The Clan should be out hunting, not waiting for their leader to make a decision. Frostpaw looked at Owlnose. Surely he must have some idea about the warrior he wanted as his deputy. But he looked as uncertain as ever.

Mothwing cleared her throat. "You need to decide," she prompted.

"Can't I think about it for a day or two?" Owlnose asked her.

Mothwing's tail twitched impatiently. "If you don't know now, I don't see how thinking for a day or two will help."

Frostpaw felt a twinge of pity for Owlnose. She knew what it was like to be under this sort of pressure. As his gaze flitted around the Clan once more, she willed him to make a good decision.

Owlnose's abrupt mew took her by surprise. "Splashtail."

"*Splashtail?*" Sneezecloud echoed the tabby tom's mew in surprise.

Splashtail pricked his ears, his eyes widening with surprise.

"He's too young," Duskfur snorted.

Frostpaw bristled defensively. "He's strong and brave," she mewed.

Splashtail puffed out his chest, then seemed to shrink a little as Shimmerpelt sniffed.

"That might be true," she snapped. "But he has no experience!"

Minnowtail was staring at Owlnose as though she could hardly believe her ears. "It's bad enough having an inexperienced leader, but a deputy too?"

Splashtail's eyes rounded with hurt, and Frostpaw blinked at him reassuringly. He hadn't asked to be dragged into this.

Owlnose stared like cornered prey at Minnowtail. "I—I just chose the cat I thought I could work best with."

"That's not how you choose a deputy!" Minnowtail growled. "You're supposed to choose a warrior who will challenge you and make up for your weaknesses."

Duskfur sniffed, and Frostpaw guessed what she was thinking. *Owlnose has a lot of weaknesses to make up for.* She blinked at Minnowtail. "Splashtail is very decisive," she mewed. The Clan had seen by now that decisiveness was not Owlnose's greatest quality. She was relieved to see Breezeheart and Harelight nodding approvingly.

Yet Minnowtail hadn't finished. "But Splashtail hasn't had an apprentice," she pointed out. "How can he be deputy?"

"He might have had one if RiverClan had more kits," Mothwing pointed out. "Graypaw and Mistpaw have been our only apprentices in moons." She fluffed out her pelt. "We'll have to be practical and overlook that requirement."

"*Overlook* it?" Duskfur asked. "Is the warrior code merely a suggestion now?"

Mothwing glared at her. "Of course not. But we desperately need a leader and a deputy, and now that we have them, we should support them."

Graypaw's ears pricked. "If we have a leader and deputy now, can Mistpaw and I get our warrior names?"

Mothwing hesitated. It was a good question. Could a leader without nine lives name warriors? RiverClan seemed to be swimming in unknown water.

Owlnose spoke, taking Frostpaw by surprise. Perhaps, now

that he had a deputy, he really was finding his paws as leader. "I will hold your naming ceremonies as soon as I have my nine lives," he mewed.

Graypaw and Mistpaw exchanged glances. Were they satisfied with his promise? *At least*, Frostpaw thought, *Owlnose is acting like he will get his nine lives soon.* The tom's optimism gave her a glimmer of hope.

But Duskfur was still glowering. "What do we tell the other Clans?" she asked.

Mothwing met her gaze steadily. "We'll tell them that Mistystar and Reedwhisker died and that Owlstar is our new leader and Splashtail our new deputy."

"And you don't think the other Clans will object?" Duskfur asked. "Or have . . . questions?"

"What say do they have over RiverClan's choices? RiverClan runs RiverClan," Mothwing spat back.

"Owl*star*?" Shimmerpelt looked disapproving.

Mothwing looked at her sharply. "Would you rather tell the other Clans that our leader hasn't been given his nine lives yet?" she demanded.

Shimmerpelt dropped her gaze. Anxious murmurs rippled around the Clan.

Splashtail puffed out his chest. "We can't appear vulnerable. The other Clans must believe for now that Owlstar has StarClan's blessing. I'm sure it won't be long before he does." He glowered at the Clan, as though daring them to challenge him. No cat spoke, but Frostpaw could see pelts prickling uneasily.

RiverClan was taking a risk by carrying on without being sure StarClan approved of her choice of leader, but what else could they do? Frostpaw had done her best to follow Curlfeather's advice to look for a new leader beyond the obvious choices. She had to believe the Clan was following the right path.

Mothwing whisked her tail. "I suggest Splashtail finish organizing the dawn patrols." She ignored Duskfur's scowl. "And Owlnose can—"

Before she could finish, the reed tunnel shivered and Nightsky hurried into camp. The RiverClan she-cat looked worried, and Frostpaw stiffened as she saw Tawnypelt follow her in.

"I was making dirt," Nightsky explained as the Clan turned to stare at their unexpected visitor. "And I smelled ShadowClan scent. I found Tawnypelt waiting on the other side of the river."

Tawnypelt dipped her head low. "I'm sorry for intruding," she mewed. "But Tigerstar wanted me to bring a message."

Harelight and Brackenpelt exchanged glances.

Minnowtail rolled her eyes. "What does he want *now*?"

Mothwing hurried forward, beckoning Owlnose and Splashtail to follow with a flick of her tail. She stopped in front of the ShadowClan warrior. "What's the message?"

As Owlnose and Splashtail stopped beside the RiverClan medicine cat, Tawnypelt scanned the clearing.

"Is Mistystar here?" she asked.

Frostpaw caught Mothwing's eye. Was it time to announce RiverClan's new leader to a warrior from another Clan? Mothwing gave her a warning look, then answered Tawnypelt.

"I can pass your message along," she mewed.

Tawnypelt's gaze sharpened for a moment, but she didn't press Mothwing for an explanation. Instead, she mewed, "Tigerstar wants an emergency Gathering of the Clans."

"Why?" Mothwing narrowed her eyes.

Owlnose stepped in front of the medicine cat. "Has something happened?" he asked Tawnypelt.

The ShadowClan warrior's gaze was darting around the clearing, as though searching for something. She answered distractedly, without looking at Owlnose. "He wants to discuss the catmint shortage."

Frostpaw frowned. "But the mission to find some was a success," she mewed. "Alderheart brought some to RiverClan."

"They found some catmint . . ." Tawnypelt looked at her. "But not in time to save Rowankit."

Frostpaw's breath caught in her throat. A kit had died of greencough. "I'm so sorry." Guilt jabbed her heart. RiverClan had been so wrapped up in their own troubles, they'd been little help to the other Clans.

Tawnypelt's gaze was hard. "It's a little late for RiverClan to worry about Tigerstar's kit," she mewed sharply. "But he hopes that you'll be willing to discuss ways of preventing shortages in the future."

Frostpaw felt the sting of her words and was relieved when Splashtail moved closer and met the ShadowClan warrior's gaze.

"RiverClan will help," he told her.

Tawnypelt narrowed her eyes curiously, as though wondering why he was speaking for his Clan.

Mothwing swished her tail. "Send our condolences to Tigerstar," she mewed.

"You can give them to him yourself," Tawnypelt told her. "The Gathering will be tonight, and it's for all cats, not just leaders." She glanced at RiverClan's warriors, who were watching her nervously. "We hope to see you there."

Without waiting to hear more, Tawnypelt turned and headed out of camp. As she disappeared through the reed tunnel, Frostpaw's breath quickened. There was to be a Gathering of the Clans tonight. RiverClan couldn't avoid the announcement they'd been delaying for so long: Mistystar and Reedwhisker were dead. And Owlnose would have to stand beside the other leaders. Was he ready to be Owl*star*? Were any of RiverClan's warriors ready to face the Clans with such a lie?

CHAPTER 13

❧

Were there more cats at this Gathering than usual? Sunbeam gazed across the sea of pelts. The island clearing rang with mews as warriors, elders and apprentices shared tongues. Their scents filled her nose, the peaty musk of WindClan clashing with the fishy tang of RiverClan. Perhaps it only *seemed* crowded because it was so dark. Tigerstar hadn't waited for the sky to clear before he called the meeting, and Silverpelt was hidden behind thick cloud. *Does that mean StarClan won't be watching over the Gathering?* What if the Clans fought?

They won't fight, Sunbeam told herself. They were here to plan how to avoid catmint shortages. Surely no cat would fight over that!

Sunbeam had hung back at the edge of the clearing as her Clanmates melted into the crowd. She'd been avoiding Berryheart, unsure what to say to her since the meeting about the so-called Clan-swappers. Her mother was somewhere in the crowd now, and Sunbeam hoped she wasn't sharing her thoughts and, with them, her anger about the changes to the warrior code. Sunbeam hadn't openly disagreed with Berryheart's views. She wasn't sure if she should. Berryheart was her mother, after all, and a senior warrior. And she might be right that changing the code could have unforeseen and dangerous consequences for the Clans. But for now, it seemed easier to keep her mother at tail's length.

Sunbeam wished she had some cat to confide in, but Lightleap was keeping her distance, as though she'd given up on trying to repair their friendship. She and Blazefire preferred to hang out with only each other rather than with Sunbeam, and Sunbeam tried not to feel hurt. Blazefire had told her that he wasn't interested in Lightleap as a mate, but knowing that didn't help. She'd been friends with them both; now neither of them seemed to want her around at all, and it was hard watching them share prey and scramble to join the same patrols. She felt lonelier among her Clanmates than she'd ever felt in her life, and she found herself wishing she were still on the mission to find catmint. At least then she'd had Nightheart to confide in.

She pricked her ears eagerly as she saw his pelt moving through the crowd. It was as though thinking about the ThunderClan tom had made him appear. His amber gaze flashed, catching hers and lighting up. He looked pleased to see her too.

She lifted her tail in greeting as he headed toward her. "Hi, Nightheart!"

"Hi!" He squeezed between a WindClan warrior and a RiverClan elder and stopped beside her. "Wow, it's crowded tonight." He looked across the shifting pelts. "I've never been to a Gathering that wasn't at the full moon. Tigerstar must be pretty upset to call one." He blinked at her anxiously. "Is it true Rowankit died?"

"Yeah." Sunbeam looked away guiltily. "We came back too late."

"We couldn't have traveled any faster," Nightheart told her.

"If we hadn't slept—"

"Or stopped to eat?" There was a challenge in his mew, but he wasn't waiting for an answer. "We'd have collapsed from exhaustion," he told her. "We're just regular warriors, not StarClan cats."

She blinked at him. He was right, and she was grateful for his reassurance. "Tigerstar is really upset," she mewed.

"Losing a kit must be hard," Nightheart mewed.

Sunbeam changed the subject. She didn't want to feel sad tonight, not now that Nightheart was here. It was her first chance to talk to a friend since the mission. "How are things in ThunderClan?" she asked. "Last time I saw you, you said you weren't really comfortable there." She knew how he felt.

"It seemed better when I got home," he mewed. "I think a few of the warriors respect me more now. But it . . ." He hesitated, and Sunbeam leaned closer. "It's strange there right now."

"Strange?" What did he mean?

He frowned, as though he was trying to work it out.

"How?" she pressed.

"It's like something's going on with Bra—"

A snarl sounded from the Great Oak. Sunbeam jerked her gaze toward it.

Leafstar and Tigerstar were staring at Owlnose, their hackles high as the RiverClan warrior scrambled onto the low branch beside them. Bramblestar blinked at him, and Harestar let out a warning growl.

"What's he doing?" Surprise sparked through Sunbeam's fur. "He's not a leader."

Nightheart's eyes had narrowed. "Perhaps one of his Clanmates dared him to do it."

"Even RiverClan cats must know you don't joke around on the leaders' branch." Sunbeam was puzzled. The RiverClan warrior wasn't backing down, even though Leafstar had pulled back her lips and looked ready to swipe his muzzle with her claws.

"Are you lost?" The SkyClan leader hissed at him.

Owlnose blinked back at her. "No." There was a tremor in his mew.

Harestar's eyes were slits. "What are you doing up here?"

"Where's Mistystar?" Tigerstar demanded.

Owlnose stared at the ShadowClan leader, his ears twitching nervously.

"What in StarClan is happening in RiverClan?" Tigerstar glared at him harder. "The whole Clan has been acting weird for a moon, and now you turn up without your leader and start climbing the Great Oak like you belong here!"

Sunbeam saw Mothwing pushing her way through the crowd.

"He's *does* belong there," the RiverClan medicine cat called up to the leaders. "Mistystar is dead."

Around the clearing, warriors lifted their heads sharply. Elders' eyes rounded with shock. Apprentices exchanged anxious glances.

How could this be true? Mistystar had missed the last Gathering because she'd had whitecough. Could it have progressed to greencough and killed her that quickly? And, if it had, why hadn't RiverClan been more invested in the quest for more catmint? It didn't make sense. That very day, Tawnypelt had visited the RiverClan camp, and Mothwing had promised to pass on her message to Mistystar. Was Mistystar alive then? Or did they lie to her?

In the Great Oak, Tigerstar's pelt was ruffling along his spine. "Did Mistystar's whitecough turn into greencough?" he asked. "And you never mentioned it until now, knowing that Rowankit was dying of the same? I can't believe it! And where on earth is *Reedstar*, if Mistystar has suddenly died?"

"He's dead too," Mothwing told him.

Around the clearing, surprise fluttered around the clearing in gasps and mews of disbelief.

"What happened?"

"How did he die?"

Sunbeam leaned forward, her ears pricked. Why hadn't RiverClan let on until now that greencough was devastating their Clan as well? *How many cats have they lost?* She glanced anxiously at Tawnypelt. Could the ShadowClan she-cat have been infected? Greencough hadn't been an issue in ShadowClan since Rowankit's death. but all it would take was one cat to bring it back.

Mothwing stopped below the leaders' branch and looked up. There was no grief in her gaze, only determination. Wasn't she upset? Losing both leader and deputy must have been traumatic. But perhaps she'd already come to terms with the deaths. Perhaps she didn't want to show weakness.

"Owlstar is our leader now," Mothwing mewed. Frostpaw stopped beside her. The RiverClan apprentice had followed her mentor, but she was keeping her head low as though she didn't want to be noticed. Mothwing went on. "It's been a difficult moon for RiverClan," she mewed stonily. The River-Clan medicine cat seemed determined to endure her Clan's suffering without complaint. "But we've seen difficult moons before, and no doubt we'll see difficult moons again. Our duty is to live through them like true warriors. And so Owlstar is our leader and Splashtail is our deputy."

Sunbeam noticed for the first time that Splashtail, the brown tabby RiverClan tom, was sitting beside Cloverfoot and Squirrelflight. The other Clan deputies, Hawkwing and Crowfeather, were staring at him as though a bird had settled between them.

Tigerstar stared down at the RiverClan medicine cat, not hiding his disbelief. "*When* did this happen? How bad is the outbreak now? Do you need catmint? And why didn't we know about this?"

Mothwing didn't answer his questions. Instead she pointed her muzzle toward Owlstar. "Ask our leader."

Harestar's tail was flicking. "How can he be Clan leader?" he mewed. "You have far more experienced warriors."

Leafstar's gaze was on Splashtail. "How can such a young tom be a deputy? Have you even had an apprentice, Splashtail?"

Splashtail looked at his paws. Leafstar's disbelief seemed to be shared by the watching Clans. Warriors, apprentices, and elders were pressing closer, their gazes fixed on the leaders' branch.

Spireclaw called from among a group of ThunderClan warriors. "When did Mistystar die?"

"Who chose these cats to take over?" Harrybrook mewed.

His SkyClan Clanmates yowled around him.

"Is this what Mistystar wanted?"

"Has *either* of them even had an apprentice?"

Owlstar stared back at them from the leaders' branch like a kit being quizzed on warrior skills—one who didn't know any of the answers.

Mothwing lashed her tail. "Our *leader* will explain everything." She glared at Owlstar.

Sunbeam felt a rush of sympathy for the RiverClan tom. His eyes were glittering with panic. He closed them for a moment, as though gathering his thoughts, then spoke.

"Mistystar died a moon ago." His mew was husky, and Sunbeam wondered if he was grieving or just terrified to be addressing the five Clans for the first time. Whatever it was, he didn't seem like a leader. His tail was quivering and his ears twitched. He looked like he wished he were anywhere but here.

Leafstar was watching him thoughtfully. Her gaze had

softened a little. Did she feel sorry for him too? "What happened to her?" she asked him gently.

Owlstar blinked at her eagerly, as though grateful for her encouragement. "Greencough," he mewed.

Tigerstar stared at him. "A moon ago? Then why did you lie at the last Gathering? Surely it had progressed to greencough by then."

"I was at their camp today and they acted like nothing was wrong!" Tawnypelt was glaring up from the crowd. "Why hide their deaths?"

Tigerstar leaned closer to Owlstar. "If your leader and deputy had greencough, why didn't you help us find catmint?"

Owlstar shifted his paws.

Harestar's tail was whisking impatiently. "What does it matter now how they died?" he snapped. "I'm more interested in why they chose cats like *these* to replace them!" His gaze flitted disdainfully from Owlstar to Splashtail. "For StarClan's sake! They might as well have chosen *kits*!"

Splashtail bristled.

Sunbeam frowned. It seemed unfair to assume that a warrior was useless just because they were young. RiverClan wouldn't have chosen Owlstar unless they believed he would be a good leader. And yet RiverClan's new leader was looking anxiously at Mothwing. Was he asking his medicine cat for permission to speak? She nudged Nightheart. "Did you see that look?"

"Yes." Nightheart's ears pricked with interest. "It makes me wonder who's *really* in charge of RiverClan."

Mothwing gave a tiny nod and Owlstar looked once more at the gathered cats. "Reedwhisker named me deputy before he died."

"*You?*" Crowfeather gave a snort of disgust from the bottom of the oak.

But Tigerstar's gaze had sharpened. "Reed*whisker*?" he mewed. "Surely if Mistystar died and he was made leader, he'd be Reed*star*."

"Um—yes," Owlstar mewed haltingly. Then he quickly added, "I'm just used to calling him Reedwhisker, that's all."

Tigerstar's gaze didn't leave him. "So, Reedstar was given his nine lives before he died?"

Leafstar's eyes narrowed suspiciously. "Are you telling us that greencough killed him *nine* times?"

"It was really bad," Owlstar offered hopefully.

Tigerstar snorted.

"He . . . kind of died and . . . then he didn't come back to life," Owlstar mewed. "So we figured perhaps StarClan took the lives back. Maybe?" It sounded like a guess, and the new RiverClan leader glanced around the gathered cats as though trying to decide if they believed him. "Maybe they were punishing him," he went on. "Because . . . because he supported the impostor . . ." His gaze settled beseechingly on Mothwing. Was he hoping she'd save him from this interrogation? But Mothwing didn't speak.

Tigerstar's tail flicked ominously. "Did he have nine lives or not?"

Sunbeam was glad she wasn't Owlstar right now. Her

thoughts flitted back to her visit to the RiverClan camp with Hollowspring. The RiverClan cats had seemed weird then, and the camp had been a mess. Had they been grieving? If they had, why hadn't they said anything? She could understand her leader's frustration. Why was RiverClan's new leader having such a hard time explaining what had happened in his Clan?

"Well?" Tigerstar pressed.

Owlstar blinked at him. "I think so. To start with, yes . . ."

Questions erupted from the crowd.

"How long was he sick?"

"How long was he leader?"

"Did he name you deputy straight away?"

Owlstar tried to answer. "Not long . . . A quarter moon ago . . . Not straight away, but . . ." He seemed to run out of words and simply stared into the crowd, clearly too confused to speak.

Tigerstar looked at him. "So, Reedstar became sick with greencough—sick enough to *die*—but still managed to make it to the Moonpool for his nine lives, but then StarClan took them back the first time he died."

Owlstar stared at him, his ears flat with alarm. "I—I guess."

"You *guess*." Tigerstar curled his claws into the oak branch so hard that splinters of bark showered onto the deputies below.

"They don't seem to know what's been happening in their own camp," Sunbeam whispered to Nightheart.

"I know, right?" he mewed back. "And I thought *Thunder-Clan* was messed up."

Mothwing's mew rose above the yowling crowd. "We didn't

come here for your approval." The fury in her voice silenced the Clans. She glared at Tigerstar. "*Or* your permission. We came here to tell you that Mistystar and Reedwhisker are dead. What happens in RiverClan is RiverClan's business, and Owlnose doesn't need to answer anyone's questions but his Clanmates'."

"Owl*nose*?" Leafstar's gaze flashed toward her. "You called him Owlnose."

"She said Reed*whisker* again too," Tigerstar mewed.

Leafstar turned to look suspiciously at Owlstar on the branch beside her. "Do you really have your nine lives?" she asked. "Did Reedwhisker?"

Tigerstar cut in before the RiverClan leader could answer. "Wait." His ears pricked. "RiverClan sent a patrol to Shadow-Clan a little while ago asking if any cat had seen Reedwhisker."

Harestar's eyes widened. "They came to WindClan too, asking the same question."

At the bottom of the Great Oak, Squirrelflight swished her tail. "They asked ThunderClan as well."

"And SkyClan." Leafstar narrowed her eyes.

Tigerstar looked down at Mothwing, ignoring Owlstar now, his gaze flashing in the night shadows. "Was Reed-whisker ever *found*?"

"He—he—" Mothwing seemed lost for words.

"Was he missing? Or was he sick? Or was he both?" Tigerstar kept pressing, and Mothwing's eyes clouded with confusion. "What's going on here?" Tigerstar stared at her. "Because it looks to every cat here as though RiverClan is, at best, trying to hide something and, at worst, *lying*."

On the branch beside the ShadowClan leader, Owlstar looked suddenly weary. His shoulders slumped, and he looked toward Mothwing, defeat in his gaze. "I don't have my nine lives," he confessed. "Neither did Reedwhisker. There wasn't time. But I am RiverClan's leader. It's just that when I went to the Moonpool, StarClan didn't share with me."

The gathered cats murmured to one another. Every cat seemed calmer now, despite the shocking news, as though relieved to have the truth.

"So you're Owlnose, not Owlstar." Leafstar looked at him. "Who chose you to be leader?"

Owlnose stared back at her, and Sunbeam wondered if he was going to say Reedwhisker again. If he did, she wouldn't believe him. *No* cat here would. Something very unusual had been going on in RiverClan, and with so many lies already, it was hard to trust anything they said.

"Who was it?" Tigerstar echoed Leafstar's question.

"*StarClan* chose him," Mothwing called from below. Beside her, Frostpaw stared at her paws as though frightened of catching any cat's eye in case she'd be asked to speak.

Leafstar's gaze flashed toward the RiverClan medicine cat. "*You*—a cat with no connection whatsoever to our ancestors— are telling us that *StarClan* chose RiverClan's new leader?"

"They shared with Frostpaw," Mothwing snapped.

"An *apprentice*." Leafstar sounded unimpressed.

Frostpaw seemed to shrink deeper into her pelt, but

Mothwing held the SkyClan leader's gaze without flinching. "I trust her completely."

Tigerstar shifted on the branch, his pelt ruffled. "All this is highly irregular," he mewed. "And if Owlnose can't get his nine lives, shouldn't—"

Mothwing interrupted him. "That is between Owlnose and StarClan," she growled.

"Really?" Tigerstar's gaze narrowed. "But surely if they'd chosen him, they'd have given him his nine lives by now."

Mothwing bristled. "Not necessarily—"

Tigerstar didn't let her finish. "Clearly, they have doubts. And so do I."

"It's none of your business," Mothwing hissed.

"A weak Clan is always my business," Tigerstar snapped back.

Mothwing stared at him. "Are you planning to interfere? Because if you are—"

"Have you forgotten already?" Tigerstar's mew grew icy. "You recently sought refuge in ShadowClan with two of your Clanmates. Surely you better than anyone should know that what affects one Clan affects them all." His gaze hardened. "So perhaps you will indulge me by hearing me out."

Sunbeam shifted her paws. Tigerstar's concern was beginning to sound like a threat.

"If one Clan is weak, then all the Clans are weak," Tigerstar went on. "We saw what happened when Ashfur undermined ThunderClan. It endangered every Clan, even StarClan."

"RiverClan will sort out its own problems," Mothwing growled.

"I think RiverClan needs help," Tigerstar mewed.

Sunbeam shifted her paws. Tigerstar was offering support. Mothwing should be grateful. And yet there was a darkness in her leader's mew that made her uneasy. She narrowed her eyes as he went on.

"Since we share a border, and a history, I think Shadow-Clan should take over the running of RiverClan for a while."

Sunbeam stiffened. What did he mean? She glanced at Berryheart. If her mother wanted the Clans to keep to themselves, what did she think about their leader becoming so involved in RiverClan's affairs?

Around the clearing, gasps erupted from the crowd. River-Clan pelts bristled, but the other Clans seemed just as alarmed.

"You can't take over RiverClan!"

"A Clan's borders are their own!"

"Five Clans, five leaders!"

The calls came from every Clan.

Tigerstar ignored them. He hadn't taken his eyes from Mothwing. The RiverClan medicine cat glared back at him with a stony gaze, but her pelt was twitching uneasily.

"You need a leader," Tigerstar told her. "And I can lead you. Until you get back on your paws."

Tawnypelt shouldered her way to the front of the crowd, staring up at her son. "Have you forgotten the first Tiger-star?" she yowled, her gaze fierce. "My father led ShadowClan and then tricked RiverClan into following him. His thirst for power led every Clan into battle. No cat has the right to lead more than one Clan."

Sunbeam looked at Nightheart, surprised. "What does she mean?"

"The original Tigerstar fooled one of the old RiverClan leaders into agreeing to unite ShadowClan and RiverClan," Nightheart explained. "They formed TigerClan. But Tigerstar was just using RiverClan. He killed their deputy and turned their leader into little more than a rogue. RiverClan was nearly destroyed forever."

Sunbeam had heard whispers in ShadowClan of the dark history of the first Tigerstar, but no cat had ever explained to her what exactly had happened. "Surely that's not what *this* Tigerstar is planning to do?" Sunbeam's pelt prickled nervously. The Tigerstar she knew would never do anything like that. Would he?

"Who knows?" Nightheart's gaze flitted back to the Great Oak.

Judging from the yowls of outrage from the crowd, Nightheart wasn't the only cat suspicious of Tigerstar's intentions.

Mothwing hissed at the ShadowClan leader. "RiverClan has already suffered at the paws of one Tigerstar. We have no intention of suffering at the paws of another!"

Tigerstar swung his gaze toward her. Sunbeam stiffened in surprise. Was that *hurt* showing in his amber eyes?

"I am *not* the first Tigerstar," he snapped. "I'm nothing like him, and I don't want to take over RiverClan. ShadowClan doesn't need more mouths to feed. We don't *want* them. In the past, we've given sanctuary to cats driven out of their Clans, but we've always been happy to let them return home once it was safe. And RiverClan is clearly struggling. They've lost their leader and their deputy, and it looks like their attempts to find proper replacements are floundering." He lifted his gaze and looked out, over the crowd. "All I am offering is help for a Clan that seems incapable of helping itself."

Brackenpelt, a RiverClan warrior, spoke up. "Have you forgotten Darktail?" she called up to Tigerstar. Her eyes glittered with fear.

Tigerstar glared down at her. "I'm no rogue!"

Sunbeam had heard of the vicious rogue who'd taken over ShadowClan and then RiverClan. Berryheart had lived through those days, and even though she never talked of it in detail, Sunbeam knew that her mother had seen Darktail murder warriors and terrorize all the Clans, nearly destroying them from within.

"He took over ShadowClan," Brackenpelt cried. "And then RiverClan. He nearly destroyed them both. Do you want to be remembered like him?"

"Let RiverClan take care of themselves!" Tawnypelt called.

"Borders are borders!" Crowfeather yowled.

"No ShadowClan cat tells us what to do!" snarled Duskfur.

Mallownose's tail was lashing. "You'll never set paw in our camp!"

Mothwing's yowl was the loudest. "We don't need your help!"

Tigerstar was pacing on the branch, his ears flattened

against the barrage of objections.

Leafstar stepped forward as RiverClan yowled angrily below the Great Oak. "Tigerstar has made his proposal," she called over their snarls. "And I'm sure he did it with the best of intentions. But borders are borders, and Clans should run themselves." Her firm mew seemed to settle the crowd. "Perhaps I can offer a better solution."

Sunbeam leaned forward, curiosity pricking in her paws as Leafstar went on.

"It seems to me that if Owlnose had been given nine lives, we wouldn't be having this discussion." She dipped her head respectfully to Mothwing. "You are a good medicine cat, but your lack of connection to StarClan may be the reason StarClan has not yet given their blessing."

"*Frostpaw* has a connection to StarClan," Mothwing reminded her.

Frostpaw looked up nervously.

"Yes," Leafstar agreed. "But she is only an apprentice. StarClan may wish for a more experienced cat to be involved." Mothwing's ears twitched irritably as the SkyClan leader went on. "SkyClan is fortunate enough to have two medicine cats. We can spare one to help RiverClan. I would be happy to send Fidgetflake to help. He can go with Mothwing and Frostpaw when they take Owlnose to the Moonpool." She looked at Fidgetflake, and the black-and-white tom dipped his head solemnly.

Sunbeam saw Mothwing frown. Why? Medicine cats helped each other all the time. How would this be different from lending and borrowing herbs? Besides, Leafstar's solution would keep Tigerstar out of their camp. It seemed like a perfect compromise.

Leafstar was gazing hopefully at Mothwing. "If you have Fidgetflake's help, you can avoid more drastic action from the other Clans." Her gaze slid toward Tigerstar for a moment, then flicked back to Mothwing. "Do you agree? Will you accept my offer?"

Beside Mothwing, Frostpaw's eyes were round with alarm. Leafstar's solution seemed to frighten her as much as Tigerstar's, and Sunbeam half expected the medicine-cat apprentice to speak out. But she didn't move as Mothwing dipped her head.

"We'll accept it."

Mothwing sounded less than enthusiastic, and Sunbeam couldn't help thinking that the leaders had given RiverClan little choice. But it seemed to close the matter, because Harestar stepped forward on the leader's branch.

He looked at Tigerstar. "Now that that's sorted—"

"Is it?" Tigerstar stared back at him challengingly.

Harestar didn't answer the question. "You called us here to discuss the catmint shortage," he went on. "You wanted to find ways to protect our supply in future."

Tigerstar's tail was flicking. "We'll worry about catmint supplies *after* the RiverClan issue has been resolved." He dug his claws into the branch. "I just hope Fidgetflake's help will be enough."

But Harestar wasn't the only leader who clearly wanted to move the discussion on.

"We can only wait and see," Leafstar mewed briskly. "Let's hope that the coming moons are easier than the ones we've just had."

Harestar dipped his head to the ShadowClan leader. "WindClan is sorry for your loss," he told Tigerstar gravely. "Rowankit would have been a brave warrior."

Bramblestar, who had been quiet up until now, lifted his muzzle. "It was an unnecessary death."

Leafstar swished her tail. "Let's discuss the catmint short-age at the full-moon Gathering," she mewed. "For now, it's time we went home."

Leafstar jumped down from the Great Oak and headed across the clearing. Harestar leaped down too and led his warriors toward the tree-bridge, while Squirrelflight beck-oned Bramblestar down from the leaders' branch with a nod and padded beside him to the clearing's edge.

Sunbeam's eyes widened. The Gathering had ended so suddenly. Did the SkyClan leader hope to finish it before any more pelts were ruffled?

She looked at Nightheart, disappointment jabbing her heart as she realized he'd be leaving too. Being with him felt easier than being with her own Clanmates right now. She blinked at him. "Do you think sending Fidgetflake to help Mothwing will really solve RiverClan's troubles?" She didn't care about his answer; she just didn't want him to leave yet.

"I hope so." Nightheart glanced at his Clanmates as they began to push their way into the long grass. But he didn't hurry to follow. "It looks like RiverClan needs all the help it can get right now."

"Nightheart!" Lionblaze called him from the edge of the clearing.

"I'd better go," he mewed.

"Yeah." Her tail quivered. "I hope things are better for you soon."

"You too." Turning, he hurried toward Lionblaze.

Sunbeam wondered if he'd look back at her. But he didn't. Perhaps he was worried what Lionblaze would think. Besides, they'd see each other again soon. At least, she hoped they would.

Her own Clanmates were waiting in the clearing, and she rushed to join them. Lightleap and Blazefire were already heading for the long grass. Berryheart had fallen in beside Tigerstar and Dovewing. Sunbeam was happy to trail slowly at the back of the patrol as it made its way to the tree-bridge. By the time she reached it, RiverClan was disappearing among the reeds, while ThunderClan and SkyClan were no more than specks in the distance. She hurried across the tree-bridge, jumped down, and raced to catch up to her Clanmates as they headed for the pines.

As she reached them, Tigerstar's tail was twitching. "I don't know how Leafstar thinks she can fix this by sending a medicine cat to help," he growled.

Dovewing looked at him. "But if it does—"

"How can it?" Tigerstar glared at her. "If StarClan didn't give Owlnose their blessing the first time, why would they give it the second time?"

"A more experienced medicine cat might make a difference," Dovewing reasoned.

"He's not a *RiverClan* medicine cat," Tigerstar argued. "I can't see why he'll make any difference. It's a waste of time and Leafstar knows it. She's just helping RiverClan play for time."

Berryheart's tail swished. "Why should we even care?" she snapped. "We should be worrying about our own Clan, not theirs."

Sunbeam shrank inside her pelt. Why did her mother have to be so argumentative?

Tigerstar glanced at Berryheart. "A weak Clan on our border makes us vulnerable," he told her.

"RiverClan shares a border with WindClan too," Berryheart argued. "Let Harestar worry about them. ShadowClan should keep to itself. Every time we get involved with another Clan, it just makes *our* lives hard."

"If we just sit and watch, we'll have to deal with the fallout," Tigerstar told her. "It's better to head trouble off now before the situation has a chance to get worse."

But Berryheart's tail was still twitching. "It might not get worse—"

Dovewing cut in. "Perhaps it's better to save this discussion for the morning," she mewed. "We're all tired and need some sleep."

Sunbeam dropped her gaze. Berryheart seemed to be more and more outspoken. Now she was even arguing with the Clan leader. Sunbeam wished for a moment that Berryheart were some other cat's mother. She knew, with a tug of foreboding, that eventually Berryheart would make her choose sides—and whichever side she chose, Sunbeam suspected it would be an ugly fight.

CHAPTER 14

☘

"Stupid moss." Nightheart nipped a *dried-up* strand from between his claws and spat it out. He'd been clearing the bedding from the elders' den since sunhigh. Now he was shaping bracken into fresh nests.

At least the elders had gone out. Thornclaw, Brackenfur, and Cloudtail were hunting in the forest, while Brightheart was just getting over the last of her greencough in the medicine cats' den. The catmint had helped her enormously. Nightheart couldn't help wondering what three such old cats could catch. They might get lucky and find a three-legged mouse or a squirrel too ancient to climb a tree. Nightheart twisted a bracken stem crossly and poked another underneath. Why did he even care what they caught? They weren't *here*, that was all that mattered; he didn't have to make conversation while they watched him fix their bedding.

He tried to work out how many moons were left until Stemkit, Bristlekit, and Graykit became apprentices. The stems unraveled in his paws. "Dumb bracken." He sat back on his haunches and looked at the nest. *It's good enough to sleep on.* So what if it was a little loose around the sides? If he made a mess of this one, they might stop asking him to fix nests altogether. Besides, he'd finished the other three. They were fine. Thornclaw, Cloudtail, and Brackenfur, would just have to fight over who got this one.

He heard mews in the clearing.

"What's she doing here?" Blossomfall sounded ruffled.

Myrtlebloom's mew was anxious. "She must have news."

Nightheart smelled SkyClan scent and hurried to peer through a gap in the den wall. Outside, in the sunshine, he could see Poppyfrost and Molewhisker escorting Leafstar into the clearing. Squirrelflight was padding to greet the Sky-Clan leader.

"She was waiting at the border," Poppyfrost told the ThunderClan deputy.

Leafstar dipped her head. "I've come to talk about River-Clan," she mewed.

"Fetch Bramblestar," Squirrelflight told Poppyfrost.

As Poppyfrost turned and leaped up the rock tumble, Squirrelflight gestured for Molewhisker to leave with her tail and guided Leafstar away from the ThunderClan warriors who were sharing prey beneath the Highledge.

They're coming over here. Nightheart dropped low. Were Leafstar and Squirrelflight going to talk in the elders' den? He was relieved when they stopped outside. It was bad enough doing 'paw duties without being shooed out like a kit so that the senior warriors could talk.

What had Leafstar come to say? At last night's Gathering, she'd calmed an awkward situation. Tigerstar had ruffled nearly every pelt on the island with his plan to help RiverClan. Even Sunbeam had seemed shocked by her leader's proposal. But RiverClan did seem to be a mess. Perhaps Leafstar had plans of her own to help them.

"How's SkyClan?" Squirrelflight asked her politely. "Any sickness?"

"A case or two of whitecough," Leafstar answered vaguely. "Nothing serious."

"You must be relieved to have catmint," Squirrelflight mewed.

"Yes."

Was Bramblestar coming yet? Nightheart strained to see the Highledge, but it was hard to make out from this angle. The ThunderClan leader was resting in his den as usual, although he had, for a change, joined a dawn patrol today. *Just as well,* thought Nightheart. *Before he forgets how to hunt.* He wished Bramblestar would start acting like a proper leader again.

Nightheart had been on edge since he'd told Bramblestar that Squirrelflight had taken a patrol to WindClan to talk to Harestar about the stolen vole. He'd expected the Thunder-Clan leader and his deputy to argue fiercely about it, but they hadn't—not in front of the Clan, anyway. He could sense the tension between them: they rarely shared tongues or prey, and when they did speak, there was a bitter edge to their mews. It seemed sad after Squirrelflight had fought so hard to save Bramblestar when Ashfur stole his body. Couldn't they be happy just to be together after being separated for so long?

Guilt still wormed in his pelt. It was kind of his fault they were angry with each other. But he hadn't meant to betray Squirrelflight, and he half wished she and Bramblestar *would* argue, just to clear the air.

Pebbles clattered from the rock tumble as Bramblestar scrambled down from the Highledge. His pelt was unkempt, as though he'd just woken. Nightheart watched through the bramble wall as he approached. Would Leafstar notice that the ThunderClan leader seemed sad and distracted? Bramblestar had been quiet at the Gathering, but he'd looked calm and freshly groomed even though his gaze, at times, seemed to drift. As he greeted Leafstar now, Squirrelflight's pelt ruffled uneasily. Was she worried too that Leafstar would notice his unwashed fur?

"Leafstar." Bramblestar dipped his head. "What brings you to the ThunderClan camp?"

Nightheart wondered again if he should finish making the nests. Perhaps he should go outside, greet the leaders politely, and then leave them to talk. But he'd been here too long already. It might seem odd if he left now. They could guess that he'd been listening. He might as well stay until they'd left. Besides, he was too curious to hear what they would say.

"I'm worried about Tigerstar," Leafstar mewed.

"Me too." Squirrelflight sat down. "He was edgy even before the RiverClan trouble. He always seemed to be demanding meetings or proposing missions. Now he wants to start running RiverClan."

"He's trying to help," Bramblestar mewed.

Nightheart's eyes widened. Did Bramblestar really believe that?

Squirrelflight eyed her mate sharply. "I wish he'd confine his help to his *own* Clan."

Leafstar's tail was flicking. "I can't imagine why he thought any Clan would support his idea of taking over RiverClan."

"He didn't say he plans to take over for good," Bramblestar mewed.

Leafstar blinked at him. "Does a hawk say it wants to hunt? Does a fish say it wants to swim? From what I hear, ambition is in Tigerstar's blood. He can't help himself."

Bramblestar cleared his throat. "Tigerstar and I share blood." He stared at Leafstar.

"Of course." Leafstar's eyes widened in recognition, and she shook her head awkwardly. "But Tigerstar leads ShadowClan, like the first Tigerstar did. I would never imply that *you . . .*"

Bramblestar's whiskers twitched with amusement as Squirrelflight dipped her head respectfully to the SkyClan leader. "Anyway, you did well to head Tigerstar off."

"For now," Leafstar mewed. "What if Fidgetflake doesn't solve RiverClan's problem?" Leafstar fretted. "StarClan might have a good reason for not granting Owlnose his nine lives, and if they do, Fidgetflake's presence won't change anything."

"In which case Tigerstar will march into RiverClan and start giving them orders," Squirrelflight growled.

"We don't know that," Bramblestar objected.

Nightheart pressed his muzzle closer to the wall, trying to hear more clearly.

"Besides," the ThunderClan leader went on, "it might be a good thing."

Nightheart blinked. Did Bramblestar *want* Tigerstar to run RiverClan?

Squirrelflight stared at the ThunderClan leader.

Leafstar's eyes widened. "A *good* thing? Have you got bees in your brain?"

"I really don't think he wants to *lead* RiverClan," Bramblestar argued. "He just wants to advise them. And they sound like they need advice."

"Not from ShadowClan," Leafstar grunted.

"He backed down at the Gathering, didn't he?" Bramblestar reminded her. "After the Clans objected. He clearly doesn't want to do anything that upsets the balance of the Clans. He was just running his idea past us. He probably didn't realize the rest of the Clans would object so strongly."

Leafstar looked unconvinced. "This is *Tigerstar* we're talking about," she mewed. "He knew exactly how the rest of us would react."

"Let's see how it plays out." Bramblestar looked at her steadily. "It's not like Tigerstar is planning to invade River-Clan."

"Not yet," Leafstar mewed darkly. "But I can't help feeling that he was more than just running an idea past us, as you put it. I think he was preparing us, getting us used to his plan, so that when he does act, it will seem less shocking."

"You're being paranoid," Bramblestar told her.

"Am I?" Leafstar looked at Squirrelflight, clearly expecting the ThunderClan deputy to back her up.

But Squirrelflight looked away. "If Bramblestar thinks we should let it play out, then that's what we'll do."

Surprise lit Leafstar's eyes. "You're going to let Tigerstar do what he likes?"

"We're going to wait and see," Bramblestar told her.

Leafstar shook out her pelt, but Nightheart could still see it bristling. "Then let's wait," she mewed sourly. "But I think you're being naive. I can see all too clearly how it will play out." She shot Squirrelflight a reproachful look, then headed for the camp entrance.

No wonder she was angry. She'd come here for support and left with nothing. Nightheart wondered what the SkyClan leader would tell her Clan. Why was Bramblestar hesitating? ThunderClan had never stepped back when a Clan was in trouble. Why start now?

As Leafstar disappeared through the thorn tunnel, Squirrelflight turned on Bramblestar. Nightheart tensed. Her green eyes were blazing. Why was she so furious? Hadn't she just backed Bramblestar up?

"'See how it plays out'?" she snapped. "Is that the best you can come up with? RiverClan is in trouble and Tigerstar is preparing to move in. And you want to do nothing?"

Bramblestar didn't move. "Let's not underestimate Tigerstar."

"It's not me who's underestimating Tigerstar—it's you!" Squirrelflight's pelt was bristling. "Who knows what he'll do if he gets his claws into RiverClan?"

"I don't think he wants to get his claws into any cat," Bramblestar mewed. "Tigerstar is a good leader. And River-Clan is a mess right now. They might actually benefit from his advice."

Squirrelflight's eyes widened. "Do you really think advice is all he's planning to give them?"

Nightheart's pelt prickled nervously. Was it normal for a deputy and leader to disagree so fiercely? But he understood Squirrelflight's frustration. ThunderClan had never sat back and let ShadowClan take the initiative before. It felt like a sign of weakness—the wrong signal to be sending to the other Clans.

Bramblestar met Squirrelflight's gaze squarely. "I'm the leader, no matter what you think," he growled. "And if I say we should see how it plays out before we act, that's what we'll do."

Squirrelflight looked ready to swipe a blow at Bramble-star's muzzle. Instead she growled and stalked away.

Bramblestar sat down, his pelt pricking along his spine. Clearly the argument with Squirrelflight had shaken him more than he'd let on. Nightheart wondered what to do. If he went back to fixing the nests, the ThunderClan leader might hear him. He'd guess at once that Nightheart had been listen-ing. There was no way he could have missed the conversation from here.

Nightheart crept away from the den wall. If he didn't want to be discovered, he'd have to stay here until Bramblestar left.

But Bramblestar wasn't moving. He was staring into space, clearly lost in thought. As the sun began to sink toward the treetops. Nightheart shifted nervously. He was supposed to be going on patrol with Bayshine. If he didn't leave the den soon, Bayshine would come looking for him.

Since Bramblestar didn't look like he would be moving any time soon, Nightheart came to a decision. Fluffing out his fur, he ducked out of the den. With any luck, Bramblestar would be so lost in thought he wouldn't notice him. Lifting his tail, he padded casually past the ThunderClan leader.

Bramblestar's muzzle swung toward him. "Hi, Nightheart."

Nightheart froze as Bramblestar's gaze reached him. "Um—hi," he mewed weakly. Was the ThunderClan leader going to lecture him about eavesdropping? He dipped his head apologetically. "Sorry," he mumbled.

But Bramblestar looked far from angry. Surprise flickered through Nightheart's fur as Bramblestar got to his paws. "You look like you've been busy." He brushed a scrap of bracken from Nightheart's shoulder with his tail-tip.

"I've been fixing nests for the elders." Nightheart looked guiltily back toward the den.

"Still doing apprentice chores, eh?" Bramblestar sympathized.

"I guess they need doing," Nightheart mewed.

"It's just for a while," Bramblestar mewed. "We'll have apprentices again soon." He glanced toward the camp entrance. "I was thinking of going for a walk. Would you like to join me?"

"Okay." Nightheart felt a flicker of foreboding. Bramblestar had never asked him to go for a walk before. Was the lecture going to start as soon as they left camp? He glanced across the clearing. Bayshine was watching him from beneath the Highledge. The golden tabby's eyes rounded questioningly. He was clearly wondering why Nightheart was talking to Bramblestar instead of joining him to hunt. But hunting would have to wait. Nightheart couldn't say no to the Clan leader.

He nodded apologetically to Bayshine and followed Bramblestar through the thorn tunnel.

Outside, birds were twittering excitedly. The smell of rotting leaves and damp moss sweetened the damp air, and Nightheart could taste prey-scent. There were squirrels nearby. "Should we hunt?" he suggested hopefully. It might distract Bramblestar from the lecture Nightheart suspected was coming.

But Bramblestar was already heading out of the hollow. He leaped the last few tail-lengths where the trail steepened, and Nightheart bounded after him. At the top, Bramblestar padded between the trees. Nightheart fell in beside him, bracing himself. But the ThunderClan leader's pelt was smooth and his gaze reached deep into the woods. He didn't seem ready to deliver a lecture on eavesdropping.

"What did you think of last night's Gathering?" Bramblestar asked suddenly.

Nightheart glanced at him. "Me?"

"You." Bramblestar looked at him.

"I guess—it felt strange," Nightheart mewed haltingly. "It

sounded like RiverClan has been in trouble for a while, and we had no idea."

Bramblestar padded on, looking thoughtful. "When I was younger, the Clans only saw each other at Gatherings," he mewed. "We didn't expect to know what was happening in another Clan."

Was that why Bramblestar was so reluctant to get involved in RiverClan's problems? "But the Clans are closer than they used to be," Nightheart ventured. Perhaps he could persuade the ThunderClan leader to step in and help RiverClan before Tigerstar interfered. "And even before that, ThunderClan helped out Clans that were in trouble." He glanced at Bramblestar. "I've heard stories about Firestar helping SkyClan at the gorge, and you helped ShadowClan when Darktail took over."

Bramblestar kept walking. "True."

Nightheart went on. "And didn't ThunderClan and WindClan join with RiverClan to drive away a band of rogues when Firestar was leader?"

"What are you trying to say?" Bramblestar slowed.

Nightheart hesitated. Was it wise to suggest that a Clan leader might have made the wrong decision? He lifted his chin. "I think we should help RiverClan."

Bramblestar halted and looked at him. "Why?"

"Because we don't know what Tigerstar is planning. We don't know if he really wants to help RiverClan, or if he's taking advantage of their weakness."

"You don't trust him?"

"Do you?"

"What if we knew exactly what Tigerstar was thinking?"

"That would be great, but it's impossible."

"Really?" Bramblestar's gaze narrowed. "Is there really no way we could find out?"

Nightheart frowned, thinking hard. "I guess we could send a warrior to find out what's going on in ShadowClan," he mewed tentatively.

"You mean a *spy*?"

"Not exactly." Nightheart thought harder. The idea he'd felt glimmering at the edge of his thoughts grew brighter. "The Clans are closer now, right? It's not unusual for warriors from different Clans to know each other." He was thinking of Sunbeam. "We don't need to spy. We just need to ask the right warrior the right questions to find out what's going on."

Bramblestar's gaze hadn't moved. "And you know a ShadowClan warrior," he mewed. "Don't you?"

Nightheart stiffened.

"I saw you sitting with her at the Gathering."

Nightheart's pelt felt hot. Bramblestar had noticed him with Sunbeam. "She was on the mission to find catmint," he mewed quickly. "We became friends. Kind of."

"Friendly enough to ask her what's going on with Tigerstar?" Bramblestar asked.

Nightheart suddenly wondered if this was what Bramblestar had been planning all along. Was this why the ThunderClan leader had invited him on this walk? "I guess."

Bramblestar leaned closer. "You'd have to sneak into ShadowClan territory," he warned. "Could you do that?"

"Yes." Nightheart's pelt twitched excitedly. Bramblestar wanted him to go on another mission. This was way better than cleaning dens.

"If you could talk to this friend . . . ," Bramblestar mewed.

"Sunbeam," Nightheart told him.

"Sunbeam." Bramblestar nodded. "And maybe to some of her denmates, we'd have a better idea of Tigerstar's intentions."

"I could do that."

"Really?"

"Really." Nightheart fluffed out his fur. He didn't blink in case Bramblestar saw his doubt. Would Sunbeam really help him? He knew they were friends, but she was also a loyal ShadowClan warrior. He'd have to convince her that she'd be sharing information for the good of all the Clans. He just hoped he'd be able to find the right words.

"Take a Clanmate with you," Bramblestar told him.

Nightheart wondered whom to choose. Did Sunbeam know any of his Clanmates? He doubted it. He needed someone who would put Sunbeam at ease, who wouldn't seem threatening, who would seem sincere. "Bayshine?" he ventured.

"Sure."

Nightheart couldn't wait to get back to camp and tell Bayshine. This would more than make up for missing today's hunt. They could plan the mission tonight. The *secret* mission. Nightheart swallowed back a purr. For the first time in a long time, he felt like a real warrior. Suddenly his future in ThunderClan seemed clear. He belonged here, and he was going to become a great warrior, trusted by his leader and admired by his Clanmates. No one would even care that he'd once been named Flameheart.

"Tigerstar mustn't know you're there," Bramblestar cautioned. He leaned closer, his mew dropping to a whisper. "And neither should Squirrelflight."

CHAPTER 15

Frostpaw dropped a bunch of comfrey leaves beside the other piles. The collection of herbs looked small and withered, laid out in the evening light on the sandy floor of the RiverClan medicine den. Embarrassment sparked in her pelt as Fidgetflake looked them over.

"Is this all the marigold you have?" he asked.

"We were going to pick more but—"

"Surely you must have more thyme than this." Fidgetflake poked the two thin tendrils, whose shriveled leaves were barely more than dust.

"Things have been difficult." Frostpaw wished that Mothwing were here to explain, but her mentor was in the clearing, keeping an eye on Splashtail as he sent off the last patrols of the day. RiverClan's new deputy was more decisive than its leader, thankfully, but Mothwing had wanted to observe for one more day. "We haven't really had time to collect fresh herbs for a while," she finished weakly.

"But leaf-bare's coming," he mewed. "There'll be no herbs *to* collect soon."

Frostpaw's claws itched with annoyance. Did he think

she didn't realize? "I *know*." She swallowed back a growl. She shouldn't be ungrateful. In the days he'd been here, the SkyClan medicine cat had checked every RiverClan cat for illness, treated their ticks, and made sure that the whole Clan groomed itself meticulously for fleas. He'd helped fix the medicine den—mending the sagging wall, patching up the roof, and weaving new nests. Frostpaw had let him do that in order to distract him from examining RiverClan's herb stores. She was painfully aware of the woeful state they were in. Fidgetflake had worked hard and without judgment, for which Frostpaw was grateful. But now, as he picked up a desiccated yarrow leaf with his claw and examined it, he was less gracious. "This must grow plentifully beside the river."

"It does," Frostpaw agreed. "That's why we haven't bothered collecting fresh leaves. There didn't seem . . ."

Her mew trailed away as Fidgetflake dropped the yarrow and moved on to the poppy seeds. "These wouldn't be enough to cure a headache." He looked at her. "Where do you collect fresh seeds?"

"Beside the water meadow."

"Is that far?"

"No." She knew he was asking indirectly why they'd allowed their supply to fall so low. She looked away guiltily. "I guess we could have gathered more by now, but it's been hard organizing patrols."

Fidgetflake sat back on his haunches. "I can see you've been having a difficult time," he mewed. "I just wish you'd asked for help earlier."

"We thought we could manage." Frostpaw blinked at him apologetically. This was humiliating, but she'd had so much on her mind.

Fidgetflake gazed back at her sympathetically. "Mothwing said you lost your mother recently."

She looked away again, trying to stop her eyes pricking with grief. "Yes."

"I'm sorry," Fidgetflake mewed softly. "Losing kin is hard enough at the best of times. She must have meant a lot to you."

Frostpaw's throat tightened. "She did," she whispered. *And if she'd become RiverClan's leader like she was supposed to, we wouldn't be in such a mess.*

Fidgetflake gazed at her silently, as though allowing her a moment for her grief, then spoke again, this time briskly. "Owlnose will get his nine lives soon," he promised her. "Then RiverClan can get back to normal."

"I hope so." Frostpaw couldn't help thinking that getting back to normal might not be as easy as it sounded. But at least the trip to the Moonpool would be a step in the right direction, and with Fidgetflake there, she wouldn't be solely responsible for making sure Owlnose received StarClan's blessing. "It's been hard without a leader."

Fidgetflake's tail-tip flicked. "How long exactly is it since Mistystar died?" He looked thoughtful. "Mistystar missed the Gathering a moon ago, didn't she? Was she already dead then? Is that when Reedwhisker died too?"

Frostpaw's mouth grew dry. She tried to remember exactly what lies had been told and when. She didn't want to contradict Mothwing or Owlnose. "They both died a while ago," she mewed vaguely. "Not long, but enough for us to get behind on herb gathering." She began to gather the herbs. "I should put these away. They're all we've got." She made herself busy collecting the bundles and stowing them among the woven reeds of the herb store, relieved when Fidgetflake padded to the den entrance and looked out without asking any more awkward questions. Then she joined him, wondering what was holding his interest.

Outside, the sky was beginning to darken. The clearing was slick with mud after the afternoon's rain. Owlnose stood at its edge, Splashtail beside him. RiverClan's new leader looked anxious, his fur ruffled, while his deputy's tail twitched impatiently. Their Clanmates shifted from paw to paw as they waited for orders, and Mothwing hung back, watching quietly.

"Gorseclaw." Owlnose seemed to come to a decision. "Take Nightsky and Havenpelt hunting in the water meadow."

Shimmerpelt pulled a face. "We hunted the water meadow this morning," she called out.

"Yes, but—" Owlnose began, but Shimmerpelt didn't give him a chance to explain.

"If we hunt there twice a day, the prey will leave for good," she told him.

"I know, but rain has swollen the river," Owlnose mewed.

Duskfur snorted. "We're RiverClan cats, for StarClan's sake," she snapped. "We're used to swollen rivers."

"What if another riverbank collapses?" Owlnose's ears twitched nervously.

"What-ifs don't fill the fresh-kill pile," Shimmerpelt grunted.

Splashtail stepped forward. "Fish in the gorge instead," he told Gorseclaw.

Gorseclaw dipped his head and turned to leave. Nightsky and Havenpelt began to follow.

"The gorge?" Owlnose's eyes widened. "The current is too fierce there."

"Gorseclaw is an experienced warrior," Splashtail reminded him.

"But isn't it better to be safe?" Owlnose's gaze clouded with confusion.

Gorseclaw glanced back at him. "Where do you want us to hunt?"

Owlnose blinked at Mothwing. "What do you think?"

Impatience flashed in her amber eyes. "Send them to the gorge," she mewed. "Shimmerpelt and Duskfur can check the WindClan border with Icewing and Mistpaw. Splashtail can take Breezeheart and Graypaw to the ThunderClan border."

Shimmerpelt scowled at Mothwing. "Why do you even let them try to organize patrols when you're going to make the final decision?" Her gaze flitted irritably toward Owlnose and Splashtail.

As Fidgetflake watched through narrowed eyes, Frostpaw shrank beneath her pelt. She wanted to tell the SkyClan medicine cat that the Clan wasn't always like this, that sometimes Owlnose and Splashtail organized the patrols easily and with authority. But it wouldn't have been true.

It was a relief when the SkyClan medicine cat seemed to have seen enough and ducked back inside the medicine den. Then indignation began to swell in her chest. What business was it of his? Fidgetflake was here to help them contact StarClan, not to judge how Owlnose and Splashtail ran the Clan. His opinion meant nothing. And yet her belly was tight with worry. Even if it was none of Fidgetflake's business, it was obvious to her own Clanmates that Owlnose was struggling to lead them. He couldn't give orders; he wasn't even close to winning the respect of his warriors.

Had she made the right choice? As the patrols headed for the entrance, she watched Owlnose pad heavily to the leader's den. Mothwing followed him and disappeared inside. Was she going to give him advice?

Splashtail was leading his patrol to the camp entrance. He caught Frostpaw's eye. Frowning, he waved Breezeheart and Graypaw ahead with his tail and padded toward her. "Are you okay?"

"I guess."

"You look worried." He stopped beside her.

"Fidgetflake was watching you organize the patrols." She wasn't sure how much to confide in him. She didn't want to hurt his feelings by pointing out how disorganized he and Owlnose had appeared.

"It was kind of messy," he mewed. He looked disappointed. "I hoped we'd be better. But it's hard. Owlnose is so scared of upsetting the warriors that he can't stick to a decision."

She looked at him. "Do you think I made the wrong choice when I chose him as leader?"

"Of course not." Splashtail whisked his tail. "He's just new to this, that's all. And so am I. Owlnose will be a great leader once he learns how to deal with the senior warriors, and I'm going to get better and do everything I can to help him."

Frostpaw felt a glimmer of relief. Splashtail was willing to admit his mistakes and was determined to do better. He sounded like a real deputy. She just wished *Owlnose* would do or say something to reassure her that he'd be a good leader one day. "But what if Owlnose never improves?"

"He will," Splashtail promised.

Frostpaw wasn't so sure. "Perhaps StarClan wanted me to choose a different cat."

"No way." Splashtail argued. "You have a stronger connection with them than any cat in RiverClan."

"That's what Curlfeather used to say. But what if she was wrong?" Frostpaw felt a fresh pang of grief.

Splashtail must have seen it. He touched his nose to her ear. "If she were here right now, she'd tell you she has faith in you and that you're going to be a great medicine cat."

Frostpaw blinked at him gratefully. Suddenly she realized how much she missed her mother's encouragement. "I just wish I could hear her tell me again."

"*I'm* telling you." Splashtail blinked at her. "You're destined for great things, Frostpaw. You're the only one who can't see it."

His eyes shone with such warmth that her heart lifted. A rush of affection for Splashtail took her by surprise. She stiffened. Had her feelings for Splashtail gone beyond friendship? She pushed the thought away. *Medicine cats don't have mates,* she reminded herself. But, for the first time since she'd become a medicine-cat apprentice, the thought tugged at her heart.

Fidgetflake stuck his head out of the medicine den. "Where's Mothwing?"

Fidgetflake sounded touchy, and Frostpaw jerked her muzzle toward him, aware of how close she was standing to Splashtail. Guiltily, she stepped back, her pelt hot. "She's in Owlnose's den. Why?"

But Fidgetflake didn't answer. Instead, he called across the clearing. "Mothwing!"

The RiverClan medicine cat ducked out of Owlnose's den. "What is it?"

"We need to talk about your herb supplies," Fidgetflake mewed.

Frostpaw sighed. Hadn't he already said enough about them?

Mothwing padded toward the medicine den. "Is there a problem?"

The SkyClan medicine cat frowned. "Yes."

As Mothwing passed Splashtail, she glanced at him. "Shouldn't you be on patrol?"

"I'm just leaving." Splashtail dipped his head. He blinked reassuringly at Frostpaw and headed for the entrance. But

Frostpaw's attention was on Fidgetflake. What was his problem now? She followed him as he headed inside the den with Mothwing.

The SkyClan medicine cat stopped beside a pile of shriveled leaves on the floor.

Frostpaw looked at it in surprise. *Catmint!* And this was much older than the fresh catmint Alderheart had brought. That meant they must had had some before . . . but she'd thought they'd run out. "Where did you find it?"

Fidgetflake nodded toward a gap in the reeds at the edge of the herb store. "It was shoved in there," he mewed.

Mothwing inspected the gap. "With everything that's been happening, I forgot I put it there," she mewed. "It must have been moons ago. Look how dry it is."

Fidgetflake's pelt ruffled along his spine. "Was Tigerstar right? Were you hoarding it?"

"Of course not!" Mothwing looked outraged. "We forgot it was there, that's all."

"You forgot you had *catmint*?" Fidgetflake stared at her. "Do you expect me to believe that while your leader and deputy were dying of greencough, neither one of you remembered that you had the one herb that could save them?"

Frostpaw glanced at Mothwing. How were they going to explain this? She could think of no excuse. The truth was, Mistystar hadn't died of greencough. Neither had Reedwhisker. Even if Mothwing had remembered this supply was here, it wouldn't have saved RiverClan's leader and deputy.

But if she told Fidgetflake that, she'd have to tell him every-thing and admit to all the lies Owlnose and Mothwing had told at the Gathering.

Fidgetflake was still staring at them. "Well?"

"Mistystar was old," Mothwing mewed defensively. "Cat-mint wouldn't have saved her."

"But Reedwhisker wasn't," Fidgetflake snapped. "He'd have survived with this much catmint." He poked his paw into the pile, anger glittering in his gaze. "Rowankit would have survived too, if you'd shared it."

Guilt pierced Frostpaw's heart. They had been so caught up in the disasters that had hit RiverClan that they'd let a kit die. She looked helplessly at Mothwing.

But Mothwing's gaze hardened. She lifted her chin. "River-Clan doesn't have to explain anything to you," she snapped at Fidgetflake. "You're here to help Owlnose get his nine lives. That's all. You're lucky I even let you into my medicine den. We forgot we had catmint, okay? And look—" She lifted a dry catmint leaf with her claw, and it crumbled into fragments. "This herb is so old, I doubt it could cure anyone."

Fidgetflake's eyes narrowed. But Mothwing glared back at him, unflinching.

It was clear he wasn't going to get an explanation from her. He dipped his head. "Fine," he growled. "Since I'm only here to see Owlnose receive his nine lives, let's do it now so I can go home."

Frostpaw's fur pricked uncomfortably. Fidgetflake had helped RiverClan selflessly since he'd arrived, and now

Mothwing seemed to be sending him away without even thanking him.

And yet it would be a relief to have him gone. "I'll fetch Owlnose," she mewed. She wanted to get out of the camp and think about something other than herb supplies. Once Owlnose had been given his nine lives and Fidgetflake had left, RiverClan could fix its problems without outsiders poking their whiskers where they weren't wanted.

Mothwing led the way as they followed the stream toward the Moonpool hollow. Fidgetflake barely spoke, and Owlnose was even quieter than he'd been the last time they'd come this way.

Frostpaw glanced nervously at the RiverClan tom. His tail was down and his shoulders low, like an apprentice heading for a stern lecture from his mentor. "I'm sure StarClan will share with you this time," she reassured him. It felt more like a hope than a promise. "Fidgetflake will make sure of that." She blinked at the SkyClan medicine cat, but he kept his gaze on the trail, and Owlnose eyed her doubtfully.

"What if they don't?" he mewed.

"Fidgetflake." Frostpaw called to him, hoping the SkyClan cat might put Owlnose at ease. "Tell Owlnose what Leafstar's nine lives ceremony was like."

"I wasn't there." Fidgetflake sounded distracted. Was he still thinking about the catmint he'd found in the medicine den?

"You must have heard about it," Frostpaw pressed. Her ears

twitched self-consciously. She seemed to be the only cat trying to reassure Owlnose.

She felt relieved when Mothwing joined in. "Tell Owlnose what you know," she told Fidgetflake. "It might help if he knows what to expect."

"All I know is that Cloudstar was there," Fidgetflake answered.

Cloudstar? Frostpaw pricked her ears. Wasn't he one of Sky-Clan's first leaders? She'd never met such a legendary warrior when she'd shared with StarClan. She'd seen Mistystar, of course. But she'd never met a leader she'd only *heard* about.

Fidgetflake went on. "Leafstar saw her mother too."

Owlnose lifted his head. The thought that he might see his mother seemed to cheer him up, and he quickened his pace a little, but not for long. He looked at Fidgetflake. "Frostpaw says it might hurt."

"It might," Fidgetflake told him. "But that's not the part you'll remember. You'll be surrounded by the whole of StarClan."

"All of them?" Owlnose's pelt rippled nervously.

Frostpaw frowned. She'd never seen the whole of StarClan. Not clearly, at least. Perhaps this was something that only happened at nine-lives ceremonies. "Have you ever seen the whole of StarClan?" she asked Fidgetflake.

"Of course," Fidgetflake answered.

Butterflies seemed to flutter around Frostpaw's heart. Her visions suddenly seemed vaguer than ever. Was that normal? She wanted to ask Mothwing, but Mothwing wouldn't know.

She pushed the worry away. Moonlight was silvering the heather, and the Moonpool hollow cut into the star-specked sky ahead of them. With a rush of dread, she recognized this part of the trail. They were passing the place where Curlfeather had been killed. Even though she'd passed this spot the first time she brought Owlnose to the Moonpool, it still sickened her to be here. Sharply and suddenly, she missed her mother. *If it hadn't been for those dogs, none of this would be happening.*

Mothwing must have noticed her shrink beneath her pelt. "Is this where it happened?" she asked softly.

"Where *what* happened?" Fidgetflake spoke before she could answer.

"Curlfeather died here," Frostpaw told him quietly.

His eyes rounded with sympathy. "I'm sorry." He glanced toward the tree jutting from the heather, where Frostpaw had sheltered while her mother led the dogs away.

"She was a loyal Clanmate," Owlnose mewed. "And she loved Frostpaw and her littermates very much."

She would have been leader if she hadn't died, Frostpaw thought. She suspected Owlnose would have preferred that.

"What happened to the dogs?" Fidgetflake asked.

"I sent patrols to track them," Mothwing told him. "But they'd disappeared."

Fidgetflake's eyes had narrowed. "This is WindClan land," he mewed. "Have you spoken to Harestar about it?."

"Not yet," Mothwing told him.

"Perhaps you should," he mewed. "At the Gathering, a

WindClan warrior said that patrols have found piles of prey bones on the moor."

"Probably left by hawks or foxes," Mothwing mewed dismissively.

But Frostpaw pricked her ears. "Do you think the dogs left them?"

"Maybe," Fidgetflake replied, his mew darkening. "Or the bones were left to lure the dogs here."

Frostpaw stared at him. "Who would do something like that?"

Mothwing ran her tail along Frostpaw's spine. "It's just speculation," she soothed.

But Frostpaw's thoughts were spiraling. She'd assumed Curlfeather had just been unlucky, that she'd run into the dogs by accident. Was there a chance the dogs had been lured there deliberately? "You think some cat *wanted* Curlfeather to die?" she mewed.

"Of course not." Mothwing shot Fidgetflake a warning look. "Stop upsetting Frostpaw. It's nothing but gossip."

Frostpaw wanted to believe her, but her mother's last words rang once more in her mind. *Trust no cat.* If Curlfeather had been killed on purpose, the warning made sense. She realized, with a sickening sense of dread, that there was a connection that linked every death in RiverClan over the past moon. Why hadn't she noticed it before? It seemed so obvious.

Every cat who'd died was a leader or was about to become one.

The idea churned in her mind as they approached the steep

wall of rocks that reached up to the rim of the Moonpool hollow. Fidgetflake climbed it first. Mothwing followed. But Owlnose hesitated.

Frostpaw stopped beside him. "I'm sure it will be fine this time," she mewed as he looked up, round-eyed, at the hollow. She hoped it was true. But what if it didn't work this time? What if StarClan didn't show up, even though Fidgetflake was with them, because she'd made the wrong choice? Her chest tightened. *What if I did* misunderstand what StarClan was trying to tell me?

Mothwing and Fidgetflake were waiting at the top of the rock wall. Frostpaw took a deep breath. *StarClan is watching over me. They wouldn't have let me choose wrong.*

Mothwing peered over the edge. "Come on," she called, her mew echoing over the silent moor.

Frostpaw blinked at Owlnose. "You can do this," she encouraged.

He stared back at her, his eyes as dark as the sky. "I'm sorry," he mewed. "I can't. I don't think I'm supposed to be leader." He backed away. "I just want to be an ordinary RiverClan warrior." His mew was thick. "I'm not going to the Moonpool."

CHAPTER 16

♣

Sunshine filtered through the pines, warming the ShadowClan camp
for what might be the last time before leaf-bare. Sunbeam lay
beside her denmates, an untouched squirrel in front of her, as
they played with their food.

Flaxfoot grabbed the mouse he'd chosen from the fresh-
kill pile and tossed it high above his head, then lifted himself
on his hind legs to snatch it between his jaws.

Pouncestep swished her tail appreciatively. "Higher," she
dared. "See if you can throw it over that branch and still catch
it." She pointed with her muzzle to a low bough jutting over
the clearing.

Flaxfoot looked doubtful. "If it gets caught up there, it'll be
a waste of good prey."

"You can climb up and fetch it," Pouncestep mewed.

"One piece of prey in my paws is worth two in a tree." Flaxfoot took a bite from the mouse. "Besides . . ." He glanced at
Cloverfoot, who was frowning at him from the other side of
the clearing. "I don't think the gray-pelts approve."

Sunbeam knew her denmates were trying to distract her,

but she was still aware of Lightleap and Blazefire on the other side of the clearing, sharing a sparrow, their whiskers almost brushing as they took turns to take a bite.

"How high can you throw yours?" Flaxfoot asked her. The brown tabby tom blinked at her encouragingly.

"It's too big to throw." Pouncestep nodded at Sunbeam's squirrel. "Do you want to swap it with my shrew?"

"You can have it." Sunbeam pushed the squirrel toward Pouncestep. She wasn't feeling very hungry. She wished she hadn't taken such a large piece of prey from the pile, but Blazefire and Lightleap had arrived as she'd been choosing, so she'd grabbed the closest fresh-kill and hurried away.

"Just a bite." Pouncestep licked her lips and reached for the squirrel. "If you insist."

The camp entrance shivered. Berryheart hurried in, Whorlpelt and Yarrowleaf at her heels. They were carrying prey from their hunt, and Fringewhisker was following, a mouse between her jaws. Berryheart dropped her vole near the entrance and looked around the camp.

Sunbeam narrowed her eyes as she saw the grim expression on Berryheart's face. Her mother was angry.

"I need to speak to Tigerstar." Berryheart puffed out her chest.

Around the clearing, their Clanmates looked up from their meal.

At the head of the clearing, Tigerstar stopped washing. Dovewing, lying beside him while Birchkit clambered over her, narrowed her eyes as Tigerstar got to his paws and crossed the camp.

The ShadowClan leader stopped in front of the patrol. Whorlpelt's fur was ruffled. Yarrowleaf was swishing her tail indignantly. Something had clearly upset them. But Fringewhisker only looked puzzled as she padded quietly to the fresh-kill pile and dropped her catch.

"Has something happened?" Tigerstar asked Berryheart.

The black-and-white she-cat's gaze flashed accusingly toward Fringewhisker.

Sunbeam got to her paws. What had the former SkyClan cat done?

"*She*—" Berryheart's mew was sour with contempt. "*She* gave prey to SkyClan."

Tigerstar looked at Fringewhisker, surprised. "Did you?"

Fringewhisker blinked at Berryheart in surprise. "But you—"

Berryheart cut in. "We were hunting on the border, and she gave a squirrel to Harrybrook. I saw her do it. So did Whorlpelt and Yarrowleaf."

Her patrolmates nodded.

Sunbeam narrowed her eyes. Something felt wrong. Yarrowleaf and Whorlpelt held their heads high. Their eyes shone. It almost looked as though they were enjoying their indignation. She scanned the camp for Spireclaw, feeling anxious. Berryheart had made a serious accusation. Fringewhisker was going to need support.

Her mother's tail flicked ominously. "This is why we shouldn't let cats swap Clans like they're swapping nests. Switching dens is easy, but switching loyalties isn't." She scowled at Fringewhisker. "At least it shouldn't be."

Whorlpelt nodded. "If Fringewhisker doesn't know which side of the border her loyalties lie on, what will she do when she faces SkyClan in battle?"

Yarrowleaf's ears flattened. "How can we fight beside a cat who can't choose a Clan?"

Cloverfoot padded to Tigerstar's side. The ShadowClan deputy's eyes were dark. "You chose to live here," she told Fringewhisker. "You can't live on both sides of the border."

Fringewhisker's eyes glittered sharply.

Say something! Sunbeam willed her to explain, but the former SkyClan cat didn't seem to be able to find the words. Instead she glared at her patrolmates.

It didn't make sense. Fringewhisker must have known that giving prey to SkyClan would risk her place in ShadowClan. She wouldn't do that. Even if she wasn't entirely comfortable yet, she wouldn't want to be separated from Spireclaw.

Sunbeam stepped forward, avoiding her mother's gaze. "We should let Fringewhisker explain what happened," she told Tigerstar.

Tigerstar turned to Fringewhisker. "Is it true?" he asked. "Did you give away prey?"

"Yes." Fringewhisker didn't flinch. "But it was SkyClan prey. A squirrel ran over the border. There were SkyClan warriors on its tail. All I did was—"

Tigerstar cut her off. "If it was on ShadowClan land, it was ShadowClan prey," he told her firmly.

Cloverfoot growled. "Giving prey away isn't your decision to make once it's on ShadowClan land."

Fringewhisker looked back at them. Her gaze narrowed, as though she was wondering what to say. Then she bowed her head. "I'm sorry," she mewed. "I made a mistake."

Berryheart whisked her tail. "We should review our decision to let Fringewhisker join ShadowClan."

Dovewing got to her paws. "We can't throw her out now that we've accepted her."

Berryheart dipped her head politely to the pale gray she-cat. "She's not like you, Dovewing. The Clan was a mess after Darktail. You had nothing to gain by joining. You helped rebuild the Clan and proved your loyalty over and over again." Her gaze darted back to Fringewhisker. "*She* just walked in because she felt like it."

Dovewing blinked at her. "She joined ShadowClan because she loves Spireclaw."

"And she passed a test!" Sunbeam added.

Berryheart snorted. "An *apprentice* could have passed that test!" She turned back to Tigerstar. "All I'm saying is that a Clan-swapper will never be as invested as a warrior who's shared a Clan's history."

Dovewing looked worried. "I'm not sure that's true."

"Then why is she giving *our prey* to SkyClan?" Berryheart demanded.

Sunbeam narrowed her eyes. Her mother looked *pleased* that Fringewhisker was in trouble. Whorlpelt and Yarrowleaf moved closer to Berryheart, and all Sunbeam could see was how satisfied the three warriors seemed. *Did they plan this?* Or was it just a coincidence that Fringewhisker had been hunting with three of most vocal cats from the Clan-swapper meeting when she'd decided to give prey to SkyClan?

But Tigerstar seemed oblivious to the pleasure the patrol seemed to be taking in Fringewhisker's denunciation. He glowered at Fringewhisker. "I expected more of you," he growled. "You must have known that as a cat who just joined ShadowClan, you'd be held to higher standards, and yet you can't even obey the most basic of Clan rules. Would you have given prey to a ShadowClan warrior when you were in Sky-Clan?"

"It wasn't like—" Fringewhisker tried to defend herself, but Tigerstar wasn't listening.

"I'm not throwing you out of ShadowClan this time," he mewed. "But there will be consequences." Sunbeam's belly tightened. "You will leave camp and not return until you've caught three pieces of prey to replace the one you gave away. I'm giving you a chance to make up for this mistake, but that's all. Next time you break a rule, the consequences will be more severe."

This time Fringewhisker didn't try to argue. Instead she dipped her head meekly and headed for the camp entrance.

"Is that all?" Berryheart stared at Tigerstar.

"It's enough," Tigerstar told her.

Sunbeam saw disappointment in her mother's eyes. As Fringewhisker disappeared into the forest and the rest of ShadowClan returned to sharing prey, her pelt twitched uneasily.

"Eat your squirrel," Flaxfoot mewed, nudging it toward her.

"We can give the kits a badger ride afterward." Pouncestep nodded toward the nursery where Firkit and Whisperkit were chasing each other under Slatefur's watchful eye. Cinnamontail, Streamkit, and Bloomkit were napping in a sunny patch of pine needles. It gave Sunbeam some comfort to know that the catmint they'd brought back from the Twolegplace had cured Cinnamontail and her kits, who were now just working on getting their energy back. *Because of us, ShadowClan lost only one kit to greencough. But that's still far too many.*

Sunbeam returned her thoughts to Fringewhisker. She wanted to find out exactly what had happened. "I need a drink of water," she told Pouncestep.

"But we stopped by the stream on the way back from patrol," Pouncestep mewed.

"I'm thirsty again." Sunbeam headed toward the camp entrance. "I won't be long."

She ducked out of camp and followed Fringewhisker's scent along the trail that led to the ditches.

Fringewhisker was stalking along the edge of the widest ditch, scanning it for prey. Something scuttled in the shadows beneath her, but Fringewhisker didn't move. She didn't even prick her ears. Her attention was clearly not on hunting.

"Fringewhisker," Sunbeam called to the white-and-brown she-cat, and Fringewhisker looked up.

"What?"

"I just wanted to make sure you were okay." Sunbeam hopped the two ditches between them and stopped beside her. "And to hear your side of the story."

Fringewhisker met her gaze. Her amber eyes shone with anger and hurt. "I already told it."

Sunbeam felt a pang of sympathy. She was more certain than ever that there was more going on than Berryheart had claimed. "What *really* happened?"

Fringewhisker searched her gaze as though deciding how much to share. Seeming to make up her mind, she raised her head defiantly. "They told me to do it," she growled.

"Who did?" Suddenly Sunbeam wondered if she really wanted to know. She braced herself.

"Berryheart and Whorlpelt," Fringewhisker told her. "And Yarrowleaf. They were all in it together. The squirrel crossed the border, just like I said, and there was a SkyClan patrol. But it was *their* idea to give them the squirrel, not mine."

Sunbeam's heart pounded hard in her chest. How could Berryheart be so spiteful?

Fringewhisker went on. "They said it would be better to give up one piece of prey than risk a fight," she mewed. "It seemed weird at the time. Normally, they hardly talk to me. But I just figured that they were finally trying to be friendly." Her whiskers quivered with anger. "'Tigerstar doesn't have to know.'" She mimicked Berryheart so closely that Sunbeam could picture her mother speaking. Fringewhisker's gaze hardened. "And then, the moment we got back to camp, they said it was my idea and that I betrayed the Clan." She stared angrily at Sunbeam. "They set me up."

Sunbeam's pelt burned with shame. "Why didn't you say something?"

"As if Tigerstar would believe *me*. I've just joined the Clan. Nobody's going to take my word over the word of three Clan-born warriors." She flexed her claws. "I don't want to hurt Spireclaw, or I'd be fighting those cats now." Then her anger seemed to fade. She sat down heavily. "How can I challenge his mother?"

"Do you want me to have a word with Tigerstar?"

"And get Berryheart in trouble?" Fringewhisker looked defeated. "The Clan would hate me even more, and Berryheart would never accept me as Spireclaw's mate."

Sunbeam's heart ached. She was beginning to doubt that Berryheart would ever accept Fringewhisker, no matter how many tasks the former SkyClan cat completed. "I'm glad you're Spireclaw's mate," she mewed sincerely. "You clearly care for him a lot."

Fringewhisker glanced at her. "Thanks."

"Let me help you catch the prey," Sunbeam offered.

"You'd better not," Fringewhisker told her. "I don't want to get into more trouble. And I don't want to get you in trouble too. Berryheart hates me enough already."

"I'm sorry." Her mother had done something cruel and dishonest. "Things will get better," she promised. *I'll make sure of it.*

She headed back to camp. *I don't care if she is my mother. Berryheart can't get away with this.*

"Berryheart?" She padded to where her mother was lounging beside the clearing with Yarrowleaf and Whorlpelt. The three cats looked pleased with themselves, and Sunbeam had to force her pelt to stay smooth.

Berryheart looked at her. "Are you okay?"

"I need to talk to you," Sunbeam mewed. "In private." She nodded toward the camp entrance and waited for Berryheart to get to her paws before leading her into the forest.

"How could you do such a mean thing?" she demanded once they were too far away from camp to be overheard. "Fringewhisker said you told her to give SkyClan the squirrel. Is it true?" Was her mother going to deny it?

Berryheart eyed her sharply. "Are you planning to tell Tigerstar?"

"No," Sunbeam told her.

Berryheart sniffed. "I guess you're loyal, at least," she mewed.

Sunbeam felt a prick of guilt. She *was* being loyal, but to Fringewhisker, not her mother. She'd promised the former SkyClan warrior she wouldn't tell. She stared at Berryheart. "So?" she demanded. "Is it true?"

"It's true." Berryheart sounded unapologetic. "But we

only made the suggestion. It was Fringewhisker who gave the squirrel away."

"Only because you told her to!"

"She should have known better."

"She trusted you!" Sunbeam snapped. "You're Clanmates!"

Berryheart glared at her. "She's no Clanmate of mine."

Sunbeam could hardly believe her ears. Was this the cat who had raised her? What had happened to the cat who had given her badger rides after a long day's patrolling, and sat beside her through the night when she'd had whitecough, and taught her to share prey with her littermates? She stared help-lessly at her mother. "Why are you being so cruel?"

For the first time, Berryheart looked away. "You're too young to understand," she mumbled.

"Even a kit understands what it is to be bullied!" Sunbeam flattened her ears. "Fringewhisker's a good cat and a true war-rior. She's your son's mate, for StarClan's sake. She doesn't deserve this."

Berryheart's gaze snapped back to Sunbeam. "*Darktail* pre-tended to be a good cat and a true warrior too!"

"Darktail?" Sunbeam frowned. What did that fox-hearted rogue have to do with this?

"It was before you were born, so you don't know what it was like," Berryheart mewed. "Darktail came to Shadow-Clan, pretending he wanted to be part of ShadowClan. He made every cat trust him. He convinced them with lies that he had ShadowClan's best interest at heart, and then he brought his friends." There was a flash of fear in her mother's eyes.

"Before long, ShadowClan wasn't ShadowClan anymore, and Darktail was our leader." She paused, as though the memory hurt too much to go on. "He killed so many cats."

Her mother looked suddenly lost and frightened. Sunbeam had heard tales of Darktail's cruelty, but she hadn't ever wondered how Berryheart had lived through those days.

"He tried to drown me," Berryheart mewed. "In the lake. He held me under until I thought I would die for sure." She shuddered. "It isn't safe letting outsiders in."

Sunbeam hesitated. Part of her was relieved that there was a reason for her mother's unkindness. And yet Berryheart was being unfair. "Darktail was a rogue," she reminded her. "Fringewhisker is a warrior. You can't compare them. They're nothing like each other."

Berryheart held her ground. "But Fringewhisker wasn't born here. She wasn't raised here. Who knows what's in her heart? We should never have taken her in. If she *were* a true warrior, she'd never have abandoned her Clan."

"But Spireclaw loves her."

Berryheart didn't seem to care. "The moment we let a cat from another Clan into ShadowClan, we risk losing everything. Is it worth it just so a few cats can be happy?"

"It's more dangerous to turn Clanmates against each other," Sunbeam challenged.

"I'm only turning them against an intruder."

"You're splitting the Clan!"

"Nonsense," Berryheart mewed. "I'm protecting the Clan. You'll see that I'm right in the end."

Sunbeam's heart sank. Her mother looked so sure of herself. Nothing she could say would change her mind. She lifted her chin. *I have to choose.* "I'll never believe you're right," she told Berryheart. "Not over this. Not ever." She looked her mother in the eye. "From now on, leave me out of your meetings. Keep your opinions to yourself. I don't want to hear them."

CHAPTER 17

Nightheart had woken before dawn, his heart racing. Excitement fizzed beneath his pelt. Tonight was the night when he and Bayshine would sneak into ShadowClan territory and ask Sunbeam and her denmates what Tigerstar was planning. At last he had a real warrior mission.

But Bayshine had been less excited about it than he'd imagined. In fact, the golden warrior had hardly spoken as Nightheart had gone over the plan to leave the ThunderClan camp after dark and sneak around the shore to ShadowClan land. He figured the ShadowClan camp wouldn't be too deep into the pine forest, and even if it was, all the scent trails would lead there, wouldn't they? Bayshine had only nodded unenthusiastically. Now, as Nightheart hopped out of his nest, he hoped his denmate would be grateful that Nightheart had picked him to join the special patrol.

He ducked out into the clearing. The sky above the hollow was beginning to lighten. Squirrelflight was stretching on the Highledge. Jayfeather was eating a stale piece of prey, left over from last night, outside the medicine den. He nodded in Nightheart's direction, then returned to his meal. Nightheart padded to the fresh-kill pile. He nosed through the leftover mice and voles, looking for something still soft enough to take to the nursery for Spotfur and her kits.

"You're up early," Squirrelflight called from the Highledge.

Nightheart stiffened. Had waking so early betrayed his excitement about his secret task? She was looking at him curiously. What if she'd guessed? "I—I was hoping I'd be assigned to an early patrol," he mewed.

Her whiskers twitched with amusement. "Are you worried I might put you on den-cleaning duty again?"

Nightheart's pelt prickled irritably. It was nice to know that she found assigning him apprentice chores funny.

Birchfall slid from the warriors' den. "Good morning." He nodded to Nightheart and Squirrelflight.

Alderheart padded, yawning, from the medicine den.

Nightheart grabbed a mouse from the fresh-kill pile and carried it to the nursery. By the time he'd dropped it beside Spotfur's nest, said hi to Stemkit, Bristlekit, and Graykit, and returned to the clearing, the camp was awake.

Bayshine poked his nose from the warriors' den and glanced at the sky before padding out.

Nightheart hurried toward him. "Are you ready for tonight's mission?" he hissed as he reached him.

Bayshine rubbed his nose sleepily with his paw. "Let's get today's patrols out of the way first."

Disappointment jabbed Nightheart's belly. Bayshine didn't seem any more excited about the mission than he had last night. As the other warriors milled about beneath the

Highledge, waiting for Squirrelflight to assign the morning's patrols, he nudged Bayshine closer to the camp wall.

"What's wrong with you?" he mewed. "This mission is special. And Bramblestar chose me to lead it." Bramblestar clearly trusted and respected Nightheart in a way he didn't trust and respect his older warriors. He must see something in him, and it felt good, for a change, to feel special. At last he was being treated like a real member of the Clan. "Aren't you glad I asked you to be part of it?"

"But what's the point of it?" Bayshine mewed.

"Bramblestar needs to know what Tigerstar's up to." Nightheart wondered why he had to explain something so obvious.

"But the Gathering is soon. We can ask Sunbeam and her denmates anything we like without having to sneak onto another Clan's territory without permission."

"We have *Bramblestar's* permission."

"It's not his land," Bayshine grunted. "And he's not the one who might have to explain himself to a ShadowClan patrol."

Nightheart swallowed back frustration. He wasn't going to let Bayshine spoil his excitement. Perhaps his friend was jealous that Bramblestar had chosen him to lead the patrol. "We won't have to explain ourselves to any cat," Nightheart told him firmly. "We'll just slip in and out without any cat noticing."

"And ask a bunch of ShadowClan warriors what their leader's planning." Bayshine looked unconvinced. "Don't you think they'll just report us to Tigerstar?"

"Sunbeam won't betray us."

"But she'll betray her Clan by telling us secrets?"

"It's not like that," Nightheart mewed hotly. "No cat's betraying any cat. We're just collecting information for the good of the Clans."

Bayshine flicked his tail. "It sounds more likely to start a battle than help the Clans." He looked closer at Nightheart. "Are you sure this is what Bramblestar wants?"

"Do you think I'm making it up?" Nightheart bristled defensively. Was it so unbelievable that Bramblestar would ask him to undertake a special mission?

"No, but it just seems risky." Bayshine looked thoughtful. "Do you think Bramblestar was always so impulsive? We were still kits before the impostor, so we've never seen him being a proper leader. Every cat says he was great. Do you think he was? Because he doesn't exactly seem great now."

Nightheart's eyes widened. "He was great when I was doing my assessments!" he mewed hotly. "He was practically the only one who encouraged me. And don't forget he survived Ashfur. And the Dark Forest. He beat *death*, for StarClan's sake."

"Only with Squirrelflight's help," Bayshine reminded him. "It's like he needs Squirrelflight's help with everything now."

How could Bayshine be so disloyal? Sure, Bramblestar seemed a bit confused sometimes. Nightheart, too, had doubted the Clan leader. But perhaps that confusion was just part of his greatness. Perhaps it was just him working things through. Nightheart wasn't going to question it; Bramblestar had given him a chance to help his Clan. "He's our leader, and our leader's word is the *code*! If Bramblestar tells us to go on a mission, then that's what we do."

Bayshine still looked uncomfortable. One of his ears was twitching. "Don't you think Bramblestar is a bit . . ." He hesitated, as though searching for the right word. "A bit disconnected?"

"He's just busy, that's all."

"Even though Squirrelflight does most of the leadership stuff?"

"A deputy's supposed to do leadership stuff sometimes," Nightheart mewed hotly. "But Bramblestar's our leader."

"I know, but . . ." Bayshine seemed to be weighing the idea. "I think I'd rather take orders from Squirrelflight."

Nightheart could hardly believe his ears. "Are you saying you want to disobey Bramblestar's orders?"

Bayshine shifted his paws uneasily. "No," he mewed. "Of course not. But—"

Nightheart wasn't going to listen to anymore. "We're going on the mission tonight," he mewed fiercely. "Just like we've been ordered."

"I guess." Bayshine looked wary.

"We meet up after dark outside camp, just like we planned."

Bayshine blinked at him. "Sure."

The day stayed clear, and by the time Nightheart returned from the afternoon hunt, he was worrying that the lack of cloud cover would make their secret mission difficult. He'd be able to blend in with the shadows, but Bayshine's golden pelt would stand out in the moonlit forest.

The sun was already setting as he followed Finleap, Shell-fur, and Fernstripe through the thorn tunnel and padded into camp. The mouse he was carrying smelled sweet, and his belly was grumbling with hunger, but there would be no time to eat before they left. As he headed toward the fresh-kill pile to drop his prey, he saw Squirrelflight watching him. His fur lifted on the back of his neck when he noticed that Bayshine was with her. His denmate was looking guilty.

Alarm sparked in Nightheart's chest. Bayshine had told Squirrelflight about the mission. He knew it as surely as he knew the mouse he was holding was dead.

"Nightheart." His heart sank as Squirrelflight beckoned him over. "Can I have a word with you, please?" She nodded to Bayshine. "Will you fetch Bramblestar?"

Bayshine glanced apologetically at Nightheart and headed up the tumble of rocks. With a sinking feeling, Nightheart laid his catch on the fresh-kill pile and padded slowly toward Squirrelflight. She looked more worried than angry, but his heart was still pounding as he reached her.

"Bayshine says Bramblestar asked you to sneak into ShadowClan territory," she mewed.

He hesitated. Frustration sparked beneath his pelt.

"Well?"

His pelt grew hot as her gaze sharpened. "Yes," he confessed.

Bramblestar scrambled down from the Highledge, Bayshine at his heels, but Squirrelflight didn't take her eyes from

Nightheart as they stopped beside her. "You realize that's a terrible idea, right?"

Nightheart lifted his chin. "We need to know what Tigerstar's thinking." Bramblestar was here now. He'd back him up. But Bramblestar said nothing. Nightheart looked at him. "We need to know what Tigerstar's thinking, *right?*" he repeated.

But Bramblestar was watching Squirrelflight, his pelt rippling along his spine.

"If I want to know what Tigerstar's thinking," Squirrelflight mewed, "I'll ask him myself."

"But he might lie," Nightheart argued.

"And so might your ShadowClan friends." Squirrelflight turned on Bramblestar. "You want to send two of our most inexperienced warriors on a spying mission." She didn't try to disguise her anger. "Do you realize the trouble they'd cause for every cat if they got caught?"

"We won't get caught," Nightheart mewed.

Squirrelflight ignored him.

"They're just two young toms sneaking out to visit their ShadowClan friends," mewed Bramblestar.

Just two young toms? Nightheart looked at him, shock sparking in his chest. Was that why Bramblestar had chosen him? Because ShadowClan wouldn't see him as a threat? Squirrelflight refused to be swayed. "It's not going to happen."

Bramblestar stiffened. "Isn't that up to me?"

"I'm thinking of the Clan," Squirrelflight snapped.

"And I suppose you were thinking of the Clan when you

went behind my back and took a patrol to see WindClan."
Bramblestar's tail was flicking angrily now.

Nightheart could hardly believe his ears. Were they
going to have the argument they should have had days ago?
Why now? This was supposed to be about *his* mission. "We
wouldn't get caught," he mewed, trying to refocus their attention. "Honest."

But neither of them was listening. "A deputy is supposed
to support their leader, not undermine them!" Bramblestar
snapped.

Birchfall looked up from the fresh-kill pile. Outside
the nursery, Spotfur's attention darted away from her kits.
Around the clearing, their Clanmates turned to look at their
leader and deputy, pelts prickling uneasily.

Squirrelflight lowered her voice. "We shouldn't be having
this conversation here," she hissed.

"Really?" Bramblestar was still glaring at her.

Squirrelflight nodded to Bayshine. "Thanks for letting me
know what was going on," she mewed. She looked at Nightheart. "I'm sorry, but there's not going to be a mission." She
bounded up the rock tumble and looked back at Bramblestar,
clearly waiting for him to follow.

Bramblestar glowered at her. Nightheart tried to catch his
eye. "We won't get caught," he mewed again, pleading this
time. Surely Bramblestar wasn't going to let Squirrelflight
take charge! This mission was too important. But Bramblestar didn't even look at him. Instead he bounded up the rock
tumble and followed Squirrelflight into his den.

"Sorry." Bayshine glanced at his paws. "I didn't know what else to do. I just felt in my gut that Bramblestar had made the wrong—"

Nightheart turned away. "Whatever." He'd been mouse-brained to trust any cat. Disappointment clawed at his belly. This had been his chance to be a real warrior, and Squirrel-flight had ruined it. He headed for the fresh-kill pile. He wasn't hungry anymore, but his Clanmates were watching him, and there was nothing else to do now.

Bayshine hurried after him. "You're not still planning to go, are you?"

"It doesn't seem like I can." Nightheart poked the pile with his paw.

Bayshine blinked at him anxiously. "So you'll stay in camp, right?"

"I have nowhere else to go," Nightheart growled bitterly, and he grabbed a shrew and carried it to a patch of grass beside the camp wall.

Bayshine watched him for a few moments, then chose a sparrow and carried it to where Myrtlebloom and Finch-light were eating below the Highledge. He kept a wary eye on Nightheart for a while, but as Myrtlebloom and Finchlight drew him into their conversation, he seemed to forget that Nightheart and the mission had ever existed.

The camp grew darker as the sun sank behind the forest, until Nightheart could hardly make out his denmates through the shadows. He hadn't touched his shrew. His appetite had died. For a moment, he'd thought Bramblestar had believed

in him. But the ThunderClan leader had let Squirrelflight
snatch his mission away from him without even caring how
Nightheart felt. Bramblestar had been more interested in
their argument about WindClan. *There's no place in ThunderClan
for me.* His Clanmates had made it clear that he was good only
for cleaning dens or filling out patrols, and now Bramblestar
had made him feel invisible. How had he been so flea-brained
as to believe he was important to ThunderClan?

He felt a rush of rage. *It's not fair!* He kicked the shrew away.
If his Clanmates didn't value him, then he'd value himself.
What did they know anyway? He should find a Clan that
would appreciate him. Look how well he'd gotten along with
the other cats on the mission to find catmint. Especially Sunbeam. He should move to ShadowClan and become her mate.
Then, at last, he'd have a chance to be happy. She'd really
seemed to like him on the mission to bring back catmint. And
he'd really liked her. They'd hunted as though they'd trained
together for moons, and she'd been easier to talk to than any
of his Clanmates.

Perhaps he *should* go and find out what she thought of the
idea. He got to his paws. What was he waiting for? He'd go
now and ask her straight out. It would be his own mission.
Squirrelflight couldn't steal it from him. He'd sneak over the
border as he'd planned. It would be easier alone.

He padded into the deepest shadow beneath the camp wall
and followed it to the entrance, keeping an eye on the other
warriors sharing prey and tongues around the clearing. But

no cat noticed him. He wasn't surprised. No cat ever noticed him. It was easy to slip out of camp, unseen.

He'd talk to Sunbeam. Even if she wasn't ready to be mates, she always cheered him up. And he could ask her what Tigerstar was planning after all. If he brought back the news Bramblestar had wanted until Squirrelflight argued with him, they'd have to admit it was a useful mission. He wasn't breaking any rules. *Bramblestar* hadn't told him not to go; *Squirrelflight* had. But Squirrelflight wasn't Clan leader.

It was an easy trek to the lakeshore. When he reached it, Nightheart kept to the waterline and skirted SkyClan territory. He cut back across the pebbly beach into the trees when clouds covered the moon. His black pelt was no more than a shadow on the shore, and once he reached the cover of the pines, he only had to worry about his scent. As he passed a patch of comfrey, he had an idea. He lay down and rolled in it, rubbing his fur into the thick, fragrant leaves until he smelled more like Jayfeather's den than a ThunderClan cat. Then he looked for a track that might lead to the ShadowClan camp.

Broken bracken stalks showed where warriors had passed recently, and he followed their trail between the pines. The birds had ended their day's chatter, and the forest was quiet but for the wind whispering in the branches. Far in the distance, a fox barked, and Nightheart fluffed out his pelt, his eyes wide as he scanned the woods.

Another trail joined this one, and he felt sure he must be heading the right way. Only now, as his anger began to ease, did he wonder how he'd find Sunbeam. Perhaps she'd be on guard duty. Or out hunting. Perhaps he could locate Shadow-Clan's dirtplace and wait in the shadows until she showed up there. Surely she'd make dirt before she slept.

His thoughts spun with so many possibilities that the sound of paw steps on the trail took him by surprise. His heart lurched as he glimpsed white fur on the path. A ShadowClan warrior was heading toward him.

Nightheart froze. Should he duck for cover, or would movement give him away? As he dithered, the warrior halted. It was a ginger-and-white tom, and he was tasting the air.

Nightheart held his breath.

The tom's gaze flashed toward him. It glittered in the moonlight.

"What are you doing here?" The ShadowClan warrior's hackles were high.

Nightheart swallowed. "H-hi." He forced his pelt to stay flat. Perhaps Bramblestar was right—a young tom sneaking out to visit his ShadowClan friend might seem less threatening. And he was being honest. "I came to talk to Sunbeam," he mewed. "We were on the mission to find catmint together. I just wanted to see how she's doing." He rounded his eyes, trying to look innocent.

The white-and-ginger tom padded closer and stopped a tail-length away. Nightheart recognized Blazefire. He'd seen him at Gatherings. Wasn't he the one Sunbeam had wanted to be mates with?

Blazefire was looking at him curiously. "You're friends with *Sunbeam*?"

"Yeah."

"And you crossed the border just to speak to her?"

"Yeah."

Nightheart blinked in surprise. The ShadowClan tom looked pleased to see him. Had Sunbeam mentioned him? Did she like him that much?

"I can fetch her for you, if you like," Blazefire offered.

"Really?" Nightheart stared at him. "Won't you get into trouble?"

"Not if you don't get caught by any other ShadowClan warriors." He nodded toward a thick swath of brambles a little way from the path. "Wait there. I'll bring her to you."

Before Nightheart could answer, Blazefire turned away and disappeared between the shadowy pines.

Nightheart nosed his way gingerly through the prickly branches and crouched among them. Was he really going to ask Sunbeam to be mates? His heart pounded. Perhaps he should try to see how she felt first. Maybe he should stick to his original mission and ask about Tigerstar. He waited, growing more and more nervous until, at last, he heard paw steps and then Blazefire's mew.

"I told him to hide here."

The brambles rustled, and Sunbeam pushed her way through, wincing as the thorns tugged at her fur.

Her eyes lit up as she saw Nightheart. "I've found him,"

she called back to Blazefire.

Nightpelt fluffed out his fur. "Hi." He tried to read her gaze. Was she happy to see him?

"Don't stay out too long," Blazefire called to Sunbeam through the branches.

"He won't tell any cat, will he?" Nightheart asked Sunbeam anxiously as Blazefire headed away. "I don't want to get you in trouble."

"I think he's happy you came to see me," Sunbeam told him.

"Are *you* happy I came to see you?"

"Sure." She purred. "But why are you here? It's dangerous."

He hesitated. *I want to become your mate and move to ShadowClan.* "I just wanted to see a friendly face," he mewed weakly.

Her eyes rounded sympathetically. "Are you still having a hard time in ThunderClan?"

She was so kind. His heart seemed suddenly to burst with the hurt that had been festering there. "No cat appreciates me there," he blurted. Bramblestar, Squirrelflight, Bayshine— they'd all been so dismissive of his special mission. "I don't fit in at all. Even Sparkpelt and Finchlight don't want me around."

"I'm sure that's not true," Sunbeam mewed.

"It feels true." He sat down. "Do you remember when we caught the rabbit on the way to Twolegplace?"

"Yes." Her whiskers twitched happily.

"You didn't boss me around or tell me I didn't have enough experience," he told her. "You were the first cat to treat me like a real warrior."

"You *are* a real warrior," she mewed.

"If only my Clanmates thought so," he mewed. "It's like you're the only cat who really *sees* me."

"I know how you feel." She sat beside him. "Blazefire and Lightleap are being friendly to me again, like nothing ever happened. It makes my pelt burn." She flexed her claws. "It's like they don't even know they betrayed me. Like it's fine with them if they want to hang out with me sometimes and then, other times, just hang out with each other, like they're the only two cats in ShadowClan. My feelings are totally invisible to them."

"At least you get along with your mother and littermates," Nightheart reminded her.

"I get along with my *littermates*," Sunbeam told him. "But Berryheart is acting weird right now. She's got this thing about Fringewhisker—"

"She used to be a SkyClan cat, right?" Nightheart narrowed his eyes.

"Yeah." As Sunbeam stared into the brambles, he suddenly remembered that Sunbeam wasn't entirely approving of cats who joined other Clans. His belly tightened. *She won't want me to join ShadowClan.*

Sunbeam went on. "She joined ShadowClan to be with my brother, Spireclaw. But Berryheart thinks she should never have been allowed to join, and she's trying to drive her out. This afternoon, she even lied to get Fringewhisker in trouble. Spireclaw is going to be so upset when he finds out. And I can't believe how many of our Clanmates feel the same way. If

Berryheart keeps going on about *Clan-swappers* and loyalty and the warrior code, she could end up dividing the whole Clan."

Nightheart looked at her. Did this mean Sunbeam herself had changed her mind about cats that switched Clans? "And you . . . don't agree with Berryheart?" he asked.

"Of course not," she mewed. "Berryheart is being totally unreasonable. And *mean*. Fringewhisker is a really good warrior, and she's trying so hard to fit in. Spireclaw will be heartbroken if she leaves." Her eyes glittered with worry. "What if he leaves with her?"

Nightheart moved closer. It sounded like Sunbeam, at least, might be okay with him joining ShadowClan. "So you want Fringewhisker to stay?"

"Of course."

"And you think inter-Clan relationships are fine?"

"I think they make the Clans stronger," she mewed. "Berryheart is stuck in the past, that's all. She thinks that all cats from outside ShadowClan must be rogues, even if they're warriors. But the Clans have changed since she was young. We're all closer now, and it makes sense for cats to choose who to love and where to raise their kits."

Nightheart shifted his paws nervously. "So if one day I, say, wanted to join ShadowClan . . . that would be okay with you?"

"Sure." Sunbeam looked at him, her large, round eyes shining in the moonlight. "We need all the strong, young warriors we can get."

Relief swept through Nightheart's pelt. She wanted him to join ShadowClan. Suddenly he had choices and the possibility of a happy future. He kept his tail from quivering with excitement. He didn't want to push his idea too far yet. Sunbeam would need time to get used to it.

She looked at him. "Shouldn't you get back to your camp?" she mewed. "Someone might notice you're missing."

He got to his paws. She was right. "I guess I should go." But he wanted to find out about Tigerstar and RiverClan. He wanted to see the look on Squirrelflight's face when he proved that this wasn't a useless mission after all. She might start to respect him at last. He hesitated, wondering how to ask. He didn't want Sunbeam to think Tigerstar was the only reason he'd come. "It's just that Bramblestar's kind of worried," he mewed hesitantly.

She looked puzzled. "What's he worried about?"

"RiverClan," Nightheart told her.

"RiverClan?" She frowned. "What's that got to do with Bramblestar?"

"He's just wondering what Tigerstar's plans are, that's all." He tried to sound casual, but her gaze looked suddenly guarded. "You don't have to tell me anything," he added quickly. "Bramblestar just wants to be sure nothing's going to destroy the peace between the Clans." He glanced at his paws, then back at her. "I don't suppose you know whether Tigerstar's planning to go ahead and advise RiverClan? You know . . . like . . . *intervene*."

"I don't see why." She eyed him thoughtfully. "The other Clans were pretty clear at the Gathering that they thought it was a bad idea."

"But is that enough to deter Tigerstar?" Nightheart pressed gently.

"I *guess* so." She tipped her head to one side, as though she hadn't really considered how far Tigerstar might go. "But he *did* seem pretty angry on the way home."

Nightheart leaned closer. Sunbeam clearly trusted him enough to share her thoughts with him; he felt surer than ever of their connection. They'd be *great* mates.

She went on. "He thinks some cat should do something about RiverClan since they're such a mess. And he was annoyed the other Clans didn't trust him."

"But he's not planning to invade RiverClan, right?" Nightheart searched her gaze.

"I guess if the other Clans are going to wait, then Tigerstar will wait too." Her gaze suddenly fixed on him, sharpening with alarm. "Isn't it *horrible* that RiverClan lost their leader and deputy so close together? Can you imagine how scary that would be?"

Nightheart tried to picture ThunderClan without Bramblestar *or* Squirrelflight. ThunderClan had come close to losing them both in the Dark Forest. What if they had? Who would have replaced them? Lionblaze? Birchfall? His pelt prickled uneasily. He didn't like the idea of either warrior leading ThunderClan. "Let's hope we never have to find out," he mewed.

"Nightheart?" Sunbeam gazed distractedly into the brambles.

"Yeah?"

"Is it mouse-brained of me to be hurt that Lightleap and Blazefire like each other more than me now?" She looked at him so sadly that his heart pricked with sympathy. "Sometimes I think I'm just acting like a jealous kit."

"They were your best friends, weren't they? And they broke your heart."

"Yeah."

"Then of course it hurts." Nightheart padded closer and touched his nose to her ear. He remembered Bayshine standing beside Squirrelflight earlier. His so-called best friend had ruined his mission. "I know what it feels like to be betrayed. It really hurts."

She looked at him. "I hate the thought of any cat hurting you," she mewed. "You're so kind and so easy to talk to."

"Am I?" He felt warmth seeping through his pelt.

"Yes."

"So are—"

Before he could finish, he heard mewing along the trail. His pelt rippled nervously. It sounded like a ShadowClan patrol.

"You'd better go." Sunbeam got to her paws and nudged him away. "I'll distract them. You go that way." She nodded to where the brambles opened into a gully. "Follow the path until it gets rocky, then head for the lake. You'll be able to see it through the trees."

He nodded his thanks, not daring to speak in case he was heard. As she turned in the direction of her Clanmates' voices, he hurried toward the gap in the brambles.

He ran until he could see the lake sparkling between the pines, then raced down the slope to the shore. Once he reached the lake, relief swamped him. His paws felt suddenly light. The cold night air felt refreshing. Sunbeam wanted him to join ShadowClan. His heart seemed to shine. Hope rose his chest. He belonged with her, didn't he? He could make a fresh start with some cat who believed in him.

CHAPTER 18

❧

Sunbeam pricked her ears. The mews on the trail that had sent Nightheart scurrying home were moving closer. And yet she couldn't drag her thoughts from his question. *He's not planning to invade RiverClan, right?* Did Nightheart really think that was a possibility? Was ShadowClan on the verge of war?

She nosed her way from the brambles, still unnerved by his words, but she'd promised to distract whichever of her Clanmates were coming along the trail. Her thoughts wandered back to Nightheart as she stood in the moonlight and squinted to see who it was.

His suspicions about Tigerstar weren't the only reason he'd crossed the border to see her. He'd sounded unhappy in ThunderClan. Unhappy enough to suggest moving to ShadowClan. And he'd wanted to talk about it. She felt a twinge of pity for the ThunderClan tom. He deserved to be happy. Why couldn't his Clan see what a great cat he was?

What if he does move to ShadowClan? Her heart quickened. Without Blazefire's and Lightleap's companionship, she'd been feeling lonely. But if Nightheart joined the Clan, she'd have a real friend again. ThunderClan's loss would be her gain.

Two figures padded from the shadows of the pines, and she shook out her pelt. Spireclaw was talking to Berryheart, and though their mews were hushed, she could hear anger in them. Her brother must have found out that his mother had tricked Fringewhisker into giving prey to SkyClan in the hope that Tigerstar would banish the former SkyClan cat from ShadowClan. He was furious.

"Leave Fringewhisker alone!" Spireclaw growled.

"She shouldn't be here," Berryheart snapped back.

They hadn't noticed Sunbeam, and she moved back into the shadows while they talked. *Berryheart wouldn't listen to me, but maybe Spireclaw can make her see reason.* She hoped so, even though they seemed furious with each other.

"Would you rather I went to SkyClan?" Spireclaw demanded.

Berryheart stiffened. Had Spireclaw's threat surprised her? Surely she'd considered that Spireclaw might follow his mate if Berryheart succeeded in driving her out. But the idea only seemed to make her angrier. "Have you no loyalty?" she spat.

"I'm loyal to Fringewhisker!"

"And what about your Clan?" Berryheart was bristling.

Spireclaw glared at her. "You know I'd die to protect whatever Clan I belong to," he hissed. "And if I end up fighting for SkyClan rather than ShadowClan, you'll only have yourself to blame."

Sunbeam's belly tightened. She had to stop this before they said something they couldn't take back. She padded into the moonlight once more and stood in their path.

"Hey, Berryheart." She tried to look unconcerned, as if she hadn't heard any of their argument.

Her mother's eyes narrowed. "What are you doing here?"

"Just getting some air," Sunbeam told her.

But Berryheart's nose was twitching. "You smell strange."

"Do I?" Sunbeam asked innocently. She forced her pelt not to ruffle. Could Berryheart smell Nightheart's scent on her?

Spireclaw padded around her, his mouth open to taste the air. "You smell like Puddleshine's den."

Puddleshine's den? Sunbeam was confused. Then she remembered the strong comfrey smell on Nightheart's pelt. He must have rolled in some to disguise his scent. She felt a rush of gratitude for his cleverness. "I walked through a patch of comfrey."

"Where?" Berryheart's gaze sparked with suspicion.

"Back there somewhere." Sunbeam nodded vaguely toward the shadows beyond the bramble bushes.

Spireclaw seemed satisfied. He looked back at camp. "I'm going to finish my meal," he mewed. "Fringewhisker will be waiting for me."

"I'll come with you," Sunbeam told him. She didn't want to be left alone with Berryheart. Her mother might ask more questions. Instead she followed Spireclaw along the track toward the entrance, relieved that she'd stopped them from arguing.

"Is Fringewhisker okay?" she asked.

"Yeah," he mewed. "I guess. Thanks for sticking up for her."

"Berryheart was out of line," she mewed. "I mean, I can

understand why she's worried, after Darktail and everything."
She wanted Spireclaw to know that Berryheart had her reasons to hate change, even if they were making her behave like
she was fox-hearted. "But it was wrong of her to get Fringewhisker in trouble on purpose."

Spireclaw glanced at Sunbeam. "She needs to get her whiskers out of the past," he mewed. "Fringewhisker's not a rogue,
and the Clans aren't enemies anymore."

I wonder if RiverClan agrees. Nightheart's question about
Tigerstar's intentions toward the troubled Clan was still worrying her as they reached camp and Spireclaw ducked through
the entrance tunnel. She followed, flicking her tail in greeting
to Fringewhisker, who was waiting for Spireclaw, a juicy rabbit at her paws.

Around the clearing, ShadowClan was eating. Cloverfoot
and Tigerstar were sharing a pigeon. Dovewing was outside
the nursery with Birchkit, Whisperkit, and Firkit, and Cinnamontail reclined nearby, enjoying a vole as her kits wrestled
a few tail-lengths away. *They must be feeling stronger,* Sunbeam
mused. Yarrowleaf scratched fleas from her pelt in front of
the warriors' den, and Flaxfoot washed his face beside a fresh
heap of mouse bones.

As Spireclaw crossed the clearing to join his mate, Flaxfoot
beckoned Sunbeam with a nod.

"I saved you this." The brown tabby tom pushed a shrew
toward her. "I know it's your favorite." The warm scent of prey
billowed in his breath. "Where have you been?" He tasted the
air. "You smell like herbs."

"I walked through a comfrey patch." She sniffed the shrew, grateful that Flaxfoot had thought of her. Perhaps she wasn't as friendless in ShadowClan as she'd thought. Could she ask him about Tigerstar's plans? Even if he didn't know, it might be reassuring to talk about it with a Clanmate.

Flaxfoot blinked at her. "Do I have mouse blood in my whiskers?"

Sunbeam realized she was staring at him. "Something's worrying me," she mewed tentatively.

Flaxfoot narrowed his gaze. "What?"

"I heard a rumor." She didn't mention where.

Flaxfoot leaned closer. "What about?"

"You know what Tigerstar said at the Gathering," she mewed. "About helping RiverClan until they found a proper leader."

"Sure." Flaxfoot nodded.

"I heard that he's actually planning to invade."

"Invade?" Flaxfoot's eyes widened. "Where? RiverClan?"

"Yes." Sunbeam shifted her weight. "Have you heard anything like that?"

"No." Flaxfoot glanced at Tigerstar and Cloverfoot, as though looking for clues in their expressions.

"Do you think he will?"

"Invade?" Flaxfoot frowned. "I don't know. RiverClan must be pretty weak right now, but why would Tigerstar want river land? ShadowClan cats don't eat fish."

"Will you keep your ears open?" Sunbeam asked him. "In case you hear anything."

"Sure."

"It's probably nothing," Sunbeam told him. She didn't want to start a panic.

"Okay." Flaxfoot began to wash his muzzle once more.

Sunbeam felt relieved. Nightheart's suspicions felt less scary now that she'd shared them with a Clanmate. And if Flaxfoot hadn't heard anything about invasion plans, she felt more confident that it was just an empty ThunderClan rumor.

"Enjoy." Flaxfoot got to his paws and nodded at the shrew. "I'm off to use the dirtplace."

As he padded away, Sunbeam took a bite. She was hungry, and the shrew tasted musky and sweet. The moon was high now, its light dappling the camp, and she settled down happily to enjoy her meal.

Was Nightheart really considering joining ShadowClan? Her heart quickened again. She could teach him how to be a ShadowClan warrior—the best places to hunt frogs, how to climb pine trees without getting needles in his pads. It would be fun. And they could hang out after patrols and talk as much as they liked instead of hiding in brambles or only see-ing each other on emergency missions or at Gatherings. She could really get to know him. A purr gathered in her throat and she took another bite of shrew. Her mind was buzzing by the time she finished it, still picturing Clan life with Night-heart. Lost in her thoughts, she forgot to wash, but lay happily on her flank and let her imagination drift.

"My plans are none of your business!" Tigerstar's angry hiss made her look up.

She hadn't noticed her mother return to camp, but Berry-heart was facing the ShadowClan leader, her tail swishing accusingly as she glared at him.

Tigerstar was on his paws now, his hackles raised. "Don't forget, I'm the leader of ShadowClan, not you."

"I'm not disputing that!" Berryheart's pelt twitched along her flank. "But you're *our* leader! Not RiverClan's!"

Sunbeam's heart lurched. What did Berryheart mean? She got to her paws, her fur sparking with alarm.

Tigerstar was staring at her mother. "No cat said I was RiverClan's leader!"

"Not yet," Berryheart growled.

"What in StarClan are you talking about?" Tigerstar stared at her, furious and bewildered.

"You want to invade RiverClan," Berryheart snapped. "But ShadowClan won't support you. It would be reckless and pointless." Her eyes flashed accusingly. "I know that you're angry you lost a kit because RiverClan wouldn't share their catmint. But your need for revenge for Rowankit shouldn't endanger your Clan."

Tigerstar flinched as though she'd lashed out at him with her claws. Then the muscles on his shoulders flexed ominously.

Sunbeam froze. Was he going to attack Berryheart? Rage was burning in the ShadowClan leader's eyes. She'd never seen Tigerstar so angry.

"How dare you," he hissed. "I would never use my own grief to send my Clan to war."

Dovewing scrambled to her paws, her eyes round. Birchkit, Whisperkit, and Firkit were play fighting beside her, unaware of the argument at the other side of the camp. But the rest of the Clan had looked up. Even Cinnamontail and her kits sat at attention. Yarrowleaf watched through narrowed eyes. Spireclaw and Fringewhisker exchanged looks. Flaxfoot, back from the dirtplace, halted beside the warriors' den, his ears flicking nervously.

The tip of Berryheart's tail twitched. Tigerstar was still glaring at her in undisguised fury. She must have realized she'd gone too far. "I didn't mean—"

Tigerstar cut her off. "And what in StarClan are you even talking about?" he snarled. "Where did you get the mouse-brained idea I want to invade RiverClan?"

Sunbeam's heart seemed to skip a beat. That was exactly what she'd told Flaxfoot. She glared at the brown tabby tom, and he eyed her guiltily, then looked away. *You told her what I said!* Berryheart's gaze flashed toward her just long enough to accuse her with a look. A chill spread beneath Sunbeam's pelt.

Tigerstar hadn't finished. "I don't want to invade any Clan," he growled. "Certainly not for revenge. Wherever you got the notion, it was wrong. RiverClan is in trouble, and if I can do something to help them, then I will." He shifted his paws and allowed his pelt to smooth before adding, more softly, "I don't blame any Clan for what happened to Rowankit. I only want to protect ShadowClan. And that may mean helping RiverClan."

Berryheart's tail twitched again. "RiverClan's troubles are

their own," she mewed testily. "I don't see why we have to get involved."

"What affects RiverClan affects us," Tigerstar told her firmly. "Look how fast ThunderClan's turmoil spread to every Clan after the impostor took over. If they'd been honest about what was happening, we could have helped before it threw all of us into chaos."

"Helping is one thing." Berryheart gazed back at him steadily. "But stepping in where we're not welcome will stir up a wasps' nest of trouble, and we're the ones who'll get stung."

"Let me worry about that," Tigerstar mewed. "And next time you hear rumors about what I'm going to do, check that they're true before questioning your leader." He looked around the clearing at the watching ShadowClan warriors. "Go back to your meals or your washing or whatever you were doing," he told them. "Berryheart has said her piece and so have I. I hope it's put an end to the matter."

Sunbeam didn't move, but her heart was pounding. Flaxfoot had betrayed her confidence. And to her *mother*. Didn't he realize she'd make a meal of it? She certainly wasn't going to be pleased that she'd looked like a fool in front of the Clan.

Sunbeam already knew who Berryheart would blame for her humiliation. Her mother's fur was rippling along her spine as she turned away from Tigerstar, and she wondered whether to hide until her mother calmed down. But indignation kept her paws rooted to the ground. Why should she be sorry? She'd told Flaxfoot in confidence. She lifted her chin as Berryheart marched toward her, her amber gaze as hard as stone.

"How could you pass on *lies!*" Berryheart demanded as she reached Sunbeam.

"It wasn't a *lie*," Sunbeam mewed. "It was something I heard. And I didn't ask Flaxfoot to tell every cat he met. I thought he realized it was just a rumor."

But Berryheart wasn't ready to be appeased. "You should find out if rumors are true before you go spreading them around!" she snapped. "Where did you hear such nonsense?"

Sunbeam froze as she pictured herself huddling behind the brambles with Nightheart. Guilt swept over her. "I just heard it."

"Not in ShadowClan you didn't," Berryheart mewed. "No cat in ShadowClan has mentioned such a thing. If they had, I'd have known about it already." She thrust her muzzle closer. "Where did you hear it?"

Sunbeam dropped her gaze. "ThunderClan," she mumbled.

"ThunderClan?" Outrage edged Berryheart's mew. "What were you doing in ThunderClan?"

"I wasn't," she mewed. "It was just a cat I met at . . ." She couldn't say she'd met him on the mission to fetch catmint. Berryheart might guess who it was. "At the Gathering."

Berryheart snorted. "Don't you know ThunderClan cats are liars? This cat probably made up this rumor just to spread fear in ShadowClan."

"They'd never do that!" Sunbeam fluffed out her pelt.

Berryheart glared at her. "Do you trust a ThunderClan cat more than your own Clanmates?"

"It's not like that!"

"Then what is it like?"

Sunbeam stared at her mother, not knowing what to say. She guessed her best option was to admit her mistake and change the subject. "I'm sorry I embarrassed you," she mewed. "I didn't know you'd go straight to Tigerstar. I told Flaxfoot in confidence. I didn't know if it was true or not. I was just worried about it and I needed to share."

Flaxfoot was watching meekly from the other side of the clearing. Frustration surged in Sunbeam's chest. Was there no cat in ShadowClan she could trust?

Berryheart's tail was lashing.

This wasn't fair! None of it was fair. Sunbeam ducked past her mother and raced out of camp. She knew her Clanmates would be watching, but she didn't care. She couldn't trust any of them. No cat was on her side. If she had to be alone, she'd rather be alone *by herself.*

As she stormed out of the bramble tunnel, she heard fallen leaves rustling beside the camp wall. She turned her head and saw Blazefire and Lightleap. Scrambling to a halt, she stared at them. Their pelts were touching and their muzzles were so close they must be able to taste the prey on each other's lips.

Lightleap saw her and stiffened.

Blazefire moved away.

At least they had the decency to look embarrassed. Sunbeam swallowed back a growl. *Friends!* It was obvious they were more than friends. Not only had they excluded her, but they'd lied to her too.

She waited for an explanation, but Lightleap only looked

away. Sunbeam felt breathless with hurt. Her former friend wasn't even going to apologize. She turned away and raced into the woods, rage and grief pounding in her ears. Was every cat in the Clan going to betray her today?

"Sunbeam!" Blazefire's yowl rang through the woods. "Stop! We have to talk!"

She pushed harder. She didn't want to talk to any cat, let alone him.

"Please!" He sounded desperate.

Okay, then. He could explain himself. He could tell her why he'd lied. And why he had feelings for Lightleap and not her. She skidded to a halt and turned to glare at him.

He pulled up. "I'm sorry," he puffed. "I'm really sorry."

"Are you?"

"I didn't want you to find out this way."

"You said you were just friends."

"We were, but . . ." He hesitated, clearly finding this difficult. "Our feelings grew. We didn't mean for them to. We just couldn't help it."

Sunbeam felt her breath slowing. To her surprise, the pain in her heart was dissolving. She gazed at him, wondering if his words had eased it, but that wasn't it. As the shock wore off, she realized she didn't care. Of course she was upset that Lightleap had gone behind her back after promising that Blazefire was only a friend. And her pride was wounded; after all, Blazefire had chosen Lightleap over her. But the idea that their relationship had moved past friendship into something more serious didn't hurt her as much as she'd thought it would.

Blazefire was staring at her apologetically, his expression so worried that she knew he was genuinely concerned about her. She blinked at him, realizing that she'd barely thought about him in days. There was another tom, from a Clan two borders away, who'd been occupying her thoughts: a tom who'd crossed into forbidden territory just to talk to her. Her heart felt suddenly warm. Happiness surged beneath her pelt.

"It's okay," she told Blazefire. And she meant it.

He stared at her. "Are you sure?"

"Yes." She lifted her tail. "You'd better go back and talk to Lightleap. She's probably worried. Besides . . ." She shook out her pelt. "I've got more important things to do." She turned away and headed into the woods. For the first time in a moon, her heart felt as light as thistledown.

CHAPTER 19

Frostpaw felt the chill of the night air even more sharply as Owl-nose walked away. Shadowed by heather and with the stream glittering in the moonlight beside him, the brown tabby tom looked suddenly stronger and more confident than he had in days, no longer a leader but a warrior. Frostpaw felt a rush of respect for him. It must have been hard to admit he wasn't cut out to be RiverClan's leader. Now he was going home to explain his decision to his Clanmates. They might approve. She hoped they'd at least be kind. But it didn't solve River-Clan's problems. They had no leader now, not even a leader they didn't entirely believe in.

But this must mean that StarClan hadn't meant Owlnose to be leader. *How could I have gotten it so wrong?*

Fidgetflake scrambled down from the edge of the hollow and stared after Owlnose. "Where's he going?"

"He doesn't want to be leader," Frostpaw told him.

Mothwing landed beside them, her tail bushed in alarm. "He can't leave!"

"You can't force a cat to be leader," Frostpaw mewed.

Fidgetflake looked at her. "What are you going to do now?"

"I don't know." Frostpaw watched Owlnose disappear into the darkness. She felt numb. *If not Owlnose, who?*

Mothwing's eyes glittered with disappointment. "I thought he was the answer."

Guilt stirred in Frostpaw's belly. *This is my fault.* She'd misunderstood StarClan and chosen the wrong cat to be RiverClan's leader.

How could this have happened? Her chest tightened, and suddenly she felt like she couldn't breathe. *I've never seen all of StarClan. My visions aren't like the other medicine cats'.*

What if she hadn't *misunderstood*? What if she'd only *imagined* what StarClan had told her? What if she had never spoken to StarClan at all?

Her head was spinning. *I was RiverClan's last hope, and I failed.*

Fidgetflake looked grim. "We must tell the other Clans."

"None of them can know we're vulnerable!" Mothwing glared at him. "It's bad enough *you* know. You have to keep this secret."

"But the other medicine cats could help you," Fidgetflake insisted. "If we all come here tomorrow night, we can figure this out."

"I don't want the other Clans to know," Mothwing growled. "You heard Tigerstar at the Gathering. He wants to run RiverClan. Isn't that why Leafstar sent you to us? To stop Tigerstar?" She snorted. "The moment he finds out we still don't have a leader, he'll take over. And how long before

SkyClan and ThunderClan stick their paws in?"

Fidgetflake held her gaze. "RiverClan needs help," he pressed.

"We can sort it out by ourselves," Mothwing snapped.

"Can you?" He stared at the RiverClan medicine cat.

Mothwing didn't answer.

Frostpaw shivered. Sorting it out by themselves meant she'd have to choose another leader on her own. If she'd been wrong the first time, she might be wrong again. She no longer trusted her connection with StarClan to guide her. *I might be the problem.* Perhaps Fidgetflake was right. Perhaps they *did* need help.

Fidgetflake shifted his paws. "I'm going back to SkyClan," he told them. "I'm going to call an emergency meeting of the medicine cats." He looked encouragingly at Mothwing. "We can fix this, I promise."

She stared bleakly back at him. "I don't know if any cat can fix this."

"Of course they can." Fidgetflake turned to Frostpaw. "Go to the Moonpool," he mewed. "Share with StarClan. Your ancestors might help you now that Owlnose has walked away."

Frostpaw hoped he was right, but doubt tugged in her belly. If StarClan could help, wouldn't they have done so by now? *What if I can't share with them? But who else is there?* She watched as the SkyClan medicine cat headed toward the lake. "Wait." Her mew caught in her throat as she called after him. "What if I can't reach them?"

He glanced back. "You won't know unless you try."

"Come on." Mothwing padded to the bottom of the rocks.

Frostpaw watched her, her heart pounding. "Now?"

"Fidgetflake might be right," Mothwing told her. "StarClan might help now."

Reluctantly, Frostpaw followed. The whole Clan depended on her sharing with StarClan, and she wasn't certain she could. All this time, she'd been swiping at butterflies, trying to hook one in her claws, but they'd always been just out of reach. Now everything seemed to depend on her catching one, and she felt suddenly very young and small, and she wasn't at all sure she knew what she was doing.

She followed Mothwing down the spiral of paw prints that led to the Moonpool, imagining the countless cats that had worn away the stone—wiser cats than her, with a more powerful connection to StarClan that had drawn them here moon after moon. She wondered if she even deserved to set paw on this ancient path. If only Curlfeather were here to reassure her that her connection with StarClan was strong . . . that it was even *real*.

Mothwing touched her nose to Frostpaw's head as they reached the bottom. "You can do this," she breathed.

Frostpaw felt a wave of gratitude. Mothwing seemed to believe in her connection to StarClan as much as Curlfeather had. Frostpaw tried to believe in it herself as she lay down beside the water and touched her nose to its glittering surface.

She closed her eyes and strained to see into her thoughts. Blackness screened them, and she wondered if she was simply looking into her eyelids as they blocked out the night.

She strained harder, struggling to see beyond the flesh and fur that made her no more than an ordinary cat. Her heart thumped. Her breathing grew shallow as panic quickened in her blood. There was nothing to see. There was no cat here. StarClan was unreachable.

Surely they *must* come. RiverClan was in trouble. Tigerstar had more or less threatened to take over if they couldn't find a leader. Why wasn't Mistystar reaching out? Why was Curlfeather silent? Frostpaw's panic deepened, snatching her breath until she thought she would explode with it.

She scrambled to her paws. "I can't do it!" Horror swirled around her. "I can't speak to StarClan! I can't see anything except my own thoughts. I can't feel anything except my body." Why had she ever believed she was a medicine cat? The real medicine cats' visions had been clear, sharper even than a dream. They'd seen ancestors from before they'd even been born. They'd walked in StarClan's hunting grounds. It had never been like that for Frostpaw. Mothwing's eyes flashed with fear, and Frostpaw's panic quickened. "I thought I had a connection with them," she mewed desperately. "Really, I did. But I was wrong, and now I can see that. My visions always felt wrong, and the more I hear other medicine cats talk about StarClan, the more I see that I haven't spoken to them at all!" She wanted to drop to her belly and sob into her paws. How could she have been so wrong?

Mothwing seemed to gather herself. She ran her tail along Frostpaw's spine. "Take a breath," she mewed. "You're still just an apprentice. You need to give it time."

"But we don't *have* time!" Frostpaw shook off Mothwing's tail and blinked at her in alarm. "RiverClan is depending on me, and Fidgetflake is about to tell every cat about Owlnose. What if—" She couldn't even find the words to describe the disaster she felt sure would engulf RiverClan if she didn't contact StarClan right now.

"Look at me." Mothwing's eyes were dark as she met her gaze. "You mustn't tell *any cat* about this. We'll figure something out. But for now, no cat should know that you can't reach StarClan. It's happened to medicine cats before," she mewed. "It doesn't mean you don't have a connection to them, only that you can't reach them right now." Her eyes glistened. "I'm sorry I can't help you with this. I'm your mentor. I should be able to teach you. But you have to master this skill alone. That means it'll be harder for you than for an ordinary medicine-cat apprentice. But you're smart, and you're quick, and your heart is in the right place. You can do this. I know you can. You just need to keep trying."

Frostpaw stared back at her mentor. She was desperate to believe her. *Of course* she didn't know how to contact StarClan properly. Mothwing hadn't been able to show her. She'd had to figure everything out by herself. But if she kept trying, she might find a connection. She forced herself to hope. Maybe it was just a question of practice.

And yet that didn't help RiverClan now. "I need to share with them," she whimpered. "RiverClan has no leader." She blinked hopefully at Mothwing, but Mothwing's gaze had drifted away.

"RiverClan needs *one* medicine cat with a connection." Mothwing seemed to be talking to herself. "If the other Clans think we can't even contact StarClan—" She broke off and looked at Frostpaw once more. "No cat can know." She nudged Frostpaw toward the water. "Try again. You might find the way."

Every hair on Frostpaw's pelt seemed to shrink from the idea. But she knew she had to try. *I can do this,* she told herself as she lay down beside the water. *I have to do this.* She closed her eyes and touched her nose to the shimmering surface once more. But she couldn't relax. She was aware only of the blood pulsing in her ears and behind her eyes. Her thoughts raced, too fast to even reach for StarClan. Memories of her mother darted through her mind. Curlfeather's frantic face flashed before her. *Trust no cat.*

Frostpaw was suddenly aware of the great, cold space around her and the wind whispering above the cliffs. The moor stretched, bleak and empty, to the horizon, and she felt very far from home.

Trust no cat. Her mother had died here. *What if I die too?* She remembered the piles of bones Fidgetflake had mentioned. Had some cat *wanted* Curlfeather to die? *Perhaps they want me dead as well.*

Fear was rooted deep inside her now, pressing tendrils around her heart and twisting in her belly. *What if I'm not a real medicine cat? What could I be? A warrior?* She'd have to start her training, moons behind Graypaw and Mistpaw, and learn skills she'd never even thought about. Could she fish anywhere deeper than the river shallows? Could she stalk birds in the water meadow?

Of course I can. She pushed back panic. *I'll be a warrior if I have to.* She let a new future unfurl ahead of her, one where it didn't matter if StarClan didn't share with her. She'd protect her Clan. She'd be strong and brave. Nothing would scare her ever again. She'd have a mate. Her heart quickened. *Splashtail.* At last, she could explore her feelings for him. She wouldn't have to pretend she didn't care. They might fall in love and become mates and have kits. She could name one after her mother.

Her heart sang and her fear ebbed. Suddenly, she felt stronger and more certain than she had in ages. There was no need to hide the fact that she had no connection with StarClan. Whatever Mothwing said, she was going to be honest. What was the point in lying? Fidgetflake already suspected that Mistystar and Reedwhisker hadn't died of greencough. Now she would tell him everything. This was a problem that needed a *real* medicine cat to fix—a medicine cat who could reach StarClan.

Frostpaw knew Mothwing would be disappointed, she might even be angry, but in the end it would be best for River-Clan. There would be no more secrets to confuse and frighten her. She was so tired of watching every word and living with the desperate hope that if she just kept her mouth shut long enough, everything would work out.

She was certain now. StarClan wasn't going to share with her. They never had. She opened her eyes and got to her paws. "We should go home," she told Mothwing.

"Couldn't you see them?" Mothwing's ears twitched nervously.

"No." Frostpaw headed toward the edge of the hollow. She felt a pang of guilt. She was going to disobey her mentor. But she needed to disobey. *Trust no cat.* Her mother's words were set deep into her heart, and they seemed to ring in her mind with every beat.

Mothwing's intentions were good. Frostpaw was certain of it. Her mentor only wanted the best for RiverClan. But Mothwing was expecting too much of her, and Frostpaw knew that she wasn't strong enough to carry the fate of RiverClan on her shoulders. *I'm only an apprentice.*

She stopped at the top of the dimpled slope and looked back.

Mothwing was following, her gaze sharp with curiosity.

Frostpaw turned away. *I have to tell the truth.* It was the only way to be free of this fear. No cat should expect an apprentice to decide the fate of her Clan.

Mothwing barely spoke on the journey home. She asked once if Frostpaw was sure she hadn't contacted StarClan, as though she might have spoken to them without realizing. But Frostpaw said no and hurried ahead, and kept up the pace the whole way so that Mothwing had no chance to ask again. The sun was rising beyond the reed beds as they neared the camp.

Only now did Frostpaw slow. If she was going to be honest, she'd begin by being honest with Mothwing.

As they neared the river's edge, she lifted her chin. "I'm going to tell them I can't reach StarClan," she mewed.

Mothwing stopped and stared at her. "You can't." She sounded frightened. "If the other Clans see how vulnerable we are, we'll be in danger."

Frostpaw looked at her for a moment, then waded into the river. "Lying won't make us strong," she mewed as she pushed out into the chilly water and swam to the other side.

Mothwing followed. Her eyes were shadowed with foreboding as she climbed out of the river. "You *must* have a connection with StarClan," she mewed. "How else will we choose a leader?"

Frostpaw didn't answer. It wasn't her problem anymore. Without even shaking the water from her fur, she headed along the path that led to the camp entrance.

A familiar scent touched her nose. *That shouldn't be here.* Her belly tightened as it grew stronger. ShadowClan stench hung in the air, thick and warm, as though this were their camp, not RiverClan's.

Mothwing caught up with her. Her hackles lifted as she tasted the air. She ducked through the entrance tunnel, and Frostpaw raced after her, alarm shrilling through her pelt as she burst into the clearing.

Tigerstar stood at the center, his broad head and shoulders silhouetted against the pink dawn sky. His pelt gleamed, and around him a patrol of ShadowClan warriors scanned the camp. Their eyes were slitted with determination. RiverClan was watching from the edges of the camp as though frozen to the earth. Frostpaw smelled fear-scent, and dread hollowed out her heart. Was Tigerstar making good on his promise to help RiverClan? If he was, why had he brought so many warriors?

CHAPTER 20

Nightheart raced through the dark. The moon was high and shining through the canopy of branches. As he neared the Thunder-Clan camp, his paws were still fizzing with excitement. At last, his future seemed clear and bright. He was going to be free of ThunderClan's suffocating hollow; in ShadowClan, he would find the respect he deserved. *And* he'd have Sunbeam as a mate. She'd encourage him more than any ThunderClan cat ever had. And he'd encourage her in return, of course. They'd support each other, and right now it sounded like she needed the support as much as he did.

He leaped over a fallen branch and swerved around a hawthorn. ThunderClan wouldn't mind. They'd been fine with Fernstripe moving to ThunderClan to be with Shellfur; how could they object to him moving to ShadowClan to be with Sunbeam? They'd probably be relieved that he'd found somewhere he could finally fit in.

Nightheart slowed as he reached the steep trail into the hollow. He slithered down the loose rocks at the top, digging his claws in until he found his paws. Breaking his slide, he leaped nimbly down the last few tail-lengths. Now that he'd made the decision, he felt warm toward ThunderClan. His time with them hadn't been *all* bad. He'd never gone hungry, and he'd always felt safe. He'd even had fun occasionally. He didn't want to leave the Clan on bad terms, so he'd stick it out for a while longer and prepare his Clanmates for his departure. He'd tell them gradually, hinting at first and then perhaps telling one or two in confidence. Bayshine to begin with, then Myrtlebloom. Maybe Finleap too. He'd always liked the brown tom.

At some point he'd have to tell Finchlight and Sparkpelt. He'd wait for the right moment, even if it meant sticking it out for another moon before he switched Clans. They were bound to disapprove—they disapproved of all his decisions. And they might make a fuss. But he'd ride it out. They couldn't stop him. He was making the right choice.

He shook loose gravel from between his claws, then padded into camp.

The clearing was empty. ThunderClan seemed to have gone to their dens already. He was relieved. He could sneak into his nest without anyone asking any questions. He doubted anyone had even noticed he'd been gone.

"Nightheart!" Squirrelflight's mew took him by surprise. She padded from the shadows beneath the Highledge, her eyes flashing with anger. "Where have you been?"

"Out." He faced her, sticking out his muzzle. Why did she suddenly care where he'd been?

She stared at him. "*Out?* Without telling any cat where you were going?" She narrowed her eyes. "Did you go on Bramble-star's mission after all?"

Nightheart's pelt bristled defensively. "So what if I did?" Why was she so determined to stop him doing anything important? It was like she didn't want him to be a warrior at all.

"It was dangerous, that's what!" she snapped.

"I was careful!" Nightheart was aware of his Clanmates beginning to peer from their dens. They were probably enjoying watching him being lectured. Peering wasn't enough for Sparkpelt, clearly. She'd padded into the moonlight and was watching from the edge of the clearing. Finchlight ducked out behind her, eyes glittering with interest.

"What if you'd been caught?" Squirrelflight's tail was lashing angrily. "You could have started a war!"

Was that the only reason she cared? Not because he might be in danger, but because it might affect the rest of her precious Clan. "I'm not mouse-brained!" he snapped.

"Really?" She glowered at him. "Right now you seem to have no more sense than an apprentice."

Fury exploded in Nightheart's chest. "That's all you'll ever let me be," he hissed. "For some reason you hate the idea of me being a warrior. You think I'm only fit to fix nests and pull ticks out of elders' fur. I'm *so* glad I spent all those moons learning how to hunt and fight," he mewed sarcastically. "It really helps when I'm doing all the nastiest tasks in camp."

Squirrelflight's eyes flashed a warning. "You know full well that ThunderClan has no apprentices right now. Every warrior has to help out, and that includes you."

But Nightheart wasn't listening. Blood was roaring in his ears. "Is that why you noticed I was missing tonight? Did you have some important den cleaning for me to do?"

"It doesn't matter why we needed you here! You shouldn't have left without permission." Squirrelflight padded closer. "You pushed and pushed for your assessment—before you were even ready—because you wanted to be a warrior so badly. But your attitude stinks like crow-food. You'd better improve it soon or—"

"Or what?" Nightheart couldn't believe his ears. "You'll give me apprentice duties? You don't realize how much I could do for this Clan. You won't give me a chance. Tonight I got the information Bramblestar asked for. Without getting caught. And I get home to *this*!"

"You disobeyed my order!" Squirrelflight hissed. "From now on, you will—"

Nightheart wasn't going to let her finish. This was so unfair. "You can't tell me what to do anymore! I'm not part of ThunderClan!"

Sparkpelt's eyes widened. "What are you talking about?"

He glared at her. "I'm leaving!"

"Leaving?" She padded toward him. Nightheart blinked at her. Did she actually care? He stiffened in surprise as she said it again, her mew hardening. *"Leaving!"* She was *angry*. "How dare you make such a threat!" she snapped.

Finchlight trotted after her. "He's just being dramatic," she mewed. "He won't do it. He'll have calmed down by morning."

Nightheart hissed at them. "I'm not going to calm down," he yowled. "Not as long as I'm stuck in this hollow. This Clan treats me like a mouse-brain. I get no respect, and no cat cares what I think or how I feel." He whisked his tail. "I'm not going to put up with it any longer. I'm a good warrior. I'm strong and I'm smart and I deserve Clanmates who value me." Fury was pulsing beneath his pelt. "I'm going to join a Clan that'll appreciate me."

He stared around the camp, challenging anyone to defy him, and saw Bayshine watching from outside the warriors' den. The golden tom looked crestfallen. Nightheart felt a glimmer of surprise. Bayshine seemed to care more than Nightheart's own kin. He should have broken the news to him more gently, but Squirrelflight hadn't given him a chance. Now he'd made his decision, and he wasn't going to go back on it.

He headed for the camp entrance, ignoring the stunned expressions of his Clanmates as they watched him leave. Lifting his muzzle, he padded through the thorn tunnel, relieved as the forest shadows swallowed him.

"Nightheart!" He heard Bayshine's wail from the camp.

"Come back!" Finleap was calling to him from the entrance. "Sleep on it. You'll feel differently in the morning."

But Nightheart refused to look back. He scrambled up the steep trail and broke into a run, heading for the lakeshore. He reached it and followed the water's edge until Shadow-Clan scent touched his nose. His heart began to thump like a trapped rabbit in his chest. Was he doing the right thing?

Could he really leave his Clan for good? If he left now, Spark-pelt and Finchlight might never forgive him. Whatever mean things they thought about him now and in the past would be all they remembered. He could forget whatever hopes he'd had that one day he'd be close to them.

And Bayshine had looked so sad.

Nightheart paused at the top of the shore. The pine forest stood in front of him, as dark as his pelt, the branches too tightly pressed together for moonlight to pierce. *I should go back and face whatever Squirrelflight wants to throw at me.* He turned and gazed toward the ThunderClan shore. *But if I back down now, ThunderClan will never respect me. I'll be cleaning out dens for the rest of my life.* He turned his tail on the oak forest and looked at the pines. They were dense, but they grew straight and strong, in neatly ordered rows as though ancient paws had arranged them. ShadowClan would be fair. His Clanmates would respect him. At last he'd have a chance to become the great warrior he'd always dreamed he'd be. It was where he belonged.

He didn't sneak through the forest this time. Instead he waited. He was going to stand here quietly until a Shadow-Clan patrol found him, then announce his decision. They would see he was serious and respect him from the start.

An owl was calling to its mate nearby. A fox screeched in the distance. Nightheart felt the chill of the night settling into his pelt as he stood at the edge of the trees. Surely Shadow-Clan would send out a border patrol before they went to their dens. He shifted from one paw to another. Perhaps they were already asleep. Should he wait here until dawn despite the cold?

Perhaps the courageous thing to do would be to cross ShadowClan territory and walk straight into their camp, his head held high, and ask to join. That would be impressive, wouldn't it?

Yes. That was what he'd do.

He fluffed out his fur and padded into the forest. His heart was beating hard as he followed the trail that had led him toward the ShadowClan camp earlier that evening. The owl had stopped calling and the fox had grown quiet. Even the wind made no noise, muffled by the trees, and the forest was silent. The hairs lifted along Nightheart's spine. Around him the pines seemed to watch him as he padded past them. He had an eerie sense that he was the only creature alive.

His paws pricked nervously.

Once you get to the camp, everything will be okay, he told himself. And yet bats seemed to swoop inside his belly. By the time he saw the bramble wall of the ShadowClan camp looming above him, his mouth was dry. *I'm going to do this.* He lifted his chin and, finding a tunnel in the camp wall, ducked through it, hoping he hadn't sneaked in through the dirtplace tunnel. That wouldn't be a very dignified way to make his first entrance into the ShadowClan camp.

Dark shadows swept across a dark clearing. He stopped at the edge and looked around. He could hardly make out the dens. They were low and woven from brambles, half swallowed by the camp wall. The grass around the clearing was long and tangled. Pine branches stretched overhead, and rocks jutted here and there like badgers' spines pressing up through the earth. He swallowed. This gloomy-looking camp was going to be his new home.

He cleared his throat. Surely some cat had detected his scent and woken. Didn't Tigerstar post at least one guard at night? He looked around, suddenly aware that the dens were silent. In ThunderClan, the warm scents of his Clanmates would be filling the air along with their snoring. Bracken would be rustling as they shifted in their nests.

Unsure, Nightheart hesitated. He had the strange sense that no cat was here. Perhaps he should return to the border and wait until morning after all.

But ShadowClan must be here. Where else would they be?

He heard paw steps scuff the earth. Alarm pricked in his fur. He spun around.

Blazefire was staring at him. The ShadowClan warrior's eyes flashed with surprise. "You came back." He looked puzzled.

Nightheart squared his shoulders. "I've left ThunderClan," he announced as confidently as he could. "I'm here to join ShadowClan. I want to become Sunbeam's mate."

Blazefire's eyes widened in amazement. He stared at Nightheart as though lost for words.

Nightheart kept his chin high. It would probably take

Blazefire a moment or two to understand. "I'm here to join ShadowClan," he mewed again.

"I heard." Blazefire didn't disguise his disbelief. "I just wondered if you were serious."

CHAPTER 21

Frostpaw froze at the camp entrance. Tigerstar stood so still in the moonlight that he reminded her of a heron poised in the river, waiting for prey. Her chest tightened. *What's he doing here?* Around him, his warriors shifted uneasily. She recognized Cloverfoot, the ShadowClan deputy, and Tawnypelt. Sunbeam was here too, and Berryheart, Spireclaw, and Fringewhisker.

Mothwing padded quietly to the head of the clearing, where Owlnose and Splashtail faced the ShadowClan patrol. Half hidden in shadow, the rest of RiverClan glared at the intruders.

"What are you doing in our camp?" Mothwing demanded.

Tigerstar looked at her calmly. "We've come to help," he mewed.

"We don't need help." Splashtail bared his teeth, and Frostpaw could see his muscles tight beneath his pelt. He was ready to fight; it frightened her to see the usually gentle warrior looking so fierce.

The damp air was thick with ShadowClan scent. More

of it rolled in through the entrance, and she glanced behind her, her heart lurching as she saw figures moving in the dark beyond the camp wall. "There are more warriors outside," she called to Mothwing.

Her mentor's gaze did not shift from Tigerstar. "How much *help* do you think we need?" she growled.

"I just wanted you to know that ShadowClan is committed to seeing RiverClan through its troubles," Tigerstar mewed.

Mothwing curled her lip. "Go home and take your warriors with you."

Tigerstar's gaze flicked to Owlnose. "Shouldn't you be doing the talking?" he mewed. "You're the leader, after all."

"I'm not—" Owlnose began, but Splashtail cut him off.

"It doesn't matter who does the talking," he hissed. "The words will be the same whoever says them. We want you out of our camp."

Frostpaw felt exposed, alone near the entrance. She skirted the clearing, catching the eyes of Duskfur and Shimmerpelt as she passed. She could see from their rage that they weren't going to back down.

She stopped beside Splashtail. "When did they arrive?" she whispered.

"After Owlnose got back." He kept his mew low, and Frostpaw wondered whether Owlnose had told him yet what had happened at the Moonpool.

"Owl*nose*?" Tigerstar pricked his ears. "Does that mean StarClan still hasn't given him nine lives?"

Mothwing lifted her muzzle. "It's none of your business."

Tigerstar glanced around the camp. "Where's Fidget-flake?" he asked.

"He's gone home," Mothwing snapped.

"Does that mean he couldn't persuade StarClan to give Owlnose their blessing?" Tigerstar sounded genuinely concerned. Frostpaw searched his gaze. Had the ShadowClan leader really come to help?

Splashtail padded closer to Tigerstar, every hair on his pelt twitching with fury. "You have two choices," he snarled. "You can leave, or you can fight."

Tigerstar gazed back at him, his pelt still and smooth as water. "We all know that RiverClan is in trouble," he mewed quietly. "You have no leader, and StarClan doesn't seem to be helping. You've been relying on your medicine cat to lead you, and it's not working. She's been so busy trying to hold the Clan together that she didn't even know how much catmint she had in her herb store."

Frostpaw stiffened. When had Fidgetflake found time to tell him that?

Tigerstar went on. "If she had, Rowankit wouldn't have died. StarClan only knows what else has been neglected." His gaze slid around the camp. Frostpaw shifted uncomfortably. It was obvious to any cat how tattered the dens had become, and the river was glittering through holes in the camp wall. "Face it," Tigerstar mewed. "You're a mess. Why don't you accept help until you find a real leader and sort yourselves out?"

Splashtail flattened his ears. Duskfur lashed her tail. A

growl gathered in Shimmerpelt's throat. Around the clearing, RiverClan warriors shifted into battle stances.

Frostpaw glanced toward the medicine den. Did they have enough herbs to deal with battle injuries? She hoped it wouldn't come to that. Perhaps there was a way to persuade Tigerstar to leave before a fight broke out.

Harelight stepped forward. Frostpaw held her breath. Was the RiverClan tom going to attack? But the white tom's fur remained smooth.

He looked around at his Clanmates. "It might not be a bad idea," he mewed.

Duskfur stared at him, disbelief in her eyes. "You'd let a ShadowClan cat tell us what to do?"

"Are you crazy?" Mallownose yowled across the clearing.

Icewing padded to Harelight's side. "Hear him out," she mewed. "Tigerstar might be able to help us." The she-cat's Clanmates began to yowl her down, but she pressed on, raising her voice to be heard. "Harelight and I lived with Shadow-Clan for a while—"

"Perhaps you should go back there!" Mallownose spat.

Icewing ignored him. "Tigerstar took us in and treated us well." She turned to Mothwing. "He took you in too when the impostor made Mistystar exile you. He treated you like a Clanmate. You trusted him then, and he lived up to your trust. Don't you think you might trust him now?"

Mothwing met the she-cat's gaze. "That was different. We were Clanless. We chose when to stay with ShadowClan and when to leave. But Tigerstar isn't offering us a choice. This isn't *help*, it's a takeover, and RiverClan will never surrender to another Clan. Either Tigerstar leaves or we fight to the death."

Tigerstar's tail began to flick. "This isn't a takeover!" He was losing patience. "There's no need to fight. It's in your best interests to let me step in and advise while you find your paws again."

"'Advise!'" Duskfur's growl became a snarl.

"Go home!" Mallownose hissed.

Around the clearing, the RiverClan warriors raised their voices in anger.

Frostpaw flattened her ears against their yowls as they began to close in on the ShadowClan patrol.

Tigerstar glanced toward the entrance. "Stonewing." He lifted his tail, and on his signal more ShadowClan warriors filed into camp. They moved slowly, but there was determination in their gazes. Moonlight gleamed on their muscled pelts as they surrounded the RiverClan warriors.

"How dare you!" Duskfur's eyes blazed.

Shimmerpelt looked at Owlnose. "Give the signal and they're crow-food," she snarled.

Owlnose glanced at Splashtail, but the RiverClan deputy didn't take his eyes from Tigerstar. Mothwing shifted her paws uncertainly. Without leadership, no cat knew what to do.

Frostpaw moved closer to her mentor. "Perhaps if you take Tigerstar to the medicine den to talk," she whispered, "you can persuade him to—"

She couldn't finish her sentence. A yowl split the night air. Frostpaw's breath caught in her throat as Duskfur leaped at

Cloverfoot. With a snarl, the RiverClan she-cat dug her claws into the ShadowClan deputy's scruff and dragged her to the ground. Berryheart lunged at Duskfur. Shimmerpelt went for Spireclaw. The clearing exploded with the screech of battle, and terror shrilled through Frostpaw's pelt as, all around her, RiverClan and ShadowClan began to fight.

CHAPTER 22

❧

This wasn't supposed to happen! Sunbeam's pelt spiked as the River-Clan camp blazed into battle. Within moments, the clearing was a mass of writhing bodies. In the moonlight it was hard to make out one from the other, but the iron tang of blood was already clear.

Shimmerpelt barged past her and sliced open Spireclaw's muzzle. Fury surged through Sunbeam's pelt and she lunged at the RiverClan she-cat, hooking her claws into her pelt and hauling her away. Spireclaw shook the blood from his nose, but before he could retaliate, Mallownose barreled into him and knocked him to the ground. Sunbeam's heart lurched. Was he okay? Before she could find out, Shimmerpelt ripped free of her grasp and turned on her.

Rage blazed in her eyes. "Intruder!"

We came here to help! Sunbeam dodged clear of Shimmer-pelt's lunge. The RiverClan she-cat slammed her paws onto empty earth, and Sunbeam sank her teeth into Shimmer-pelt's scruff. Tugging Shimmerpelt backward, she wrapped her forepaws around the RiverClan warrior's chest and, when they'd thumped together onto the ground, began to churn at her spine with her hind claws.

How did this become a battle? Tigerstar had said he wasn't planning to take over RiverClan. Sunbeam had heard him promise Berryheart in front of the whole Clan. *So why are we fighting now?*

With a surge of anger, she kicked Shimmerpelt away and scrambled to her paws. *We had a chance to leave in peace, but Tigerstar didn't take it.*

Berryheart pushed past, driving Owlnose backward, swiping at his bloody muzzle, one paw after another. She pushed him through the heart of the battle and Sunbeam watched, rooted to the spot, as Owlnose hit back at her mother, catching her on the jaw, and then began ducking and weaving like a snake. Berryheart seemed confused. Uncertain where to aim, she reared; Sunbeam guessed she planned to slam her forepaws onto his back. But the RiverClan tom darted forward and sank his teeth into her hind leg.

Sunbeam shouldered her way through the fighting cats, trying to reach her mother. As Berryheart struggled to rip her paw free, Owlnose bit down harder and she screeched in pain.

"I'm coming!" Sunbeam pushed harder, but a muzzle-length from her mother a broad head slammed into her flank. She staggered, fighting to keep her balance, and turned to see who'd hit her. Gorseclaw was glowering at her, his eyes burning with anger. She shifted her weight, preparing to meet his attack with a powerful swipe, but he was too fast. Fire seemed to scorch her forehead as he sliced her open. Blood streamed into her eye. He'd cut a gash above it, but rage throbbed too fiercely beneath her pelt to feel pain. She hit out at him, catching his cheek with her claws. A surge of satisfaction filled her belly as she opened a wound that he'd remember for moons.

Berryheart had torn free of Owlnose and was once more driving him backward, her swipes more vicious now, anger burning in her eyes.

We're the ones who'll get stung. Her mother had predicted this. But Tigerstar had refused to listen. Then Nightheart's question flashed in Sunbeam's mind: *Tigerstar's not planning to invade RiverClan, right?* If ThunderClan had guessed what Tigerstar was planning, why hadn't she?

Her thoughts whirled. She dropped onto her belly, preparing for Gorseclaw's counterblow. Then she saw that the RiverClan tom had frozen. He was staring at her, his cheek bloody from her attack as though he couldn't believe he'd been wounded. Suddenly she wondered if the RiverClan tom had ever fought in a battle before. She glanced around. How many of these young RiverClan warriors had seen a real fight? Each of them seemed to be fighting alone, as though battling only for themselves, while ShadowClan worked together, warriors ready to dive in where a Clanmate had failed to land a blow or been tripped before they could reach their target.

Tigerstar's yowl rang over the battle. "Push them toward the reeds!"

As Sunbeam shifted her position, she spotted Tawnypelt fighting Breezeheart and Graypaw. The tortoiseshell warrior was parrying blows with great skill, but she was outnumbered, and they were pushing her back. *She needs help.* As Sunbeam turned toward her, Gorseclaw snapped out of his trance. He reared, but she was faster. As soon as he lifted his forepaws from the ground, she dived beneath them, pushed up, and flipped him onto his back.

She turned, ready to finish the fight, but Spireclaw was already on top of the RiverClan warrior and pummeling him with his hind paws. Sunbeam nodded thanks to her brother and darted to Tawnypelt's side.

Tawnypelt glanced at her gratefully, and together they began to drive Breezeheart and Graypaw toward the tattered camp wall. Berryheart and Flaxfoot fell in beside them, Whorlpelt and Lightleap too, until a wall of ShadowClan warriors was pushing RiverClan toward the reeds as Tigerstar had ordered.

Frostpaw's terrified wail sounded from beside the medicine den. "Please stop!" She stood beside Mothwing in the moonlight, her pelt spiked and her eyes wide with horror.

But her Clanmates didn't even look at her. Their panicked gazes were on their attackers.

"Please!" Frostpaw wailed.

Splashtail's growl rose above the shriek of battle. "Never."

RiverClan seemed to harden and push back harder. Mistpaw and Icewing surged forward, claws slashing as they tried to shoulder their way through the ShadowClan line. Sunbeam felt a glow of respect. RiverClan's fighting was chaotic, but they had courage.

Tawnypelt caught her eye, and Sunbeam understood her

Clanmate's silent command. She pressed closer, and together they blocked Mistpaw's and Icewing's escape.

Sunbeam ducked a blow and threw one back that sent Mistpaw reeling. Tawnypelt kicked out with her powerful back legs, catching Icewing in the belly with such force that she staggered back into her Clanmates.

Panic seemed to spark like lightning through the River-Clan warriors. Shimmerpelt lashed out wildly. She was looking around as her Clanmates were corralled into the shadows beneath the reed wall. Was she hoping some cat would give an order to tell her where to aim her blows?

Duskfur surged forward, trying to break through the ShadowClan line, but Cloverfoot and Whorlpelt closed ranks and drove her back.

Fur flashed at the edge of Sunbeam's vision as Mallownose leaped over the line. He landed behind Stonewing and grabbed the white tom's tail between his jaws. Sunbeam ducked from among her Clanmates and raced to help. As Stonewing fought to rip free, Sunbeam barged into Mallownose, unbalancing him long enough to duck low and bite down hard on his hind paw. He shrieked and let go of Stonewing's tail.

Stonewing spun and swung a paw at his head, slashing the RiverClan tom's ears as Sunbeam released his hind paw and fell in beside him. They reared and began to bat the River-Clan tom backward with a flurry of well-timed strikes that didn't give him a chance to find his balance. Confused and hissing with anger, Mallownose lifted onto his hind paws, staggered, and collapsed through the reed wall of the camp.

He plunged into the moonlit river and disappeared beneath the surface. Sunbeam turned away. *He's a RiverClan cat. He'll be safer there than in camp.*

She returned to the ShadowClan line. It was pressing RiverClan harder against the reed wall. Shimmerpelt crashed through, and so did Breezeheart. Harelight and Icewing dove through by choice, disappearing into the water, hoping perhaps to circle back and come at the ShadowClan cats from behind. The only cats left fighting looked fresh from the apprentices' den. Sunbeam kept swiping at them but sheathed her claws now. It was like batting away prey.

"Give up!" Tigerstar's hiss sounded from the edge of the camp.

In a pool of moonlight near the entrance, the ShadowClan leader was pressing Duskfur to the ground. His claws dug in around the old tabby's throat.

Duskfur glared at him, her gaze lit with fury, her hind legs thrashing as she tried to break free of his grip.

Sunbeam felt the battle slow around her as every warrior turned to watch the ShadowClan leader.

He bared his teeth. "Do you want to die?" he snarled.

Duskfur stared back at him defiantly. "I would always choose death to save RiverClan!"

Tigerstar glanced at her Clanmates, bloody and trembling beside the camp wall. "Will you let them die too, just to save your pride?"

Duskfur twitched, blood welling in her fur where Tiger-star's claws pierced her flesh. "This isn't pride," she growled. "This is survival."

"We're here to *help* you," Tigerstar hissed.

Duskfur's tail was lashing. "Is killing us part of your plan?"

"I gave you a choice," Tigerstar growled back. His claws were so deep now that Duskfur could barely move.

"Surrender or die?" Duskfur croaked. "Is that a choice?"

Sunbeam felt a chill in her fur as silence descended over the clearing. Was the RiverClan warrior right? Would Tigerstar kill any RiverClan warrior who refused to go along with him?

"Sometimes cats need to be shown when they need help," Tigerstar hissed.

Duskfur struggled to turn her head. She looked desperately toward Splashtail.

The RiverClan deputy had padded away from his Clan-mates and stood alone in the moonlight. He stared back at Duskfur, then dipped his head. "It's over," he growled. "No cat should die today."

Duskfur grew limp in Tigerstar's grip. In the shadow of the reed wall, her Clanmates collapsed, panting, and Sunbeam backed away, relieved that the fight had ended.

Tigerstar let go of Duskfur's throat. As the battered River-Clan she-cat struggled to her paws and limped away, he gazed around at his warriors. "You fought well," he mewed. Above him, the sky was specked with stars. "Now we can start to rebuild." He nodded to Mothwing. "Fetch all the herbs that you have," he told her. "Your Clanmates are hurt."

Sunbeam felt a surge of pity for the RiverClan cats. They looked as tattered as their camp, their fur hanging out in clumps just like the frayed walls of their dens. Fixing this place would take time and energy, and she wondered how much of either ShadowClan would have to spare now that leaf-bare was coming. When the cold weather hit, it would be hard enough feeding their own Clan without having to worry about RiverClan.

Tigerstar nodded to Flaxfoot and Tawnypelt. "Gather moss," he told them. "Soak it in the river and bring it here. There are wounds to be cleaned." He turned to Cloverfoot. "Take Lightleap and Spireclaw and hunt." His gaze flitted to the empty fresh-kill pile. "Take more warriors if you need. I want enough food for every cat by dawn."

Sunbeam watched them go, surprised that he would leave the remaining ShadowClan cats so outnumbered. Was he so certain he'd won RiverClan's cooperation? She looked around. The RiverClan cats were clearly in no state to fight. They limped away from the reed wall and sat down in the clearing, avoiding each other's gazes as though too ashamed to acknowledge their defeat.

"Owlnose." Tigerstar nodded to RiverClan's leader. The tabby tom blinked back as though in a daze. "Check on your Clanmates," Tigerstar told him. "Find out their injuries and fetch whatever they need."

Owlnose dipped his head and began to move among the

RiverClan cats, stopping beside each one to speak.

"Mistpaw." Tigerstar switched his attention to the River-Clan apprentice. "It is *Mistpaw*, right?" The gray she-cat looked too old to be an apprentice, but she nodded. "Catch up with Cloverfoot," he told her. "Help her hunt." He looked at Gray-paw. "Go with her."

The two apprentices exchanged glances but didn't argue. Instead they padded out of camp.

Splashtail hadn't taken his eyes from Tigerstar. The RiverClan deputy was scowling with a look of hatred at the ShadowClan leader. The moonlight caught the wet patches of blood on his tabby pelt and made them shine. Sunbeam's heart ached for the beaten tom. She tried to imagine how she would feel if warriors had invaded ShadowClan and forced them to surrender. Her pelt burned with indignation at the thought, and she shifted her paws as Tigerstar padded across the clearing and stopped in front of Splashtail.

The RiverClan deputy's pelt bristled, but he didn't move as Tigerstar swept his tail along his bloody spine. "Trust me," the ShadowClan leader mewed. "It's for your own good."

Sunbeam saw a flash of rage in Splashtail's eyes before he dropped his gaze, and she shivered. *Does Tigerstar really think RiverClan will ever believe he wants to help them?*

CHAPTER ONE

Leaf rolled over and stretched her paws out in front of her, raking the thin soil with her claws, then rolled again onto her back and slowly opened her eyes. The sky above was a soft gleaming gray, pale and unmarked by clouds. All she could see was the very top of one tall tree at the edge of her vision. Leaf felt almost as if she could tumble into the sky.

Her stomach rumbled.

There'll be time for sky-gazing after the First Feast, she thought, letting out a huge yawn and flopping back onto her stomach again. She got to her paws and loped over to the big tree and scratched the back of her ears against its gnarled trunk.

Through the sparse trees that grew on the northern slopes, she could see Aunt Plum and all the other Slenderwoods rising from comfy piles of leaves and clambering down from flat rocks, heading over to the thin bamboo stalks that pushed up between the trees. Leaf shook herself and padded toward the place where she had seen some growing the night before. Sure enough, every few paw-lengths she was able to break off a bunch of tender shoots with thin green leaves sprouting. But she stopped before she had gathered them all.

Greedy cub now, hungry cub later, Aunt Plum always said, and she was right.

Leaf held the bunch of shoots tightly in one paw and hurried across the forest floor to the big clearing. The other Slenderwood pandas had all gathered there already, each sitting with their back to a tree, a respectful distance away from one another.

"Come along, Leaf," said Plum, with a yawn. "The Great Dragon won't wait for you."

She said that a lot too. Leaf grinned and sat down at the base of the same tree as little Cane and his mother, Hyacinth. Cane wriggled on his stomach toward the small pile of shoots in front of Hyacinth, but she gently reached out a paw and rolled him away.

"Not quite yet, little one," she said. Cane squeaked in disappointment, and Leaf knew how he felt. The bamboo in her paws smelled delicious, but no panda could begin to eat before the blessing.

Aunt Plum scratched her back against the tree trunk and cleared her throat. "Great Dragon," she said, holding her own shoots out in one paw. "At the Feast of Gray Light your humble pandas bow before you. Thank you for the gift of the bamboo, and the wisdom you bestow upon us."

Leaf bowed her head, and so did all the other pandas in the clearing, including Cane, who dropped his muzzle until his nose rested on the forest floor. There was a short pause before they all looked up again, and the sound of happy crunching filled the clearing. Leaf brought her bamboo to her nose, smelling the fresh, cool scent, and then started to pick off the leaves. She formed them into a small bundle before chomping down on the tasty green ends. Hyacinth stripped the tougher bark from the outside of her bamboo, and passed the softer green shreds from the inside down to Cane, who gobbled them up with gusto.

"The Dragon could be a bit more generous with his gifts," one of the older pandas grumbled, his mouth full of bamboo splinters.

"And you could be more grateful for what you have, Juniper Slenderwood," said Plum, eyeing him sternly through the pawful of green leaves.

"Juniper *Shallowpool*," Juniper muttered.

"There is no shallow pool now, Juniper," said Hyacinth gently. "We're all Slenderwoods now."

"Yeah, if you won't be a Slenderwood, you ought to be *Deepriver*, or *Floodwater*," said Grass, with a snide look over her shoulder toward the edge of the river. Juniper got to his paws with a huff and turned his back on the other pandas, settling on the other side of his tree and chewing on the woody stems of his First Feast.

Leaf watched him with a pinched feeling growing in her heart. That was mean of Grass. Juniper was a crotchety old panda, but she couldn't exactly blame him—she couldn't imagine what it would be like to have her home there one day and vanished the next, swallowed up by the rising river. She had never known any home but the Slenderwood, with its tall, wavering trees and sparse bamboo.

"All of you are stuck in the past," Grass snorted, rolling over onto her back and licking her muzzle. "Nine times a day we thank the Great Dragon for feeding us, but why? Who has seen so much as a dragon-shaped cloud since the flood? Juniper's right—the Dragon has abandoned us."

"Not what I said," grumbled Juniper, without turning around.

Leaf turned to look at Plum, and so did several of the others. Leaf half expected her to snap at Grass, but she just shook her head.

"That isn't how it works, Grass," she said calmly. "The Dragon cannot abandon us. The Great Dragon *is* the Bamboo Kingdom. As long as there are pandas, and there is bamboo to feed us, the Dragon is watching over us." She held up the next long stem of her feast, as if that settled the matter. For a while there was silence, only broken by crunching.

"Do you remember that summer," Crabapple put in, using a long black claw to pick a bamboo shoot out of his teeth, "before the flood, when Juniper's pool dried up? The Dragon Speaker warned us all. You found a deeper pool in plenty of time—remember that, Juniper?"

Juniper just grunted again, but Hyacinth smiled to herself as she nudged a pawful of leaves toward Cane. "Oh, remember the time with the sand foxes?" she said. "Old Oak Cragsight had to take the message to them by foot, right up to the White Spine peaks. Only just made it in time to warn them about the avalanche."

"I thought it was a blizzard?" said Grass, her cynical expression melting a little.

"No, it was an avalanche," grumbled Vinca, wriggling his back against the tree to scratch between his shoulder blades. "*Beware the white wave*—that was the Speaker's message. I remember it distinctly."

Leaf wriggled onto her back again, trying to take her time over the last mouthfuls of her feast. Once they started on this topic, the older pandas could go for hours—they would still be here reminiscing when it was time for the Feast of Golden Light, and the Feast of Sun Climb after that.

Leaf knew that Plum was right, that the Great Dragon was still out there, watching over them. She believed it, truly, she did. But when Plum and the others told their stories of the time before the flood, when the river had been calm and narrow enough to cross, the bamboo plentiful, and every panda had had enough food and space to have their own territory, Leaf couldn't help wondering why things weren't like that anymore.